What Makes Us Stronger

A Well Paired Novel

Marianne Rice

Published by Star Hill Press, 2018.

Also by Marianne Rice

A Well Paired Novel
At First Blush
Where There's Hope
What Makes Us Stronger

The McKay-Tucker Men
False Start
False Hope
False Impressions

Standalone
Smoke & Pearls
Marshmallows & Mistletoe

Watch for more at www.mariannerice.com.

To Natalina and Alisha, my sprinting buddies. Without you I'd never get any writing done.

CHAPTER ONE

TY PARKER STEPPED OUT of the Sunrise Diner and couldn't help his gaze from glancing down the road to the Sea Salt Spa. This time it had nothing to do with the gorgeous blonde owner and everything to do with the black ominous cloud of smoke billowing from the third story window where her apartment was.

"Shit." He barely heard Cameron's *oompf* as the door smacked his friend in the face. Ty had always been a fast runner, even with a load of artillery jacked on his back and four-pound combat boots on his feet buried ankle deep in Iraqi sand.

Today, a bit out of shape since leaving the service five years ago, and even with his steel-toed work boots on, he sprinted toward the spa. Yanking the door open, he stormed inside the spa, hoping to find Lily still alive. The reception area was quiet, the girly music playing softly in the background. Annie looked up from the table where she was polishing someone's nails.

"You alright, Ty?"

"Lily? Where is she?"

He heard Cam come in behind him. "Everyone okay?"

"Sure. You guys in need of a desperate cut or something?" Ty's sister, Mia, asked from the sink where she was washing someone's hair. Hell. His first thought should've been the safety of his sister and not the woman who occupied his dreams every night.

"Smoke. I saw smoke. There's a fire upstairs. You ladies need to evacuate." Ty took in the rest of the room. The three other chairs were empty. He'd never been on the second floor, but he knew that was where Lily offered massages and facials.

And the third floor, filled with smoke, was where her apartment was.

"You sure?" Mia sat her customer up and placed a towel on her head.

2

"Hell, I'm sure. Cam, take care of the women. I'm going up-stairs." He started for the stairs, and Cam yelled after him.

"I'll be right behind you."

Ty didn't wait and, taking the stairs two at a time, reached the top in a matter of seconds. His trained eyes scoped out the area; not for enemy snipers, but for smoke, fire, and the sound of survivors.

Lily.

He opened the two closed doors and, not seeing anything, ran to the end of the hall, hoping the heavy door at the end led to the third floor. Turning the knob, he cursed when it stopped. Locked.

He banged on the door and called out for her, "Lily?"

Ty heard a scream and a stream of curse words he'd never imagined coming from the stunning, sophisticated spa owner.

"Lily!" he screamed again. He heaved his shoulder into the door and got nowhere. Searching for something, anything to break the door down, he came up empty. Each of the rooms on the second floor held a small massage table and a tray of lotions and oils.

There was no time to search for an ax. His heart heaved in his chest as the worst possible scenarios ran through his head.

"Lily! You need to leave. Can you make it to the door?"

The door opened, and he was greeted by a coughing, swearing, gorgeous blonde wearing nothing but a skimpy tank top—sans the bra—and shorts that were too indecent to wear out in public.

The tang of an electrical fire stung his nose but did nothing to erase the image of her perky nipples pointing at him through the pale pink silk top.

"There was a small fire." She coughed. "It's out now."

Snapping back to attention, he lifted his gaze to her face. Hair that he'd never seen out of place before was knotted and rumpled around her shoulders. Her face, clean of makeup, was smudged and rosy from the heat of the morning.

"You're okay?" he managed to croak out.

"Yeah. My dryer, on the other hand, is not." She turned her back on him and glided up the stairs, her shorts riding up to indecent proportions, and he kicked himself for gawking.

Ty stood at the bottom of the stairs not sure if he should follow her or not. This was unchartered territory. Her apartment. The lack of clothes. The tightness in his jeans.

This was Lily Novak.

"Ty?" she called from the top of the stairs. "Can you take a look?"

He cleared his throat and jogged up the stairs. "Sure."

He found her in the living room. Her hands lifted above her head as she pulled down the top windowpane. The miniscule piece of satin crept up, revealing slim hips and what promised to be the softest skin he'd ever seen.

"Today's my late morning, so I've been doing chores around my apartment." She fanned the air with her hands in an attempt to push the smoke out the window. "I tossed my laundry in the dryer about twenty minutes ago and was working on breakfast when—oh, crap." She dashed to the left and he followed behind, worry etched in his chest.

While the electrical burn permeated the air to his right, a new smoky, burnt smell filled the left side of the apartment.

He glanced about the small yet tidy living room, the cobalt blue couch and white pillows bringing a brightness to the tight quarters and into an efficient kitchen. Lily's back was to him and he appreciated the pull of her shirt as she dumped a pan into the sink, steam and smoke rising above her head.

"I've never been a great cook, but I don't usually burn my underwear and my eggs in the same day. Heck, the same hour." Lily coughed and waved her hand in front of her face as she turned to face him. "Sorry. My apartment doesn't usually smell this bad either."

Ty couldn't say he enjoyed the stench of burnt wires and eggs, but he'd wake up every morning to the aroma if it meant seeing Lily like this.

Loud footsteps echoed on the wood floor and stopped short behind him. "Hey. Everything under control in—oh, uh. Yeah."

He turned around and watched Cameron cover his eyes with his hand. If Ty was a gentleman he would have done the same. Hell, instead, he'd been ogling Lily and wishing she was more than an untouchable friend of his sister's.

"Ohmygod. I can't believe I'm dressed like this." Lily gasped and covered her chest and passed them, her fresh as flowers scent slapping his nose and making him forget why he'd come up here in the first place.

"So, uh. She's okay?" Cameron jerked his head back, and Ty did his best not to let his eyes follow her down the hall.

"Yeah. Sounds like her dryer fried out. Then a kitchen disaster."

"Want me to take a look?"

Even though Cam was an electrician of sorts and Ty the carpenter, he wanted to be the one to fix whatever was wrong with Lily. Or, rather, her appliances.

"I've got it. I'm sure Hope is worried. Why don't you let her and the girls downstairs know everything's okay?"

Cam snorted. "Sure thing, man."

"What's that supposed to mean?"

Holding up his hands with a smirk, Cam backed up. "I'm not about to infringe on your territory. I've got Hope and Delaney. Lily's all yours."

Hope and Ty had been best friends in high school. She was his anchor while he was overseas and while he'd have liked to have confided in her about the mess he'd gotten himself into, she'd beat him to the punch, unloading her burdens on him.

She'd gotten pregnant her freshman year in college and when the guy died and his twin brother was sent to jail, she dropped out and returned home. It wasn't until Cameron was released from prison and showed up in town last fall, setting some of the misconceptions straight, that the two of them fell in love and were working on the happily ever after thing.

He'd been wary of him at first, but Ty was a good judge of character and figured him to be a good man. Still, he stood by Hope's side and would strap Cameron to an A-bomb if he did anything to hurt Hope or her daughter, Delaney.

Cam may have become one of his closest friends, but he didn't like the man thinking he had an interest in Lily.

"She's not my territory."

"Sure thing, Ty. Gotta go check on my ladies. Don't do anything I wouldn't do." Ty flipped him off, and Cameron chuckled on his way out.

Lily came out of her room and stopped Cameron with a hand to his forearm. "Thanks for coming to my rescue. Is everything okay downstairs?"

"The girls were spooked at first, but they're good. I'll let them know it's okay to come back inside. Mia already called 911. I'll take care of things downstairs. I'm sure Ty can tend to things up here."

Could he sound a little less obvious? Ty didn't think he'd made his interest in Lily *that* evident. Sure, Mia had teased him about Lily, offering to set them up, but he'd refused. And, according to his sister, Lily was completely against it as well. No need to be rejected to his face. He accepted her lack of interest with a speck of pride and fantasized about her instead.

"Thank you, Cameron."

And could she sound a little less grateful to Cam? He hadn't done anything. It was Ty who tried to bust down her door and rescue her. His mood quickly soured from rescuer to pissed off and sexually frustrated.

"Where's your dryer?" He didn't mean to bark at her, but the sooner he could get out of her apartment the better.

"Uh, in the bathroom."

He unglued his eyes from her long, lean legs and brushed past her, heading toward the smell. The opened window had let out most of the smoke, but the stench still lingered. Thankfully she stayed back, although leaning against the doorjamb like a model in a Victoria's Secret ad wasn't helping the tight space in his jeans.

Pretending she wasn't there—which he deserved a freaking medal for attempting—he pulled the dryer away from the wall and unplugged it. Squatting behind it, he inspected the back, black from smoke.

Without his tool belt there was only so much he could do. Wiring wasn't his specialty, but he could change a fixture and replace a wire or two if necessary. Seeing there wasn't any damage to the outlet, he deduced the fire must have come from within the machine.

Ty crawled around to the front of the dryer and opened the door. A waft of electrical burn mixed with fabric softener accosted him. He coughed and cleared his throat. He didn't mean to paw through her clothes, only wanted to search inside for anything suspicious.

The only thing suspicious was the amount of white and pastels in the dryer. Lots and lots of undergarments. Not something he needed to see or think about right now.

"Uh, how old is the dryer?"

"I'm not sure. It came with the apartment. I can ask Melissa Button. I'm leasing the building from her."

The Button Agency owned pretty much every building in town. They were a respected couple and agency, and Ty doubted they'd keep out of date appliances in any of their buildings.

"There had to be a reason for the smoke and fire. Maybe a loose wire inside the machine? You'll want to look online for any recalls."

"Sure. I'll grab my laptop."

The lint trap was in an unusual place, toward the back of the machine. He slid it out and inspected it. There wasn't too much accumulation; no more than what he'd expect from the current load. Sticking his hand in the tight space where the mesh trap goes, he felt around for an obstruction and felt something larger than a ball of lint. Tugging, he yanked until the material came free.

Dangling from his fingertips, inches from his nose, was a black lace thong. Ty gulped.

Sweat formed above his brows and dripped into his eyes. Instinct moved his hand to wipe it away and only stopped when the lace touched his cheek.

"Damn." He dropped the panties and crab crawled backward until his head hit the windowsill. Swearing, he rubbed his head and gawked at the scrap of lace staring at him from the white linoleum floor, taunting him. Teasing. Tempting.

Ty rolled his shoulders and lengthened his neck, trying to get a hold of himself. He'd fantasized too many nights about what Lily Novak wore under her clothes. She had a body meant for a runway, yet she never wore anything flashy. Simple jeans and t-shirts. They fit her differently, though. Like the clothes were made for her body, hugging every curve, showing off every muscle.

Lily wasn't waif-like thin like a model, though. She had muscles that Ty could appreciate. Toned and in shape, yet she often held her body like she was hiding something. A deep, dark secret that no one knew.

Mia had alluded to Lily's mystery numerous times, but Ty always pretended to be indifferent and kept his distance.

It was becoming harder to stay away from her as their circle of friends began to overlap, so he remained quiet, aloof. He'd been burned too deeply by another woman with dark secrets, and Lily with her golden looks and skimpy undergarments held her own closet of mysteries he didn't want to get messed up in.

The dark thong stared him in the face, and he leaned forward to pick it up and toss it to the side. Pinching a small piece of fabric between his fingers, he held it out in front of him as if it were a serpent ready to strike.

Long, bare legs stood in front of him and his eyes took forever to travel their length and make contact with their owner.

"I, uh, found the problem."

Her blonde mass of tangled hair was pulled back in a bun, her manicured fingers clutched at her chest. And that mouth. Normally her lips were lightly glossed and pursed in a soft smile, but she'd tucked them inside her mouth.

And those eyes. Those stunning blue eyes were glossed over in fear. And then he noticed her shoulders begin to shake. He'd spooked her, and he didn't have a freaking clue how.

• • • •

LILY CLUTCHED HER SHIRT in her fist, fear running through her veins. She instantly calculated the eight steps it would take to get to her door. The fourteen stairs that led to the second floor and fourteen more to the main floor. Hopefully the front door was unlocked and she had a clear path to...

No. This was Ty. He was in her bathroom trying to fix her dryer. He wasn't Malcolm looking for...

Shaking her head clear of the past, she loosened her grip on her shirt and released her lips from between her teeth. She could feel them swell from the tight hold she had on them.

"Are you okay?" Ty stood, his tall, powerful body filling up her tiny bathroom.

Instinct had her stepping back into the hall. Her eyes darted to the erotic image of her black thong dangling from his fingers.

"Lily?"

The close proximity of Ty and his leather and woodsy scent was too much. She barely noticed the smoky smell anymore and, for a moment, she wished for it back. Anything to distract her from Ty Parker.

"You said... you said you found the problem?" She reached out and grabbed the panties from him.

"Yeah." He swiped his arm across his forehead.

Was it hot in here? The window was open, and the cool spring air felt good on her tense muscles. If there weren't four buildings to her left she'd have a fantastic ocean view. Still, the breeze off the Atlantic filled her third-story apartment enough to make it bearable even when August humidity hung thick. Not that Crystal Cove, Maine ever got too hot in the summer.

"Looks like your, um, undergarments got stuck in the lint trap. Probably caused the belt to clamp up and overheat. I don't see any wiring issues, but I'd like to take the back panel off to check. Just in case."

"You don't have to do that. I can call a repairman."

"I suppose I won't take offense to that."

Ty's charming smile did her in. He didn't flash it often. He was like her, the quiet one of the group. Often the loner. Granted, she'd made quite a few friends over the past year, most having some sort of connection to Ty.

Mia, his sister, helped out as her receptionist and cut men's hair. She'd shampoo and style women's but didn't cut their hair. Hope, Ty's best friend, had become one of her close friends as well, so running into him was inevitable.

They'd danced around each other. Both polite, but never holding a real conversation.

"I didn't mean—"

"I'm kidding." He shuffled his feet and slid his hands into the pockets of his worn jeans. "I'm no appliance expert, but I don't mind taking a look. I have a feeling it's just the belt."

She didn't mean to offend him. Ty was a reputable carpenter in the area. His finishing work, especially, had been praised by many in the town. Lily didn't know if he worked with appliances and machines, but if he said he'd take a look, she might as well let him.

"Okay. That would be great. Thanks."

"Sure. I just need to grab my toolbox from the truck. I'm parked down at the diner."

He whisked past her before she could ask why he was parked down the block and what he was doing at the spa. Maybe to stop in and say hi to Mia? Although he'd never done that before. In fact, Lily couldn't remember if he'd actually ever been to the Sea Salt Spa before.

Remembering the rest of her underwear and sports bras were in the dryer, she quickly scooped them into her arms and plopped them on her bed. Bringing a sports bra to her nose, she sniffed and scrunched her nose in disgust. The load would need another washing—maybe two—to get the smell out.

Gone were the days of luxurious lingerie that would never touch a commercial washer and dryer. With the exception of her underwire bras, everything she owned went into her standard washer. No more dry cleaning. No more specialty services.

And she was fine with that. She didn't miss any of it.

Crystal Cove had been her home for nearly two years now, and she was surprised at how quickly she'd adapted to this new lifestyle. Life moved slower and was more relaxed in mid-coast Maine.

Her apartment was small yet had character. She loved her privacy and the proximity to her spa.

The dark sage walls in her bedroom comforted her at night, as did her tan and sage comforter. A bed-in-a-bag deal she found at one of the bix box stores when she first relocated. The concept was new to her.

All of it was. Laundry. Cooking. Cleaning. Shopping. Well, shopping for linens and practical items.

"Lily?" That strong, yet soft voice sent shivers down her spine.

Tossing the smelly clothes back in the hamper, she stepped into the hall and took in the view. Ty had turned the dryer away from the wall and squatted in front of it fiddling with something, with what she didn't care. His jeans stretched in all the right places. With thighs so thick and powerful she didn't know how he squeezed them into his jeans. They rested slightly below his hips but not so low where it sagged in the back. Not with that backside. Oh, how she appreciated how the denim molded to his butt.

And the tool belt strapped around his waist.

Lily gulped.

The image was one straight out of one of those romance books Celeste was always pushing on her. She liked Ty's mom. A lot. She ran the local bookstore, Books by the Ocean, and was a wonderful supporter of their book club. Most of the time Celeste didn't join them, but let the girls use her store for their meetings, which often turned into fun gossip and girl talk.

It was funny. Their idea of gossip was nothing like what she was used to in her former life. Hope, Alexis, Jenna, and Mia only gossiped about each other. And to each other's faces. It was all in good fun.

Ty shifted and his navy shirt came loose from the waistband of his jeans, revealing his lower back. The indent of his spine accentuated how muscular he was. Her gaze traveled higher to his arms that were flexed as his big hands worked at removing the back of the dryer.

Triceps, biceps, and forearms. Oh my. While she'd appreciated his good looks over the years, she never took the time to appreciate his powerful body. Not wanting to be caught staring, she'd toss him a casual greeting and look away. But now with his back to her, she didn't have to worry about being caught staring.

His body was one used for hard, physical labor. She'd bet his hands were rough and calloused, and that his body had scars from being in the military. He was as far from a *suit* as could be.

As opposite from her past as one could possibly be.

Grunting, Ty got the panel free and cocked his head to the side. "I'll need to set this somewhere."

Realizing she was hovering over him and was in the way, she scampered backward out of the bathroom and stood in the hall.

"Sorry. Didn't mean to..." *gawk?*

"No problem." His dark eyes flicked over her quickly and returned to his task at hand.

Remembering she hadn't eaten yet, she ran through a mental list of what she had in her fridge. Not much.

"I'm going to toast a bagel. Would you like one?"

"No thanks." Ty didn't even look up at her and continued working on the dryer.

"Okay." She felt bad leaving him. This wasn't his problem yet here he was, giving up his Wednesday morning to fix her appliance while she ate a leisurely breakfast down the hall. It didn't seem right. She wanted to do something for him. "Can I make you a cup of coffee?"

"No thanks," he said again, still not lifting his head.

Okay, Mr. Personality. She did a mental eye roll and walked away. Ty was nice to look at. From what she'd heard from Hope, he was a good guy. From what she heard from his sister, Mia, he needed to get laid. Lily cursed the tingles between her thighs and sliced her French Toast bagel and put it in the toaster.

So much for titillating conversation. Ty Parker would continue to be eye candy she thought about from afar. Maybe he wasn't a shy loner like her. Maybe he just didn't care for her. They didn't have anything in common anyway.

He was a military vet who worked for his father's carpentry business and didn't talk much. A born and bred local. She was... Lily didn't know who she was anymore. There was her old self whom she wanted nothing to do with and had worked incredibly hard to banish, and the new Lily.

The new Lily wanted to be real, not a fake product of her upbringing. But it was times like these when she doubted herself; when she gave up hope that she'd ever have a normal life or any type of future.

The toaster dinged, and she opened the refrigerator for the tub of whipped cream cheese. Once her bagel was done, she made herself a cup of hazelnut coffee and sat at her small round table and picked at her food. The noises from down the hall made her feel less alone, but she'd rather have Ty sitting across from her. Or simply talking to her.

Lily was a social person, even though she didn't often come off as one. Relocating and starting over was the hardest and most wonderful thing she'd ever done.

For a few minutes she pretended she wasn't alone. That the sexy man down the hall was part of her life and would be joining her at the table when he was done.

That he'd give her a chaste kiss the next time he brushed by her, hold her hand while walking down the street. And at night, he'd warm the empty side of her bed and cover her body with his.

Suddenly feeling warm, Lily pushed her coffee aside and finished her bagel. Glancing at the clock, she cringed. Her ten o'clock would be here soon, and she still hadn't showered or done her hair.

After a quick wipe down of the table and counter, she tossed the dishrag in the sink and turned, slamming into a chest of steel.

"Oh." She staggered back, and Ty dropped something before reaching out his strong hands to grab on to her upper arms. Yeah. Rough and calloused just like she imagined.

"You okay?"

She couldn't help inhaling his woodsy scent. Tempted to lean forward into his muscled chest, she bit at her lower lip and stood still.

"Yeah. Sorry. Didn't see you there."

Dropping his hold from her, Ty crouched down and picked up whatever he'd dropped. She stared down at the top of his head, hair a dusty brown, cut short enough so he didn't have to style it, but not so short she could see his scalp.

He stood and nearly bumped his head into her chin. She stepped away and intertwined her hands together in front of her. "What's that?"

"The belt. It wore thin which caused the smoke. I'll order you a new one. I didn't see any signs of an electrical fire, but I'll ask Cameron to take a look."

Cameron worked on boats, but she'd heard he'd done some wiring work in Hope's house when she first moved in. Wires were wires she supposed. She'd rather have Ty in her apartment—to work on her dryer. Purely for practical reasons, she lied to herself.

"You've already done more than enough. I'll call him and figure out how to replace that." She curled her nose at the smelly piece of rubber he held. Only twenty minutes ago he held her black thong in his hands.

No. Don't go there.

"You'll need the make and model number of the dryer. I wrote it down." Ty fished around in his tool belt and pulled out a piece of paper with pencil marks all over it.

"What does this say?" She tried to decipher his handwriting, but it was atrocious.

"Probably easier if I call it in."

"Were you a doctor in your past life?" she teased. "I can't read a single thing on this."

The corner of Ty's lip lifted. "Something like that."

Oh. That smile and the crinkling around his eyes.

"Thank you so much, Ty. Really. I can't imagine how late I've made you for work. Speaking of, I need to get downstairs."

Ty took the scrap of paper back and shoved it deep into the front pocket of his jeans. She couldn't help her eyes following his movement. The tool belt covered his front, but she knew from previous gawkings that he filled out the front of his jeans just as nicely as he did the back.

"I'll order a new belt."

"I like your belt." *Crap. Did she say that out loud?*

His smile grew, and her cheeks burned in embarrassment.

"Kidding." She laughed at herself hoping he'd think she was teasing. "You sure? I don't mind ordering it." He nodded. "Okay. Great. I need to go shower."

Ty's smile dropped, and he took a sharp breath before doing a one-eighty. His heavy work boots were loud as he practically ran down the stairs of her apartment. Needing one final glimpse of him, she went to the living room and peered out the window next to her couch.

It wasn't long before Ty came into view. He had both hands on his head and was moving quickly down the road. Right before he turned the corner and out of sight, he stopped and turned, looking up at her window.

Lily startled and moved to the side, out of view. Giggling like a schoolgirl, she peeked out the window and watched him shake his head. His lips moved like he was talking to himself, and then he glanced her way again. She couldn't help the grin that erupted when he waved.

Busted and not caring, she stepped into the window and waved back. Ty stood there at the corner for a beat looking up at her before walking away.

The rest of her day moved quickly. With the warmer weather coming, she had back-to-back-to-back highlight appointments, and Annie's pedicure chair was booked solid for the rest of the week as well.

The massage tables didn't typically get booked up until the summer, but the locals would treat themselves every now and then. She sold a lot of gift certificates around the holidays and had a spurt of sales during last week's Mother's Day promotion.

Getting her masseuse license had not only increased the flow of traffic to her spa, but gave her those quiet moments during the day when she needed them most. Lily loved starting her day out with hair appointments, chatting with her customers, learning about their families and asking about their children's activities.

Some hairdressers were self-absorbed and talked solely about themselves; she'd experienced many over her years. Since she didn't like talking about herself, it made her customers feel special and remembered when she asked about their lives. She'd often jot down little notes in their files so she wouldn't forget grandbabies names and birthdays. It was fun.

And ending her day on the second floor giving a tired mother a well-deserved massage was the icing to her day as well. Gentle music, lavender and oils, peace and serenity filled the room and allowed Lily's mind to focus. To wander. To go wherever it wanted to go.

Today as she worked out the kinks in Debbie Flint's shoulders, her mind drifted to a pair of shoulders strong and wide and capable of carrying the heaviest burdens.

There was something sweet and fragile in Ty's dark eyes. He had secrets and pain hidden behind them that she wanted to soothe and comfort. If he'd ever talk to her, share his stories with her.

Although she wouldn't be sharing hers. Ever.

CHAPTER TWO

HOPE MAY HAVE WANTED her wedding to be a simple affair, but Mia and Lily wouldn't hear of it. She deserved to be pampered and spoiled, and Cameron had been more than supportive in giving his fiancé "girl time" before the wedding.

Since the Sea Salt Spa had all the makings of pampering, Lily closed it to the public on Friday at noon in preparation of Hope's mini-bachelorette party the night before her wedding. There was no need for a rehearsal since Hope and Cameron would be saying their nuptials in the gazebo at Alexis' winery, Coastal Vines. The reception would be in the banquet center on the property as well.

"Knock, knock." Mia used her hip to push open the front door, her hands laden with shopping bags. "I come bearing food."

"And I have drinks," Alexis said from behind her, a case of wine in her hands.

"I set up a table in the corner for dinner." Lily took three of the bags from Mia and set them on the floor. She'd moved the chintz chairs around and covered a folding table she'd borrowed from Jenna with a linen tablecloth. It wasn't damask, but the closest thing she could find at Target.

"The flowers are gorgeous." Mia bent over and smelled them.

"It's surprising what the grocery store carries these days." Three years ago she would have been embarrassed by a floral arrangement from a food store. Today, she was proud of her bargain shopping and how much she could get for so little.

"I've got a crockpot in the car. I'll be right back." Mia jogged out the door, and Lily began unpacking her bags.

"Where would you like the wine?" Alexis held up two bottles of her vineyard's specialty, Lobster Red and Crystal Ice.

"How about over on the counter? I set up some glasses, two ice buckets, and a corkscrew. Not that I doubted you wouldn't come prepared."

"You're always thinking. It's why I love you. I have backups in the car, but we might as well use what you put out." Alexis picked up the pink tin bucket. "This is cute."

"I bought it last month when all the Easter stuff was on clearance." Another new tip she'd learned over the past months. "I figured I could decorate them almost year round. Maybe put a plant in them in the summer. Or keep them as ice buckets."

"Got the weenies," Mia's loud voice boomed through the doorway. "Figured we couldn't have a bachelorette party without weenies."

"Seriously." Hope stepped around Mia and slipped off her sunglasses. "Leave it to Mia to bring the dirty."

"What?" Mia placed a hand over her chest and forced an innocent face. "Everyone loves little weenies. I prefer mine big, but—"

"Enough." Hope covered Mia's mouth with her hand. "What else did you bring? Tell me there's something healthy. I need to fit into my dress tomorrow."

"I've got a veggie platter, cheese and crackers, olives, some cute little ham pinwheel things Mom made, and of course, weenies."

"I think she just likes saying that word."

"Which is why she's still single," Grace snorted as she breezed inside, leaving the door open behind her. The gentle breeze blew through her hair and loose blouse making her look like a movie star. Alexis' sister returned to Crystal Cove a few months ago, and Lily didn't know what to think of her.

She'd spent the past five years in Europe. According to Alexis, Grace spent those months traipsing around, working just enough to support her shopping habit and doing nothing with her life. There was too much familiarity in her lifestyle, so Lily had kept her respectful distance.

It wasn't like Grace had ever done or said anything to offend or anger Lily, she just didn't know how to read her. And, according to Mia—who prided herself on knowing all the goings-on—Grace was quite interested, too interested, in finding out about Lily's past.

Keeping her distance was best for everyone around.

"Pot. Kettle. I don't see the boys storming down your door. At least not like they did in high school. Rumor had it you spread—"

"Woah. Easy, girls. This is my party, and I'll have no catfighting."

"Geesh, sorry, *Mom*. You're quite dull now that you've got your ball and chain." Mia wadded up the saran wrap and tossed it at her.

"How about some wine?" Alexis held up both bottles. "White or red?"

"Both," they all said in unison.

"Thanks for waiting for me." Jenna closed the door with her foot, while her loose skirt billowed around her ankles. "I guess the girl bringing the presents isn't as important as the food and wine-bearer."

"I brought a present too." Grace held up the pink gift bag with white and pink striped tissue paper tastefully exploding from the top.

"You guys." Hope swiped her hand across her eyes. "You didn't have to do this. You went to so much trouble."

"Not really. We did the divide and conquer thing. Besides. You deserve it. You've been a single mom for twelve years and have finally found your true love. Cam is sexy as sin and is awesome to Delaney and you. You're like the perfect little family." Mia clicked her tongue and pointed at Alexis. "Pour the drinks, bartender. Spa girl, get the footbath going. Our bride needs a pedicure."

Two hours and five bottles of wine later, they all had pretty toes and were working on round two of the food. Lily brought Hope up into one of the massage rooms while Mia painted Jenna's fingernails and Grace painted Alexis'.

"This was really sweet of you, to close the spa and host my party. I appreciate it, Lily."

"I'm having so much fun and am glad I could do this for you. You've been... very kind to me since I moved here."

"With the exception of not having any blackmailing stories from your high school years and not knowing your family, it's like you've been part of Crystal Cove your entire life. And without you, we wouldn't have book club. Great idea, by the way."

Lily had only been in town for a month and hadn't opened up the Sea Salt Spa yet for business when she'd met Celeste Parker at Books by the Ocean. With no friends, no family, and no one to talk to, she spent any free time that she wasn't working on the spa at the bookstore. Celeste had suggested a new women's fiction novel, and they were talking about it a few weeks later when Hope had come in. Next thing she knew, an hour had gone by and the three of them had dissected the plot, the characters, and the theme of the novel.

Hope recommended another read and introduced her to Mia. Then came Jenna and finally Alexis. Grace stopped by for the socializing but had yet to actually read anything.

"You and Celeste were very gracious in your friendship. I've never really had girlfriends. These past two years have been... nice."

She shut the door behind them and turned on the music, just loud enough to fill the room with background noise. Crashing waves and soft violins and flutes.

"Lavender, eucalyptus, or orange oil?"

"Let's go with eucalyptus. It sounds so Zen."

"I'll step outside while you slip under the sheet. You can keep your underwear on."

"I'm not shy. And even if I was, I've had enough wine to make me not care." Hope giggled and stripped, sliding under the sheet. "I haven't had a massage in years. This is going to be awesome."

Lily gently moved Hope's hair to the side and worked the tension out of her shoulders. "Let me know if it's too much pressure or if you want more."

"Mm."

She pressed the heels of her hands into Hope's tight muscles, working out the kinks, and dripped more oil on to her skin.

Hope's voice was low and throaty with her face looking down at the floor through the open hole of the rest. "So you and Ty." Lily's heel slipped across Hope's oiled skin, and she nearly fell on her back. "That's what I thought."

"There's nothing to *think*."

"Cameron said he came to your rescue a couple days ago."

Lily worked her thumb under Hope's shoulder blade. "I didn't need rescuing." She bore down harder, annoyed that anyone in town thought she needed to be rescued. Lily Novak was not some weak, simple-minded, distressed female. She could handle a simple appliance malfunction.

"Ouch."

"Sorry." She eased up the pressure and used all of her fingers on Hope's lower back.

"Maybe rescuing wasn't the right word. Cameron said you had things under control by the time he and Ty got to your apartment."

"I did." She may have burnt her eggs as well, but she wouldn't have if Ty hadn't come up and distracted her.

"Ty didn't need to stay then. You could have figured out your dryer issue on your own."

"Yes. I could have."

"But he worked on it anyway."

Because he didn't think she could take care of herself. She wasn't some pampered princess. Not anymore.

"He didn't give me much choice." She used her elbow on Hope's lower back.

"That feels good," Hope moaned and was quiet for a few minutes. Unfortunately, the silence didn't last long. "He likes you."

"I'm a nice person." She moved to Hope's thighs and poured more oil on her hands, working them up and down her hamstrings.

"That you are. Which is why he likes you."

She ignored the compliment, concentrating on the muscles in Hope's legs.

"I'm very protective of Ty. He's been my best friend for nearly fifteen years."

"I remember how jealous he was of Cameron and vice versa."

"Yeah. Now they're best friends. Sometimes I feel like the third wheel around the two of them. Which is fine. They're good for each other."

"You're good for both of them."

"Listen to us with all the compliments. When we get back from our honeymoon we should double date."

"I don't think so." Lily moved to her other leg.

"Why not?"

"You're getting married tomorrow. I wanted to give you a relaxing massage, but with all your chatter it's hard for me to concentrate, and your muscles are tense. Why don't you lay still and try to drift off to sleep?"

Hope propped herself up on her elbows and looked over her shoulder with a grin. "That's the same response Ty gave me when I mentioned the double date."

"He was giving you a body massage? I didn't think you were *that* close."

Hope shook her head with a laugh and rested her head again. "I won't push it, but don't be surprised when I say I told you so."

Yeah. That wasn't going to happen. While Ty had everything she was looking for in a man—family orientated, honest, hard-working, genuine, caring—he would be too demanding. He'd want to know more than she was willing to share. He was the kind of guy who wanted it all, and she only had so much to give.

And by the sound of it anyway, Ty wasn't interested in her. He'd come to her rescue because he was a nice guy. He'd do the same for anyone else.

The smoldering look she'd caught in his eyes was from the overheated dryer, not his interest in her.

It couldn't be.

• • • •

THE FOLLOWING MORNING Hope and her daughter, Delaney, came to the spa so Lily could do her hair for the wedding.

"I have complete hair envy, Delaney." Lily picked up the twelve-year-old's waist-long hair and let it slip through her fingers. It was thick and wavy. Every woman's dream.

"I'm thinking of cutting it. I have to wear it in a bun for many of my dance recitals, and it's getting out of control. The thing is massive. Mom said I can donate to one of those charities that makes wigs for cancer patients."

"Your hair is in such healthy condition it would be perfect to donate."

"Can we do it today? That way you can do something really cool with my hair for Mom and Cameron's wedding."

"How do you feel about that, Hope?"

"My girl makes me prouder and prouder every day." Hope sniffed back tears and leaned over to hug her daughter.

A lump formed in Lily's throat, and she stepped away to give them their moment. A moment she'd never experienced. There were no motherly hugs, not even before her mother got sick and died. And no fatherly hugs to make up for them. No wonder she was so easily swept off her feet.

"Lily? Can you do it?"

Thankful for the interruption to her unpleasant trip down memory lane, Lily picked up the black cape and draped it across Delaney's body.

"If the Windward girls say—"

"We're going to be the Smithfield girls after today. Cameron's adopting me, and I'm going to change my name to his."

"You are the luckiest girl in the world. Both of you are."

"I know," Hope sighed, and she wasn't the sighing type of woman. Strong, independent, feisty, yet over the moon in love.

It wasn't jealousy or envy in a negative way, Lily was truly happy for Hope. She wished it would happen for her one day as well. To find a man who would accept her as she was and not ask for anything more; not expect her to relive her past. That man would be hard to find.

The time went by fast with Delaney's chatter and with just enough time to spare to do her own hair in a quick up-do before the rest of the girls came clattering into the spa. Lily made fast work of their hair, and Mia assisted.

Mia cracked Lily up and frightened her a bit too. She was still looking for her niche. She'd made it through eight weeks of cosmetology school but dropped out when she realized it wasn't what she wanted to do for the rest of her life.

She waited tables and acted as an assistant manager at Hope's restaurant, The Happy Clam, when she wasn't at the spa. And when she wasn't working, Mia was out on dates or doing something. Always busy, she was.

Lily peered over at the fancy twist Mia was working on with Grace's hair. "I didn't know you were so good at this. I've got a wedding party in a few weeks. Want to work it with me? The bride's been great, but her maid-of-honor is high maintenance."

"I'll take the m-ho then. High maintenance is my specialty." Mia tugged hard, and Grace yelped.

"Mia," Hope reprimanded.

"Don't correct her. She's right. I'm a diva and proud of it. But I'm not a bitch. Shut it," she quickly added when Mia snorted. "I know what I want and am not afraid to speak my mind."

"You two are more alike than you're willing to admit," Alexis said from her chair where she waited for her turn. Not that she wanted one. She preferred her hair in a braid or ponytail.

"Am not," they both said in unison.

The front door opened, and Celeste Parker and Hope's mom, Diane, came through, arm in arm.

"Oh, sweetie." She cupped Hope's face in her palms and sniffed. "You're gorgeous." Diane looked over at Delaney and gasped. "And what happened to my twelve-year-old granddaughter? You look like you're ready to walk the runway."

Delaney giggled and hugged her grandmother tight. Again, something Lily had never done. Forcing the negatives away, she focused on the beautiful memories being created in her spa. If she couldn't have her own, at least she could create them for others.

Placing the last bobby pin in Jenna's French twist, she sprayed her hair and called it good. "You're stunning as well. The men in Crystal Cove are going to flip when they see you."

Jenna's dark hair only intensified the glow of her green eyes. She had a simple beauty inside and out. So sweet, so reserved. She seemed more comfortable painting or working on her pottery than socializing, but who was Lily to judge?

Socializing had been her thing. *Had* being the operative word.

"We need to get the bride in her dress." Alexis took charge and brought Hope's dress from out back. "You ladies need to get dressed as well."

"As do you," Hope pointed out.

"It'll take me ten seconds to zip up."

"I still need to do your hair." Mia picked up the curling iron and pointed at the empty seat.

"Nu, uh. I'm not a frou-frou kind of girl. You're lucky I agreed to even wear a dress. My ponytail is fine. Ben's not going to recognize me as it is out of jeans and my flannel."

"Oh, I'm sure he's seen you out of them plenty of times," Grace snickered, and Alexis' cheeks bloomed red.

With so many helping hands, they managed to get Hope into her simple off-the-shoulder dress and gave her a few minutes alone with her mother in the nail room.

Celeste came over and placed a hand on her arm. "It was so kind of you to open your spa to Hope and the girls."

"I'm happy to help her out. She's done so much for me since I came to town."

"You're a dear friend to all these girls. And to... well, the whole town loves you." She gave Lily a motherly pat and sidled away with a knowing smirk on her face.

* * * *

TY APPRECIATED BEING asked to be the best man in Cam's wedding. He was marrying Ty's best friend after all, and it only made sense for him to be in the wedding party. And having Lily in the bridal party wasn't too shabby either.

Since the wedding was informal, there wouldn't be too many moments when they'd be paired up. They'd stand up front with Hope and Cam under the gazebo then pose for pictures in the vineyard. The bride and groom, five bridesmaids, Alexis' husband, Ben, and Ty would sit at the same table for dinner. Chances were he'd hang out with Ben and let the ladies gaggle around together.

He kept his hands in his pockets and roamed the grounds while he waited for the groom to finish dressing inside the function hall. The man should be a ball of nerves, but he was as calm as Emerald Pond on a warm June night. Not a ripple of unease in the man.

If he'd been nervous, Ty would have questioned his promises to Hope. Would have drilled him about second-guessing, taking off, leaving his commitments behind. Hope and Delaney deserved stability and love in their life, and Ty believed they had found it with Cameron.

Much like Ty, Cam didn't have many friends, but for different reasons. He was new to the area and didn't have family, where Ty preferred to keep to himself. Less likely to get screwed over by those he trusted. Besides his family, Hope, and now Cameron, were the only people he truly trusted.

The only other guy he saw much of was Ben. He and Alexis had married last year, and they'd all hung out a few times in a big group, but Ty wasn't a going out and having a beer type. Ben seemed to be, so did Cam. Maybe over time, once Ty could get past his demons, he'd open up a little. For now, this was good.

Small groups. No commitment. Distance. Less chance of getting hurt. Again.

Ty turned when he heard the door open and close and let out a low whistle. "You clean up nice, pretty boy."

Cam tugged at his tie. "I'm glad Hope didn't want the monkey suit thing. I would have worn one for her, but damn. This tie. I'm not used to wearing one."

Hope had picked out light brown suits for the men to wear. White shirts and purple ties. Lavender, she called them. They looked purple to him. Girl colors weren't his thing. Like Cam, though, he'd wear anything for Hope.

"She here yet?"

"Easy, man. Enjoy your last few minutes of bachelorhood. You'll be tied down soon enough."

"I'm looking forward to being tied down."

"I don't want to hear this." Ty covered his ears with his hands. Hope was too much like a sister to him. Sometimes more of a sister than Mia. Sure, he was close with his sister, but he didn't understand her. Mouthy and full of sass, the girl had no boundaries. She'd finally stopped pestering for war stories a few years ago when she realized he didn't want to talk about his time overseas.

It could've been the roughness of his words or the fact that he wouldn't let her in his house for months. Whatever it was, Mia finally stopped pushing. Hope, however, never asked, only offered her ear, her shoulder, her arms for a hug if and when he needed them. She understood him better than Mia.

He loved both women with all his heart though, and would do anything and everything to protect them. Hearing about their sex life, however, was crossing the line.

Cars started filling the parking lot, and people made their way up the slope by the gazebo. There were no chairs as the ceremony would be quick. Ty recognized some of the business owners and a few other townsfolk gathered around.

His parents pulled in, and he watched as his father hugged his mother close as they walked up the hill.

Then the tires of a long white limo crunched across the dirt driveway and stopped in front of Ty and Cameron.

Delaney got out first and ran into Cam's arms.

"You're going to be my dad as soon as you and Mom say *I do*, right?"

"Even before that, princess." Cameron spun her around, and she giggled.

"Uncle Ty!" Delaney wrapped her arms around his waist and hugged him tight, and his chest swelled with pride. He loved this girl like she was his own.

"Don't tell your mom, but I have a feeling you're going to be the prettiest girl here. I like your fancy hair."

"Thanks. Lily cut a ton off, and we're donating it to charity."

Before Ty could respond, Delaney ran over to join her grandparents who had just pulled in.

"You gonna give her a little brother or sister? She has so much energy. I think she needs one."

"Been working on it," Cam said with a gleam in his eye. Again, TMI.

"Hope'll kick my ass if I don't get you up to the gazebo before she gets out of the limo. Let's go."

For some reason Ty felt like a proud father. Or brother. Maybe uncle. He didn't know, but he was proud to be part of this day, to stand with Cam and Hope. Just because he didn't believe forever would be a thing in his life, didn't mean he didn't want it to happen for his friends.

He and Cam took their spots in the gazebo and watched as the women started piling out of the limo. First Grace got out. Then Jenna, Alexis, and Mia. And finally Lily. The pale purple, hell, the lavender dress cupped her curves, and even though it stopped modestly at her knees, it showed off the longest legs he'd ever set eyes on. Damn, they were long.

The tank style dress had thick straps, thicker than the spaghetti looking ones that held up her silky top the other morning. And while it didn't dip too low, he could see a hint of her cleavage, even from so far away. Granted, he was looking. Looking hard. Totally zeroing in.

Ty couldn't help his gaze from following her up the three steps to the gazebo. When soft blue eyes met his she faltered a little, and he leaped over to make sure she didn't fall.

"I got it," she muttered under her breath and took her spot next to Mia.

"Nice save, hotshot."

Yeah, he may have over-reacted. Just a little. Ty smoothed his tie and glared at Mia who smiled back at him. He took a moment to make eye contact with each bridesmaid. They were all beautiful women, but Lily was mesmerizing.

"Damn, she's cute."

"Yeah." Realizing Cam wasn't talking about Lily, he shifted his gaze to the lawn and watched Delaney practically skip down the aisle to the gazebo taking her place next to Cameron.

"How's your mom doing?" Cam asked.

"She said the justice of the peace better make this fast."

"Oh yeah? She hungry?"

"Seriously. I'm not a child. I know she wants to get to the kissing part and take off for the honeymoon."

They all laughed and Cam sucked in his cheeks, which turned pink.

"Didn't know I was adopting such a cheeky kid."

"Mom says you're in trouble when PMS hits."

Ty couldn't help the loud snort that came out his nose. Even the JP was laughing. Yeah, the Smithfield trio would be one of the lucky families.

"Hot damn." Cam let out a loud sigh. "My wife is freaking gorgeous."

And that she was. Hope could walk down in a paper sack and she'd still knock Cam off his feet. The love that radiated off her was blinding. Ty cocked his head to the right and studied Lily. She dabbed her eye with a tissue, her focus on Hope right up into the gazebo and was in the crosshairs of their view.

Ty felt the rush in his chest when her eyes met his, and this time he was the one who almost stumbled. Lily blinked rapidly and moved her gaze to Hope's back. There were words being said, but Ty didn't hear any of them until Cam smacked his arm.

"Rings?"

"Yeah. Yeah. Right here." Ty pulled them out of his coat pocket and handed them to the JP.

A few minutes later Cam and Hope were kissing, and there were loud whoops from the crowd. A group hug was had with the new family of three, and Ty barely remembered what came next. He went to the stairs and held out his arm for Lily, helping her down the steps, and led her and the other bridesmaids around to the barn for pictures.

Heat radiated off Lily's delicate arm; even through his jacket he could feel her soft, delicate features. Being so close, he could smell her fragrance again. She smelled like... her spa. Not something he'd smelled before. Some sort of incense and flower. He didn't do flowers so he couldn't identify it, not that it mattered.

Lily had her own unique scent, which matched her perfectly. They stood arm in arm while the others lingered behind.

"That was a lovely ceremony." Lily licked her lips, and Ty held back his groan.

They glistened more than ever under the sunlight, and the highlights from her hair practically glowed. "Yeah."

"Delaney is wonderful."

"She is." His fingers itched to reach over and stroke her hand that was still lightly draped through his elbow.

"Hope is gorgeous."

"Yeah." He stared down at Lily's lavender nails and wondered what they'd feel like raked across his back.

Lavender? Had he just identified her nails as such? Ty let his gaze follow her downy white skin, traveling up her arms and resting on her bare neck. Her hair was pulled up and back in some sort of intricate twisty thing. While he loved it down, this allowed him to see her neck and imagine what she'd taste like right behind her ear.

Lily's breath caught.

Busted. She'd caught him staring, which was sure as hell hard not to do.

Loosening her grip on his arm, Lily stepped away and fiddled with the earrings dangling from her ears. He hadn't noticed them before, too caught up with her arms and neck, but her ears. Yeah, he wouldn't mind nibbling on those as well.

"Do you two need a minute?" Grace asked, her arms folded across her chest, and a wicked grin on her face.

Busted. Again.

"No. I, uh, we, are they doing pictures now?"

"Yeah. The photographer already got a bunch of the happy couple. Now they want the singles. Well, and Alexis."

It was better with more people around. So caught up in Lily, he hadn't realized they'd walked well past the meeting spot. Now, with the photographer posing them in odd combinations—paying up the single groomsman and five bridesmaid angle—the mood had been lightened. Which was a good thing or Hope and Cam would be mortified when they got their wedding photos back and spotted Ty pitching a serious tent in his pants.

The rest of the evening was more relaxed with distractions at every turn. Ty had taken the seat to Cam's left and asked Ben to sit next to him. This saved him from the temptation of Lily and from Mia and Grace's smart mouths.

When the couple's first dance was called they invited the entire bridal party. Alexis pulled Ben, but Ty was still stuck with four bridesmaids. Most men wouldn't have any problem with this situation, granted one was his sister, but Ty wasn't most guys. He wasn't a flirt. Wasn't a player. And wasn't interested in having any type of relationship.

Taking the easy way out, he pulled Delaney to her feet and danced with her while the four bridesmaids paired off and danced around Hope and Cameron to Christina Perri's "A Thousand Years". The song was fitting for the couple. He spun Delaney around and around the dance floor, doing his best to forget about the beautiful blonde who smelled of her spa and had his mind spinning in fifty different directions.

CHAPTER THREE

LILY REPLAYED THE BEAUTIFUL wedding through her mind for the next few days. It was easy to escape into the magical feel of romance while putting foils in her client's hair or giving a massage. There were times when she enjoyed the conversation, and she allowed her clients to control how much chatter went on with their appointments.

While some came to socialize and beautify, others wanted to have a quiet and relaxing experience. It was during those quiet moments when she daydreamed.

She'd attended literally hundreds of balls, galas, and charity events over the years wearing designer gowns and some of the most expensive jewelry on the planet. Yet it was in her simple lavender dress that Hope had found online through a discount retailer that made her feel truly like a princess.

Or maybe it was the way Ty's dark eyes kept glancing her way during the ceremony. Or the way he rushed to her aid when she'd almost tripped up the steps. She wasn't even close to falling, yet he'd appeared at her side in an instant like a true gentleman. Lily touched her upper arm where he had grabbed on to her.

"Don't tell me you're cold, Lily. The ocean breeze feels darn right heavenly. You'll lose your tip if you close the front door."

Priscilla tsked her while flipping through the magazine in her lap. Good 'ol Priscilla. She was a character for sure. Running the Sunrise Diner for the past four decades, she prided herself on knowing all the goings-on in town and claimed to be somewhat of a psychic. Some called her a matchmaker, but she never pushed couples together, only claimed to know of the match before the lucky souls fell in love.

Whether her ability was premonition or pure coincidence, Lily wasn't sure. The only couples she'd heard of Priscilla predicting were

Cameron and Hope, and Ben and Alexis, but it didn't take a rocket scientist to figure out how each couple would end up.

The girls at book club predicted the same without seeing the aura Priscilla claimed to pick up on around two destined souls.

"I can't believe these two are back together. Again. Must be the third time in the past decade." Priscilla flipped the pages of Hollywood gossip and tossed the magazine on Lily's workstation table.

Once upon a time, Lily had been caught up in the gossip as well. Only she got her news from reliable sources, not popular magazines.

"What about you, sweetheart. You've been in town nearly two years now. I think it's time Scilla reads your aura."

"I'm all set. But thanks." Lily laughed as she painted on the last of the red hair dye.

"It's not like you can hide it from me. I don't like to be nosey or nothing."

"Ha!" Ruth shouted from two chairs down.

"Never mind her. Ruth's curlers must be in too tight. Go easy on her, Annie. She doesn't have much common sense left in that head of hers."

Ruth and Priscilla had been best friends and worst enemies for as long as they'd known each other. At least, that's what Lily had learned in her short time in Crystal Cove. Town characters they were. Ruth stayed mostly in her house, only coming out for her twice a month hair appointment and Sunday brunch at the Sunrise Diner after church.

Like clockwork, she'd scold Priscilla for working on the Lord's day, and Priscilla would say something inappropriate and sometimes anatomically impossible. But since Ruth was married to Bruce, Priscilla's husband's best friend, they held off on completely ringing each other's necks.

Everyone knew they had each other's backs though, in time of need. From the stories Lily had heard, Ruth had saved Priscilla from a capsized boat when they were in their twenties. She didn't know how to swim, and Ruth held her above water for thirty minutes while they waited to be rescued.

And back in 1989, Priscilla gave Ruth the Heimlich maneuver during the Sunday rush at the restaurant, yelling at everyone to back away and give Ruth some space. There were other stories Lily had heard, but their banter was just as much fun to listen to as their heroic stories.

"If your mouth didn't run so much you might not have so much gray in your hair. Don't know why you try to hide it. You're old as dirt."

"Says the woman whose birthday is six weeks before mine."

"And four years later."

No one knew exactly how old they were. Somewhere between sixty and eighty. Lily placed a cap over Priscilla's head and tugged off her gloves.

"You never was any good at math."

"And you don't know your colors. Still pretending to see them swirling around the young folks in town as if you're some psychic."

"Haven't been wrong yet."

Lily turned on the dryer and led Priscilla to the chair. "About fifteen minutes under the heat and then I'll check on you, okay?"

"You only say something when the couple's already together."

Priscilla stuck her head out from under the dryer. "Not true."

"Is so."

Annie was used to the ladies bickering and chuckled as she warmed up the dryer next to Priscilla. "You only need five minutes, Ruth."

Ignoring her, Ruth tapped her foot on the floor and pointed at Lily. "So tell us who Lily's going to fall in love with."

"Oh, no. Don't get me in the middle of this."

They both ignored her, and Lily made herself busy washing out the coloring trays.

"It's not like I know the name of the couples. I see their colors and find a match."

"Uh, huh. Likely story." Ruth sat under the dryer next to her and took out her knitting.

Lily didn't want to be fodder for their latest challenge. The least she could do was throw her friends under the bus. "I'd love to see Mia settle down. Maybe you can find a nice guy for her?"

Priscilla shook her head with a *tsk*. "No, that girl isn't ready to settle. You, however, have those yellow and violet colors wrapped around you so pretty."

The violet had to have come from her dress this past weekend and the white and yellow and purple flowers she'd decorated the spa with to go along with Hope's color scheme. Priscilla had been at the wedding and seen her in the dress.

"Those are pretty colors," Ruth noted next to her, studying Lily with a keen eye. "I can see her in yellow and purple."

"Not wearing them, dummy. It's all around her."

"Of course it is, dumbass. They're the flowers from Hope's wedding."

Lily rolled her eyes and picked up the broom. "I'll check on you as soon as I finish sweeping." She managed to stay out of ear's reach, tidying up the place and prepping for closing. Ruth and Priscilla were the last two appointments of the day and then Lily could rest.

What she wouldn't do to soak in a hot tub. Unfortunately, her tiny apartment only had a single stall shower. In another month or so she'd take her beach bag and walk down to the shore.

She went back into the stylist room and checked on Priscilla's hair. "Looks good. Let's go wash." She helped her out of the chair and led her to the sink. Lily folded up a towel and placed it in the hollowed out area for the client's neck and turned on the water. "Let me know if it's too hot or too cold."

Pulling off the plastic cap, Lily tossed it in the trash and ran her hands through Priscilla's hair. Almost lost in her thoughts again as she lathered shampoo and massaged her scalp, Priscilla spoke up.

"Lots of yellow. Lemon. Pale. And some violet."

"Hm?" Lily looked around, spotting the vase of flowers on the receptionist desk. "Yes. They're pretty, aren't they?"

"It's you. You're a complex girl, but most people have color combinations. Very few are one solid color."

"Oh." Lily didn't know how to take that. Good, she supposed. That meant she was normal, right?

"I'd figure you for lots of reds. A girl with your looks is typically quite sexual."

Lily gasped and accidentally squirted Priscilla's face with the water. "Sorry." She picked up a dry washcloth and blotted her face.

"It's the violet in you."

"Um. Thank you?" Lily wanted to roll her eyes but making nice with her clients was part of her job.

"You're a daydreamer and able to change the world with your spiritual love."

Daydreamer, yes. Spiritual love, not so much.

"Sure. I guess." Still, Lily didn't know what that had to do with finding her match. Not that she was looking. Or wanted Priscilla to look.

"You've lost someone close to you. Or have lost something close to you. A loved one, a job, a lifestyle change."

Lily stilled. She didn't believe in these psychic things. It was all a stab in the dark. Priscilla had listed a bunch of untruths. A loss of a loved one? Sort of. It wasn't like she and her mother were close. And her father, yeah. Not going there. She never had a job to lose until now, so Priscilla was way off the mark there.

The lifestyle change. That one was a little more specific and dead on. Yet, it could mean a bazillion things. Lily had moved to Crystal Cove two years ago, so of course she had a lifestyle change. Everyone knew that.

Granted, she could have come from a similar town or upbringing. No one knew. And no one would.

"You have a fear of losing control over your destiny."

"Do I have to pay extra for the psychic reading? I thought you did colors?" Lily teased, trying her best to distract Priscilla from the truth.

"The pale yellow. Hmm." She closed her eyes as Lily finished rinsing. "There's a renewed sense of excitement and hope for your future. You're going to do well, Lily. I can sense it."

"I hope so. You can sit up now." Lily placed a towel on her head and patted her hair dry. "I'll give you a trim, style your hair, and you'll be all done."

Priscilla remained uncharacteristically quiet in her chair while Lily trimmed her hair. It wasn't until she'd finished drying it and unsnapped the cape around her neck that she seemed to come to life.

"You'll pair well with blues. You two will compliment each other. He'll have trust issues, but with your pale yellow, your optimism and hope for the future will set him free."

"Just what I always wanted. A guy with trust issues."

When the wacky psychic and her negative friend were finally gone, Lily took the bottle of wine out from the work fridge and poured herself a glass. "Want some?" She held up the bottle to Annie.

"No thanks. Dani is home from college, and I promised we'd go to a movie tonight."

"You should have told me. I would have sent you home hours ago." Annie's daughter was working on her law degree in Boston and didn't spend much time at home anymore. Lily knew how much Annie missed her.

"And miss all the fun with those two? Never. Besides, I'm off for the next three days. Unless you need me to come in."

"No. Enjoy your daughter. I'll see you on Monday."

"I'll flip the sign in the window."

Lily slunk into the wing-back chair in the waiting area, kicked off her sandals, took a healthy sip of her white wine, closed her eyes, and rested her head against the wall.

The door opened and the breeze, much cooler now that the sun was beginning to set, swirled around her ankles.

"Back so soon?"

"I put a rush order on it."

Ty's deep voice startled her and she lifted her head too quickly, sloshing the wine over her glass and onto her pale blue top. "Ty?" She brushed at the wet spot and calmed the rush of excitement his voice stirred in her. "I thought you were Annie."

"I saw her in the parking lot."

"Yes. She's done for the night."

"I can come back later."

"Come back? Why are you here? I mean..."

"No worries." Ty chuckled, and her heart flipped. It wasn't a sound she heard from him very often. Ever, really. And from the gossipy chatter from the girls at book club, many didn't ever hear Ty relaxed enough to laugh. Maybe Hope, but even then, she'd said it'd been years.

He held up a box, and she read the label on the outside. "The part for the dryer."

"I can come back another time if now's not good."

"No. Now is fine. Sorry for lounging. Thursday is my long day, and my feet are killing me."

She watched as Ty's gaze drifted down her body, stopping momentarily on the wet spot on her chest, and then working its way down her legs to the tips of her toes. They wiggled of their own accord. That was what Ty's chocolate eyes did to her parts. Made them squirm. The bill of his ball cap shielded his face, and she could only imagine how dark his eyes had turned.

Clearing his throat, he tucked the box under his arm and opened his mouth before closing it again. He did that a lot, as if he wanted to say something and then thought better of it.

"Let me lock up and we can go upstairs." She didn't mean for her voice to sound so throaty. Picking up her sandals, she walked as quickly as she could down the hall and up the two flights of stairs without spilling her wine. "Oh." She stopped in front of her door and turned. "I didn't ask you if you wanted a glass of wine."

They stood nearly eye level with each other, her on the top step, Ty one step lower. She was tall for a girl. Five nine in flats. When she used to wear heels all the time she'd clear six feet easily.

"I'm good," he whispered, his eyes following her tongue as she darted it out to lick her lips.

"Okay."

She watched as he closed his eyes and sighed. His face was strong and defined, his features strong and sharp as if molded from granite and speckled with a day's growth of facial hair. His dark brows sloped downward in a serious expression, almost as if he were in pain. Realizing she was staring, she fumbled in her pocket for her keys and unlocked her door.

Once inside, she held the door open and waited for him to take the last two stairs. His muscled legs moved slowly as if they were anchored with cement blocks, or Ty was incredibly tired.

"You've probably had a long day too. You don't have to spend your evening fixing my dryer. I'm sure you have plenty of other things to do."

"I don't mind." Ty didn't look at her as he brushed past her and made his way toward the bathroom.

"Okay. Um. Do you need anything? Tools or...?" He'd turned his baseball cap backward and was already crouched on the floor fiddling with the dryer.

"Do you have tools?" A genuine grin spread across his face turning it from handsome to holyfreakingcow.

"Sort of."

"Sort of?" He cocked a brow, and she had to lean against the doorframe for strength. When he was relaxed like this, with his hat on backward and his boyish grin taking over his face, she forgot about how standoffish he'd been and sunk a little deeper into her Ty fantasies.

Sipping, or rather gulping, the rest of her wine, she came up for air and nodded. "I have a toolbox of sorts."

"Of sorts."

"You keep repeating me."

"I'm just trying to understand what you're saying."

Yeah. She didn't have a clue either. Toolbox. Yes. "I have a hammer and a screwdriver."

"Anything else?"

"A tape measurer."

"A tape measurer."

"You're repeating me again."

Oh, that grin. It crinkled little lines around his eyes that she wanted to lick. No. Not lick. That would be inappropriate. Kiss. Maybe just touch. Look. She could look and not touch.

"All I need is a screwdriver and a socket wrench."

"I have a screwdriver." Needing to get away from the heat of Ty, Lily jogged to her kitchen and scrounged around her junk drawer for it. Smiling in victory, she raced back to the bathroom and held it out for him.

"Is it a Phillips?"

"Who?"

"Or a flathead?"

"It's a screwdriver."

Ty chuckled and hopped to his feet. "Let me see." He took it from her, their hands skimming across each other in the exchange. "It's a Phillips. But I don't need it." He handed it back to her.

"You said—"

"I came prepared." He winked and pulled out two tools from his back pocket.

"I'm assuming the other is a socket wrench?"

"You're a fast learner."

"So what's the Phillips thing?"

Ty touched the end of her screwdriver and pointed it toward her. "See the X? That's a Phillips. A flat head is just that. Flat. The next time you see a screw, pay attention to the indent in the top. It will determine which one you need."

"Why don't they make all screws the same?"

"Are you sure you really want to know?"

"Why? Is there some secret men are keeping from women?" Lily crossed her arms over her chest, forgetting she had a wet spot until her arm came into contact with it.

"Hardly. But it dates back to the fifteenth century. It's an interesting story, if you're into carpentry and how things are made." Lily scrunched up her nose. "I take that as a no."

"Maybe some other time. I really need my dryer fixed."

"I'll get right on that." The smile left his lips, and he turned his back to work on the dryer.

"I didn't mean to sound so... bossy. I just meant... I'd like to hear about it some other time, maybe."

"The history of screws really isn't that interesting."

Now she'd hurt his feelings. Not wanting to sound like she was using him for his repair services, she thought of a way to thank him.

"Have you had dinner yet?"

"No," he grunted, his hands busy doing... stuff.

"Me either." She wasn't one for asking a guy out, especially not Ty who'd paid little attention to her since they'd met and went from seeming interested to annoyed with her in a matter of seconds.

Her culinary skills were less than stellar, which was why she relied on Lean Cuisine and take out.

"I can order a pizza or something."

Ty paused, sliding his back along the yellowing tile until his face came into view.

"You don't have to do that."

"You're giving up your Thursday night. And you gave up your morning last week. It's the least I can do."

"Well then. Sure." He slid back around and banged on the machine.

Once again, she didn't know what she did to offend the man. He was harder to read than *War and Peace*, which she had been forced to read in seventh grade.

Realizing their conversation—if she could call it that—was over, Lily pushed off the doorframe and went to retrieve her phone. There were no missed calls or texts, which she'd grown accustomed to. Two years ago, a silent phone meant freedom. Peace. Serenity.

Now, however, she looked forward to group chats from the girls. With Hope away on her honeymoon, the texts were minimal. They were holding out for next week's book club when they'd grill Hope about newlywed bliss. They had bets on how long the newly married couple would wait before adding to their family.

Alexis and Ben's Sophie had been walking for quite a few months, and there was a side wager when they'd have another as well. The betting pool wasn't as big for them, though. Alexis was a tomboy and although she claimed to never want children, when Ben introduced her to his newborn daughter, Sophie stole her heart in seconds.

Hope and Cameron, however, were destined to have a few more kids. Being a mom wasn't something Lily had thought much about. Her family had been all about business and wealth and social status. If having children helped, they'd be supportive. But if being pregnant and chasing around toddlers would interfere with business, there'd be no talk of it. Which was what her twenties was all about.

Now that she'd hit thirty and was free from *them,* she could take the time to figure out what she wanted in life.

Was it a family? Kids? The white picket fence she'd read about in so many novels and seen in the Lifetime movies? Maybe. But to have those, she'd need a man.

And the man down the hall didn't seem like he was interested in anything other than sex. He hadn't crossed the line, but she could read the hunger in his eyes, saw the way his jaw clenched when they'd accidentally touched. And then he'd push away as soon as they started to have a conversation.

Talking wasn't Ty's thing, and she refused to be a toy to be played with in the bedroom and forced to shut up and look pretty the rest of the time. Been there. Done that.

Not wanting to brood about her past, she scrolled through her phone for some local pizza places. She didn't go out much, other than to the Sunrise Diner and The Happy Clam. The book club hung out at the bookstore or at Alexis' place, and more recently, Hope's new house. Other than that, Lily was a homebody.

Since Crystal Cove didn't have any pizza places, she looked up the number for one in Woodbine, the next town over. Not knowing what Ty liked, she ordered a large veggie. Screw him if he didn't like his vegetables. Part of her hoped he didn't.

Making sure she had her wallet in her purse, she slid into flip-flops and checked on Ty. While he may not be the most talkative or interesting person, she trusted him alone in her apartment. He had good stock: his parents were genuine, and his sister was... spunky. And he was honest and loyal. Otherwise, she'd be more hesitant at leaving Ty alone in her apartment while she went to pick up their dinner.

"I'll be right back."

Ty's head turned, and he squinted at her over his shoulder. "Leaving?"

Not even a full sentence. The man was infuriating. "I'm picking up the pizza."

"Where?"

"Does it matter?"

Ty stood, his six feet something frame filling up the small space. Lily instinctively stepped back, and he scrunched up his face again. "I'll go with you."

"I'll be back in twenty minutes."

"If you can wait five, I'll be done." He didn't wait for her response and turned his back on her again, fitting the inner drum of the dryer back in the cavity.

So he either wanted to spend time with her or didn't want to be left alone in her apartment. Or something. She didn't know and would never know. The man was closed up tighter than a clam unless he was talking about screws and carpentry stuff.

Which was kind of a turn on.

Lily chewed on her bottom lip as she watched the muscles in Ty's back flex and bunch under his shirt. After a few grunts, a couple curses she'd heard him mutter under his breath, and a little more banging of tools, he sat back on his heels and wiped his brow with the back of his hand.

"That should do it." He scooted the dryer back against the wall and hooked the heating vent then turned the knob.

They both stared at the machine as it tumbled.

"I don't smell anything."

"Sounds good." Ty pocketed his tools and brushed his hands across his jeans. When he lifted his head and his eyes met her, she spun around and left the bathroom. No sense in getting lost in his eyes if all he wanted was sex. And pizza.

She locked up the apartment, and he followed her down the stairs in silence. Once outside, they both held their keys and Ty did that opened mouth thing again where no words came out.

"I can drive."

"So can I."

"I'm assuming you've had your license since you were sixteen, so I'm sure this isn't about showing off our driving skills, but more a showdown of sexism."

"Excuse me?" He turned his hat around so the bill shielded his eyes.

"I'm not a damsel in distress. Just because you rescued, well, you didn't rescue. My place wasn't burning down; it was just some smoke. And my eggs. Well, I wouldn't have burnt those if you hadn't distracted me. And at Hope's wedding. I didn't really trip. I—"

"Lily."

"I'm not an invalid."

"I never said you were."

Now she felt like an idiot, going on that tirade. "I'm perfectly capable of taking care of myself."

"I don't doubt it."

She waited for the clanging around in her chest to settle down before apologizing, only Ty spoke up first.

"Will you feel more comfortable taking two cars?"

It wasn't about being uncomfortable. Well, sort of. Sitting in an enclosed space so close to Ty, breathing in his manly, woodsy scent, and keeping her thoughts pure and clean were the problem.

"We might as well since you live out that way. You won't have to drive back into town."

"I don't mind."

She hated sounding like a ninny. "You don't mind what? Taking two cars or driving back into town?"

Ty removed his cap and ran his hair through his hair. "I'm sorry if I offended you." He tugged his hat on tight over his head again. "That wasn't my intent. Just being polite."

Maybe she'd been too harsh on him. Her mind had done its usual trickery twisting words and intentions around. Letting go of the past wasn't something she could easily do, yet Ty didn't deserve her bitchiness. From what she'd heard from Hope and Mia, he had manners and was most likely acting like a gentleman.

"I suppose if you're dead set on doing the chivalry thing by driving, I'll accept the ride." She tossed her keys in her purse and watched that mouth. Those lips. They opened and closed and she swore his jaw ticked. Maybe he didn't want to drive her but wanted to go separately. "Or not."

"No. It's fine. Come on." Without waiting for her reply, he hustled down the sidewalk and around the corner of the spa to his truck, which was parked on the side of the road. He opened the passenger side door for her and waited for her to reach him.

Without saying a word, she hefted herself into the truck and waited for him to close the door. She did a quick inspection of the cab. It wasn't littered with takeout wrappers or trash. The back seat was fairly empty as well. A clipboard and some rope on the seat and a five-gallon bucket filled with carpentry looking stuff on the floor.

"Do you mind if we stop at my place first?" Lily lifted a brow. So much for the chivalry. They were back to pizza and sex now. "I need to let out my dog."

"Oh. Sure."

A dog. Of course he had one. It was a good thing Ty didn't have a personality or he'd be the perfect guy, and her heart would be at risk of needing some major therapy.

He started up the truck and cracked the windows. "Feel free to roll them up or down."

Ty was hot. He had a body that even Sports Illustrated wouldn't photoshop, a smile that was rare, but when he shared it, holy hot between the legs. And then there was the family loyalty thing. The manners. And the dog.

If only he knew how to carry a conversation, or seemed interested in getting to know Lily.

It didn't take long to reach his house. She'd never been before but had an idea where he lived. Her listening may have perked up when Mia and Hope talked about him. He turned down a dirt driveway, the oak and maple trees providing a shady canopy until it opened up to a cute little country cape-style home.

"Not what I was expecting."

Ty quirked his head to the side. "No?"

"I figured you had a sprawling log cabin by the lake. Something more... woodsy."

"Sorry to disappoint you." The edginess to his voice was her fault. She offended him. Again. Ty jumped out of the truck and slammed the door behind him.

"I didn't mean it in a bad way." She scrambled out of her seat and hurried after him. She'd caught up to him on his front porch as he fumbled with his keys.

"I'll be right out." Ty slipped inside and literally closed the door in her face.

CHAPTER FOUR

THE WOMAN HAD TY IN knots. He couldn't get a read on her. Besides being elusive and mysterious, there was sexual awareness he'd never witnessed before, which he hadn't expected from Lily.

Closing the door behind him, he squatted low to pat his dog behind his ears. "Hey, Meatball. Sorry I'm so late. Let's go out back."

Meatball was is in no hurry. He never was. Legs too short and a belly too fat, his bulldog didn't do much besides sleep, drool, and fart. When he'd brought him home from the shelter four years ago he was a feisty guy. For a bulldog. But lately, he'd been a big grump, not wanting much to do with Ty.

Just like the woman on the other side of the door. He felt bad about closing the door in her face, but if she was going to judge him for his simple lifestyle, she could stay out on the porch.

For two years now he'd tiptoed around her. Normally when he entered her space her bright eyes would cloud over and lower, as if she were incredibly shy or possibly afraid of him. Not of him, of men.

She kept to her spa except when his sister or Hope or one of their other friends dragged her out to the bookstore or to dinner. With a town as small as Crystal Cove, and a sister as nosey as Mia, if Lily had entertained any men or was into anything wild, he'd have heard. Hell, the whole town would have heard.

It wasn't like he spent every day in town. Days were spent wherever his jobsites were. Lately, that had been in Lincolnville refurbishing an old Victorian right on the ocean. The Sea Salt Spa and Seaview Drive weren't exactly on his way, yet he'd driven into town to pick up a coffee and muffin at the diner on his way to work each morning.

It wasn't because he was hoping to catch a glimpse of Lily. He knew she'd be inside her spa or upstairs in her apartment. He pictured her getting ready, naked and wet in her shower stall in her bathroom, her silky lingerie littered on the bathroom floor.

He opened the back door and waited for Meatball to stroll down the stairs and out onto the back lawn. He was particular about where he did his business, a private dog to say the least. Ty kept an eye on him as he sniffed the perimeter of the property and waddled down his doggy path in the woods.

His dog took his time sniffing around, checking out the plants that he'd sniffed four thousand times before.

"Come on, Meatball. Find a tree and mark it."

"Meatball?"

Ty jumped at the sound of Lily's voice behind him. Slowly he turned and took in her natural beauty. Creamy white arms crossed and tucked under her chest, and long legs showcased in fitted white pants that stopped above her ankle. The pale blue of her shirt made her eyes pop even more against her alabaster skin.

His hands twitched at his sides and he stuffed them in the pockets of his jeans. "My dog." He pointed toward the woods with his head.

Lily padded across the lawn and stood next to him. He did his best not to inhale too deeply and turned his head away to avoid being intoxicated by her.

"You named your dog Meatball?"

"No." She lifted that perfectly shaped eyebrow at him. Again. She did that a lot. "Delaney did."

"Oh." Her shoulders relaxed and her face softened. "Does he need to go for a walk? I don't mind waiting. Or bringing him."

Ty snorted. "Good luck with that."

"You don't think I can handle your beast of a dog?"

He couldn't help the tug at his lip. "I'd love to see you attempt to bring Meatball for a walk."

Apparently offended, Lily placed her delicate hands on her hips and let out a loud *huff*. "Care to place a wager on it?"

Not one to bet with a woman, he bit at the inside of his cheek. This could be fun, though.

"Sure."

Lily narrowed her eyes at him. "If Meatball lets me walk him, you pay for dinner. If I can't handle him, dinner's on me."

Ty would pay for dinner regardless, but he'd love to see this through nonetheless.

"Deal."

With a roughness that surprised and totally turned him on, Lily placed two fingers in her mouth and let out a piercingly loud whistle. "Come on, Meatball. Lily's going to bring you for a walk."

They stood shoulder-to-shoulder waiting for his lazy dog to traipse out of the woods. Lily cast a questioningly glance at him and whistled again.

"He's not one to come when called."

"All dogs love attention. Unless you don't talk to him either," she mumbled, but he heard her loud and clear.

Yeah, Ty wasn't known for being a conversationalist. It wasn't because he was shy or intimidated by people. The closer people got to you the more they wanted to know. And then you opened up to them, and then they betrayed you. Better to let everyone assume you were incapable of carrying on a conversation. Or, at least, this was his approach with women.

The few he'd gone out with had no expectations of a relationship. His lack of words was quite clear about how he felt about continuous dates, sleepovers, commitments.

"Maybe he got lost."

"Doubtful." Meatball wouldn't wander off. It would mean he'd have to walk further to get to his next meal. The only thing he did care about. His vet had diagnosed Meatball with depression. Ty had scoffed at him and refused the medication or therapy. Dogs didn't get depressed. People did. He would know.

"I'll go get him. He doesn't bite, does he?"

"Only if you're kibble."

Lily rolled her eyes and sighed, venturing off into the woods. Ty could see where Meatball was by the movement in the bushes. Chances were he'd found a dead mouse or something to keep him occupied for a few minutes or an hour.

"Meatball?" he heard Lily call and then. "Oh. Look at you. Aren't you the cutest?"

Her blonde head disappeared as she lowered herself to Meatball's height and was obstructed by the bushes.

The bushes were a good twenty yards away, but he could hear her giggling and the rustle of the leaves underfoot. She finally emerged from the brush, Meatball at her heels.

"Do you have a leash?"

"Sure." He'd never used it. Well, once or twice when he first got Meatball. He'd hooked the blue leash to his collar and forced him outside. They made it to the mailbox on the first day, and then Meatball sat. Then lay down in the warm sun. The following day he did the same. Seemed he enjoyed napping outside. Walking, not so much.

Ty went inside and grabbed the leash, still hanging on its hook by the basement stairs. Exactly where it had been and unmoved for nearly four years. The screen door slapped behind him, and he held it out for Lily.

"Here you go."

There were about twenty minutes left of daylight, but Lily wouldn't need that long. Meatball was already asleep at her feet.

"Hey, buddy. Want to go for a walk?" She scratched his back and rubbed his head and ears as she attached his leash. "Come on, boy." Lily started walking and tugged at the leash.

Meatball didn't budge.

Ty sniffed and attempted to hide his grin. This would be fun. The only thing that would make him get to his stumpy legs was the sound of food. Ty would hold that card to his chest for a little bit.

"Meatball. You need to exercise. Come on." She tugged again. And again, nothing. This time Lily got down on her knees and lowered her head to the dog, lifting his head up, and looked him in the eyes. "Buddy, let's go. Come on." She clicked her tongue and started crawling on all fours, obviously hoping Meatball would follow suit.

He couldn't help the laugh that escaped his lips.

"You knew he'd do this."

"Yup."

She got up and brushed the dirt off her knees. Crawling around in the dirt with white pants wasn't something he'd ever imagine someone like Lily doing. It made him like her even more, if that was possible. "I thought your dog would be... bigger."

And here come the insults. Again. She thought his house would be different and then his dog. What else would he disappoint her with today?

"He's not." Ty went to the back door. "Come inside, Meatball. Dinner time."

It was the only time he obeyed commands. Meatball shimmied to all fours and trotted up the steps and in through the door Ty held open for him, and instead of closing the door on Lily again, he waited while she brushed past him and into his home.

He'd never been self-conscious of his home before. There wasn't anything wrong with it. The living room was a decent size, and fit his brown leather couch and matching recliner. The flat screen wasn't obscenely large, just big enough to fill the space above the fireplace.

The kitchen was quaint. At least that's how his mom described it. The appliances were stainless steel, the counters a dark gray granite, and his cabinets a deep cherry. Custom. They took him nearly a year to design and build, but they were worth it.

Over time he'd refurbish the rest of the house. The oak hard-wood floors were in solid condition, as were the railings to the up-stairs. The bathrooms were next on his list. First the downstairs, then the upstairs and master. He didn't need three bathrooms, but since the house came with them, there wasn't much he could do about it. The downstairs one wasn't large. A pedestal sink and toilet. The laundry off from that room.

And besides the three bedrooms upstairs, there wasn't much else to his place. But it was his. Always a project to do, but in good enough condition that he didn't feel like a bum living in it.

He had a yard, some privacy, and was only fifteen minutes from his parents. Ty opened the pantry door and popped the lid to the kibble. Taking out a hefty scoop, he carried it over to Meatball's bowl.

Meatball's stumpy legs scurried across the wood floor and he slid into his bowls, sloshing water over the side. As always.

"So he can move," Lily chuckled and picked up his bowl, filling it with water.

"Food is his only motivator. Speaking of, I'm sure our pizza is ready."

"Oh. Should we stay with Meatball a little longer?"

Ty liked how she looked in his kitchen. Her light colors contrast-ed well against his the darkness of the cabinetry. He could picture her propped up on the counter, him standing between her legs.

"Damn." Scraping his hand across his face, he wiped the image clear. "He's fine. He likes to be alone after he eats." Which was a good thing because the gas the little guy emitted was torturous.

"Are you sure?"

"Trust me. I'm sure our food's ready by now anyway." Ty held out his hand, gesturing Lily to the front door.

When they were buckled up and in the cab of his truck, Lily spoke. "You two are good for each other."

"Me and Meatball?"

"Yeah."

"What makes you say that?"

"You both like to be alone and are grumpy."

"I'm not grumpy."

Lily shot him a dirty look, and he smiled in return.

"Maybe it's just me then."

"I wouldn't say you're grumpy either."

"Oh, I know I'm not grumpy. But I seem to bring it out of you and your dog. You two don't seem to like people very much."

Again with the insult, only this time it was the truth. He had been especially grumpy around her. Only it wasn't because he didn't like her.

It was because he liked her too much.

Ten minutes later he pulled into Pizza Dough. He thought about asking Lily if she wanted to take the pizza back to his place and eat there, but he didn't think she'd agree and there was only so much rejection he could handle in a day. Or a week.

Slipping out his wallet, he handed the cashier his credit card.

"Pizza's on me." Lily took out her wallet and fished around for money. The cashier paused, his eyes bouncing from Lily to Ty.

"Put it on my card and add two drinks as well," he told the cashier.

"I lost the bet."

"You had no chance."

Lily held out a ten-dollar bill. "At least let me pay for half."

Ty shook his head and picked up a pen, signing the receipt and shoving his card back in his wallet. The cashier handed him the pizza box and two paper cups.

"Here." He gave one to Lily. "I'll find us a table."

When they had their drinks and pizza cooling on paper plates, Lily spoke again. "This was supposed to be my treat. To thank you for fixing my dryer. Oh." She stuck her hand in her giant purse again. "What do I owe you for the part? The belt thing."

"I don't remember," he lied. "I have the receipt at home." Which he sort of did. It was on his computer, which was at home.

"If you don't end up telling me, I'll look up the part and figure it out. I'm going to pay you back."

"Sure."

Tapping her nails on the table with one hand, she picked up her lemonade with the other, that eyebrow of hers shooting up again.

"What?" He used his napkin to wipe his face.

"Nothing." She picked up her plastic fork and knife and cut the tip of her pizza.

"You eat your pizza with a fork?"

"Just half of it. When I get closer to the crust I pick it up."

She ate her pizza like a classy lady. Not to say those who bit the end of their pizza didn't have class. But there was something about Lily. She had an air about her that was almost... clearer or more sophisticated than the people he knew. And it wasn't high-class snobbery.

Even her initial comments about his house and his dog weren't from a high horse attitude, more like he'd surprised her. Which, now that he had some time to process, he kind of liked. It wasn't like they knew each other well. Whatever her initial impression of him was, he'd changed it over the past week.

They'd never been alone together, always surrounded by their mutual friends, and he couldn't recall a time when they had a conversation between just the two of them.

Maybe he came across as a snob as well?

"Can we start over?"

Lily paused, the fork resting on her lips. "Start over?"

"Yeah. I have a feeling we got off on the wrong foot." Although he wasn't sure how.

Lily set her fork on her paper plate and put her hands in her lap, leaning slightly forward. "I'm listening."

Shit. He didn't know what else to say. Ty opened his mouth to tell her just that, then shut it again thinking that wasn't the best way to start over. With nothing to say. Looking for a distraction, he ripped another piece of pizza from the box and shoved the pointed end in his mouth.

"Like I said earlier, you and Meatball are a lot alike." She sipped her lemonade and crumpled her napkin on her plate then slid out of the booth, clearing the plate from under him.

Ty chewed and swallowed his pizza, washing it down with a gulp of Sprite. He tossed his dirty napkin in the pizza box, closed the lid, folding the box in half, and stuffed it in the trash.

Lily gave him another shake of her head and walked out the door. Unlike Meatball, Ty followed right at her heels. Clicking the button on the key fob, he unlocked the door to the truck and opened it for her.

"Thank you," she said before climbing up. When her butt stared him in the face, so beautiful and round, Ty closed his eyes backed away.

The country music on the radio was the only sound in the truck. Neither one of them attempted to make conversation. When he pulled in front of her spa, Lily hopped out and he quickly turned off the ignition and chased after her, moving between her and the front door.

"We are not," he said. That eyebrow of hers. He wanted to trace it with his tongue. Lowering his gaze to her eyes, he continued, "Meatball and me."

Lily played with her purse straps, clutching her keys in her fist. "Meatball needs more attention. With a little TLC, I'm sure he'll come out of his shell."

"I guess in that sense, Meatball and I *are* a lot alike."

Lily's eyes rounded. Her tongue darted out, and she slowly licked the corner of her mouth then glided along her lower lip. Ty closed his eyes and groaned.

"You're saying you need TLC?" she whispered, her breath feathering across his face.

"I..." Ty swallowed. If he leaned in a few inches he'd be able to taste her lips. If he moved his hand he'd be able to touch her fingers. If he stepped closer he'd be able to feel the heat of her body against his. "I should go."

Like a fool, he backed away and retreated to the safety of his truck. He waited until she unlocked the front door and slipped inside before driving away.

Yeah, it wouldn't take much TLC from Lily to completely get him to come out of his shell.

CHAPTER FIVE

"SO THE DATE WENT WELL?" Lily had only gotten one foot through the door and Mia was already questioning her.

"It wasn't a date." She brushed past Mia, avoided Hope's knowing smirk, and set her mini-cooler on the coffee table in the back of Books by the Ocean. Over the past year, their monthly book talks had slowly turned into girl talk.

First, it was Alexis joining their circle of friends and distracting them from their monthly read with her sexy Italian who'd come to Maine to help her family better market her winery. Then it was Hope and Cameron's drama until they fell madly in love.

Lily refused to be the next center of attention. She'd moved to this little corner of Maine to escape the limelight.

"Ty doesn't date much. At all really. I'm glad my brother is finally getting out."

"We shared a pizza after he fixed my dryer. It was a thank you dinner. That's all it was." Lily opened her cooler and took out the cherry vodka and diet soda, glad she opted for the hard stuff tonight.

"How would you feel if it was something more?" Hope opened up a package of large plastic cups and held one out to be filled.

"If what was more? Vodka?" Jenna fluttered in, her wispy skirt blowing around her ankles. "It's Mia's turn to be designated driver, right? So fill me up." She plopped herself on the couch and held out her hand for a cup.

"She wants something more with Ty." Mia snagged a water bottle and sat across from Lily.

"I do not." Lily continued pouring the drinks, going easy on the vodka for Alexis, who'd already texted saying she would be a few minutes late.

"Is there something wrong with Ty?" Hope asked, sipping her drink.

"No. We're not... he's not... interested. And neither am I."

"Liar," Mia snorted, not even trying to hide behind her water bottle.

"Ty hasn't shown an interest in any woman since he's been home from the Special Forces. I think it's great if you two hook up." Hope grabbed the bottle from Lily and added another splash of vodka in a cup. "Here. This one's for you."

"We're not hooking up."

"Just for the sex?"

"Mia," Jenna scolded.

"I'm not having sex with Ty!" Lily said more forcefully than intended.

Mia looked up over Lily's head and smirked. "Hey, Ty."

Lily stilled, her eyes wide and her heart began to race. Maybe it was the vodka.

"Ladies."

Nope. It was Ty. Closing her eyes, Lily lowered her head and tucked her chin to her chest. Maybe if she crouched down small enough he wouldn't notice her sitting there.

"What brings you by?" Hope made a poor attempt at hiding her smile behind her plastic cup.

"Mom said a shelf in the backroom fell down."

Lily still hadn't turned around or acknowledged Ty. She'd been trained on proper etiquette in all sorts of situations, but never had this one come up in her etiquette classes. Should she greet him and pretend he hadn't heard her? Continue ignoring him and pray he'd leave soon? Or address the comment and tell him that she really did want to have sex with him? It was pretty much a lose-lose situation.

"Sorry to interrupt your party. I'll be out back."

"It's a book club," Mia called after his retreating back.

"Maybe I should go." Lily set her cup down on the table and tucked her book back in her bag.

"If it was just dinner then there's nothing to be embarrassed about. There's no doubt my brother has the hots for you. But if you're not interested you should probably tell him soon. He doesn't need his heart broken again."

"Again? Ty's never told me about a girlfriend. I'd have known if he'd ever had his heart broken." Hope eyed Mia suspiciously who actually looked apologetic for the first time in her life.

When Lily first moved to Crystal Cove she thought Hope and Ty were a couple. He spent a lot of time at her restaurant and with Hope and Delaney. It wasn't until Cameron came to town that Lily learned they were only friends. Best friends, but not lovers.

And that was when Lily allowed her fascination with Ty to grow deeper. She hadn't told anyone about her infatuation with him.

Part of what appealed to her was his sense of loyalty. Ty cared about this family, about Hope and her family. He was a hardworking man and spent time in the military. All admirable attributes. And he wasn't cocky or arrogant about his looks. Instead, he seemed shy, unlike the men she'd associated with for so many years.

There were no designer suits and ties, fancy cars, priceless jewelry or high-end liquor with Ty. Just honest to goodness, what you see is what you get. Take it or leave it Ty, rough around the edges and wrapped up in a country song.

And the fact that she could make that analogy almost had her cracking up. Country music was so far off her radar two years ago, and here she was, sitting in a cute little bookstore surrounded by working middle-class women ogling a carpenter who knew how to fill out a pair of Levi's.

Lily much preferred this life to champagne and caviar.

"Forget I said anything, okay?" Mia's voice was low and regretful. "Please don't say anything to him about this."

"Why wouldn't he tell me about his girl problems?" Hope inched closer to Mia, the apparent hurt etched into her brow.

While she was grateful the focus was off her, Lily felt bad for Hope who seemed hurt about not knowing this piece of Ty's past.

Mia scooched to the edge of her seat, and Jenna and Lily did the same while Hope dropped to the sit on the coffee table.

"It was a long time ago. While in the military. That's all I can say, okay?"

"Hey, girls. Sorry I'm late." Alexis dropped to the sofa next to Jenna. "What did I miss?" They all looked around the circle not saying a word. "What's wrong? I'm only ten minutes late. I told you I couldn't get here until—"

"Ty has the hots for Lily," Mia blurted out.

"What?" Lily snapped her head up and would have glared at Mia had she not seen the hurt in Hope's eyes. Not knowing about Ty's broken heart had to be eating her up inside. If being in the spotlight helped Hope, she'd take one for the team.

"Tell me something I don't already know. That's old news." Alexis reached for a cup and sipped. "Diet Coke and cherry vodka. Nice change. Good work, Lily."

"Um, thanks."

A series of loud bangs echoed down the tiny hall to the backroom. "My brother doesn't seriously think he's going to work on the shelving during our book group, does he?"

"He's your brother. You tell him to stop," Jenna said, reaching for a chip to dip in the guacamole.

"Maybe Lily can get him to stop." The hammering continued. This time even louder. "Although then we'd be hearing different sounds from out back."

Her friends laughed, even earning a slight smile on Hope's face.

"Joke all you want." Lily sighed and settled into her chair. "But remember, payback's a bitch."

This time even Hope barked out a loud laugh. They managed to discuss the characters in the crime novel they'd read throughout Ty's hammering.

"Desire reminds me of you, Lils. Gorgeous, mysterious heroine comes to town and stirs up all sorts of trouble."

"What is it? Pick on Lily night? Not offended at all."

"As long as you don't turn into a serial killer like Desire." Jenna tucked her legs under her loose skirt and leaned away from her.

"You girls keep taunting me and anything's possible." Lily lifted her cup to her lips and pretended to give each of her friends an evil glare.

"Even see a resemblance here." Hope pointed to the cover.

"Gee. Thanks. Besides, she's a brunette. I'm blonde."

"I could see you with brown hair. You'd look good. You'd look good with any color and style hair, serial killer bitch," Mia muttered under her breath with a smile.

Yeah, she had looked good as a brunette. Copper and auburn highlights were added every five weeks from her stylist with a micro cut to keep her hair looking perfect. Needing a change, she went blonde and while she didn't mind it, she could probably safely go back to her natural color.

"Thanks for the backhanded compliment."

"I hear blondes have more fun though," Hope added.

"Ty, what do you think? Should Lily dye her hair darker or do you like her as a blonde?"

Lily glared at Mia across the seating area.

"I, uh...whatever she wants will look good, I'm sure."

"Aww, you're so good with words, bro."

"Sorry about the noise. I'm all done and will be out of your way."

"You sure you don't want to hang out with us? We've got food and drink. I'm DD tonight, so I can drive your sorry ass home later if you want to get a little crazy."

From what Lily had heard over the past year, Ty wasn't one to let loose. His sister had inherited all those genes.

"I'm good. Thanks. Ladies, if Mia doesn't stay sober, give me a call."

"All of us or just Lily?"

"Mia!" She was taking it too far. It was one thing to poke fun at her brother and to tease Lily when he wasn't in the room, but she was crossing the line and making them both uncomfortable. Even Alexis, Jenna, and Hope cringed.

"Sorry. My bad. Lack of alcohol is having the reverse effect."

"I'm out." Ty left, leaving an uncomfortable silence in his wake.

"I may have gone too far, huh?"

"You think? One of these days all this teasing is going to catch up with you. When you finally find a guy you want to be serious with, Ty is going to enjoy making you suffer." Hope bunched up her napkin and threw it at Mia.

"I can't imagine Ty doing that. He's too sweet." Alexis unscrewed the vodka bottle and poured herself another drink.

"I know. That's why I can give him a hard time. I know I can totally get away with it."

"Well, someday you'll have a sister-in-law who may not be as understanding." Hope glanced apologetically to Lily.

Jenna snorted and bless her, changed the subject. "So about our favorite psycho heroine, Desire..."

* * * *

FRIDAY AND SATURDAY were so busy at the spa even Mia didn't have a chance to tease Lily about Ty. Soon Lily would need to hire another stylist.

Mia had been incredibly friendly and helpful when Lily first opened. While she admitted to not having a beautician's license or knowing anything about nails, she did the less fun grunt work Lily didn't care for as much. She answered the phone and booked appointments, did the laundry, kept the floors clean, and washed Lily's client's hair while they waited for her to be free.

Last year Mia took a course to earn her barber certificate. She said she'd cut her dad and brother's hair all the time, and it wasn't too hard to learn a few tricks with an electric razor. Mia's popularity in town brought in the first drove of customers, and now Lily had an established clientele.

She'd been open about not wanting to settle for too long and would help out as long as Lily needed her services. Hope also hired Mia as an assistant manager of sorts at The Happy Clam. Between the spa and the restaurant, Mia kept busy, but never so busy it interfered with her social life outside of Crystal Cove.

There wasn't much nightlife in the quaint town. One had to drive twenty minutes to Rockland for any type of entertainment. And that was a drive Lily had no desire to make. Getting lost and flying under the radar was all part of her new life.

"You sure you don't need anything else?" Mia closed the door to the broom closet and dusted her hands off on her thighs.

"All set. Thanks for sticking around. I know you don't have much time in between your shift at the restaurant."

"Might as well stay busy to keep my mind off working on a Saturday night. Beats being home alone I guess."

Which is exactly where Lily would be. The alone part hadn't bothered her until recently. Only when she discovered what being with someone was like. Or rather, being with someone who wasn't controlling and manipulative.

"Sometimes Ty pops in and sits at the bar. Keeps me company while I close up. He used to do the same for Hope until Cameron came around and stole her from him."

"I didn't think Hope and Ty were an item."

"Yeah. Not like that. Just BFFs. Still, I think Ty feels left out. I'll text you if he swings by. Unless, of course, you two already have plans?" Mia swirled her key ring around her finger and clicked her tongue.

Lily rolled her eyes and flipped the sign on the front door to *Closed*. "My dryer's been running perfectly, so I don't need him anymore," she lied.

"There are plenty of other appliances he can work on." Mia shuddered. "Okay. I can't go down that road. He's my brother. No sexual innuendos allowed. Gross. I mean, it wouldn't be gross if you two hooked up, just—"

"No need to explain." Lily opened the door for Mia. "There's no hooking up, so no heebie-jeebies are necessary. Have fun at work tonight. See you on Wednesday."

"Keep your phone handy," Mia called over her shoulder as she practically skipped down the sidewalk toward The Happy Clam.

Chuckling, Lily locked up and took the clip out of her hair, enjoying the feel of the soft waves caressing her shoulders as she headed toward the back staircase and made her way up to her apartment.

It was only five o'clock. Too early to call it a night and most likely too late to make plans. With Alexis and Hope married off and Mia at work, Jenna was her only hope at being available.

Lily sent her a quick text and made a small snack while she waited for a reply. They'd all learned not to panic when Jenna didn't answer her phone or reply to a text for a few days. When she got caught up in her work, whether it be pottery or painting, she completely shut out the outside world. Besides, she had Jerry to care for.

He was such a sweet man and treated Jenna like a granddaughter instead of a live-in caretaker. She had to find babysitters of sorts to stay with him when she went out, which wasn't often.

The evening was warm and still bright, so Lily opened her living room window and settled on the couch to read, keeping her phone nearby. Three chapters later, it buzzed. Mia's name filled the screen.

Can you stop by for a sec? Need to talk.

Talk? On a Saturday night? Tourist season was in full swing, and the restaurant had to be busy. Lily knew what Mia was up to.

Ty. He had to be at the bar. And alone.

She bit her lip in anticipation. Should she go? Plead ignorance to Mia's not-so-subtle way of hooking her and Ty up?

Yeah. If nothing came out of it, she at least owed him an apology for... for what she wasn't sure. She couldn't say, *Sorry for telling the girls I don't want to have sex with you. Because really, I do.*

Fake ignorance it was. Lily leaped off the couch and rustled through her closet looking for the least obvious hook-up outfit. Casual. Nothing out of the ordinary or Mia would call her on it.

Opting for a pair of cut off denim shorts and a cute teal chevron striped halter top, she slipped them on and lathered her arms and neck with her lavender scented lotion and added a pair of silver hoops in her ears.

The night was too warm and the distance too short to need a car. Lily slid into her black flip flops and gathered her keys and wallet. The walk would do her good. Hopefully her nerves would calm down a few notches before seeing Ty.

There was a line of customers at the door, and she worked her way through them and toward the bar. There was no sign of Mia, but she had to be running around like crazy, as were all the wait staff.

"Hi, Lily," Jessica said as she loaded her tray with beverages. "You look cute. If you're looking for Mia, she's in the kitchen. She'll be right out."

"No worries. I can come back later. You guys look swamped."

"Yeah, but it's all under control. Gotta run." Jessica picked up the tray and hurried off.

Still no sign of Mia. Or Ty. There weren't any open seats at the bar, and she felt awkward standing around waiting for Mia who had to be running around like crazy.

She was about to leave when Ty pushed through the swinging doors and emerged from the kitchen carrying a tray of glasses. Lily watched him as he said something to Ken, the bartender, and put the clean glasses away.

Ty slid a wine glass in place and looked up, his dark eyes locking on hers. The trace of a smile tugged at his lips, and he hesitated before coming over to her end of the bar.

"Hey." He dropped the tray to his side. "Mia's pretty busy, but I can tell her you're here."

"Oh, no. That's okay. I was just..." *Hoping to have dinner with you.* Not knowing how to explain it, she opted for a distraction. "I didn't know you were working here as well."

"Me? No. I stopped in for a beer. Mia's dishwasher got into an accident, nothing major thankfully, and is going to be late. I offered to pitch in until he got here."

"She texted me too. Maybe she needs another helping hand?"

"She did?" Ty seemed surprised.

Crap. Maybe she shouldn't have said anything. "Or it could be about... about..." Mia came bustling through the kitchen doors and perked up when she saw Lily.

"Hey, girl. Glad you stopped by. Corey is on his way, so you're free from dish duty, Ty. You two go out and have dinner somewhere. Or here if you want. It'll be about forty minutes until we have a free table, though."

"Don't I get special treatment since I'm your brother? And I did the dishes?"

Mia's grin grew from cheek to cheek as she looked from Ty to Lily. "Nope. You two will have to wait until the crowd dies down before I give you a table." She spun around and hustled off to wait on customers.

The little brat was still doing her matchmaker thing. And Lily didn't mind one bit.

"So, uh." Ty tucked the tray under his arm and scratched his jaw. "Have you eaten yet?"

"No."

"Do you want to?"

"Do I want to eat? Yeah. I like dinner."

"I mean, do you want to have dinner... together?"

If two adorable pink spots hadn't colored his cheeks she would have teased him some more. And if he really thought she wasn't into him—especially after overhearing her comment at the bookstore the other night—she needed to let him know she was. Totally.

"I'd love to."

The tension she hadn't noticed in his shoulders before relaxed. "I'll be right back."

"I'll wait for you outside."

Lily made her way through the crowd and out the front door. The breeze picked up off the ocean cooling the night air. She picked up a copy of the local paper and skimmed through it, stopping to read the ad for the Sea Salt Spa. Next to it was an article about the new drive-in a few towns over.

"Sorry to keep you waiting." Ty's tall frame blocked the setting sun from her eyes, and she studied his silhouette. What a gorgeous view. The sun reflecting off the ocean, sailboats peppering the horizon, and Ty in the foreground, handsome and nervous as ever.

"Not a problem."

"Where would you like to go?"

Lily looked down at the paper in her hands and figured she might as well take a leap. "How about the drive-in?"

"For dinner?"

"We can pick up subs or something on the way. I've never been to one before. It'll be fun."

"You want to go to a movie with me?"

She didn't like how hesitant he sounded. Maybe she had been giving off snobby vibes. If Ty wasn't going to be the aggressor in this relationship or this pairing, then she'd take the bull by the horns.

"Yeah. Unless you don't want to go. We could just do dinner. Or if you have other plans tonight I can head home. No worries." She wasn't *that* aggressive. If Mia's pushing had turned him off, she'd let him loose before her heart got involved.

"Well. Sure. I guess."

Lily snorted. "You don't sound overly enthused. Seriously. It's not a big deal if you say no. It was just an idea. I'll see you around."

She only managed two steps before Ty's strong hand wrapped around her bicep, stopping her in her tracks.

"I didn't mean to sound so..." his voice, sad and deep, whispered on the back of her neck.

"Hesitant?" Lily turned and studied his chocolate eyes. A trace of skepticism, mixed with interest and a dash of lust, was etched in his face.

Ty loosened his grip on her arm and turned it into a light caress with his fingers. He must have realized what he was doing and gasped, dropping his hand away and stepping back. "I wouldn't mind checking it out. The drive-in."

Her arm still tingled where he'd touched her, and little butterflies danced in her belly. A date. A real date. Whether Ty wanted to call it that or not, they were going on one.

"I need to go home and let Meatball out first. I'll pick you up in a half hour or so?"

"Sounds like a plan. I need to change into something warmer anyway." Ty's gaze dropped to her arms and made its way slowly down her front, stopping at her toes before skimming up her body again. Before she did anything stupid, like lock her lips to his, she started down the sidewalk toward the spa.

"Do you want a ride?" he called after her.

Lily turned, walking backward. "It's only a half mile. I'll still get home before you. Go take care of Meatball. I'll see you soon." She waved and spun back around, the happy smile on her face warming her inside and out.

· · · ·

HIS SISTER WAS A ROYAL pain in the ass, yet he had to appreciate her tenacity. She'd never been so obvious trying to hook him up with someone. Hell, she'd never tried to seriously hook him before.

Mia had hedged, had asked him on too many occasions to go out with her on weekends, to meet up with some of her party crowd. A crowd she kept outside of Crystal Cove. They weren't her true friends, he knew. They were her escape. Escape from what, he wasn't sure.

Just like his escape was unknown to many as well. Most assumed he was a quiet man. One who'd experienced and seen too much in Afghanistan. True. But it wasn't war that made him close up.

"Meatball," he called, opening the front door to his house. "I don't have all night. You gotta go do your business fast so I can get going." Ty crouched and rubbed his unappreciative dog's ears and back. "Come on, boy."

He led his dog to the back door, opening it wide and impatiently waiting for him to follow. "You don't get dinner until you pee on a tree, so make it snappy." Ty went back into the kitchen and prepared Meatball's dinner and filled his water dish.

A few minutes later he checked on his dog, still moseying around the backyard. "Dinner's ready." Meatball cocked his head toward Ty and lifted his leg, christening an oak. "Good boy."

Once he was back inside, Ty took a quick shower to clean off the restaurant smell and went over to say goodbye to Meatball. "You be good." His dog rolled over, and Ty rubbed his belly. "I'll be home late. No wild parties, and don't let any strangers in our house."

Fifteen minutes later he parked outside Lily's spa. She was out the front door before he had time to turn off the ignition, and helped herself into the front seat before he could do the gentlemanly thing and open the door for her.

"Sorry if I kept you waiting."

"No. Not at all. It didn't take me long to change."

Ty glanced at her legs. Thankfully they were covered in denim. Sitting in close quarters with long, bare-naked legs would test his self-control more than he wanted.

"I'm sure there'll be a Subway or store where we can get sandwiches along the way, if that's okay with you?"

"Sounds perfect. I would have packed something but my fridge is a little bare."

If he'd thought of it he would have tossed a few beverages in a cooler. Instead, his mind had one track. Lily. She trumped food any day of the week.

He headed south out of Crystal Cove. They found a deli still open and bought some snacks and drinks as well. There was a line of cars at least a quarter mile long outside the drive-in.

"Think they'll have room for us? I wasn't expecting it to be so busy." Lily scooted to the edge of her seat and peered out the window. Ty got a glimpse of her back and saw the markings of a tattoo above the waistline of her jeans.

He clamped his eyes shut and looked away before his hands got away from him and did something stupid like reach out and trace the tattoo with his fingers.

"The line's moving." Lily's excitement was contagious. He didn't want to think about a Plan B if they couldn't get in.

It didn't take long until they reached the front, paid the ten dollars to get in, and drove to the back of the lot to the area designated for trucks and big SUVs.

"This okay?"

"Absolutely. I've never been to a drive-in before."

"Actually, neither have I."

"I didn't even think about looking up to see what movies they were featuring tonight."

The sign outside listed the new Bruce Willis action flick and some other movie he'd never heard of.

"We don't have to stay for both if you don't want to. By the time the first one starts it's going to be close to nine." The days were still long this early in the summer, which Ty appreciated. Even more so tonight meaning he'd have more time with Lily.

"Actually, the second one is supposed to be pretty good. A romantic horror."

"Sounds like an oxymoron." Or the truth for some.

"Which is what makes it all the hype."

"Hungry?" Ty rolled down the windows and turned the radio station to the one that would play the movie.

"Starved." Lily dove into the bag and handed him his roast beef sub and opened her turkey sub on her lap.

They listened to the commercials while they ate, and not long after they finished, the movie started.

"That's so inaccurate," Ty mumbled under his breath as he sat back to watch the movie. He hated how every movie depicted Afghanistan as blazing hot sun and dry sandstorms. He'd spent too many Christmases there cold and shivering in his barracks.

"Hmm?" Lily reached for her water bottle and leaned toward him while still facing the movie.

"They cut from Thanksgiving in the States to a hot sandstorm in Kabul. The average temperature is forty in December."

"You spent a lot of time there?"

"Eight years."

"Thank you." Ty tilted his head toward her. "For your service. Thank you for giving eight years of your life to our country."

The way she spoke, the sincerity in her voice and in her eyes had him all turned up in knots. It wasn't a polite *thank you* but one that sounded genuine. Hell, everything Lily said sounded genuine.

But so had Kristi's words. He'd believed her every time she said *I love you*. What a crock that was.

Erasing her from his mind, he focused on the big screen again. "Don't pull a Rambo mission, guys. Make it real."

"Do war movies bother you?"

"No. Just when they Hollywoodize the war. There's a lot of sitting around waiting for action. And action is never good in war. Sure, it gets the adrenaline pumping, but it also means danger. You never know if you're coming back alive. If your team will be whole when it's over. Mostly it's trainings, studying, being on alert twenty-four seven."

"Were you scared? Sorry. I don't mean to pry. I've never known anyone who'd been in the military. It's an honorable thing to do."

Again, she'd made his chest swell with pride. He zeroed in on the smooth skin of her neck and swallowed hard, his Adam's apple working overtime to keep his lust at bay.

"What made you want to enlist?" Lily moved her body sideways so she faced him instead of the movie. "If you don't mind me asking."

"It's fine." He didn't mind at all. Her interest in him helped curb some of the inadequacies he felt when he heard her say she didn't want to have sex with him. Well, she said she hadn't had sex with him, but his deflated ego twisted it around a bit. "I was decent at sports, okay at school, and didn't know what I wanted to do with my life. I knew working with my dad was an option, but I needed to branch out on my own for a bit. The idea, the thrill of joining the military, appealed to me. Nothing was holding me back, so I enlisted."

"Which branch?"

"Army. Eventually Special Ops." And when his heart had been crushed he sought out the more dangerous opportunities.

"Wow. Do you mind talking about any of your... missions? Is that what you call them?"

"Yeah," he chuckled. "I'm not one to tell stories, though." This was more talking than he'd done in years. It was her infectious smile, or her sincere interest in *him* that had the previously dormant words flowing.

A barrage of gunfire rang through the speakers of his truck, bringing him back to Afghanistan for a moment. The ever-changing temperature, dry heat, dry cold. Sand. Boredom. Fear. Card games. Women.

Woman. Only one. The one who had promised to spend the rest of her life with him and then... Ty lowered the volume and focused on the screen again.

Lily didn't ask any more questions as they watched the rest of the movie in near silence.

There was a quick intermission between movies. "You sure you're up for the second one? It'll be after midnight by the time it's over."

"The spa is closed tomorrow, so I can sleep in. Unless you need to get back home? Will Meatball be okay?"

"I think he likes it better when I'm gone all day. When I'm home he gives me this attitude like I'm interfering with his personal space and bothering him with my demands to go outside and get some fresh air."

"Aw, he's a cutie." Lily tucked a lock of hair behind her ear and Ty followed her movements, his gaze lowering to her neck and scoping downward to the rise and fall of her breasts. Her hands moved through the air while she rattled on about Meatball and how she'd love to try to get him to play on the beach. "Does he like the water?"

"He doesn't like much of anything. In case you didn't notice, he's a bit of a grump. Like his owner, as you pointed out so sweetly."

CHAPTER SIX

IF HE WASN'T SO ADORABLE, Lily would have bopped Ty in the head five dozen times already. He couldn't go five minutes without talking through the movie. Not talking to her, but to himself. Mumbling, but loud enough for her to hear.

Whether it be the acting, the poor interpretation of the war, or his impressiveness with the special effects, Ty had a comment for everything.

Ev-er-y-thing.

And she didn't even think he was aware of what he was doing, or rather, saying. She nearly laughed out loud toward the end of the first movie when he predicted almost verbatim what one of the characters would say after his narrowing escape from a grenade.

Ty had to have asked over fifty rhetorical questions during the second movie. After attempting to respond to the first dozen and receiving a confused glance from him each time, she kept her comments to herself. If she'd been more interested in the movie than Ty, she would've been irritated with the interruption.

But hearing him talk, witnessing his intensity—no matter how crazy—to the acting, special effects, and other curiosities, kind of turned her on.

It wasn't because she'd gone so long without a man's touch, and even longer without a man's love. It was Ty. There were layers. Not onions, cake. Each one delectable. The outside décor was something to swoon over, and the frosting underneath the decorations was smooth and sweet as well.

Well, maybe not smooth. Ty wasn't a smooth talker. Thank God. If he was she wouldn't be sitting in the cab of his truck, breathing in his woodsy scent and wishing he'd slide closer so she could touch—or taste—his layers of delicious cake. It was his bumbling honesty and trace of insecurity that lured her in. Maybe insecurity was the wrong word to use. Ty was a confident man, but not cocky or bullheaded.

Different. A change from her past, which was exactly what she wanted for the rest of her life. Not that she was thinking about wedding bells and forever with Ty. Locked lips and tangled limbs would work just fine. For now.

The credits rolled, and Ty turned on the truck. She'd completely missed the ending, staring off into space and working up some erotic fantasies that involved Ty. Naked.

Car lights turned on all around them as vehicles started pulling out of their spaces, inching into line to exit the drive-in parking lot. They were stuck in a stand-still for a while before traffic moved.

"Kind of a lame ending." Ty turned on his blinker and turned onto the road.

"You get pretty worked up over movies, huh?"

She caught Ty's shrug out of the corner of her eye. "Not really."

Lily snorted. "That's not what I'd say." He looked at her quickly before returning his attention to the road. "You talk more during the movies than in all the times I've been around you."

"No I don't."

She laughed again. "Really? You can't hear yourself?" She deepened her voice mimicking Ty's rolling narrative. "*Eminem? He's more of a Lynard Skynard kind of guy.*"

"You have to agree. The main character was sixty-five and completely old school. He wouldn't be listening to rap music in his car."

"*Stereotypical damsel in distress move,*" she mimicked again.

"It was."

"I know. I'm not saying I disagree with most of your comments, but you say what most people would only think."

"Sorry. Didn't mean to be so annoying."

Ty pulled in front of the spa and shoved the gearshift into park before jumping out of the truck. She couldn't help but giggle at the scowl he wore when he opened the door for her, helping her to her feet.

"What? Now you're laughing at me?"

"You're cute."

"I'm not *cute*."

"Yes, you are." Lily leaned into his wide chest and pressed a chaste kiss to his lips.

Strong hands gripped on to her waist, holding her against him.

"Lily." The moon illuminated the dark, empty street just enough to see his eyes turn from a milky soft chocolate to an intense and dark smoldering brown.

He wanted her. She wanted him. They were two consenting adults. "Walk me to my apartment," she whispered across his lips. She slipped from his grasp and prayed her shaking legs would hold her upright. She had two flights of stairs to go up and wished upon a star he'd follow.

She rifled through her purse for her keys and unlocked the front door. The heat radiating off Ty warmed her back, and she all but leaned back into his strength. When they were both inside the spa he spun her around, Lily's butt pressed against the front door, closing it with a slam.

Ty's mouth came down hard on hers. Gentle he was not. His hands cupped the sides of her face, almost roughly, but without force, and his fingers threaded through her hair. Lily opened her mouth to him, welcoming his kiss.

Fearing she'd tumble, she clutched at his back, drawing him in deeper, the window of the front door cold against her back. Ty pressed into her mouth, stroking her with his tongue, playing with her lips. His body was tight and tense with passion.

"Upstairs," she said when she could breathe again.

"Are you sure?" he asked between laborious breaths.

"You've gotta be kidding me." Before he could question her again, she grabbed his hand in hers and pulled him to the back toward the stairs.

At the top, he pinned her against a wall again and kissed her neck, leaving a trail from one side to the other with his lips. He slid her against the wall to the closest room, lifting his head for a second to peek in.

"That's not going to hold us."

No. A massage table would not do for what she wanted to happen between them.

"My apartment." Lily gripped the front of his jeans and tugged him toward her private stairway.

Once again Ty pinned her to the door. She stood on the top step and he on the one below her making them almost eye level. He reached for the doorknob and swore.

"It's locked."

"My keys are—" so caught up in passion she'd completely forgotten to take them out of the front door. "Still in the outside door."

"Shit." Ty nipped at her lip and ran down the stairs.

She heard him storm down the next set, the bell above the front door ringing. Did he just leave? Leaning against the wall for support, she waited for him to come back.

And waited some more.

He left. Smack dab in the middle of their hot and heavy make-out session and Ty Parker bugged out. Just as tears threatened to pool in her eyes, the bell chimed again. There was a wrestle with the front door and the familiar sound from her noisy keychain, and then Ty's loud pounding up the stairs again. When he rounded the corner and was in eyesight of her, he slowed.

Their gazes locked, and her entire body froze. The intensity radiating off Ty was enough to burn the place down. She watched his chest rise and fall with heavy breathing until her legs began to shake.

"My truck. I... moved it."

So lost in the heat of the moment she'd forgotten he'd parked haphazardly on the curb in front of the spa. Leave it to Ty to have enough control to tamp down the rush of desire and do the practical thing.

"Are you going to stand there all day or—"

As if in stealth mode Ty was on the top step with her before she had time to register he'd even moved. Just as stealthily, he unlocked the door and pulled them through. Lily grabbed on to the hem of his shirt and yanked it over his head, tossing it to the couch behind her.

"Wow." Lily slid her hands across his chest, scraping her nails down his ribcage and circling her fingers around his waistband. She knew what he wore under his clothes would be magnificent. Ty's body wasn't one made of fancy treadmills and machines but built by hard, physical labor.

She'd gawked over his arms many times, appreciating the muscle and definition, but tonight... his chest. His stomach. Wow. He didn't have that obvious six-pack ridge. Not the one you see in models who dedicate their life to diet and exercise with their one goal to have zero body fat and all muscle.

No, Ty had natural abs. Lily studied his stomach as he held his breath, the evidence of a man in shape coming through.

His hands skimmed up her arms and stopped at her face, once again cupping her cheeks and bringing her mouth to his. He backed them toward the couch and she bumped into it, sitting on the arm. Ty spread her knees with his thighs and stood between her legs, bending down to kiss her deeper.

She wrapped her ankles around the back of his knees and hugged him closer. The temperature rose steadily in her core, and she was thankful when he finally stripped her of her top. In one quick move, he removed her bra as well.

Needing him closer, Lily gripped behind his neck and drew him down until he tumbled on her, and they both fell backward on to the couch.

It wasn't a smooth move; they bumped heads, she accidentally kneed him in the crotch, and they fell to the floor with a thud. She'd have a bruise the size of the Atlantic on her hip in the morning, and she didn't care one bit.

"We need a bed." Ty didn't wait for her response and kissed his way down her torso, sucking her breast into his mouth. He tugged and played with her as she writhed against the wood floor, not caring about the hardness beneath her and thoroughly enjoying the hardness above her.

She clutched at his back and arched into his kisses. "Ty," she moaned, wanting—needing—him to take her right here. Right now.

"Bed." Swiftly, he released her breast and hopped to his feet. She looked up at him, towering over her, an appreciative and lustrous grin tugging at his lips. He held out his hand, and she gripped it tightly as he pulled her to her feet.

"This way." She led them to her room and wasn't surprised when he had her on her back in the middle of her bed the moment she opened her door.

His jeans looked mighty fine on him, but off and on the floor they'd look even better. Lily unbuttoned and unzipped, tugging them down his hips. He moved his hands from her breasts and inched off the bed, shucking his jeans the rest of the way. He stood in glorious naked beauty, his desire more than evident.

"We need to slow down or this will be over before it starts."

"I can take it slow. The question is"—Lily rolled her shoulders back, taunting him with her breasts. They were small, but the way he'd kissed and fondled them earlier told her he didn't have any problem with that—"can you?"

Ty stiffened and ran his tongue across his teeth, the struggle to contain his composure evident across his tightened jaw.

"I can do whatever you want, sweetheart."

Lily swallowed, clenching her thighs together. "I'm a go-with-the-flow kind of girl. Slow or fast works for me. But I have to say, you standing there naked is pretty hot."

His eyes narrowed. "Your turn, sweetheart." Instead of the quick haste he'd shown earlier, Ty crawled across the bed to her, hovering over her half-naked body, his gaze never leaving hers as he unzipped her jeans, bit by painfully slow bit. Lily lifted her hips so he could ease them down her legs and sighed when she was free of them.

"And these." He slipped his finger under the lace of her panties and stroked her. She closed her eyes, her head falling back on her pillow as she willingly gave herself to Ty.

They touched, stroked, kissed, and she screamed out his name as he brought her to orgasm with his mouth. "Ty. Condom."

He paused and looked at her bedside table. "Do you have any?"

"Me?" Lily propped herself up on her elbows. She had no need to purchase any. For years she was on the pill, but ever since relocating to Maine she had no need for any type of birth control. "No."

Ty rubbed his hands across his face, the tension evident in the tautness of his jaw. "I might." He rolled out of bed and reached for his jeans, digging out his wallet. When he lifted his gaze to hers, serious and intense, she knew he'd struck gold. "It may be expired."

"Is there a date on it?" She crawled across the bed to him and played with his nipples while she waited for him to finish his inspection.

"I can't see straight when you touch me."

She bit the smile spreading on her lips. "Let me see." Lily took the condom from him and squinted in the darkened room trying to find the date. "Can you turn on the light?"

He stepped away from her to click on the lamp by her bed, and she shielded her eyes with her hands when the light hit her.

"Much better." Ty's shadow loomed over her, and he walked a trail with his fingers from her ear down her neck and lower, lower toward her quivering core.

"Find it?" he whispered in her ear.

"No, but you're pretty darn close to finding it."

His chuckle warmed her heart. She blinked away the lust and studied the silver wrapper. "Found it! It expires next month."

"I've had it for a while."

The light, the condom, the searching for an expiration date should have put a cold stall to their sexual escapades, but by the sight of Ty, he was still quite ready to get it on. And so was she. Dropping the wallet he still held in his hand to the floor, he took the condom from her, tore the wrapper, and rolled it on.

Something so simple, so basic was so amazingly erotic. Lily thought she'd have another orgasm just by watching him.

"Fast or slow, Lily." Ty moved over her body. "Tell me what you want," he whispered in her ear.

"You. Just you," she panted, meaning every word.

He controlled the pace, slow and steady until he had them both at the edge of orgasm before pulling out and lowering his forehead against hers. "Not yet." He kissed her, keeping the lower half of their bodies separate.

Lily clutched his ass and pulled him to her core. "Ty. Please." Groaning, he entered her and pulled out again. "You can't tease me like this."

Once again he entered her, this time grabbing on to her thighs and thrusting faster, faster bringing them both to a toe-curling orgasm.

Their bodies were covered in sweat, and their labored breathing echoed through the room as he fell on top of her, his weight gently crushing her into the mattress.

Her body was exhausted, hot and limp, and she never felt better.

"Am I hurting you?" he asked, his voice muffled in her pillow.

"Not at all. Don't you dare move." She kept her ankles wrapped around his thighs, not wanting to end the moment.

When their breathing slowed he rolled to his side, and she instantly missed his warmth. Not wanting him to leave, she curled into his chest and draped her leg over his thigh. They lay in silence for a while until he broke the spell.

"It's late." He slipped out of bed and reached for his jeans and underwear.

Lily chuckled so she wouldn't cry. "Classic line. I'm not going to tie you to my bedpost." Although... "And I won't beg you to stay the night. I know what this was." Yet she hoped it could be something more than a one-night deal.

"That's not what I meant."

She inched to the edge of the bed and sat on her knees, unabashed by her nakedness. "I'm a big girl, Ty. We didn't make promises to each other. Your sister is my friend. We have the same—"

"Please don't mention my sister while we're naked in your room."

"I'm naked. You have your jeans on."

Ty paused while buttoning his jeans. "And here I thought you were a shy one."

"Me? Shy?" Lily rose up on her knees. Fighting the temptation to touch his naked chest, she kept her hands at her side. "Not shy. Private. I'm a private person."

"I can respect that." Ty's gaze dropped to her breasts then dipped lower to her nakedness. He rubbed the back of his neck and lifted his gaze back to hers again. "About tonight..."

"Don't worry about it. I'm not going to be all weird about it. I get that you're a private person too. I'm not the kiss and tell type of girl."

"That's not what I was going to say."

"Then what were you going to say? Or should I put on a movie to get you to talk more freely?"

"Funny." He quirked an eyebrow and reached out to play with her hair. "You're right about not making promises. I don't make those anymo—" He paused and cleared his throat. "I don't make promises, but I also don't sleep with women on a whim."

"And I don't sleep with men on a whim."

"I know."

He knew? How? Must be the shy comment. She'd done a good job flying under the radar, not giving people anything to talk about, but it wasn't because she was shy.

"I don't want this to be a one-night thing."

"Technically it's morning." Nearly two. She hadn't seen this side of night since she was twenty-one.

"And I didn't place you as a wise-ass either. There's lots to learn about you, Lily Novak."

But not too much.

"You have some mysteries yourself, Ty Parker."

"Maybe." He glided his finger across her collarbone sending tingles of need and want through her body. "If I didn't have Meatball..."

The spell was broken, and Lily snorted out a laugh. "That sounds like the cheesiest line ever."

"It's true." The man was adorable in his ignorant confusion.

"I know it's true. But your dog. Seriously. Meatball? It kind of kills the mood here."

That lickable grin tugged at his lips again. "And what mood would that be?"

"The one where I go back on my word and tie you to my bed-post."

Ty looked over her shoulder. "You don't have a bedpost." He licked his lips and hovered them over hers. "But I do."

CHAPTER SEVEN

IT DIDN'T MATTER THAT he'd only had five hours of sleep, Ty was running on a satisfying night of sex and a pot of coffee. He tossed a stick a few feet in front of Meatball knowing his lazy mutt wouldn't chase after it, but today, he didn't care.

"Come on, boy. You're getting fat in your old age. Go get the stick."

He didn't move his body, but he tilted his head around and looked up at Ty. Progress. Squatting so he was in front of Meatball, he scratched behind his dog's ears and looked him in the eye.

"Remember that pretty lady who stopped by a few nights ago?" Meatball's tongue drooped out of his mouth, a river of drool following it. "Yeah, she has the same effect on me. For some reason, she took a liking to you. She thinks she can transform you into a normal dog who likes to go for walks on the beach and chases after balls. What do you say we give it a shot?"

Meatball wiggled his butt and sat down on his haunches. Apparently standing on all four legs for more than five minutes was exhausting.

"Promise you won't do anything stupid if we go out in public. You're not afraid of water, are you? I've never taken you to the beach." The ocean was only fifteen minutes away, yet he'd never thought of bringing Meatball. If the dog hated walking to the woods to pee, why would he want to walk along a sandy beach?

It wasn't like Crystal Cove had a very long stretch anyway. It wasn't Old Orchard Beach where you could walk for miles before coming across a rocky cove. Up here in central Maine a nice sandy beach was a rare find. Often the tiny beaches would be overcrowded in summer.

But the patch of sand in Crystal Cove was only accessible to townsfolk, and even then, Ty rarely went down there. The sand wasn't smooth and soft like most beaches. Instead, it was coarse, and from what he remembered back in his high school days when he frequented it at night for bonfires and illegal beers, the pebbles grew in size as you neared the water.

Pebble Beach they used to call it. Hurt your bare feet like a son of a bitch if you weren't wearing water shoes. Ty rubbed Meatball's head and stood.

"You can handle it. Come on inside." Ty made it to the back steps and held the door open, counting to twenty-two before Meatball picked his butt up and waddled inside.

More progress. He remembered when he'd get to seventy-eight before his dog made a move to come inside.

It only took four years.

Once inside he filled the dog dish with water and placed a doggie treat next to it knowing Meatball would come and get it when he was good and ready.

Ty slid his phone out of his pocket and dialed Lily's number.

"Hello?" her voice sexy with sleep coated his brain with lust.

"Did I wake you?" He heard rustling before she answered.

"Ty?" More rustling. He stirred inside his jeans. "Hi. I wasn't expecting... hi."

"Sorry to wake you." He held his phone away from his ear and read the time. Nine o'clock. Late enough on a normal morning, but when he'd left her bed only seven hours ago, he supposed he should've given her more time to sleep.

"No. That's okay. I normally don't sleep so late. After you left I... I had a hard time falling asleep. I read for a bit and then..."

"You don't have to explain. We had a... late night. You more than earned your sleep." Ty cringed. "I didn't mean in that way." He pictured her still naked from their evening of lovemaking, wrapped in nothing but the pale green sheets on her bed. Her skin red from where he'd devoured her. Her lips plump and wet from his kisses.

Lily laughed. "Maybe not, but you're right. I think we both earned our sleep."

Ty banged the back of his head against the wall. If she was going to turn this conversation into phone sex he'd hang up and race over to her house, opting for the real thing instead of over a cellular device.

"So the reason I called. Do you have plans today?"

"Not really, no."

"I was wondering if... well, I thought about taking Meatball down to the beach and didn't know if you'd want to come with us."

"Really?" He could practically hear the smile in her voice.

"You make it sound more exciting than it really is. Chances are Meatball won't even step foot on the sand."

"Is he scared of the water?"

"I don't know. I've never brought him."

"Really? It's about time he experiences it then."

"Great. We're on our way."

"Can you give me a few minutes to get ready?"

Ty banged his head again. *Eager much?* "Sorry. Forgot you were still in bed." No he hadn't. He'd been picturing her naked during their entire conversation.

"I can be ready in half an hour if that works for you both."

"I'm not sure about Meatball, but it works for me. See you in a bit."

They hung up, and Ty all but danced around like Delaney and her ballet friends in one of her recitals.

"Dude. You gotta make me look good," he said to Meatball who'd been curled up in his dog bed since coming inside.

It took nearly a half hour to get Meatball out of the house again. Ty picked him up and put him in the front cab of his truck. He stayed there behind the wheel, not giving Ty any room.

"Come on, Meatball. Slide over." Still nothing. Ty pushed at his butt until he slid over to the middle. "Don't make me regret this."

When he got to Lily's he cracked the windows and ordered Meatball to stay, not that he was worried.

The front of the spa was locked so he knocked, but Lily's apartment was two floors up. She wouldn't hear. He slid out his cell phone to call her, and she appeared in the door as he hit send.

"Good timing," she said as she walked out the door looking fresh and perfect in a pair of running shorts and a purple tank top that showed off her slim waist and dipped just low enough so he could get a glimpse of her cleavage.

"You look nice."

Lily cocked her head to the side. "I didn't shower; tugged my hair back in a ponytail, I didn't do my makeup, and am wearing my running clothes."

"Like I said." He wanted to lean in and kiss her, but they were on the sidewalk and he wasn't sure how she felt about being seen with him in this light in public. He wasn't sure how he felt about it either.

It wasn't like he was ashamed to be with Lily. Hell, she was the kind of woman you showed off to anyone and everyone. He wasn't ready for the prodding, the questions from his family. Primarily Mia. Their relationship—whatever it was—would stay between the two of them.

Like she'd said last night, she was a private person and so was he.

"Thanks, I guess."

"I don't know how long I can contain Meatball's excitement. We'd better go." He placed his hand on the small of her back and guided her around the hood of his truck to the passenger side door. Opening it, he pretended to scold Meatball. "Calm yourself down or you'll scare Lily away. No pawing or drooling. Understood?"

The warning should have been directed at himself instead of the dog. It roused a giggle out of Lily, which was what he was aiming for.

He'd be lying if he said her comment about him and Meatball being a good match didn't bother him. It had.

Ty wasn't a grump. He liked to think he had a sense of humor and was easy to be around. It wasn't shyness that kept him quiet and fairly aloof. Just because he didn't aim to be the center of attention like his sister, or was a social butterfly like Hope didn't mean he was miserable.

There simply hadn't been many moments in his life since his return from overseas that required him to be overly social. He left Crystal Cove and joined the military a confident teenager and returned as an emotionally shattered recluse, according to his sister.

The friends he had in high school were casual; guys he played sports with, hung out with at parties. He'd never been too close with the guys or with any girlfriends. It was easy to enlist and be wowed by the excitement of the military.

Once he flew through basic training and was called to active duty, the euphoria had worn off. It turned into a job. Not something he wanted to do for the rest of his life either. He had his platoon buddies that he kept in touch with, but again, no real connections. Except with Kristi.

"Hey, cutie." Lily patted her thighs, and Meatball's head lifted. "Are you excited to go play in the water?" She rubbed behind his ears and kissed the top of his head.

Envying his dog too much, Ty closed the door and rubbed his hand across his face as he made his way to the other side of the truck and climbed behind the wheel. Meatball's head rested in Lily's lap while Ty got his back end. Figured.

"How old is he?" Lily continued massaging Meatball, her long, slender fingers glided up and down his back, and Ty shifted at the stirring in his pants.

"Uh, somewhere between seven and a hundred."

"He is pretty cute. In a grumpy, sourpuss kind of way."

Is that what she thought of him as well? Although the way she screamed out his name when he was buried to the hilt inside of her, and the smile on her face afterward told him otherwise.

He parked behind the hardware store, which hid the access path to the beach, and cracked his windows.

"Don't say I didn't warn you. This excursion may be over before it begins."

"I'm up for the adventure."

"Or lack thereof." He slid out of the truck and didn't bother turning to see if Meatball wanted out his door. When he got to Lily's side she already had her door open and the dog's sleepy head still on her lap.

"Maybe he'll wake up when I move."

Ty snorted. "We'll see."

Lily picked up Meatball's head and swung her long, toned legs that had been wrapped around his neck the night before out of the truck.

"Hey, buddy. Want to go play?" She ruffled the rolls on the back of his neck and got nothing in response.

"The truck's too high for him to hop down. I usually have to carry him in and out." Ty brushed his shoulder against Lily, gently nudging her out of the way as he scooped up his fifty-pound mutt.

Setting him on the ground, he whispered in his ear, "Can you try to show off just a little?"

Lily giggled behind him as she hopped out. Apparently, he hadn't whispered quietly enough. Rising to his feet, he shut the truck's door and clicked his tongue.

"Alright, Meatball. Let's show the lady what you're made of." The dog didn't budge. Maybe Ty should have brought the leash. He could've at least tugged on it in hopes of getting him to move.

Instead, Meatball sat on his back paws and drooled. Lily jogged in front of them a good ten yards and crouched on her haunches as well. "Come here, boy." She patted her bare knees and gave Meatball a smile that would have any man in a twenty-mile radius running to her. His dog was stupid.

Leaving Meatball's side, he stood next to Lily and sighed. "Maybe this wasn't a good idea."

"He hasn't even seen the water yet. He doesn't know what he's missing."

"I guess I can carry him down." Ty went back and picked him up. He was dead weight in his arms. Lily skipped alongside them cooing and talking with excitement to his deadbeat dog.

"Do you want to play ball? Chase a stick? Dig in the sand?" She rubbed his chins, ignoring the drool and the bad attitude.

"I told you not to expect much. Meatball isn't exactly a dog filled with emotion, energy, or life." Ty's arms tightened around his dog as his words hit home. Would Lily say the same thing about him? Again?

Was this why he didn't have a circle of friends other than Hope and Cameron? They were the best, and he didn't mind one bit being the third wheel or sitting at home alone with his uncommunicative dog. Not being overtly social, he didn't mind being home alone on a Friday night. Or all weekend.

When a woman he'd met from a construction job crossed his path, there was the occasional date or brief hook up.

And there was always work to do, a project to plan and execute. Either the Sox were on or the Pats. The Celtics and Bruins ran simultaneously from fall to spring.

And he had Meatball.

Damn. His life *was* pathetic.

When they reached the sand, Lily put one hand on his shoulder for balance and slid off her flip-flops. Ty set Meatball down and watched the lack of enthusiasm as the dog sat its butt in the sand.

"Let's get closer to the water." Lily jogged to the shoreline and splashed her feet in the gentle surf. "Come on, Meatball!" she called.

God, she was gorgeous. The light spray from her prancing dotted the front of her shirt and glistened on her skin in the sunlight. He could see the sparkle in her eyes even from twenty yards away. Lily lifted her hands above her head and danced and frolicked in the waves, looking more like a little girl than a grown woman.

Except her curves and long limbs. Yeah. Those were anything but girlish.

The sun warmed his skin, but the breeze off the ocean cooled the temps a bit making the morning air fresh and invigorating. At least for him. And Lily. Damn, she was a dream.

"Dude. Look at her. How can you not want to run your fat little legs to her and lap at her ankles?"

Not waiting for his grump of a sidekick, he kicked off his shoes and licked his lips as his legs ate up the distance between him and the woman of his dreams.

Shit. Ty stopped short of the water, his toes curling into the warm, coarse sand and rocks and took a moment to come to terms with the struggle in his head. Both heads.

There was no doubt he wanted her in the most carnal way, but it was more than that. While he hadn't had a lot of sex over the past few years, he wasn't celibate and wasn't a saint, yet he'd never wanted a woman as much as he wanted Lily.

And it wasn't just her beauty. He actually enjoyed being around her. She made him laugh, made him think, and called him on his surly mood. There was an open honesty in her he found refreshing.

And she hadn't given up on his dog. Granted, she'd only met him a few times; still, her determination tugged at his heart.

"Don't look now, but Meatball is hedging this way." Ty started to turn his head and Lily rushed to him, taking his face in her hands. "Keep ignoring him."

"That's easy to do."

"He's curious." Lily's gaze was locked over his shoulder as she watched Meatball, oblivious to what she was doing to Ty.

Her hands were soft and delicate on his face, and he reached up, covering them with his. Slowly Lily's eyes shifted toward him. They darkened, changing from sky blue to a deep, mysterious cavern of sensuality.

He didn't want everything between them to be sexual, but the tremble in her hands and the way she seductively ran her tongue across her bottom lip made it near impossible to think about anything other than getting her naked.

Something bumped into the back of his knee causing him to stumble, the physical and emotional connection now lost between him and Lily. He looked down and cursed. "Meatball."

"He came." Lily clapped her hands and squatted to dote her love and affection on the beast. "Look, Ty! His tail is wagging."

Normally a wagging tail on a dog was no cause for excitement, but when Meatball's tail wagged, it was truly a momentous occasion. Delaney had been the only one to get a stir out of the short numb on his backside, and sometimes Hope. Since Cameron came into their lives their visits to his home were more infrequent, but he didn't begrudge them. They were a new family, and he couldn't be happier for the three of them.

"He likes the water." Lily stepped away and stomped in the water, causing spray to hit Ty and Meatball.

Meatball shook his head and stepped closer to the water until his paws stumbled on the pebbles and were nearly covered with water. He barked at the waves and scurried back. Then back in following the tide. Over and over again he barked as the tide came in, and he chased it out trotting into the water before being chased by the waves themselves and backing out of the water.

"He's adorable, Ty. Look. He doesn't know whether to be afraid of the water or to play in it."

Both Lily and Meatball ignored him, finding the coming and going of the waves more interesting than him. Figures.

Not much of a beach person, he backed away and sat on the dry sand thoroughly enjoying the two playing in the water. She continued to talk to Meatball as if he were a young toddler and Meatball barked, played, and wagged that stumpy tail of his.

Ty caught himself smiling and even barked out a laugh when his dog found himself deeper in the water than he wanted to be, the waves splashing over his wrinkled face. When he shook himself free from the coating he'd received, his spray shot out, covering Lily. She shrieked and ran away from him.

Meatball, enjoying her reaction as much as Ty had, followed her down the shoreline. They couldn't go far before an outcropping of rocks stopped them. They played at the far end of the beach and slowly made their way back to Ty.

"I'm a mess." Lily stood in front of Ty blocking the sun from his eyes.

She was. A beautiful mess. Her shorts were soaked, and her tank top was more wet than dry. Meatball followed at her heels, dropping to the sand at her feet. Within seconds his eyes were closed.

"I didn't think he'd ever do enough to actually tucker himself out. Nice job." Ty patted the sand next to him. "Have a seat and dry off."

"Eww. I'm wet. The sand will stick to me, and I didn't even think to bring a towel." Neither had he. Ty really didn't think Meatball would actually touch the water. "I don't want to make a mess in your truck."

"I'm not worried about my truck."

"You sure?"

He gave her a measured look, and she plopped herself in the sand next to him.

"You seemed to enjoy yourself out there. Both of you."

"I did."

"Did you go to the beach a lot as a kid?"

Lily tucked her knees up to her chest and wrapped her arms around them. "No. Never."

The sadness in her voice pulled at his heart. "As a teen?"

She shook her head. "My parents... my dad wasn't... really the beach type."

"Your mom?"

One shoulder lifted. "Died when I was young."

"I'm sorry." He ran his hand up and down her back in what he hoped to be a comforting gesture. Since she didn't add any more information and he respected her privacy, he asked, "What about later on? Did you go to college or venture out on your own?"

Lily rested her chin on her knees and stared off over the ocean. "I went to NYU. I have a master's degree in business management. A minor in finance. Until recently, I'd never had the luxury of playing in the water."

It was the most she'd ever said about her past. The first sign of her opening up to him. While he didn't distrust her, he didn't know much about her. Granted, she could say the same thing about him.

He didn't want to push, to pry, and held back on the questions he wanted to ask. Where was her father? Did she have a family somewhere she wanted to escape from, or were they gone? Why would a woman who had a master's degree from NYU be scraping by in a low to moderate socioeconomic community like Crystal Cove?

Money didn't mean much to him. He wanted to make enough to live comfortably, have a roof over his head, eat three squares a day, and have reliable transportation. Ty wasn't one for exotic vacations or expensive toys. His four-wheeler was ten-years-old and was perfect for riding around the tote roads. Maybe someday he'd get a snowmobile, but riding alone wasn't a smart thing to do and he didn't have much of a social circle.

Men his age didn't stick around Crystal Cove. They moved to the bigger towns or out of state. The locals were an older crew; many were lobstermen and fishermen. Good, hardworking citizens. Nothing glitzy and glamorous, which was what he'd expected Lily to be interested in.

That was before they started talking. Hanging out. Having sex. He knew whatever was happening between the two of them wouldn't be forever. Despite her interest in him now, she'd tire of the simple life, the simple man he was.

Kristi wasn't impressed. At least he found out before they got married.

"What about you?" Lily turned her head, her cheek resting on her hands as she innocently batted her long lashes at him.

"What about me?" There wasn't much to tell. What you saw was what you got.

"You said you weren't much of the ocean guy. You went off to fight for our country and settled back in Crystal Cove. Why here? Do you like to travel? Explore the world?"

And this was what he wanted to avoid. Yet she'd shared a glimpse of her past. He supposed he could give her that much. "I'm a homebody. The military was something I wanted to experience, test out. After eight years I realized it wasn't for me."

"Were you interested in carpentry before you enlisted?"

In other words, did he take the easy route by working for his dad instead of exploring his own career? Kristi hadn't been impressed when he'd told her he wasn't reenlisting and would be working for—now with—his father. It wasn't something he was ashamed of at the time, but she'd made him feel like he was settling. Like he wasn't his own person if he took the easy way out by working with his dad.

Truth was, he liked his dad. His family. Nothing else really interested him.

"I like working with my hands."

"I've always been enamored by a man who can build things. Fix things. There must be a lot to learn. I'm sure you're always learning. Like my dryer. You didn't learn how to take apart the machine by building houses. You must have a gift for being able to look at something and figuring out how it works, and why it doesn't."

"I guess." Maybe. He hadn't really thought about it that way.

"Unless it wasn't your first rodeo. Finding a black thong burning up the belt in a dryer." She leaned back on her elbows and stretched out her legs, burying her toes in the sand.

"It was definitely my first."

"I'm glad."

Ty's heart did that squeezing thing again. "Will you come over for dinner tonight?" The words came out before he could think about the ramifications.

Sounding desperate. Coming on too strong. Rejection.

"I'd love to."

Damn. Hook, line, and sinker, he was putty in the woman's hands.

CHAPTER EIGHT

IT HAD BEEN TWO DAYS and Lily couldn't keep the smile off her lips, and her Tuesday afternoon appointment called her on it.

"It's Ty Parker, isn't it?" Priscilla pulled her hand out from the nail dryer and pointed her new manicure at Lily. "I told you he had an aura about him. You two have intense colors. I always knew that boy was hot under the collar. And by the gooey, lovesick smile on your face all day, I'd say he's gotten to ya. 'Bout time. Poor Celeste Parker's been waitin' nearly a decade to be a grandma."

"Grandma?" Lily covered her belly with her hands. They didn't even have sex after dinner Sunday night, even though the temptation had been strong. There was some serious kissing and grinding against her car. The condom from Saturday, though... she prayed it had done its job. "I think you're getting a little ahead of yourself, Priscilla."

"I don't think so. You've got that blue hue around you, doll, that wasn't there the last time I saw you. Blue's rubbed off from someone else. You're a passionate one. The sex—"

"Did you say you wanted nail art today?" Lily shot out of her seat and grabbed the sample artboard from the wall. "This rainbow of stars would look great on your nails. Annie, you have time to add some art to her nails, right?"

"I'm too old for that fancy stuff. I think it's a waste getting my nails done when they're just gonna get chipped anyway, but Diane gave me that gift certificate for Christmas that I didn't want to go to waste."

Annie, bless her heart, stayed quiet while she cleaned up her station.

"It's nice to be pampered every now and then, don't you think?" Lily filled the tub at the foot of the leather pedicure seats with warm water. "Let me know if it's too hot."

"I can't remember the last time I had a pedicure. Must have been before I married Henry. He was a good husband. Died too young, he did. Fishin's a dangerous job."

Lily listened while Priscilla told the story of how she met her first husband, his long hours on his fishing boat, and how his death gave her this second sight.

When Priscilla's feet relaxed under her touch, Lily let her mind drift back to Sunday night's dinner with Ty. And their morning on the beach with Meatball. Somewhere between splashing in the waves, grilling chicken on Ty's deck, and laughing while attempting to get Meatball to play fetch, her heart took a quick turn down lover's lane.

She wouldn't call it love. Love happened when two people had more of a connection than chemistry. It happened when there was communication and trust. Open honesty. Something she could never have with Ty. With anyone.

So love was out of the question.

"I'd say my feet are pretty well scrubbed now, hun."

Lily looked down at Priscilla's pruned toes and drained the water. Normally she didn't give the pedicures, but Annie was right out straight with manicures and Lily had an opening in her schedule.

"I guess I got lost in your storytelling." She picked up the file and shaped Priscilla's toes, doing her best to listen to the stories of visions and readings and not daydream about her hunky carpenter.

After the second coat of fuchsia had dried, Priscilla tipped Lily generously and waved her newly manicured nails in the air.

"You can't fight love. Neither can he." She tossed Lily a wink over her shoulder as she strolled out the door.

When the Tuesday evening rush had finally ended and she and the girls had the spa closed up, Lily climbed the stairs to her apartment and fell onto her couch.

Was it just three nights ago she and Ty were stumbling with kisses and zippers right here? The memory warmed her and Lily rolled to her side, tucking her hands under her cheek.

And then Sunday happened. First their adventure with Meatball at the beach and then dinner at his house. To say Ty was nervous would be an understatement. He'd tripped a dozen times going in and out of the house to check the chicken on the grill and asked her three times what she wanted to drink before she helped herself to a glass of water.

It was cute. Painfully adorable. Incredibly sexy. And nearly impossible not to pout when he didn't take her clothes off.

Ty didn't kiss her until he walked her to her car at ten o'clock. The spa was closed on Mondays and she'd hoped she'd be invited for a sleepover.

"I, uh, have to be at the jobsite at the crack of dawn tomorrow," he'd said apologetically.

If his kisses weren't so passionate, so full of life and laughter and... Ty, she would have been put off. Keeping their clothes on when they both wanted to strip each other down was a sign of something more.

What was happening between them wasn't just about sex. Yet she couldn't define it. Not yet. They'd both tiptoed around their past, not saying anything that would reveal who they'd been before they met.

Her past was gone, wiped out. Didn't exist anymore. But Ty was holding something back as well. Not the same kind of dark skeletons she kept locked and buried, but there was a sadness he tried to bury that rose to the surface when she prodded. It wasn't her right to do so, especially since she couldn't tell him anything that had happened in the first twenty-eight years of her life.

It still haunted her. The secrets. The lies. The betrayal. The deaths. Living in near solitude for two years had helped bury the pain and scars, and the last thing she wanted was to have them lifted again.

And that was the cost of growing relationships with girlfriends or a man. They'd want more and she couldn't give it.

Her phone vibrated on the coffee table, and her heart jolted in response. She reached out and frowned in disappointment when Mia's name flashed across the screen. A wave of guilt rushed over her. This was what she wanted: girlfriends. And the real type. The ones who appreciated her for her, not her family's name and social status.

"Hey, Mia." She rolled to her back and crossed her right leg over her knee.

"Don't say no. Hear me out first." Mia's music of choice, eighties rock, played in the background loud enough so Lily could make out the beat, but not so loud it drowned out Mia's voice.

"Way to start the conversation." Lily laughed and listened while Mia filled her in on an up and coming band playing in Rockland Saturday night.

"When was the last time we all did something together besides our once a month book club meetings? We need a girls' night out. I already got Hope to commit."

"How did you manage that? Saturday night is her busiest night at the restaurant." And if Hope had the night off, Mia usually worked.

"She's been training Alison ever since the wedding. Being married has made Hope want to stick around at night and do the family thing."

"Yet she's going to sacrifice a night with her hunky husband to hang out with us?"

"So you're in?"

Lily had been hoping Ty would call sometime this week and ask her out. Dinner. A movie. Cuddling on the couch. She didn't care what it was; being with him was enough. And a night out with girlfriends sounded fun too. Maybe someday they'd be able to combine the two.

A couples night with Alexis and Ben, Hope and Cameron. Mia and Jenna were gorgeous women who could easily find dates.

Not that Lily and Ty were anything more than that. It wasn't like they were boyfriend-girlfriend. Although it would be nice to be in a committed relationship. One where she trusted her boyfriend. Her husband.

"Lils? You in?"

"Sure."

"Don't sound so enthusiastic about it."

"I'm sorry. I had a long day at work."

"Uh huh. If Hope can go one night without Cameron, you can go one night without Ty."

"I didn't—"

"I'm his sister. I know things."

"We're not—"

"Yeah. Whatevs. Since I'm dragging you girls out, I'll drive. Jenna and Grace are in, and Alexis is a maybe. Sunday is a busy day at the winery, and Sophia's been up a lot at night. Teething I guess."

"I'm sorry she hasn't been feeling well." The baby itch hadn't hit Lily yet. It wasn't something she'd thought about growing up, and definitely not something she wanted to think about when living in Italy with—

"You're done at two on Saturdays, right?" Mia interrupted her near-flashback.

"Yeah. I'll stay open until four in July and August. The summer people are just starting to make their way up here."

"You learn fast, outsider," Mia teased.

"It's a concert in the park gig, so bring a cooler with whatever you want to eat and drink. A blanket or chair or whatever too. It'll be fun."

"I'm looking forward to it."

"Me too."

"I'll see you Saturday."

"Sounds good. Oh and, Lily? I'm gonna let you be the one to break it to Ty that you're not available Saturday night. He'll kill me for taking you away from him."

"We're not—"

The phone went quiet on the other end and Lily sighed, putting her phone on the coffee table.

Needing to eat, she made her way to her kitchenette and microwaved a Lean Cuisine. Five minutes later she had chicken teriyaki, a glass of Alexis' wine, and a Jodi Picoult novel in front of her.

She'd managed to read three chapters and sip two glasses of wine before her eyes began to droop. Realizing sleep was in order, she checked her phone—no missed calls or texts from Ty—and got ready for bed.

It wasn't until Friday afternoon when Ty called her. She'd had back-to-back-to-back-to-back hair appointments and didn't get to return his call until after six. When he didn't answer she contemplated hanging up, knowing he'd see her caller ID, but left a quick message instead.

"Hey there. Sorry I didn't get to call back until now. We were pretty busy. So um, I'm all closed up now, so feel free to call back if you want. Bye." Lily scrunched up her face when she ended the call. Ugh, she sounded like an idiot.

What happened to prim and polished Veron—no. She was gone. Lily Novak sounded like a normal human being. Just your typical girl next door who had a crush on the town hunk.

When the spa was locked up, she climbed the stairs to her apartment and paced the living room, holding her cell phone tightly in hand. Her belly growled, but she didn't want to eat if Ty wanted to have dinner together.

An hour later, her stomach started eating itself. Squirting a pile of ranch dressing in a bowl, she scooped it up with a baby carrot and munched. And munched. And waited.

The carrots were gone, and she made a strawberry banana smoothie. Usually, she preferred it in the morning, but she didn't want to heat up a frozen dinner or boil water for noodles if she and Ty were going to have a dinner date.

A bowl of ice cream later, Lily gave up and went to bed.

At midnight her phone vibrated near her head, and Lily reached blindly for it.

"I woke you."

Eyes still closed, Lily's mouth stretched into a grin. "Nah. I'm out on the town. You know how wild and crazy Crystal Cove can be on a Friday night."

"I shouldn't have called."

"Why not?"

"It's late."

Lily rolled to her side and cuddled one of her many pillows into her chest. "Not as late as it was last weekend."

"Yeah, but I didn't call and wake you up. We were already out."

And had still been clothed. It was one in the morning by the time their clothes came off. And she'd like to do it again. Soon. Real soon.

"So why did you call tonight? Not that I mind."

"I feel bad we haven't connected this week. I've had a project down in Rockland that's been taking up more time than it should."

"Are you just getting home now?"

"Sort of. I went to my parents for dinner and then met Cameron at the Happy Clam for a beer while he waited for Hope to finish working. She didn't get out of there until almost ten-thirty."

"That's a long day."

"Yeah. I was hoping I'd get to see you sometime this week, but I've been busy. Tomorrow night..." Ty's voice changed from its usual laid-back baritone to something sad or concerned. "I hear there's a girls' night happening."

"Mia told you?"

"All too happily. Made it crystal clear Cameron and I were not allowed to crash your party."

And he was upset about it. Instead of being sad about missing a date night opportunity with Ty, she giggled. Ty was jealous. Of her girlfriends.

Again, all new experiences for her.

"And a wild party it's going to be," she teased. "Dancing, drinking, all sorts of shenanigans."

"I can believe all of that from Mia and probably Grace. You and Hope, however...and Alexis, not likely."

"What are you trying to say about us?" Lily bit her lip and contained her giggles. "What category have you placed Jenna?"

"Jenna? I'm not sure. Definitely nothing like Mia, yet I see an edge to her."

"So you're categorizing me with the married hens?" She knew Ty would hear the silliness in her voice. Hope and Alexis were lucky to have such wonderful husbands.

"Well, I. I didn't mean..."

The phone slipped from her grasp when she realized the implications of his words. Ty thought of her as his. Not in a domineering way, but taken. He wasn't a man to sleep around. He was the kind of guy—based on the expiration date of his condom—who took sex seriously.

They may not have said the words or made any type of commitment, but Ty was the committed type. And Lily was as well.

"I'm not outgoing like your sister, as you know. And I'm not a shy mouse either, as you've learned. I'm planning to have fun tomorrow night with my girlfriends and coming home not drunk, but a little frisky." Lily heard a lot of cursing on the other end of the phone.

"Oh, and by the way, I have a spare key hidden under the fourth brick from the backdoor. Night, Ty."

• • • •

HOLY HELL. HE'D TOSSED and turned all night and was a bear at work all day. As soon as he took care of Meatball he'd pick up take-out and head over to Cameron's.

Ty hadn't planned on working on Saturday, but with Lily busy at the spa and then going out with her friends, he needed to stay active.

Mia's little bomb she dropped at the family dinner was intentional. She wanted a reaction and if he hadn't been at his mom's dinner table, he might have risen to her bait.

"Sounds like fun, Mia. Maybe I'll hang out with Cameron and Delaney."

"I hope you didn't have to cancel any plans with Lily."

"Lily? Nope. Haven't talked to her in a while." Which he hadn't. The Wainwright job had turned into a bitch of a project. Angelina Wainwright changed her mind and direction for her home reno more often than a fruit fly reproduces. He supposed that was what a woman—or man—with billions of dollars at their disposal could do.

Ty and his crew had to tear down and rebuild tresses for the new dormers three times. Mrs. Wainwright was addicted to home improvement shows, and every week seemed to have a new idea for her addition. She didn't realize—or didn't care—that changing the size and shape of the windows affected the studs and now the tresses as well.

The Wainwrights weren't in any hurry, but Ty had three more jobs lined up and once he went over on one, the rest were backed up to hell. He couldn't afford to have any of them cancel their contract with him.

"You're not seeing Lily tomorrow night?" Mia hedged.

"Like you said, you girls have plans. So do I. Lily and I are just friends." Although he hadn't had sex with any of his lady friends since... Kristi. Fact was, Ty didn't have lady friends other than Hope, and she was more like a sister.

He peered across the table at Mia who was nothing like Hope. He loved them both in very different ways. And none of them were anything similar to how he felt about Lily.

It wasn't love. It would take Ty years and years of knowing and dating a woman before he'd trust one enough again to fall in love with. In the meantime, what he and Lily had together was fun.

Enlightening. She made him smile and laugh again.

After dinner with his parents—and an annoyingly amount of knowing smirks and comments from his mother and father—he'd met Cameron at The Happy Clam for a beer while Hope closed up.

They didn't talk about anything substantial. Too many bent ears. The local gossip had fun with Cameron when he'd come to town last year and were ready to move on to the next juicy tidbit.

When Ty got home he'd wrestled with sleep and finally caved, calling Lily in the middle of the night. It was a dumbass thing to do, but he hadn't heard her voice since Sunday night when he'd kissed her goodbye.

Part of him regretted holding back, of not stripping her naked and making love to her after their meal. He could read it in her eyes, and she'd wanted him as much as he wanted her. But he wanted to prove to her, or to himself, he wasn't sure, that what was going on between them was more than just sex.

And at the same time he wanted it to be just sex between them. He wasn't looking for a relationship. But this was Lily. His sister's friend. Hope's friend. A member of their community. Ty couldn't take her to bed as if she hadn't been more than a one-night stand.

If he was honest with himself, he'd admit to pining away for her for months. Maybe longer. He'd been so caught up in his misery and then taking care of Hope that he hadn't left much time or energy into noticing the world around him.

Now that he could see, he didn't know how he'd stayed away from Lily for so long. Her teasing and giggle chipped at the stone wall he'd built around his heart, and he couldn't help but smile when he was around her.

Saturday night would suck not being with her, but he'd hang out with Cameron. Work on building his own network of guy friends the way Lily so easily grew her circle of friends. Having a big circle wasn't important to Ty; he'd gone more than a decade living by himself with Hope as his only real friend and Mia as his constant pestering sister.

They loved each other, but they didn't confide in each other. The fact that Mia could read him so easily freaked him out a little. Unless Lily had talked to her about them. No, he didn't think she would. She'd said she was a private person.

Unless that was a lie.

There'd always be a piece of his heart and mind that doubted, that didn't trust. It wasn't Lily's fault. It was his. Still, that nagging piece would always come in between him and a woman, which was why he didn't pursue anything more than infrequent hook-ups.

Only Lily Novak threw a wrench into the mix. She was too damn likable. Too easy to trust. Ty would need to keep his distance or he'd lose his heart to her.

If he hadn't already.

Serious meant emotions, and emotions were dangerous. They'd make him vulnerable. He needed to stay steady. Which meant everything he felt for her needed to be tamped down a thousand notches.

Once Meatball was fed and curled on his dog bed, Ty picked up Chinese and drove out to Cameron's.

"'Bout time. I'm starving." Cam took the paper bag from Ty the second he opened the door and headed into the kitchen.

"Nice to see you too. Thanks for picking up dinner, Ty. That was nice of you," Ty muttered behind Cam's retreating back.

"Hey, don't bark at me. I got stood up tonight as well. It's pretty sad when the highlight of my night is Kung Pao chicken."

"Ouch." Ty covered his heart with his hands. "Enough with the insults. You and Hope have a fight or something?"

"Just the opposite." Cam opened the carton of pork fried rice and dumped half of it on his plate. "Delaney's at a friend's house, and Hope has the night off. I had all sorts of plans for us. And then she ditched me for the girls."

Ty took the carton from him and dumped the rest on his plate. He'd make a crack about Cam not getting laid, but Hope was like a sister to him. He couldn't go there.

"I guess you're in the same place I am, huh?" Cam asked around a mouthful of chicken and noodles.

"Nowhere near close. I don't have a wife or a kid." Even though Delaney was technically Cam's niece, he doted on her as if she was his daughter.

"So you and Lily." Cam drank from his water glass and eyed Ty speculatively.

"I bring you dinner and you can't even offer me a glass of water? No wonder Hope was in a hurry to run off without you."

He slid off the barstool and helped himself to a glass, filling it up from the sink and drinking it down in one gulp. He filled it again before sitting back down.

"Back to you and Lily."

"There isn't a me and Lily."

"You sure about that?"

No. "Yeah."

"Huh. That's not what Hope said."

Ty shoveled a forkful of rice in his mouth and chewed, not taking Cam's bait.

They made quick work of their dinner and rinsed their plates before putting them in the dishwasher.

"I'd offer you a beer... maybe a glass of wine?"

"I'm good."

Cam didn't hide his past issues with drugs and alcohol. After nearly ten years in jail, he'd been clean and sober before coming to Crystal Cove to win Hope back. When he'd first come to town Ty was protective of Hope, but it didn't take long to see she had a thing for Cam. And he proved himself early on as a decent guy.

The kind of guy Ty could see himself hanging around with. Laid back, far from perfect, and easy to get along with. They spent quite a few nights hanging out at Hope's bar while she closed up. Ty would nurse a beer while Cam would nurse an iced tea.

It was never awkward. The unease in the air tonight had nothing to do with alcohol and everything to do with a woman.

"I've got some brush in the fire pit. Want to sit out back for a bit?"

"Sure."

When they were situated in their Adirondack chairs and the fire blazing, Cam brought her up again.

"Lily seems to have come out of her shell lately."

"You've known her less than a year, man."

"And you've been pining away for her for more than that."

"I don't *pine*."

"Lust?" Ty glared at Cam across the fire who chuckled in response. "Hope said—"

"I never knew Hope to be such a town gossip."

"You're headliner news these days."

"Nothing I do is newsworthy." And wasn't that the truth of it. Kristi had something along the same lines years ago.

Cam must have sensed the change in Ty's voice and leaned forward. "Listen. I know we're relatively new to this guy friendship thing."

"Guy friendship thing?"

"Friends. I don't have many and from what Hope says—" Cam held up his hand as if to ward off Ty's comeback. "It seems you don't have many either."

"I'm not into the social scene."

"Me either."

Ty snorted. "Could've fooled me. You've got that Mr. Personality thing going. It's what charmed Hope and Delaney."

"Thank you? Unless that was a stab. If so, I totally missed it. Anyway, you were gone for some time fighting overseas while life continued in Crystal Cove. That had to be hard. Then to learn of Hope's pregnancy. She said she relied on you a lot, even with you thousands of miles away."

And wasn't that the crux of it all. For some reason their friendship never faltered, even after a failed attempt at romance, and with him gone eleven months out of the year in another country. When she came home from college pregnant and her boyfriend dead, Ty had been the only one she'd completely confided in.

Her trust in him kept him going during those long desert nights in the blazing heat and bitter cold. Keeping Hope's spirits up gave him more purpose than fighting a war he didn't fully understand.

She told him everything, and he told her nothing. He hadn't told anyone about Kristi. Only a few of his squadron knew about her. They'd kept their relationship private, unsure what the repercussions would be.

When his service was up and he returned home, he spent some time in therapy. Ty hadn't agreed with the PTSD diagnosis his therapist slapped on him, granted, the guy didn't know about Kristi and her betrayal. Ty answered questions about the war, what he saw, how he felt about it, but didn't mention what it was that really had him torn up inside.

It wasn't Kristi that he mourned over for three years. It was the betrayal. The feeling of worthlessness. Ty had joined the service to figure out what he wanted in life, and he returned more confused than ever. After being home for a few years and hating his emotional lethargy, and after some prodding from Hope, he finally visited his doctor and opened up. A little.

Doctor Kimball referred him to a psychologist, who diagnosed him with depression. And that depressed the hell out of him. He was a grown man. Depression was for the weak, not a six-foot man who could bench press four hundred pounds.

Or so he thought. He'd done a lot of reading and researching and came to the god-awful same conclusion. He was freaking depressed.

Kristi's betrayal had been a trigger that sent him in a downward spiral until he couldn't get out of his own way. The medication he'd been on for the past few years seemed to be working. Or maybe it was Lily. Probably a combination of both.

While he hated to admit it, talking to friends seemed to be the best therapy of all.

Maybe now was the time to get it all off his chest.

"Hope wrote to me every month. Usually twice a month. And sent me emails almost daily. I wrote when I could. Asked her questions about Delaney. Hung up pictures of her in my tent. Hope named me the godfather. I was honored."

"From what she says, you were her lifeline."

"I know." Ty sighed and folded his hands behind his neck. "Which is why I didn't tell her much about what was happening in my life."

"The war?"

"The war was easy to talk about." Ty closed his eyes and leaned back into his palms. "There was a woman."

"Isn't there always?"

"Yeah. Pretty much." He opened his eyes and leaned forward on his knees, staring into the fire. "Kristi wasn't in my squadron but was stationed in Kabul for nine months. We seemed to be on the same schedule. Working out. Eating. Leisure time. I didn't tell Hope about her. Even though we weren't dating, I didn't know how Hope would react. She'd been through so much already."

"Understood. If you two had an agreement of some sort, that you were anything more than friends, I'd say you were an asshole to keep this Kristi woman from her. But from the way Hope talks, you guys have always been platonic."

Guilt crept up the back of Ty's neck. Did he know?

"I know about that one time before you enlisted."

"Great." Not a proud moment when a woman who has seen you naked and has had her breast in your mouth says it's not working for her. It hadn't worked for Ty either. They were too close of friends, and moving their relationship to a sexual level hadn't felt right. Still, talking about it out loud bruised his ego a smidge.

"I didn't ask for details, and if you're picturing my wife naked right now I'll hurdle over this fire and take you down in two-point-two."

"I'm not picturing her naked. Trust me."

"Lily? Kristi?"

Lily? Always. Kristi? Not in a long, long time. "Kristi and I made promises. I couldn't exactly go out and get her a ring, but I... proposed. She said yes."

"Oh, man. I'm sorry. Did she... did she die fighting?"

A sardonic laugh escaped his lips. "No. Not in the least." The next part no one knew. Not even the few who knew about their relationship. This is what stung. What ruined his spirits, his trust in women. Sent him into a deeper depression. "She got to go home to Texas on leave. Our days off didn't match up. We Skyped almost every night. I thought things were great. When she returned to base I didn't think anything was off. We picked up right where we left off."

Ty kicked at the rocks around the fire pit and reached down for a log, tossing it in the fire and watching the orange embers crackle in the dark night.

"A couple months later Kristi got sick. A lot. I was worried about her and made her check in with the medics."

"Shit. Cancer?"

He shook his head. "Pregnancy."

Cameron sat upright. "You have a—oh, man."

"I'm not sure what you're thinking, but it probably isn't this. She and I both realized the timing was off. The baby wasn't mine. Kristi admitted to sleeping with her ex-boyfriend when home for a month. Come to find out, his daddy's got some serious money in the oil business and she said Daniel could take better care of her—and the baby—than a small town carpenter."

"Wow. Shit." Cameron took off his ball cap and scratched his head before returning it again. "I had no idea. Man. That's rough."

"I never told Hope."

"Because you didn't want to burden her with your shit when she was dealing with her own."

"Yeah."

"That's noble, man."

"I wouldn't call it that." Cowardice. Shame. Distrust in humankind.

"I tell Hope everything."

"I know."

"But you have my word this stays between us. I don't keep secrets from her, but this isn't about Hope or me. If she hears about it, it'll be from you. You have my word."

Something inside Ty humbled. Getting the story off his chest relieved him of some of the pressure that had been building for years.

He still held strong to his heart, refusing to let another woman steam roll him again, but being with Lily had made him feel again.

And hell, it felt good to smile. To laugh. To have a woman's arms and legs intertwined with his. He'd had sex with other women since returning home. None, however, were Lily.

"And since Hope doesn't know I'm assuming Lily doesn't either."

"Lily and I don't have that kind of relationship."

"Uh huh." Cam chuckled. "You keep telling yourself that."

"We don't talk much."

"Oh, so it's that kind of relationship." Cam barked out a loud laugh, and Ty did all he could to keep from smiling.

"Am I late to the party?"

Ty looked over his shoulder and saw Ben making his way toward them.

"Just getting started. Pull up a chair." Cam tossed another log on the fire. "We've got all night. No point in going home to an empty bed, right?"

"Sophie's in her crib right now. Chances are she'll be in our bed once we get home. Alexis' mom kicked me out of the house once Sophie fell asleep to have *man time*. Kind of weirded me out."

"Alexis must have called her."

"Well, she hasn't called me. The girls are probably having so much fun they've forgotten about us." Ben pulled a beer from his cooler and offered one to Ty.

"You sure?"

"I'm not drinking all six or Alexis will put me on the couch tonight."

"Since Sophie'll be taking up space in your bed it may not be such a bad thing." Ty unscrewed the cap off his bottle and played with it between his fingers.

"Says the single guy. I'll take Alexis in my bed any way I can have her. Even if that means I get four square inches while she and the baby get the rest."

"Says the newlywed. I'll check back in with you in another year or so." Ty tipped his beer toward Ben in salute before he drank.

"Ah, such the skeptic. I thought Lily would have you seeing differently by now."

"What's that supposed to mean?"

When Ben and Cam laughed, Ty resisted the urge to finish off his entire beer in one swig.

"Deny it all you want, man, but you've got it bad for Lily."

"How would you know?" Ty didn't know Ben as well as Cam. He was always up at the winery or busy with Sophie and Alexis. They'd talked a few times, like at Hope's wedding and a barbeque at the winery. Other than that, they talked in passing only.

Ben shrugged. "I figured from the way things went at the wedding that you two would be an item by now."

Ty glanced at Cam and then back at Ben. "Nothing happened at his wedding."

"No wonder you're so sensitive about it then." Ben grinned into his beer.

"You guys are assholes." Ty tossed his empty in the cooler and stood. "I'm heading out."

Cam stood and pulled out his wallet. "Ten bucks says he calls Lily when he gets home tonight."

"Screw that bet. Ten bucks says he calls her the second he gets to his truck."

"Like I said. Assholes." Ty flipped them the bird over his shoulder as he walked away and couldn't help smiling when his friends catcalled behind his back.

CHAPTER NINE

TY HAD JUST FINISHED brushing his teeth and climbed into bed when headlights shone down his driveway, lighting up his room. Glancing at the clock, he swung his legs out of bed and found a pair of running shorts. Who the hell would show up at his house at midnight?

His stomach tightened. No, if his parents or sister were hurt someone would have called. Unless... the girls. Lily? When he reached the front door female voices argued loudly on the other side.

"I can't believe you did this. He's sleeping. Just bring me home."

Lily? His pulse quickened, and he opened the door. Mia's hand was wrapped around Lily's arm in an attempt to pull her back toward the house.

"Hey, bro. Your house was on my way, so I figured it would be easier to drop Lily off here. She's been drinking and shouldn't be home alone. All those stairs. You know?"

"Is she okay?" She didn't appear to be stumbling, other than from Mia's tugging. Her hair was down falling across her bare shoulders and veiled part of her face.

The purple top fit tightly across her chest and flared out around her stomach covering what he knew was skin as soft as buttery leather. And those damned long legs seemed to be shrink-wrapped in denim. The woman didn't belong in Crystal Cove. She deserved to be on the cover of a magazine. Although he was glad she wasn't. He didn't want other men looking at her and thinking the thoughts that so easily corrupted his mind.

"I'm fine. I apologize for waking you." Lily's eyes met his then dropped to his naked chest. He couldn't help but suck in his gut a little and flex his pecs.

The sliver of a moon didn't give him much light to see if her cheeks were red, or her eyes for that matter. Just enough to make out her embarrassment.

"Do you mind if she crashes here? I still have to drop off Alexis and Jenna. Bringing her here saves me a trip from going back into town."

Going into town would only be ten minutes out of her way. Ty knew what she was doing and part of him appreciated her for it, but another part was embarrassed. For him. For Lily. If Mia could be a little more subtle about her plan to get him and Lily together he'd appreciate it even more.

"Is everyone else okay?" He peered around Mia but couldn't see into the darkened car.

"Grace is passed out drunk, Jenna will be once her head hits the pillow, and Alexis is passed out from being overtired."

"If you're tired, Mia, I can drive everyone home. You haven't been drinking, have you?"

"I had one glass of wine at the start of the concert. I'm good. I gotta go, though. Ben keeps texting me about Alexis."

"Hope's already home?"

"Yeah. Dropped her off first. Can you handle Lily?" Mia smirked.

"Mia!" Lily covered her face with her hands and lowered her head.

A look of guilt—something unfamiliar to Mia—crossed her face. "Alright. Sorry. I may have crossed the line with my matchmaking skills. Hop back in the SUV. I'll take you home."

Torn between wanting Lily to stay—*really* wanting her to stay—and wanting to make her comfortable, he stepped in with an offer.

"Mia, you've got your hands full. I can drive Lily home."

"You sure?" Someone beeped her horn, and Mia looked over her shoulder. "Jenna wants to get home."

"I'm sure. If you're okay with that, Lily?"

"If you don't mind." Her voice was soft and insecure.

"Cool. Gotta run. Had a blast tonight, Lils." Mia hugged her and jogged off to her waiting vehicle.

Lily had turned to face the retreating car, her arms crossed over her body in a rigid stance.

"Come on in. I need to grab a shirt and my shoes."

Ty stepped back into the house and held the door open for her. When she shyly entered, he closed the door behind her and did his best not to stare at the way her tight jeans cupped her cute little butt.

"I'm really sorry, Ty." She turned, facing him, and bit her lip. She pushed her hair out of her face and tucked it behind her ear.

And then his body moved on its own inching closer until they were toe-to-toe. "Don't be sorry." He reached out and picked up a strand of her blonde hair, toying with the ends. "I'm sorry for my sister. She can be a bit much."

Lily laughed, lifting her gaze to his. "That she is." Her mouth froze in its smile, the crinkles around her eyes softened, and her blue irises darkened.

The spell between them would be broken if he moved. If he spoke. The urge to touch, to kiss, to ask her to stay beat feverishly through his veins. And once again the fear of rejection, maybe not tonight, but sometime in the future after he'd given his heart away to her, weighed in his chest.

Licking her lips, Lily was the first to move. And to speak. "I don't want to be an inconvenience." She tucked her already tucked hair behind her ear again. "To make you drive me home."

Was she saying what he hoped she was? If she wanted to stay the night, she was more than welcome to.

"What do you want, Lily?"

She reached out and placed her hand on his chest, and he nearly whimpered. Her fingers, cool on his hot flesh, branded him. He was hers to do with whatever the hell she wanted.

"I guess I could stay. If you don't mind. If you want me to."

Something growled deep within him, and in one swift move he lowered his mouth to hers, tasting her sweetness, her innocence, her beauty. Lily's hands slid across his ribcage and clutched at his back. Damn, it felt good to be touched. To be held.

Taking their kiss deeper, Ty cupped her face in his palms and breathed in her scent. Flowers. Something exotic. His hands and arms tingled, his groin tightened, and he pulled back before he crushed her too hard, nipping at her plump lips and trailing kisses along her jawline.

"I can take the couch if you want me to. Or we can share my bed," he whispered below her ear in between gentle bites to her neck.

Lily pulled back, wrapping her hands around the back of his neck. "You're not sleeping on the couch."

"And neither are you." Ty picked her up in his arms and carried her to his bedroom. He tried not to think about the last time he'd changed his sheets. He wasn't a slob, but washing his sheets wasn't high on his priority list when they never needed to be company ready.

Another wave of insecurities flashed to the forefront of his mind. Lily was a classy lady. What would she think of his simple bedroom? The oak headboard was passed down from his grandparents, his queen-sized bed taking up a good chunk of the bedroom. A tall bureau was the only other piece of furniture other than the matching nightstand.

The set had to be fifty years old and nothing classic. Simple. That was Ty. Just like his navy sheets and navy comforter. Decorating wasn't his gig. Building, fixing, and right now, making love to Lily were.

"I'm hoping you have condoms that haven't expired," she said while tracing her tongue across his bottom lip.

Maybe she wasn't as caught up on his lack of décor as he was.

"I may have picked up a box last week." Before she'd come over for dinner. They didn't use them that night. He didn't want her to think he was only after sex. Yet that's what he'd been telling himself this was.

He needed to keep things between them purely sexual so he wouldn't get hurt again, but since Lily was friends with his sister, he needed to respect her as well. Which he totally did.

Finding that balance was complicated. And Lily stripping off her purple top standing in front of him in a strapless bra completely threw off his balance.

Ty lowered his mouth to her bare shoulder, tasting her sweet skin before kissing it. "You're gorgeous." He set her on her feet and prayed she wouldn't go running.

"Likewise." Lily raked her nails down his chest, and he sucked in a breath as she cupped him.

"Damn." So much for going slow. Backing her to the bed, he followed her to the mattress kissing her neck and trailing his tongue down her torso until he reached her bra. Sliding his hands under her, he undid the clasp and tossed the barrier aside.

There was no more beautiful a sight than Lily sprawled out naked on his bed. Only the jeans had to go. Preferring to multi-task, he worked her button and zipper with his hands while his mouth feasted on her breasts. By the sounds of her moans and her fingers gripping into his shoulders, he'd say she was enjoying the moment as much as he was.

The zipper made it halfway down and stopped. It was stuck. He slid it up again and down, but it didn't get any further than the first time. Maybe he could slide her jeans off anyway. Lily was slim enough. Grabbing on to the waistband of her jeans, he tugged. And nothing. They didn't budge. He tugged again. With great reluctance, he picked his head up from her breast and looked down at the problem at hand.

He sat on his knees in between her legs and pulled. And yanked. And tugged. Her body jerked lower each time, the jeans not budging. "They're stuck."

A romantic he was not. He'd hoped this time he'd have a little more finesse than their first encounter. At least he didn't drop her to the floor. And he had condoms that didn't expire for another year. At this rate, he wasn't sure if he'd use them up beforehand.

Lily sat up on her elbows. "I've been wrestling with my zipper all night."

"Oh?" He held on to her thighs just above her knees and resisted the temptation to give her a possessive squeeze. He wasn't the possessive kind of guy, but the thought of Lily with another man...

"The lines for the outhouses were forever long. It wasn't until my third trip in that it got stuck. I didn't think I'd ever get out of there. Those things are nasty." She shuddered.

There was nothing as unromantic as talking about outhouses. Not that Ty did the romance kind of thing. Still, there were a few topics that should be banned from the bedroom. Outhouses had to be high up on the list.

And yet he wanted her more than ever. He only hoped she hadn't turned herself off.

"Let me try."

While she worked on her zipper Ty studied her face, all scrunched up in concentration. She wiggled her hips and lifted her butt and lowered it again trying to free herself from her jeans.

He dropped his gaze to her nakedness and saw a freckle he hadn't noticed before on her side. Hovering over her, he dipped his tongue in her belly button then made a path over to her lonely freckle.

"Uh, you're not helping any." Lily laughed and gently pushed at his stomach, which loomed over her core.

Her hands brushed against his erection. Damn. He was harder than granite and the wiggle of her slim hips, her naked breasts, and her whimsical laugh was only making him harder. If that was even possible.

Ty lowered himself until they touched core to core, still both clothed from the waist down, and braced himself with his elbows until their lips were a whisper away from each other.

"I have scissors in the kitchen. I'll buy you a new pair of jeans. But those have to go. Now."

Instead of being turned off or afraid, Lily broke into a shit-eating grin and lifted her hips, grinding into him. "If you can give me two seconds I'm sure I can get them off." She planted a chaste kiss on his lips and squirmed away.

Her body rubbed against his in all the right places, and he moaned in pleasure. In pain. In agony. Rolling to his back, he watched her hop out of bed and jump up and down in an attempt to remove her jeans.

Those breasts. Tiny and perky and made for his hands bounced around, and this time he growled. "One."

"I got them!" Lily bent over and worked the jeans down her legs.

"Two."

"Wait," she giggled.

Wait? He'd been waiting too damn long. Shuffling to the edge of the bed, he planted his feet on the floor and reached out, grabbing Lily by the waist. She shrieked when he pulled her down on top of him.

"I didn't peg you for an impatient man." Lily ran her hands through his hair and smothered him with kisses, giggling as he groped her ass.

"I've been waiting for hours for you to take off those damn jeans."

"Hours? It's been two minutes."

Actually, it had been seven days. Admitting he'd been pining away for her would scare her away so he kept that comment to himself.

"Next time wear something with elastic. It's easier to take off." Yeah. He said there'd be a next time and hadn't thought about the possible rejection. There'd be a next time. He was sure of it.

"That is true." She slid her hands between them and under the elastic of his shorts. "You know, the entire *two seconds* you were watching me fight with my jeans you could have taken these off."

Before she could formulate her next word, he grabbed his shorts and shucked them off. "See? Elastic. Next time."

"Duly noted, hot stuff. Now, you were a little anxious about my jean situation. They're still around my ankles. I'm not going to be able to..."

Message heard loud and clear. Ty rolled her to her back and slid down her legs. Taking the jeans off the final few inches was a snap. When Ty looked up again, Lily was stretched across the bed and reaching into his nightstand for a condom.

Taking it from her, he placed it next to the pillow and made love to her mouth. She tasted like cherries and wine, and he couldn't drink up enough of her.

"Ty." She lifted her hips into his again and he brought his hand between their bodies, pleasuring her, making their evening last.

After she'd clenched around him and called out his name, he tore open the condom wrapper and covered himself.

There were no more words, no more wrestling of clothes. Just the two of them, naked and joined. Loving each other into the night.

• • • •

LILY BLINKED HER EYES open in a fog. The slight throb in her head wasn't from a hangover. She wasn't that drunk last night, but she was dehydrated. Her tongue was dry and fuzzy and could use a gallon or two of water.

The clock on the bedside table read eight or six or possibly zero thirty-one. It was hard to tell with the haze in her eyes. Too caught up in everything Ty Parker, she'd forgotten to take out her contacts. Now they'd be stuck to her eyes and she wouldn't be able to see straight.

A big, strong arm wrapped around her, pulling her tight into the furnace's cavity. Or rather, Ty. His body shed off some serious heat, not only visually but in temperature too.

"You're so hot."

"Um. Thanks?"

Lily snorted. "I mean you're an oven." She rolled over to face him. He was close enough so he wasn't a blur, but she had to blink a dozen times to get him in focus. Her morning breath was rancid, so she pulled the covers up over her mouth. "And in body too." She tapped her fingers across his chest, squeezing his muscles.

"You okay? Have a headache?" Ty moved the blanket from her face. "Can I get you something?"

"A toothbrush. Water. Contact solution. Preferably in that order."

"I can do two out of the three."

"Let me guess. No contact solution."

"Twenty-twenty here." He winked.

She really didn't want to end their evening so soon, whatever time it was. A ray of light peeked through his blinds so she figured the night was over and they were knee-deep in the morning after awkwardness.

Add morning breath and glued in contacts and the awkward kicked up another notch to extremely uncomfortable.

"I'll grab you a water. I don't have an extra toothbrush but you can use mine. Or if that weirds you out, I have mouthwash in the cabinet next to the sink." He dropped a kiss on her nose and rolled out of bed.

Gah, she wished she could see better. His naked form was outlined by the crack of dawn giving her just enough of a reminder of what she'd seen quite clearly last night. Not that she needed clean contacts to remember every detail of his body. He picked up something off the floor and put it on. Probably shorts. Just as well. She didn't want to come off totally desperate and needy.

Or whorish.

Lily dragged her body up and leaned against the headboard and cuddled a pillow to her front to hide her nakedness. Her shirt had to be around the room somewhere, but she was too cozy to leave the bed.

Ty came into focus a minute later holding a glass of water in front of him. "I started a pot of coffee if you drink it."

"If? I can't function without."

The bed dipped when he sat next to her, and she gulped the water down hoping it would wash out some of the dry fuzz in her mouth.

"I'll make you a cup and bring you home."

Oh. So much for morning sex. Or hand holding during coffee. Sharing a muffin. "Sure." She shrugged the sadness away.

"Your contacts. My mom wears them. I can remember a few times growing up when she'd forgotten to take them out at night. That can't be comfortable for you."

"Yeah. My eyes feel kinda gunky right now." Way to ooze the sex appeal. "I'll probably toss the contacts out when I get home. I need to replace them in a few days anyway."

"Oh." Ty fidgeted with his hands in his lap. "How, uh, well can you see without them?"

"I don't always wear them when I'm alone in my apartment. I can't watch TV or anything, but I can read. I'm nearsighted."

"Do you need your solution to take them out?"

Lily cocked her head at the odd question. The man obviously didn't wear contacts. Why did he want to know if... *Oh!* He wanted her to stay and didn't know how to ask. Ty Parker, when not naked and rolling around in bed, was a shy guy. She liked that. Too much.

"No. In fact." She tossed the pillow to the other side of the bed and grabbed hold of the sheet, wrapping it around her body as she stood. "I'm going to take them out right now. My eyes will need to breathe, so I won't put in a new pair until tomorrow."

She let the sheet drape behind her as she left his bedroom and headed toward his bathroom. Closing the door behind her, she dropped the sheet and checked out her reflection in the mirror and shuddered.

Scary.

Smudged eyeliner and mascara, plump lips, and a thin strip of beard burn on her neck. That, she didn't mind one bit. Ty's stubble made him appear even more gruff, and she loved how it felt against her body. How *he* felt against her body.

When Ty was naked and aroused, he was a completely different man. He didn't hold back like he seemed to do when they were on a date. It was like something feral went loose in him and he forgot about whatever inhibitions he had.

It could be the friends they had in common, or small town gossip. Maybe Ty didn't want anything more than sex with her because of the complications? She understood, but she didn't want to accept it.

Lily stepped away from the mirror, did her business, then had a staredown with Ty's toothbrush. He wouldn't have offered if it grossed him out. They had their tongues down each other's throats last night.

No. She wouldn't cross that line. Yet. She reached for the mouth-wash and swirled while she unglued her contacts from her eyes.

Better. Finding a clean washcloth, she let the water warm up and washed her face, rubbing off the makeup residue from last night.

Fresh and clean, she draped the sheet around her like a toga and went back to Ty's room. Only it was empty. Noises and smells from down the hall told her he was in the kitchen. Not wanting to snoop too much, she tried the second drawer of his bureau and struck gold.

Two piles of neatly folded shirts. Taking the one on top without paying much attention to it, she slid it over her head and tossed the sheet to the bed.

The shirt hung to the top of her thighs. The last thing she wanted to do was wrestle with her skinny jeans again, but traipsing around his house with her butt hanging out wasn't ideal either. Pushing their unclear boundaries again, she tried the third drawer and was relieved when she found a stack of shorts and workout pants.

Lily was tall, nearly five-nine, but the pants would drag. She opted for a pair of running shorts and cinched them at the waist. Hopefully Ty wouldn't mind her rummaging through his things.

She closed the drawer and made her way down the hall toward the kitchen. He stood at the stove stirring something in a pot. He'd put on a shirt and had on the same shorts from last night. His feet were bare making every woman's fantasy come true.

Barefoot and cooking for her. Lily could get used to this. He must have heard her romantic sigh and turned around. A slow smile took over his face.

"You look nice."

"You compliment the grungiest outfits."

"Easy now. Nothing beats Jack's lobster pound."

Lily looked down on her chest where a bright red lobster stood out against the light gray shirt. "I didn't mean to offend Jack."

"You like seafood?"

"I'd think that was a prerequisite living here."

"Good answer. You like French toast?"

"If I don't have to make it."

"You really don't like to cook?" Ty flipped a piece of toast from the pan and placed it on a plate.

"I wouldn't say it's a matter of not liking. More like can't do."

"Your mom or dad never tried to teach you any dishes when you were growing up?" He got two forks and two knives from a drawer and set them on the counter.

"I'll help set the table. What else do we need?" They weren't taking a trip down memory lane. Not only could her heart not take it, but she wasn't allowed to anyway. She hadn't seen or heard from Agent Thorne in over eight months and didn't want to give him any reason to come back around. Not that there was anything wrong with him. But news coming from Thorne was never good.

No news was good news in her life.

Ty paused mid-flip before setting the last piece of French toast on a plate. "Okay."

Okay? Ugh. She hated how sad he sounded, like she'd run over his puppy. Lily looked around for Meatball and didn't see him. Probably moping outside, which is where Ty looked like he wanted to be.

All he was trying to do was make conversation, and she cut him off. She had to, though, and she couldn't explain that to him. Oh the irony. She inwardly complained about his lack of communication skills yet shut him down when he tried to get a conversation going.

"This smells amazing." She picked up the silverware from the counter and gave Ty a slow kiss hoping she could turn his frown around.

When his hands held firm on her hips and dragged her body into his, she figured that had done the trick. He traced her lips with his tongue and pulled her bottom lip between his teeth.

"You hungry?" He raised an eyebrow at what she was sure was meant to be a double entendre.

"Absolutely." Lily lowered her hands and squeezed his buns of magnificent steel. "Maybe one morning you can teach me how to make French toast."

Ty's hands stilled on her hips, his body tense, his eyes hooded. Maybe she made too many assumptions about the progression of their relationship.

"Or not. I know how some people can be territorial in the kitchen." She patted his buns and stepped out of his reach. Or at least, attempted to.

Strong hands held her in place.

"I'd like that." Ty leaned in and nipped her earlobe. "Making breakfast together." He released her and picked up the plate of French Toast as if he hadn't whispered sweet nothings in her ear.

Which he hadn't, but when he dropped his voice down a notch or two and did that half-grunt, half-moan, half-whisper thing—screw the math—he had her panties in a twist.

Only she wasn't wearing any panties. She'd hold that card close to her chest and let it slip if Ty did that lost puppy thing again.

They managed to eat a yummy breakfast keeping their clothes on and their conversation light. He talked about his current project, and she shared local gossip she'd heard at the spa. Nothing to get anyone in trouble; mostly about the geriatrics arguing over who had the better chowder recipes and who had the cutest grandbabies.

When they finished eating, she stood and cleared the table. "How's Meatball doing?"

"I'm sure he's got birds nesting on his back by now."

"I suppose a game of fetch or even a walk around the neighborhood is out."

"For him, yes. If that's something you want to do I'm game."

"You're going to chase a ball into the woods and bring it back to me?"

Ty laughed. "I was referring to the walk. Can you see well enough to do that?" He stroked her back while she washed the pan, only stopping when she handed it to him to dry.

"I'm not blind. I can see fine around here. Walking, I can handle. Other activities probably not."

"Other activities like what?"

That double entendre thing happened again, and Lily had to decide how far she wanted to go. Innocent flirting or another round in Ty's bed.

Five minutes later their clothes were on the floor.

Twenty minutes later they were asleep in each other's arms.

CHAPTER TEN

OVER THE COURSE OF the past two weeks, Lily and Ty saw each other almost daily. On her late days, she called him when she'd closed up and they talked for hours. On the nights when they finished working around the same time, they either grabbed a bite to eat in a nearby town—to avoid local gossip—or she peered over his shoulder while he cooked them dinner in his kitchen.

Since Ty left the house not long after sunrise on most mornings, they usually made love on his couch or in his bed shortly after dinner. Getting dressed and leaving the warmth of his arms proved to be more challenging with each day.

Somewhere between walks on the beach with Meatball—which had happened twice now—dinner, and lovemaking, they'd crossed the threshold to something more. Yet there was still the lost puppy dog look in Ty's eyes when she evaded talking about her past.

When that happened, she showered on the love and attention and asked him about his childhood.

Two loving and supportive parents, a sister who worshiped him—although he called her pesky—and an entourage of aunts and uncles and cousins sprinkled about the state. He was a lucky one, and she'd told him this on many occasions.

They'd been looking forward to Saturday night since, well, last Saturday night. Since Sunday was the only day neither of them had to work and they blocked the night before out as a date night.

And sleepover.

Lily tossed a few things in a backpack and skipped down both flights of stairs to the front door of the spa.

"Hey, Lily. Have a minute?" Grace got up from the bench outside the spa. She had bags under her eyes and her hair was pulled back in a messy bun. Very much out of character for Alexis' high maintenance sister.

Granted, no one knew too much about Grace other than what she wanted to reveal. Which was nothing other than superficial makeup and fashion advice. She knew the type and yet there was another layer to Grace buried beneath the façade of a well-put-together woman.

Lily knew those signs as well. But to confront Grace about it would mean to uncover her own scars. Scars she needed to keep hidden.

"Sure." Lily dropped her backpack on the bench and took a seat.

"Actually, do you mind if we talk inside?"

Torn between wanting to brush off the woman she barely knew to get to Ty and lending an ear to a woman who looked like she could use a shoulder to lean on, Lily stood again.

"Absolutely." She unlocked the door and let them in. A regular of the spa and all its offerings, Grace made herself at home on one of the chairs in the waiting area.

"You're on your way out," Grace stated the obvious, toying with the straps of her Michael Kors purse.

"That's okay. You wanted to talk?" Lily hadn't a clue what about. She'd never had a private conversation with Grace, much less been in a room alone with her. They'd had fun as a group a couple weeks ago at the concert in the park, and Grace had come to a couple book clubs. Other than that, she was a stranger to Lily.

"We don't know each other very well." Again, Grace stated the obvious.

"Not yet. I'm still getting to know everyone, really. It's only been the past year that I've gotten to know the women in town."

From what Lily had heard, Grace was Miss Popular before she'd gone off to Europe. Alexis had said something about her traipsing all over the country trying to find herself. It seemed like she'd found herself in fashion.

She'd been back in Crystal Cove for a few months and, according to town gossip, hadn't done much other than work in retail shops in Rockland. Not that there was anything wrong with that, but Grace never seemed happy. Her smiles and laughter were forced, not genuine.

Again, Lily was an expert in that field. If Grace needed a friend, Lily would be the most understanding.

"You're going to Ty's?" Grace nodded toward the bag at Lily's feet.

"Yeah. It's okay though. We don't have any set plans."

"All the girls had a crush on him in high school. He was older than me. A grade older than Alexis, I think. Him and Brandon Miller. They were the town hotties. There weren't any good looking guys in my grade." Grace took her hair out of her bun and wound it up again.

Lily watched and waited patiently. There was something serious going on with Grace. It wasn't drugs or alcohol. Her hands shook a little and her eyes were puffy, but more from crying or not sleeping.

"I haven't met Brandon Miller. Is he related to John and Melissa Miller who own the Sunrise on the Water Inn?"

Small talk. Make her feel comfortable, then maybe she'll loosen up and talk about what really brought her to Lily's front door.

"Yeah. They're good people. Brandon's a doctor in Portsmouth, New Hampshire. When kids graduate they either move away and make something of their lives or stay here forever and..." Grace licked her lips and slouched in the chair.

So coming back to Crystal Cove was a defeat for Grace. Okay. One step closer to the issue.

"Hope seems happy here. So does Ty." Although he often had that far away trance that she saw in Grace. "You couldn't move your sister from here if you tried. I don't even think Ben could."

"You're right. I guess things have changed since I was a teen." Grace picked at the hem of her white shorts. "I don't suppose you grew up in a place like this?"

Could Grace see through her as much as Lily could see through Grace?

"No. I was a city girl." That much was true. It was easier to keep her story straight if she kept to as much of the truth as possible. "I'm sure the grass is always greener, but I think I would have loved to grow up in a community like this. One built around families and small businesses."

"You never dreamed of traveling? Going to Europe? Paris? Italy?"

Lily stilled, thankful Grace couldn't see the turmoil in her stomach or hear the buzzing behind her eyes.

"Maine has it all. Mountains. Ocean. Farms. Wineries. Your family's winery is one of my favorite places to visit. Alexis said you've never been into the winemaking business."

"I prefer to be on the other end of the bottle. Sipping it. I don't mind filling in and pouring samples for customers, but that gets old."

"What are your plans for your future? Something in fashion?"

"Actually. Can you keep a secret?"

Lily almost laughed at the irony of the question. Her entire existence was a secret. "Of course."

"You know the Bergerons? The couple who owns the insurance company two doors down?"

"They're very sweet. My business and rental insurance is through them."

"They're retiring."

"Ruth told me last week when she came in to get her hair done, and they sent me a letter about options for other companies." She'd gone with their recommendation and transferred her plan to the Lincolns in the next town over.

"And their space will be available to rent."

"I thought they owned their building and mine?" Bergeron Insurance took up one half of the brick building next to her and Doug Chambers' accounting firm rented the other half.

"Exactly. Their space will be available to rent. Ruth said she and Herb aren't looking to make much of a profit, just enough to pay the mortgage and utilities."

"And you talked to her about it because..."

"I'm thinking about opening a boutique. I've made a lot of friends in fashion schools and thought I could have a store that showcased new designers. Like an internship in a way."

"You think there's a market for that kind of clothing around here?"

"I wouldn't sell high-end stuff. More practical wear. Cute stuff, though." Grace turned toward Lily and finally, a spark lit up her face. It was the first time Lily had seen true excitement in her. "Crystal Cove isn't a tourist trap like Camden and Rockland, but people drive through town and if we have shops, they'll stop. I've talked to Ben about it as well."

Ben had been a godsend to the town. When he'd first visited with his sights set on helping Coastal Vines, he'd met with all the small business owners and come up with a plan to bring more revenue to the town.

Building the function hall at the winery for events—like Hope and Cameron's wedding—launched the plans, and every business had seen an intake in customers and revenue since. Including the Sea Salt Spa.

"So we'd be neighbors." This could be fun. Grace needed a friend. Lily had been in her shoes not so long ago.

"Yeah." The spark dimmed, and suddenly Lily felt as if Grace were scrutinizing her, studying her reaction. Trying to get a read on her.

Uncomfortable with Grace's odd behavior, Lily reached for her backpack and stood. "I'm happy for you. Let me know how I can help when it comes time."

Grace stood as well, still serious. "You'd be okay with new designers coming in and out of my shop? Some are from the States, but some may be from Europe."

"I think it's wonderful." She hefted her bag across her shoulder and headed toward the door. "Keep me posted."

When Grace finally disappeared down the walkway, uneasiness settled in her belly. Lily didn't think Grace's visit was about her boutique. She'd appeared ragged and stressed. Something was going on with her, but Lily wasn't the right person to ask. Or to meddle.

Thursday was book club. If Grace showed up haggard like today, she'd be the center of attention, trumping the Lily and Ty gossip. It was kind of a lose-lose.

Closing the door to her worry, she got in her car and drove to Ty's.

He greeted her at the door with a kiss and an affectionate squeeze of her butt. "Long day at the office?" Ty took the bag from her and ushered her inside.

"Sorry I'm late. Grace came by as I was leaving."

"Grace?"

"Yeah. I was just as surprised." They headed to the kitchen where a bottle of Lobster Red from Coastal Vines sat on the counter next to two glasses. "Wine with dinner? Is someone hoping to get lucky tonight?"

"That's not what I—"

Ty was adorable when she embarrassed him. "Easy, hot stuff." Lily pressed a kiss to his lips and rested her forearms on his strong shoulders. "I'd planned on getting lucky with or without the wine."

"Well if that's true"—he shifted her hair to one side and kissed her neck—"did you plan on before or after dinner?"

Lily tilted her head, giving him free reign of her neck, and moaned with his touch. "Both."

"You're turning me into a sex addict." Ty worked his hands under her shirt and massaged her back.

"We haven't had sex since last week. I'd hardly call that an addict. Unless..." She knew he wasn't sleeping with other women, but giving him a hard time was fun.

His lips left her neck and he pulled back, his brows deeply furrowed. "I'm not that kind of guy. I don't sleep around."

God, he was gorgeous and stunning and rugged and manly and so, so sweet. Lily couldn't help it. Her heart had betrayed her and had fallen for Ty. There wasn't a single thing about him she didn't adore and appreciate. And respect.

Trust didn't come easily to her, and she didn't think she'd ever trust another man again. Yet here she was, dating a man for less than a month and already in love.

"I know." She traced her finger across his brows and down his cheek, landing on his lips. Lips she wanted on hers. "I'm only teasing."

On stealth mode once again, Ty picked her up in one swift move and set her on the counter. They feasted on each other, not taking the time to fully undress. Kissing with a hunger similar to their first time, yet more familiar and with a deeper connection.

Frantic hands tore at his button and zipper while he slipped his hands under her waistband.

Ty stilled, pulling back just a hair. "Elastic. No zipper."

She'd worn a pair of cute slip-on shorts intentionally. "Like I said. I had plans on getting lucky, and I didn't think you could handle another zipper." Lily gripped on to his jeans and pushed them down as far as she could reach, which wasn't far enough.

It didn't take long for her shorts to come off. The chill of the granite countertop under her warmed up as soon as Ty placed his hands on her thighs, moving them apart so he could stand between them.

Dinner would have to wait.

With their stomachs full of grilled salmon, Meatball resting at their feet, and the bottle of wine nearly empty, Ty and Lily sat on his deck and enjoyed the night air.

"I'm thinking of putting in a fire pit similar to Hope and Cameron's."

Lily curled her legs up under her and leaned her head back on the chair. The only thing that would make the evening better is if Ty had a couch outside, or a deck swing so they could sit closer.

Needing the contact, she reached over their armrests and laced her fingers in his. "That would be nice. You said you have other plans for the house? When you have time to get to them, what other projects do you have up your sleeve?"

"I don't want to bore you."

"Why do you think that would bore me?"

Ty rubbed his thumb across her palm. "Most women don't find construction talk interesting conversation."

"I don't know what women you're referring to, but I'm not them." Mia's slip at the bookstore last month resonated within. There was a woman out there who had done serious damage to Ty, and he was still fighting the battle scars.

"No. You're not." The soft sigh coming from his lips spoke of a bigger meaning behind the conversation.

Torn between wanting to help Ty with his demons and wanting to keep things as they were, she didn't know if it was her place to pry.

"You don't seem the type to date women like that. Women who wouldn't be interested in you. Your career."

"I work for my dad's construction company. Some wouldn't call that a *career*."

"What?" Lily squeezed his hand. "That's the most ridiculous thing I've heard. You work hard, you do beautiful work, and you're making a successful living for yourself. What's not to respect? You must have dated trolls in the past. Don't ever lump me in with them again."

This time she was mad. She knew too well how cruel and manipulative superficial women could be, and it sounded like Ty had been hurt by one. While she may have traveled in their pack, Lily liked to believe she was never cruel to a man. To any human being.

Setting her wine glass down on the decking, she figured she'd ask him the tough questions. If he told her to stop or changed the subject, she'd let it go.

"Tell me about her. The woman who broke your heart." She watched Ty as he closed his eyes and lowered his chin to his chest. "Or should I say the *tramp* who broke your heart?"

That elicited a tiny grin from Ty's lips. "I've never called her that, but it may be more appropriate."

"I'm sorry, Ty. I take it she's not from around here." Hope would have known about her. That meant he'd met her overseas.

"Texas."

"Is that where you had your basic training?" She could picture Ty out at a bar after a grueling week of boot camp, or whatever they called it, winning the hearts of every girl in his path.

"Not exactly."

"Is she from Afghanistan?"

"No." Ty lifted his head and released her hand, rubbing his across his face. "We were both stationed in Kabul. We were in different squadrons but were at basecamp together."

"Oh." Not what she expected. Lily didn't think she could measure up to another soldier. To a woman who fought for our country. All Lily had to offer was a heritage she couldn't claim and a past she had to forget.

"We were engaged." By the anger in his eyes she could tell he hadn't lost the woman to war. Something more personal.

He told her in brief words about the woman returning pregnant. About her choosing money and security over a man with no financial future.

Lily's heart bled for him, for the hurt he'd been harboring for so many years. Ty sharing his personal loss with her deepened her love for him even more. "I'd say you're doing pretty well for yourself." She rubbed her hands up and down his thighs in a soft and loving manner.

"I don't have the fancy car. Or a yacht. I can't afford to take exotic vacations. Or to buy expensive jewelry."

"Hm. The jewelry I can do without." If he only knew. "But the yacht. Well, had I known that I wouldn't have had sex before the wine."

"You're making fun of me?" A grin tugged at his lip.

"No." Lily scooted out of her chair and sat sideways in his lap, wrapping her arms around his neck. "I'm sorry she hurt you and caused you so much pain."

"I wasn't ready to settle down anyway."

She didn't believe him, but she understood he needed to make himself believe it. "Someday, when you're ready, you'll make an amazing husband. And father. Don't let her betrayal make you think you're not good enough. Or that all women are after a Texas oil rig."

"Just a yacht?" The light came back in his eyes.

"A stroll on the beach works for me." Lily cuddled closer, resting her head on his shoulder, absorbing his warmth, his strength.

His love.

"Tell me about this." He dipped his hand under her shirt, touching her lower back where her tattoo was.

"My tattoo?"

"I haven't been able to figure it out. Is it a cursive H? Your initials? I think it requires a closer look, which means your clothes are going to have to come off again."

"Oh really?" She wiggled in his lap. "I'm game."

"Tell me first."

It was only fair. He'd just unloaded a heavy burden he'd been carrying around for years. It was only fair for her to share a piece of herself. Just a tiny piece.

"It's a Celtic symbol for starting over. New beginnings. I got it before moving to Crystal Cove."

"What did you leave behind? Why did you need to start over?" His touch was too sweet as his words whispered across her neck.

"A bad upbringing. I needed to discover myself. Figure out who I was. Who I am."

"I'm rather enjoying discovering who you are, Lily." He pressed his lips to hers and she sunk into the kiss, thankful he didn't push her any further.

If he did, she'd have to feed him lies. The truth couldn't come out. Ever.

CHAPTER ELEVEN

TY ROLLED HIS PUSH mower out of the shed and hoped to get the back lawn mowed before the sun set and the mosquitoes came out full force. Someday he'd buy a ride-on mower. For now, the walking and pushing was therapeutic.

First Cam, and then Lily. Talking about his ultimate rejection and betrayal wasn't as hard as he thought it would be. In fact, it was almost freeing. It didn't change anything. He'd still been lied to, cheated on, and dumped because he didn't have connections to millions, but knowing he had friends who cared more about him than any of that lifted his spirits.

In fact, not since he'd been a hotshot soccer player in high school had he felt so secure in himself. Crystal Cove wasn't the pit of despair he thought it was after his high school graduation.

The town was full of good people, good families, and growing businesses. It wasn't where shallow and vain people settled down to raise a family. He'd been gung-ho about leaving the cove as soon as he graduated high school, thinking there were bigger and better things for him out in the big world.

And, yeah, there were definitely bigger, and maybe better, but not better for him. However, he didn't begrudge his time in the service. And now that he'd gotten a lot off his chest, he didn't begrudge his relationship with Kristi either.

Every relationship, every obstacle in life was a learning experience. Ty learned a lot from his first serious relationship. He'd had blinders on for months, so in love with being in love that he didn't look at all the signs of a troubled relationship.

Her questions about his future. The subtle belittling of his father's business. The pressure to work his way up in the military or pursue a high-paying job. The demand to keep their relationship a secret.

149

They weren't in the same squadron and hadn't crossed any lines, yet some did frown upon soldiers fraternizing with each other. Hell, it happened all the time.

Ty was proud their relationship was real, not a random hook-up. Yet after Kristi admitted to cheating on him and telling him the baby wasn't his, he questioned how faithful she'd been during the eight months they were in a relationship.

Stupid. That's how he had felt. Totally blindsided by the cheating. And if that wasn't already a knife in the heart, finding out about the baby was the twisting of the dagger deep in his chest until there was no point of return.

The only saving grace was burying himself in the war. In concentrating on his physical health. If he wasn't in meetings or on the battleground, he was working out. And when he could, he Skyped or sent emails to Hope and Delaney.

They'd been the perfect distraction from his problems. In comparison to what Hope had been through, his drama was miniscule. When his active duty time had been served, he was more than happy to return home. To be there for Hope and Delaney.

Ty pushed the mower off the slight embankment and turned it around again. Meatball hadn't moved from his spot in the grass. His head was shaded from the sun while his rump basked in it.

"I'm coming your way, Meatball. Move it or lose it." Even the loud mower wasn't enough to get the dog moving. As Ty neared, he turned off the mower and squatted. "Four feet to the left. That's all I'm asking. Give me ten seconds and you can rest your ass back here again."

Nothing. Rolling his eyes, Ty picked up Meatball and set him in the newly mowed grass. Shaking his head, he started up the mower again. If only the guys from school could see him now, totally owned by his mutt.

The guys he'd been close to in high school either moved away, picked up drinking as a regular hobby, or were out on the ocean from sunup to sundown. Although Brady and Carter Marshall were still in town.

Local farmers who lived over by the winery, they'd gone to school together but never traveled in the same circles. Farm boys and hard workers. They had family loyalty and manual labor in common.

From what he knew, Brady was pretty good friends with Alexis, but he never socialized much. That was Carter who went out with Mia from time to time. Just friends, she'd said, and Ty believed her. Mia was not the settling down type.

He knew the locals and the locals knew him, but like the Marshall brothers, Ty preferred to keep to himself.

Or rather *had* preferred. Hanging out with Cam and Ben and spending time with Lily was a nice alternative to sulking by himself.

It wasn't healthy, he knew, keeping to himself, working the same hours as the overworked and underpaid fisherman, and devoting the rest of his time in supporting Hope. Until Lily came around, those seemed like his only options.

He'd first noticed her when he drove by to go to The Happy Clam. She had on cut-off jean shorts and flip-flops, a bag of dirt and a tray of purple and pink petunias at her feet. He'd given his mom a hanging basket full of the same flowers the week before for Mother's Day.

After he'd parked at the restaurant, he thought about taking a leisurely stroll down the street to check out the newcomer. And then what? Ty wasn't one for small talk. He didn't randomly strike up conversations with women he didn't know.

In high school, he'd bring a girl to the movies and to Dairy Queen for an ice cream. They'd make out in his truck or at the beach. When the rare occasion happened and his parents went out for a night, he'd sneak a girl back to the house and into his bedroom. Not exactly dating.

His time with Kristi was more of the same. Only less. There weren't many places to go, and their leave never matched up. He confused their deep conversations for trust and relationship building. Instead, they were simply passing time.

She'd ruined him. Ruined the little skill he had at conversing and totally destroyed his confidence. To approach someone as beautiful as Lily, he'd need a boatload of confidence.

For weeks he'd waited, hoping Lily would stop by the restaurant. He couldn't ask anyone about her or they'd pounce on the idea of setting him up. Hope would be more tactful; Mia, however, would do just what she had done the past month. If he was going to take a girl out, he'd be the one asking, not his sister or best friend.

That tiny spec of male chauvinism was lost when Lily had initiated their first date at the drive-in.

Having patience had paid off. He'd discreetly tried to find out information about Lily: where she moved from, if she had family in Maine, siblings, an ex-husband, a current boyfriend.

Being the quiet one in the town had its advantages. Often, others forgot he was there and chatted mindlessly revealing more than they would have had they thought Ty had any interest. It still didn't give him much information on Lily.

She didn't appear to have any family. She was single—which was the most important part. His sister and Hope loved her and thought she was the sweetest, kindest soul. Yet they all agreed she had a painful past. Something about seeing it in her eyes when she first moved here.

By the time Ty had the courage to look her in the eyes, he hadn't seen any pain. Any skeletons. Just stunning blue eyes filled with humor, kindness, intelligence, and lust. Someday he'd ask her about what brought her to the cove. For now though, why rock the boat?

Lifting his arm, he wiped the sweat from his brow with his bicep and walked the mower back to the shed.

"Thanks for your help," he called to Meatball. "Let me wait on you hand and foot. Dinner will be ready in five." Ty held the back-door open and waited for Meatball to slowly rise to his legs and wad-dle his way up the steps and into the house.

Once his dish was filled, Ty stripped his jeans, tossing them in the washer, and turned on the water in the shower. He lathered up his face while waiting for the water to warm and sliced through it with his razor.

Normally he wouldn't bother shaving this late in the day, but he had a hot date at Pizza Dough with a beautiful woman.

* * * *

LILY WAS THE LAST TO arrive at Books by the Ocean. Her four o'clock highlight turned into a three-hour debacle. She'd texted the girls and told them not to wait for her. When she pushed through the door to the bookstore Mia was already pouring the drinks.

"A lot can change in a month." Mia filled five red Solo cups with the ginger beer mule drink she'd made and passed them around. "Water for you, Lils. Sucks being the designated driver, doesn't it?"

It really didn't. Especially when she had plans to drive out to Ty's after book club. They'd progressed from their Saturday only sleep-overs to whenever they felt like it. Her first appointment in the morning wasn't until nine, which gave her plenty of time to get back to the spa, shower, and pretend she'd slept there all night. Alone.

Not that it was anyone's business, but living in a small town meant gossip was easy to come by. And people loved to talk. She loved to listen and preferred the topic to be anyone but herself.

"You know I'm not a heavy drinker anyway. I don't mind driving if anyone gets too snockered off your mules."

"Snockered? That's very European." Grace sat at the far end of the couch, her legs crossed primly as she sipped her drink.

Chills pricked the back of her neck. Grace knew. The question was, had she said anything to anyone else, and how much did she know?

"It reminds me of *Bridget Jones's Diary*. We should read a comedy next." Hope passed around the plate of cookies she'd made. "We've been on this serious drama kick for too long."

"We don't even talk about books anymore," Alexis said as she took a cookie and sat next to Grace.

"I think we need to meet twice a month. Once for book talk and the other time for girl talk." This from Jenna who had yet to be the center of discussion. Being a fulltime caretaker for a geriatric man didn't give her much time to socialize.

"I'm all for it but now that Alexis, Hope, and Lily have men dominating their lives, they can barely get here in time. Was it my brother who had you storming through the door so late tonight?"

Lily didn't take Mia's bait. She knew why Lily was late and wanted a reaction. A reaction she wouldn't get. The distraction, however, was welcome. No one seemed to notice the change in Grace's demeanor. She'd always been a bit stand-offish but most times they were together as a group she tried to get along with everyone.

Their brief chat last week about opening a fashion boutique wasn't what gave Lily the chills either.

"I have to be honest," Hope said. "I didn't finish the book. I love Jodi Picoult, I really do. But this one is deep. Emotional. I didn't want to rush it. Maybe we should do like Jenna suggested and try to make more time for each other."

"Won't that cut into our reading time? With Sophie teething and the winery in full swing, I'm barely finding time to take a shower."

"It's not about the books. It's about girl time. The older I get, heck, the older Delaney gets, I realize how important friendships are. I went without for too long. Look at us." Hope set her cup down and inched to the edge of her seat. "Our friendships have budded over the past year. I've known Ty forever, but Mia never crossed my radar."

"Hey."

"No offense. You were fifteen when I was pregnant. Not exactly a lot in common there. And hell, Alexis and I have lived in this town our whole lives and only got to know each other less than two years ago. And Grace. When you left for Europe you were barely drinking age. And now you're a gorgeous woman ready to take on the world. I heard about the Bergerons leaving and your meeting with them about renting their space. Don't think you're off the hook with this piece of news."

"What?" Alexis gasped. "Why didn't you tell me?"

"I was going to."

"And she will. As soon as I'm done." Whether Hope wanted to be or not, she would always be their unappointed group leader. "Lily's new to town, and Jenna hasn't been here much longer. New friends. New relationships. We need to take care of ourselves, of each other. I didn't think having a lot of friends was important. I'm close with my parents and have a beautiful daughter. But the more my relationship grows with each of you, the more I value the power of friendship."

Lily dabbed her eye with a napkin and when Jenna sniffed next to her, she passed her a dry one.

"Shit, Hope. Marriage has turned you into a complete sap."

"I guess so, Mia. And I can't wait for each of you to find happiness as well. And I don't mean with a man, although that's icing on the cake. Or a woman, if you prefer. We need to find happiness within ourselves. I find that with each of you."

Lily wiped her eyes then blew her nose into her napkin.

"I agree with Hope. You all are becoming family to me. I came here searching for... myself, and you've all helped me do that. You mean the world to me. Really." Jenna hugged her, as did Alexis. They all stood and hugged each other.

When Grace reached for her, Lily worried it would be awkward, cold. But Grace's arms were strong around her. "We need to talk. Privately," she whispered in Lily's ears, and the chill crept down her spine again.

Yeah. She knew.

Lily's hands began to shake. Her head was heavy on her shoulders, and static blanketed her eyes. Somehow she managed to find herself back on the couch, Grace by her side. "Breathe in and out. Slowly." She handed Lily her water and rubbed her back. "I'll get us out of here," she said in a low whisper.

Standing in front of Lily and blocking her from everyone's sight, Grace made a big production about the alcohol going right through her. She rambled on about the book and how lame it was.

The voices in the room were a conjoined mass of noise, and Lily couldn't differentiate from one voice to the next. Grateful for Grace's distraction, she took her advice and concentrated on her blood flow, taking deep breaths.

Her heart thundered in her chest, and she frantically searched the room for... *him*. For *them*. She'd been too lax lately with her safety. Her name, her identity, and Agent Thorne were a constant reminder that she'd never be safe.

Ever.

Reaching blindly behind her, Grace held out her hand. "Lily said she'd drive me home, so one of you need to step up to be the DD in case someone else drinks too much of Mia's potent drink."

"I'm not having another. I'll drive if necessary."

"Thanks, Alexis." Lily had found her voice and stood, gripping onto Grace's hand for support.

"Are you okay? You're as white as a ghost." Hope rested a hand on her shoulder, and Lily forced a smile.

"Tired. It was a long day."

"Must be those late night sleepovers keeping you up. Ty's been looking a little tired around the eyes as well," Mia teased.

He didn't appear tired at all. If anything, Ty had more energy now that they were dating. Everyone had commented on it before. It was just Mia being Mia for which Lily was thankful. It alleviated some of the pressure in her chest.

"Sorry to cut the book club short and to steal Lily away. This drink isn't settling right, though."

Grace pulled her along and out the door. When they got to Lily's car, Grace took the keys from her and opened the passenger door, pushing Lily inside.

"I don't trust you on the road right now. We'll go back to your place. The walk would do you some good, but the girls will think something is up if both cars are out here when they leave."

The mile walk in the warm sea breeze would have felt good if it wouldn't lead to questions.

And possibly the end of her new life.

CHAPTER TWELVE

IN A MATTER OF MINUTES, they were walking through the front door of the spa and up the flights of stairs to Lily's apartment. Once inside, Grace boiled water then found two mugs and two tea bags.

"If you didn't look so ashen I'd suggest something strong like vodka or tequila. Something tells me that wouldn't be a good idea, though." When the water was heated, Grace filled the cups. "Kitchen table or living room couch?"

"Couch." Lily would need the space to curl up in a ball.

Carrying the mugs into the living room, Grace commented on the throw pillows, the curtains. The lavender and eucalyptus candle in the corner. "Can I light it? It smells soothing."

"Sure. There's a lighter in the drawer by the sink." Lily sipped her tea while Grace bustled about.

When the candle was lit, she made herself comfortable on the other end of the couch, mirroring Lily's position by tucking her feet under her butt.

"Should I call you Veronica?"

The tension in her stomach made her want to vomit. "No."

"I'm sorry. That was insensitive."

"What do you know?" Lily didn't want to feed Grace too much information if she didn't know the entire story. She could be one of Damian's plants. Although it was unlikely. Grace had ties to the town, and Lily didn't.

Unless Agent Thorne was one of his men as well. If so, she needed to leave tonight.

"Only what I saw on the news. Read online."

"Which was?"

"So it's true?" Grace set her tea down. "You're Veronica Stewart-Gervais back from the dead?"

The pit of despair laid heavily in her stomach. She didn't want to admit to anything. In her heart of hearts, she was *not* that woman.

"What do you know about her?"

"Daughter of the Stewart jewel empire in New York City. Heir to millions. Married—or rather *was* married to renowned French jeweler, Damian Gervais. *Her* wedding made every gossip column and entertainment show in Europe five years ago. The gown alone cost eight hundred grand."

It was a beautiful gown. Custom designed for her by one of the top wedding designers in France. Damian and her father insisted on the best. They knew the wedding would attract a lot of media attention, and Jackson Stewart and Damian Gervais were not men who shied away from the glitz.

Growing up wearing designer clothing and custom jewelry was her norm. She knew she lived the fairytale life. There were times during her young teens when she'd wished she could be normal. Go to a regular school. Hang out at the mall with friends. Eat pizza in her bedroom while gossiping with girlfriends.

The daughter of Jackson Stewart didn't behave in such a manner, though. It's not what the world wanted to see, and her father was all about impressing others. His name was worth a lot of money and he had to look the part, as did his daughter.

All. The. Time.

"I was trying to find myself in Europe. I thought the vineyards of Italy would inspire me to care more about Coastal Vines. They didn't. I appreciate wine more, yes, but still have no desire to work on a vineyard."

"That's why you went to Europe?"

"Sort of." Grace picked up her tea again, blew on it, and sipped. Lily hadn't tried her tea yet, too afraid it would come back up. Her stomach did summersaults waiting to hear what else Grace knew about her life. If it was only her identity that had been found out, she'd call Thorne and come up with a plan.

It would take fifteen minutes to pack her essentials in a duffle bag. Since Thorne had arranged for her rent and insurance on the spa, he could just as easily cancel it and find her a new place to set up shop.

A new name. A new life.

A life without her new friends. Without Ty.

The peanut butter and jelly sandwich she had for lunch hours ago threatened to resurface. Lily clenched her hands, her nails making half-moon marks in her palms.

She'd stayed away from the media, from civilization, and had no idea how much had been discovered and plastered all over the news.

"I honestly did try to enjoy winemaking. Maybe if I didn't grow up on a vineyard. However, if they had been anything like the vineyards in Tuscany, that would have been a different story. Next, I tried my hand in the fashion industry."

The seriousness took over Grace's face again. This must be the connection. Where their paths crossed or where she'd learned more about Veronica. Needing to do something, Lily tried her tea. When she swallowed and it didn't immediately come back up, she kept her mug in front of her mouth as a barrier. Of what, she didn't know. But having something to shield her made her feel a little less... threatened.

"I took a few classes, worked in some boutiques. I dated a guy whose sister co-owned Muse and got me a job filling in when one of her stock girls took a day off. I'll never forget the day you—Veronica Gervais came in with her older husband looking like they'd stepped off a runway. Everyone in the store stopped what they were doing to cater to the power couple. *Veronica* looked like I'd seen her in the fashion and gossip magazines, only different. Her smile wasn't staged. In fact, I never saw it. Her husband though, quite the charmer."

Lily didn't remember that specific store. There were so many. Too many. Damian loved to dress her up and show her off. "We're doing our duty by visiting the little people," he'd say.

Their driver would bring them from store to store where Damian would pick out items for her, which would then sell out as the next big fashion statement. He loved trend-setting with her. Or rather, using her to do so. It was all a game. See how many people he could control.

And it was also part of his cover-up. She'd bought into it when he first came to the States. She was wowed by his presence. Sixteen years her senior, he was established and glamorous in ways an impressionable twenty-two-year-old would succumb to.

Damian and her father had formed a partnership and before she realized what had happened, she'd been manipulated into marriage. Her entire life had been controlled. First by her father, then by her husband.

It was the only life she knew, living in her gilded cage, and had no idea it wasn't normal until she'd overheard Damian on the phone.

"That was you in the shop, wasn't it? Your hair was short. Darker. You were thinner. Too skinny. I wouldn't have recognized you had I not been obsessive about following you in the daily rags. I looked for social media accounts, but you never had any. I thought that odd in this day and age."

No social media for the Stewart-Gervais heiress. It would cause too much frenzy. People would learn too much about their *private* lives, Damian had said. Better to leave it to his PR people.

Needing to wash it all away, she gulped her tea, not caring how hot it was, not caring if it burned her insides.

Her father and husband had burned her from so much, from life.

"Lily?" Grace scooted closer, placing a hand on her foot. "Do you want to talk about it? About the rest?"

So she had heard. Or read. Or seen. Lily couldn't talk. Couldn't formulate words. She shook her head.

"Is it true? Did Damian kill that man? The detective or whatever they call them in France?"

Lily swallowed the ball of pain in her throat and nodding, set her tea on the table. She couldn't fight the tremble anymore.

"Some say he killed your father. Other reports are that he committed suicide."

Lily didn't know which was true and, frankly, she didn't care. After she'd witnessed Damian shooting the detective in his office, she'd snuck back to her room and threw up at least a week's worth of meals. Cold sweats and uncontrollable shakes took over her body.

Damian had found her huddled around the toilet and thought she had the flu. It was what had saved her. She couldn't face him and hide her reaction. Hide the fact she'd witness him kill a man. A police officer.

She didn't hear the gun go off, but the blood on the man's chest and his body falling to the floor in a sudden thud was clear enough a picture. And her father stood only a few feet away. She'd seen his reaction. It was of satisfaction.

Her father was just as guilty as Damian.

The toilet, the privacy of the bathroom became her saving grace. She slept there all night avoiding their bedroom. Their bed. When she heard him leave in the morning—without even checking on her—she ran to her room to change and flee.

Only there was no one to call. No one to run to.

"Do you think he killed your father?"

There was no doubt in her mind. "Yeah," she managed to say.

"I'm sorry, Lily. I'm so, so sorry. I can't imagine the hell you've experienced in life."

"The grass is always greener, huh?" Her failed attempt at humor didn't make either one of them feel better.

"Your name change, this is your way of escaping the past?"

So Grace didn't know everything. To have one friend to confide in, to tell her secrets to had always been her dream. And while Lily had the women in town, she could only share with them stories from Lily Novak's life, not anything from Veronica Stewart's.

Going against Agent Thorne's advice, she decided to open up to Grace.

"I witnessed the murder."

"Holy shit! You saw him kill that guy?"

Lily closed her eyes and nodded. "The next day I left Damian a message telling him I was spending the day at the spa. I figured he'd be too busy cleaning up his mess and figuring out what to do with the body to pay much attention to me."

"Maybe we do need the tequila."

"I don't think I could handle it now. Maybe later."

"You name it and it's yours." Grace kept earnest eyes on Lily. Yes, she'd turn into a good friend.

"I did go to the spa. I never needed an appointment. They'd bump someone to squeeze me in. I knew I had to act normal or I'd draw suspicion to Damian. Having a massage and facial meant I didn't have to talk to anyone, and it would give me time to think. By the time I was done, Bruno, one of Damian's bodyguards, was waiting for me."

"Bruno? Did he look as stereotypical as his name sounds?"

"Identical. Only instead of ushering me into the Mercedes, he gripped my elbow and said we needed to take a walk."

"He tried to kill you?"

"You and Ty should watch movies together."

"Ty knows about this?"

"No. I just meant"—Lily tugged at her ponytail—"you both love to interrupt stories."

"Oh my word. I'm so sorry. I do that a lot. I'm an interrupter. I'll shut up now."

"It's okay." Lily managed a slight smile. "At least I know you're listening."

"How can I not? I mean, your life, first it was a fairy tale and now it's a freaking mystery suspense thriller. Screw book club. You can tell us stories about your life. It's better than fiction." Grace cupped her hand over her mouth. "I didn't just say that. That's not what I meant. Your life sucks. Sucked. Seriously, Lily. I swear I'm not an insensitive bitch."

"I know you aren't. I wouldn't be telling you all of this if I thought otherwise."

"I'll shut up and let you finish. So Bruno takes you for a walk..."

The shaking in her hands had stopped, so she picked up her tea again telling the story with no emotion. She'd worked hard to compartmentalize so she wasn't living in fear twenty-four seven. "He told me Damian suspected I knew. He offered to take me away. Set me up somewhere safe."

"And you believed the guy? Sorry. I'll stop."

"That's okay. I didn't believe him at first. I figured it was Damian's way to get me out of the picture. Stage a car accident or something. I let Bruno believe I believed him, though. That night at dinner my father asked me about my day. If I was feeling better. He was heading back to New York in the morning and wanted to spend one last evening with me. I didn't want to be in the house and thought a crowd would be safer, so I suggested the opera."

"Why do all rich people like that stuff?"

"Actually, I hated it. My dad loved it, or pretended to love it. Like you said, rich, classy people are supposed to appreciate it, so he made us go quite often."

"Did you tell your dad what you saw? That your husband killed a man?"

"No." Lily shook her head and sighed. It was all she could do. There were no feelings left inside her for her father. "He knew. He was standing next to Damian when it happened."

"Dear God." Grace fell back on the couch and covered her face with her hands. "You poor girl. This story keeps getting worse. So you go out with your father not knowing if he has plans to off you? Again. Sorry. No filter here."

"Pretty much. Right before intermission, Bruno whispers to my father loud enough so I can hear. He told him Damian needed him back at the house immediately. Bruno stayed with me until the end of the opera, and I still didn't know who to trust. If I was safer sitting next to my dad or the bodyguard who knew I'd witnessed the murder."

Putting her cup down again, she grabbed a pillow and cradled it to her chest. "That night Bruno drove me to the embassy and reported what he knew. Apparently, my father and Damian had been receiving illegal shipments of jewels from Africa and covering it up for nearly a decade. They'd made their billions by stealing from those who couldn't even afford to put a real roof over their heads."

"And that's why the detective was there. When he knew he was busted, Damian reacted by killing the guy."

"Pretty much. There was some bribery going on as well. That night when officials from the embassy went to arrest my father and bring him back to the States, they found him dead from a self-inflicted gunshot wound to the head. Forensics later said it wasn't suicide. Something about the angle of the gun. At that point, I didn't care. Damian's serving life in prison. He shouldn't be a problem for me anymore."

"Shouldn't. What aren't you saying?"

This was where her future would never be the same. "The investigators discovered it went deeper than just my father and Damian. There have been at least five others arrested for consorting with them. And some have said..." she hugged her pillow tighter. "It's come out that some of these criminals think I know all the names of those involved. And there's fear that those who haven't been identified or caught, will come after me."

"Oh, honey." Grace shot up and wrapped Lily in a hug.

"My death was staged and leaked to the papers."

"Oh, Lily." She cried, her tears soaking Lily's shirt, and soon Lily's floodgates opened as well.

They rocked back and forth and cried into each other's arms until there were no more tears, only the unattractive sniffing and convulsing tearjerker aftershocks.

"You're living your life in fear. And yet you appear fresh and beautiful and happy day after day. You amaze me."

"I'll accept half the compliment. I am happy. This town, the women I've become friends with. You mean more to me than all the money in the world."

"Shit. That's a hefty compliment considering you used to have all the money in the world."

"And I mean it."

"I think it's more than that. You always looked happy, but lately you shine. It's Ty, isn't it? I won't be jealous of you anymore, not after that story."

"Jealous?"

"Sure. You make it look so easy. I know your clothes aren't designer right now, and you're barely making ends meet. Yet you have it together. And now, knowing the hell you've been through and still are so sweet and kind to everyone, wow. You're totally up there on my pedestal."

"I admire you too, Grace."

"Ah, don't feel you need to return the compliment. There's not much going on here."

"Sure there is. You went searching for something, for yourself. You knew you wouldn't be happy working on your family's winery, so you did a little self-discovery. And now you're giving back by giving aspiring designers a chance to showcase their work. I think it's a lovely idea."

"Really?"

"Really." Grace's mouth dropped open, and her eyes went wide with fear. "Oh my God."

"What is it?" The fear spread to Lily. The hammering in her chest too familiar.

"I. I." Grace ran to the kitchen and searched frantically through her purse until she pulled out her phone. "I took pictures at the concert. I posted them on my Facebook and Instagram pages. I even made a comment about how you looked like that jewelry heiress. I couldn't remember your name at the time; I'd had a lot to drink."

Lily wrapped her arms around her waist and bent over. She didn't go on social media for that very reason. While she wasn't famous, those who followed the fashion and jewelry industry, especially in Europe, could recognize her. Bile made its way up her throat but she held it at bay, reaching for a glass of water to wash it back down.

"I'm deleting it right now. No one commented back about Veronica Stewart-Gervais. I'm sorry, Lily. I'm so, so sorry. Had I known..." Grace dropped her phone back in her purse and hung her head low.

"It's okay," she said in a shaky voice. Grace didn't know. It wasn't her fault. "You didn't do anything wrong. I knew it would be a matter of time before someone recognized me. I just figured in a small town like this no one would."

"Did I put you in danger? What can I do to help? Can I call someone? The police?"

"No. The police don't know who I am. I'll call Agent Thorne in the morning to let him know there could be a possible slip. The chances are small, though."

"I've never hated myself more than I do right now."

She was scared, she'd always be scared for her life, but she didn't want to live as a recluse anymore. The relationships she'd built with her new friends and with Ty taught her about life. About living. This was living, not tossing around money as if it grew on trees. Lily reached for Grace and hugged her tight.

"I don't blame you. I'm not mad. Honestly."

"I don't deserve your kindness." Grace sniffed.

Lily heard her phone vibrate in the other room. "That's probably Ty. I forgot to call him." She needed more time to compose herself before she went over to his house. He'd be wondering where she was though, so she needed to answer it.

"Do you want me to stay?"

"I appreciate the thought. I'm okay now. I feel better. Honestly. It actually feels good to be able to talk to someone about it."

"I know I'm known for my love of gossip, but you have my absolute word that not the slightest—"

"I trust you, Grace. Last week when you came to see me you knew yet you didn't let on. Tonight you discreetly got me out of the bookstore when I thought I'd collapse. I know you didn't realize the severity of the situation. You only knew part of the story. Now that you know it all—"

"You're Lily Novak. From Arizona, if rumor is correct. Family is gone. Not sure how. That's some digging the rest of the town is anxiously awaiting to hear. When I hear the story, I'll be sure to spread it."

"Thank you. For waiting to talk to me. For being my friend." Her eyes filled again, and she sniffed back the tears.

Grace leaned in for another long hug before letting herself out the door.

Relief washed over Lily. A cleansing of the soul in a way. Now she had to figure out what to tell Ty. If anything at all.

CHAPTER THIRTEEN

THE MID-SUMMER SUN bore down on his neck, heating his body until he'd soaked through his second shirt of the day. And it wasn't even noon yet. Needing to hydrate, Ty climbed down the ladder, grateful to be off the hot as hell asphalt shingles.

The Winston house should have been a quick reno. A leaky roof from years of neglect turned into redoing the entire backside of the house. Shingling in the summer was never a fun job. Ty liked to arrive early and beat the summer heat, but the Winstons were late sleepers and wouldn't allow Ty and his crew to arrive before nine.

Two more days and they'd be done. He'd wanted desperately to take a few days off and go away somewhere private with Lily. Hell, he'd settle on a two-day lock-in at his house. Their schedules didn't mesh though, except for their Sundays off. Other than that, it was a quick meal here and there.

Their sleepovers were happening more frequently, which he had absolutely no problems with, but he wanted to take Lily somewhere. He'd never done that before. Never had the opportunity or never cared.

It wasn't like he needed to show her off, everyone in town had figured out they were together, thanks to his car being parked in her lot all night and the few times they'd had dinner at The Happy Clam and even the Sunrise Diner.

Priscilla had loved that one. She was all smiles when Ty held the door open for Lily and pulled out her chair before ordering their Sunday breakfast.

"'Scilla knows what she's talking about." She fanned herself with a plastic menu. "The colors coming off you two. Phewy! It's hot."

Ty smiled at the memory as he opened the cooler in the back of his truck and drank from his water bottle. He'd already refilled it twice from the garden hose.

"Make sure to hydrate," he said to Phil, his right-hand man on the job. "Let's break for lunch. Looks like some cloud cover will be here in a bit." Ty pointed across the horizon where a batch of white fluffy clouds would shield them from the sun.

His crew had been small this summer with many guys taking time off for family vacations. He'd never taken one before. Why bother? Where would he go? Who would he go with? It wasn't until Lily that he'd understood the importance of downtime.

"You're pushing yourself too hard, Ty." His dad carried his cooler over to a shady spot under a maple tree and sat in the grass. Ty followed him, bringing his lunch with him as well.

"Just trying to finish up the job." He unwrapped his roast beef sandwich and bit into it.

"When was the last time you took a day off? Phil says you've been working side projects on Saturdays as well."

Saturdays had turned lonely with Lily at work, and he'd used that time productively instead of moping around. It was a win-win. He wasn't as stressed about squeezing in the little projects after work and could be home in time for dinner with Lily.

"Simple repairs is all, Dad. The Chamberlains front porch stairs were rotted out. Buddy's getting up there in age and shouldn't be pushing himself and Milly can barely walk now, so I put in a simple ramp."

"That was nice of you. Milly called your mother last week to tell her what a nice boy she'd raised." His father scraped the bottom of his yogurt container. "Speaking of your mother, she'd like you and Lily to come over for dinner on Sunday."

He hadn't talked to his parents about Lily. It wasn't like he was keeping her from them; the entire town knew they were seeing each other. He'd never introduced a girlfriend to his family before. Not that Lily needed an introduction. His mother knew her before he did.

"I'll ask her."

"That would make your mother happy. She likes Lily a lot." They ate their lunches in silence until his father broke the spell. "You know, I'm not getting any younger either."

"You're sixty and in great shape. That's not old."

"I appreciate the compliment." His father slapped him on the back. "I get around just fine, but climbing ladders and putting in twelve-hour days... Well, I told your mother I'd cut back a bit. Maybe be more of the paperwork guy."

"What?" Ty crumpled the saran wrap and tossed it in his cooler. "You're retiring?" His father had taught him all he knew, and he still had a lot to learn.

"Not exactly. You hate the business side of the job. I don't mind taking the desk job. I'll have more time to budget and organize job-sites, and you can do the grunt work. When you're down a man, I'll still pitch in. I'll need to get my hands dirty every now and then."

"How long have you been thinking about this?"

"For a little bit. Not until I knew you could handle running a crew on your own. You've been doing that for a couple years. The guys respect you. Look up to you. You have a good eye and work well with the clients as well."

Pride swelled in his chest.

That had been one of Ty's biggest fears. That he'd never be looked at as his own person, but his father's son. The guy who couldn't make it on his own.

Damn, he hated how pathetic he sounded. Had he really been a complete downer since Kristi effed up his life? Lily's comment about him and Meatball being the same came to mind.

Yeah, she was right. He needed the kick in the pants to take a look around him and be grateful for all that he had.

His health. A family who loved each other and supported him. A job, a *career*, he loved and was good at. A roof over his head and a low-maintenance dog. Friends. Cameron, Ben, Hope. Hell, he'd call Mia a friend if he had to.

And Lily.

Being in a relationship, finding a woman to love, wasn't anywhere on his radar. Yeah. Love. He loved Lily. And the realization didn't scare him. He'd opened up to her about Kristi, and then a few days later he'd told her about his depression. Instead of looking at him with disgust or pity, she comforted him and hugged him tight, asking him how she could help.

But she'd been off the past few weeks. More cuddly and still wonderful, but distant and not as lighthearted as she'd been when they first started seeing each other. Maybe unloading everything on her so soon into their relationship was a mistake. It was probably too much for her to handle.

"Are you okay with this? Taking the lead on the jobsites? You've been doing that for a while now anyway. Didn't think you'd realized it, though."

"Sorry if I've stepped on your toes."

"Not in the least." His father opened up a container and offered Ty a cookie. "Your mother made oatmeal butterscotch chip. Your favorite."

"Thanks." He took a cookie and bit into it. "So when are you thinking of moving to the desk job?"

"Not until this fall. When projects slow down. Or when you're ready."

"You sure you're not sick? Something isn't wrong with you or Mom, is there?"

"Not at all." His father laughed and put the cover back on his cooler. "Just counting down the days to retirement. I wouldn't leave my company to just anyone. Parker Construction has a solid reputation. If I thought you couldn't keep it running smoothly, I wouldn't be stepping down. We're not a big corporation or anything, but around here, reputation is everything. You know that."

"I'm not going to lie, I'll miss working side-by-side with you, Dad."

"Likewise."

"And I'm honored to take over the family business." He truly meant it. Ten years ago the thought of being stuck working for the construction company made him feel claustrophobic. Today, though, it brought clarity to his future.

A future he wanted to share with Lily.

. . . .

"HEY, GORGEOUS." LILY came up behind him and greeted him with a kiss. "What ya got cooking?"

Ty closed the cover to the grill and turned, circling Lily in his arms. "Chicken thighs and baked potatoes. Nothing fancy."

"Sounds perfect." She toyed with the hair at the nape of his neck reminding him he needed a haircut.

"I want to do something fancy for you, though."

"I don't need that." Lily's fingers stopped moving, and her gaze stared out to the woods behind him.

That far off daze in her eyes was becoming more frequent. Ty couldn't figure out if he said or did something to trigger it.

"In case you haven't figured me out yet, I'm not the most, uh, romantic guy. I don't really even know what that means? Flowers? Balloons? Chocolates? What is it that you like?"

"You know what I like." She returned her gaze to him, this time the blues of her eyes were bright as the rich sky above.

"Tell me."

Her fingers stroked the back of his neck, and her body leaned closer into his. "I like this. Being with you. Having homecooked meals together. Even hanging out with Meatball."

Ty licked his lips and let out a dramatic sigh. "Hell. You're more boring than me."

Lily dropped her hands and goosed his sides. "Jerk," she said with a laugh as she slipped away. "Do you need help with dinner?"

"I'm assuming that means you think we need a vegetable."

"Does your mother know you don't eat vegetables unless I make you?"

"She's known that for thirty-four years. And speaking of my mother, she'd like us to come over for dinner tomorrow night. Is that okay with you?"

"I adore your mother. Celeste was one of the first people I talked to in town. She was kind to me from the very first time I met her while perusing through the bookstore."

"Just to let you know, I've never brought a woman to the house before."

"Really?" Lily touched her hands to his chest, and he felt instantly reassured this was a step in the right direction. Toward their future. "Well, then. I'm humbled and honored to be your first."

She rested her lips against his, and he wanted to stay like that forever. Lily in his arms, their bodies, their hearts, their lives never separating.

After dinner they went for a walk along his road, which dead ended and turned into a dirt tote road.

"This is pretty. Quiet and secluded. I can see why you love living out here."

"Is that another comment about me and Meatball being one in the same? Too grumpy for civilization."

She bumped him with her hip. "I never said you were grumpy."

Ty draped his arm over Lily's shoulder and pulled her into his side. "You implied." He dropped a kiss to the top of her head. "And you were kind of right. Although I'd call it serious and focused."

"Ty." Lily stopped walking and turned to him. Her shoulders slumped under the heaviness of his arm, and her bottom lip curled into her mouth as if the weight of the world was on her mind and she didn't know what to do. Or say.

And just like that, he went from happy and carefree to concerned and anxious. Ghosts from his past haunted the space between them. Ty dropped his arm and stepped back, not wanting her to feel how tense he was and how hurt he'd be if she misled him.

"I need to tell you something, and I'm not sure how you'll take it."

Again, the thud of his heart drowned in the sea of delusion. He'd been an idiot to trust, to believe so easily.

"Say what you have to say." He tucked his hands in his front pockets using his basic training interrogation skills to appear non-plussed by whatever ball she was about to drop.

"I've learned firsthand how short life is. We take too much for granted these days. We never know when... life will throw us a curve-ball."

Like right the hell now.

Lily reached out and caressed his chest, his thin tee not enough of a barrier to block the heat from her touch. Ty pretended to be un-affected.

"You don't have to respond. You don't have to say anything. In fact, I'd rather you didn't." She puckered her lips and exhaled, her breath loud and nervous in the still of the woods.

Like a Band-Aid, he'd rather her just be out with it. "What's the big secret you've been keeping from me?"

Her eyebrows lifted, and for a second her eyes rounded with fear and then quickly settled again. The curve of her lip sly and seductive and if he weren't about to get dumped, he'd trace his tongue along it.

Gliding her hand along his collarbone, she lifted her stunning blue eyes to his. "I love you."

Too shocked to respond, he studied her face waiting for the bomb to drop. For the final twist of the knife in his heart. Only it didn't come.

"That's your big secret?"

Lily's smile grew wider. "I don't think it's any secret. In fact, I think you're the last to figure it out." The smile wilted, and she bit her lower lip again. "I'm not asking for any type of declaration from you. I know it's hard for you to love, and I'm not asking for anything in return other than what we already have between us. I'm truly happy for the first time in my life. And you're a big part of that."

"You love me." Her eyes were sincere, her smile genuine, and his heart so full of life he didn't know how he'd gotten so lucky.

"We can go back now. Check on Meatball. I understand if you need more time." Lily started to walk away and he reached out quickly, grabbing the back waistband of her jeans.

"You love me." Tugging her into his arms, he watched as her lips curved into a shy smile, and she nodded slowly. "Damn."

He took her mouth in his and kissed her with a passion he didn't know he had. With the love in his heart he'd had tucked away for so long.

When they finally came up for air, he leaned his forehead against hers and worked on steadying his breath.

"I love you too, Lily."

CHAPTER FOURTEEN

AFTER THE MOST AMAZING evening cuddled in Ty's arms and the morning spent at the beach with him and Meatball, she left his house to go home and shower and change into something nice for dinner at his parents' house.

So this is what being in love feels like. She smiled at her reflection in the mirror as she curled subtle beach waves into her hair. When her hair and makeup were done, she slipped into a cute tangerine colored sundress and a pair of white sandals.

It was amazing what she could find at Target. To think of the hundreds of thousands, if not millions, of dollars she could have saved and donated to charities or done something good with. Instead, she and all the other too-wealthy people squandered their money as if it was easy to come by.

Which it had been. And that didn't seem fair while so many others worked countless hours day in and day out to make ends meet. This new way of life gave her a greater appreciation for all things, big and small. Lily was glad she walked away from her inheritance. Granted, claiming any of it would reveal she was alive.

Taking one final look in the mirror, she glanced at her cell phone and turned giddy inside. Ty would be there any minute. Making sure her overnight bag was packed with the essentials, she hefted it over her shoulder and made her way down the stairs to wait for him.

Ty stood on the other side of the glass door with a bouquet of flowers and the sexiest smile she'd ever seen.

Unlocking the door, she opened it and waved him in. Her heart swelled with love.

"These are for you. I've never bought flowers for a woman before."

"So I'm another first?" She took the flowers and breathed in their heavy, sweet scent.

"It's probably cliché`, giving you lilies. I know I'm not original, and I'm not the first." If he only knew how wrong he was. "But when the florist asked what kind of bouquet I wanted, I kind of froze. I don't know about types of flowers. Only the kind my mother plants in her garden."

"I love them, Ty. And I can honestly say you're the first person to give me lilies. In fact, no one has ever given me flowers before."

"Really?"

She chose her last name because it meant *new,* and she'd chosen her first name based on her favorite flower. Sure, her penthouse and many homes had been filled with flowers, but those were picked out by their staff and never held any sentimental value. Not once had her father or even Damian given her flowers.

Knowing how out of his element he was, made the gesture that much sweeter. Heck, she'd be over the moon if he picked wildflowers from the side of the road. It was the thought that counted and until Ty, she was never truly thought about.

"Really." She smelled them again and then moved them aside to give him a kiss. "So I'm the first woman you've brought to your parents' for dinner and the first to receive flowers. How did I get so lucky?"

"You're you."

A flash of guilt crept up her spine. Ty didn't know all of her, only the Lily Novak person she portrayed and pretended to be. Wanted to be. She wanted to tell him the truth, but before she did, she needed to talk to Agent Thorne. She'd called him last week, and he'd said to expect him on Tuesday. After they hashed out the details, she'd open up to Ty and tell him everything. She had to if she wanted a future with him.

Needing a moment to shake the guilt away, she stepped out of his arms. "And you're my first as well. I'm going to put these in water and then we can go."

"Want me to do it for you?"

"No." Lily stopped him with her hands. "If you come upstairs with me I'll be tempted to rip your clothes off and will make us late for dinner. Besides, I forgot the bottle of wine I wanted to bring. I'll be right back. You stay here and look pretty." She kissed him quickly and scurried off toward the back staircase.

• • • •

DINNER WITH CELESTE and Wade had been perfect. Too perfect. Even Mia had acted normal. She'd even joked about it not being fun anymore now that Lily and Ty were public with their relationship.

Between her clients at the spa during the day, and Ty at night, Lily didn't have much time to stress over her meeting with Thorne. Last week, she'd rescheduled her two-thirty foil and blocked out two hours to 'run errands', she'd told her staff.

Thorne had agreed it would be best if he waited for her in the parking lot and at two twenty-nine. She handed Charity Framingham her credit card back and printed out her receipt.

"I love the cut, Lily. As always, you know exactly what to do with this thick mop of hair." Charity signed, leaving a generous tip and handed the slip back to Lily.

"You have gorgeous hair. I'm honored you let me get creative with it." This time around she'd suggested long layers to soften the heavy curls. Charity had gorgeous hair and had done an amazing job taking care of it for over fifty years.

"I love not having to drive to Portland to get a good cut and color. The gas money I save goes to your tip every time." Charity waved her hand at the other girls and sashayed out. Rumor had it she was a bit of a cougar. She talked about Ty more than Lily, but she wasn't worried. Their relationship was solid.

One day she'd teased Ty about Charity's interest in him. She'd laughed at his reaction. Something between mortification and sheer embarrassment. No, Ty would never stray, that she was sure of. His loyalty to his family, to Hope and Delaney, and even to her was evident from the first time she met him two years ago.

She trusted him wholeheartedly and now that Grace knew about her past, she wanted to let Ty in on it as well.

Lily gathered her purse and keys. "I'll be back before closing. I'll have my cell on me if you need anything." She waved to Kendra, her new summer hire, and Annie.

Once she stepped outside, the sunshine warmed her skin and for a brief moment, she forgot about the looming dread of what this meeting with the FBI agent was all about.

His dark sedan with tinted windows was easy to spot in her small parking lot. Confirming it was him in the driver's seat, she ducked her head and rounded his car. She opened the passenger's side door and slid into the cool, leather seats. The familiar scent of new car and buffed leather had her stomach in knots. It wasn't comforting to her, neither was expensive perfume or the feel of thousand thread count sheets.

Instead, she'd taken a liking to flannel shirts, worn t-shirts, freshly cut wood, and calloused hands.

"Miss Novak. You're looking well," the agent said as he pulled onto the road and took a left onto Seaview Drive as if he knew exactly where he was going.

Which he probably did. The FBI agent was always on alert. She didn't need to look behind his tinted sunglasses to know his dark eyes were constantly flicking in the rearview and the side mirrors looking for possible tails.

"Thank you, Agent Thorne. No offense, but I was hoping I'd never have to see you again."

He made a little noise, something between a sigh, a sniff, and what could almost be a chuckle. That was a first. Lily didn't have any problems with Thorne. He'd been kind to her from the beginning. A little stiff, but she supposed all FBI agents were. Especially those responsible for keeping someone alive.

When she first met him at his office in New York, she'd been surprised by his young age. Late thirties, maybe forty. His suits were as serious as his face. And his voice never fluctuated. It wasn't monotone, but always... serious. There wasn't a better way to describe him. He didn't smile. Ever. Granted, his job didn't seem very fun. Find bad guys. Arrest them or kill them. Keep innocent people safe.

They passed through town, and Thorne took a right at Cranberry Drive and headed inland down backroads that would lead to farms and open fields. Ten minutes later he took a bumpy, dirt road Lily had never noticed before and stopped in front of a quaint cabin.

"Where are we?"

"Emerald Pond." Thorne reached behind him, gathered his briefcase, and got out of the car. Lily followed him up the stone path to the cabin.

"Who lives here?"

"No one is home. We can talk safely here."

She figured he avoided her question on purpose and wouldn't ask again. Thorne held the door open for her, and she walked past him inside.

The place was clean and furnished. Boxes were stacked along the back wall of the living room behind the worn floral couch. A row of windows overlooked a body of water. There weren't any boaters or jet skiers like she'd expect on a warm day in July. She spotted two men in a canoe far off and an old man and a little boy fishing off a dock at the neighbor's.

There wasn't much of a back lawn before it gently sloped to the water where a short dock and rowboat attached to it bobbed in the water.

"Where are we?"

"Emerald Pond." Thorne placed his briefcase on the wooden table in the kitchen and unlocked it, pulling out a laptop and a manila folder.

"I know that. But who lives here?"

Lily turned around and took in the rest of her surroundings. The living room was small, but not cramped. A brick fireplace took up much of the wall across from the couch, and a staircase peeked out from behind it.

"Does anyone else besides Grace Le Blanc know about your true identity?" Thorne sat in one of the wooden chairs, his shoulders stiff, and set back as he typed on his laptop.

"Not yet."

His typing stopped, and he tilted his head up. "Not *yet*? I thought you valued your safety. And your privacy."

Too uptight to sit, she crossed her arms, tucking her hands around her middle and paced the small downstairs. She went through the story again, this time in more detail than she had on the phone, about her conversation with Grace.

"I looked into Miss Le Blanc's background and her activity for the past six years."

Even though she didn't feel right about it, when he told her he'd do some digging, she knew he would investigate Grace. Guilt sloshed in her belly like she was slugging through wet sand digging for clams. Gross and dirty but had to be done.

"There were a few red flags."

Lily stilled. She was afraid to ask, but had to. "She's not..." She tried to swallow, the pressure in her throat making it difficult to do so. "She's not involved, is she?"

Thorne's eyes didn't reveal a thing. His face remained void of any emotion as he stared at her across the room. Lily bit her lip in worry.

"Not that I can tell. She's crossed paths with Damian Gervais and his associates before."

Lily gasped and dropped into the chair across from Thorne. "No."

"As far as I can tell, there weren't any business dealings. She flitted around Europe for a few years, working in establishments Gervais' employees, girlfriends, and wife would visit. Vineyards, shops, restaurants."

Girlfriends. She'd always had her suspicions.

"Regularly? Did you see a pattern?"

Thorne shook his head. "It appears coincidental and not regular. Miss Le Blanc worked a lot of jobs never staying long in one spot. That alone is a red flag."

"From what I've learned from her sister, Grace has always been like that. She doesn't stay in one place for very long and hasn't figured out what she wants in life."

"She's susceptible. Money hungry. Can easily be bought."

"I don't think so." Lily wouldn't believe it. Even though she wasn't close to Grace, no one was, the woman was still looking for her career path. The same could be said for Mia. Heck, Mia worked every odd job there was in Crystal Cove. The only difference with Grace was she did it in Europe.

"You can't be too trusting. Not in your position." Thorne didn't scare her, but he did throw off some pretty intimidating vibes. His tall frame filled out his suit with menacing power. Not bulk like Ty. Something different. Confidence. His lack of emotion was a shield that worked as a protection for him and ammunition for the enemy. He was a tough one to read.

"I know. I'm normally not, but the people here in Crystal Cove are different. They're good, hardworking people." Lily chewed at the inside of her cheek and tried to calm her churning belly before telling Thorne about her next move. "I've, uh, gotten close to them. Especially—"

"Ty Parker."

Thorne had never interrupted her before. He was the quiet one. The one who waited out his opponent until they dug themselves into a whole or confessed the truth.

"You know about Ty?"

"Yes." He didn't say it with cocky smugness. It was a matter of fact. Agent Throne knew about everything. "I've run a comprehensive background check on him. He served in the military. Was engaged to a woman named Kristi Longley. She had an affair with Kyle Thomas in Dallas. They have a son together." He continued with the facts Lily already knew.

Her head spun and her ears rang, drowning out Thorne's monotone list of Ty's service and his jobs and family in Crystal Cove. And then hurricane force winds hit the swamp, covering her from head to toe in a shit storm.

Lily's elbows dug into the table top and she covered her face in her hands, ashamed of the violation of privacy she brought to the people in Crystal Cove.

"Hope Windward Smithfield—"

"Stop!" She lifted her head and glared at the stoic man. "Stop prodding into my friends' lives. They deserve their privacy. Leave them the hell alone." She shot out of her chair and stormed out the backdoor until she reached the pond.

The setting was incongruous to what was going on inside the house. Turmoil. Tension. Deceit. Lies. While outside the water was calm, barely a ripple and the sun shone brightly overhead, the occasional cumulous cloud softening the sunshine, making beautiful reflections in the glasslike water.

If she hadn't heard the squeaky hinges of the door, she never would have known Thorne had joined her. The man seemed to always be in stealth mode. He stood next to her, hands dangling loosely at his sides.

Just once she'd like to see him tense. A wrinkle in his brow. Lips pursed in thought.

"You're planning on telling Mr. Parker who you are." He didn't ask. He knew. It was creepy.

"I love him. I can't keep secrets from someone I love."

"Kristi Langley said she'd loved him as well."

"I'm not going to cheat on him."

"I wasn't implying you would."

"You're saying he'll cheat on me?"

"Betrayal is as common as love."

"That's sad." Lily cocked her head to the side and studied him. While his gaze was focused on the pond in front of him, somehow she knew he wasn't taking in the beauty of their surroundings. He was scoping out the neighbors, the boaters; even the fish jumping out of the water weren't safe from his speculative glare.

"It's reality. My job is to keep you safe, Miss Novak. I've gone to great lengths to provide you with security. If you breach it willingly, I'll be forced to note that in the paperwork and pull back my protection."

"What protection? You're only here because I called you. I could have handled this on my own." Not even a cock of his eyebrow. "Wait." She stepped back, realization setting in. "You've been *spying* on me?" That's why he'd already done the thorough background check on Ty. Now she felt violated too. "Let me guess. You have telephoto lenses in your trunk or in your briefcase. Do you get off on spying on innocent people?"

Lily turned and fled. She typically wore sneakers or flats while working and today, of course, was the day she wore wedges. She ran down the driveway as far as she could before her arches gave out. Flopping to the ground, she crunched her knees to her chest and buried her face in her hands and cried. It was either that or puke.

The prickly gravel under her butt and the hot sun on her back didn't bother her as much as the invasion of privacy. Not of her. Hell, her life was an open book. To the FBI. Her friends, though, they didn't deserve to be treated as possible threats, possible criminals. But that's how it would be for the rest of her life.

The FBI lurking around the corner, hoping to catch one of Damian's men who'd slipped away. They were more concerned and focused on finding the next hit man than keeping her safe.

"I know what you're thinking." The shadow of doom loomed over her.

"You'd have to have feelings and emotions to know that." Lily wiped her eyes across the back of her hand and focused on the gravelly driveway, ignoring the polished black loafers to her left.

"My job is to keep you safe. Anyone who sparks an interest in you is an immediate threat."

"Thanks. You know how to make a girl feel special. Can't someone be interested in me for *me*?"

"That's not what I said."

"It's what you meant." Lily didn't care about being rude or crass to Agent Thorne. He may have only been kind, yet distant to her, but was still an FBI agent. A constant reminder her life would never be normal.

"I want to keep you safe."

"So you've said." Lily dropped her hands to the ground to push herself up, ignoring Thorne's outstretched hand. She wiped the gravel off her butt and crossed her arms, a common stance when the agent was around.

"I don't believe anyone in this town is a threat to your safety. If they were, I wouldn't have brought you here."

"Yet you pried into everyone's private life." Brushing past him, she marched back to the cabin. She needed to go to the bathroom and then would make him drive her back home. Or, better yet, she'd steal his keys and ditch the guy.

Even on the crunchy gravel his footsteps were silent behind her. The only way she knew he'd followed was when she caught his reflection in the gleam of the black Lexus.

She stepped into the house and let the screen door slam behind her, not caring about the rudeness in her behavior. Lily had been brought up on dignified etiquette—ironic, seeing how her father and ex-husband had been lying, cheating criminals—and was called sweet by the people in Crystal Cove, but the FBI brought out a rough side in her she didn't know existed.

Circling around the bottom floor and coming up empty, she climbed the stairs in search of a bathroom. With only three doors to choose from, she opened the closest and was relieved to find what she was looking for.

A few minutes later, after splashing cold water on her face, she opened the door. The sound of Thorne's fast and furious typing came from below. Not ready to face him, she snooped around. The door to the left opened to a small bedroom. A twin bed took up the back wall, simply made in a pale pink quilt. A tall bureau stood next to it. The room was devoid of any other furnishing or decorations. Two boxes were stacked at the foot of the bed, sealed and labeled. *Guest room.*

Lily crossed to the other room and opened the door. While it wasn't fully decorated, the nightstand did host a hardcover book and a pair of reading glasses. Another stack of boxes sat at the foot of the double bed. Someone was either moving in or moving out.

A picture frame behind the novel caught her eye. Peeking over her shoulder she craned and still heard his typing, so she crept further into the room. Lily picked up the frame and gasped at the couple smiling at each other.

"Prying, are you?"

Lily jumped and dropped the picture on the carpeted floor. Thorne stooped to pick it up and placed it back on the nightstand.

"Do they know... about... me? You?"

"You? No. Me? Yes."

Why in the world would Ruth and Herb Bergeron know FBI agent Ryan Thorne? Unless... "Are they in the witness protection plan too? Is that why they're retiring and moving?"

"Let's go downstairs." Thorne stood by the doorway, apparently waiting for Lily to go first.

"First. Tell me the Bergerons are safe. They're a sweet elderly couple. If my being in town brought them any harm..." She gulped, and that damn swelling throat of hers nearly choked her.

"They're safe and have nothing to do with this."

"Why are we here?"

"Downstairs." He closed the bedroom door behind her when she finally left.

Her feet and legs were like lead, but they finally got her down the stairs. Like a gentleman, Thorne held out a kitchen chair for her and she sat.

What was the connection? "Out of all the hideouts in the world, why did the FBI choose Crystal Cove?"

Thorne closed his laptop and sat across from her. He folded his hands together and rested them on the table as he looked at her with those serious, expressionless eyes.

"The FBI as a whole doesn't place witnesses. The fewer who know about the whereabouts the better."

"So who knows I'm here?"

"Me. And two others. Veronica Stewart-Gervais is dead. She's buried next to her mother and father in St. John Cemetery in Middle Village in New York."

How fitting that her father had purchased family plots for the family in the same cemetery that housed so many mobsters.

"You still haven't answered my question." Was that a tick she saw in his face? Maybe a glimmer of a grin? It was gone before she could register it.

"I have connections to the town."

"Which was how you found my building at an affordable price." The FBI had given her the start-up cost for supplies and the first year's rent. Well, not exactly given. She didn't take any money or possessions that she'd been entitled to, and as a thank you—sort of—they'd made arrangements for her work and apartment.

The Sea Salt Spa hadn't required much in renovations. It had been a hair salon before. While Thorne, or whoever, took care of sprucing the place up and slapping a fresh coat of paint on the walls, Lily had taken on her new identity and attended beauty school in South Carolina. She flew through the classes and spent every minute she wasn't in class on the floor of the beauty school, earning her hours.

Beauty and fashion were her *thing* growing up. If the profession wasn't so beneath the Stewart family's expectation, she probably would have gone into it. She had a good eye for what looked good. All she needed was the training. And she got that.

By the time the Sea Salt Spa was ready, she had her certificate.

"If your cover has been blown, it's not from anyone who's been in town for the past few years. Miss Le Blanc did wipe out most of her social media account as you'd told me, but there's a chance her pictures of you are still circulating out there."

"You think Grace is a threat?"

Again, his eyes didn't reveal any of his true thoughts. "Not intentionally."

"I want to know what your connection is to the Bergerons. Do they know we're in their house right now? This is a total invasion of their privacy, you know. Or do you have them locked up in the basement?"

"There isn't a basement."

Lily scowled. "Is that your poor attempt at a joke?"

"It's a fact."

"So you scoured the place before bringing me out here?"

"You could say that."

"What the hell? You said we'd talk once downstairs. Well, hell, since there isn't a basement, I'd say we're downstairs. I deserve to know everything. This is my life you're trying to ruin!" Lily pounded the table with her fists while her heart beat erratically in her chest.

"I'm not ruining your life. I'm protecting it," he said calmly.

"Go to hell." She tugged at her scalp and scratched her nails down her face in frustration.

"Ruth and Herb Bergeron are my grandparents."

"What?" Lily's eyes widened in shock. She couldn't picture the stoic agent with grandparents. Heck, with a family of any sort.

"I spent my summers here growing up."

"Do they know you're..."

"An FBI agent? Yes. That's no secret."

"Do they know who I am?"

"No." Thorne shook his head. "The rental agreement was signed by Lily Novak's lawyer, Chip Franklin."

Lily snorted. "Total fake name. Couldn't you come up with something a little more believable than that?"

Again, an almost smirk from Thorne. "That's his real name. He's in the agency with me. One of the others who knows about you."

"Have I met him?"

"No. The less contact, the fewer connections the better."

"Yet you bring me to your childhood getaway? Not smart, Agent Thorne."

"Safer than some of our safe houses."

"Until I blew it. Is that why your grandparents are retiring? Have I brought danger to the town?" Regret boiled in her gut.

"No. They'd planned on retiring three years ago."

"Why didn't they?"

"You should still be safe in Crystal Cove. I strongly urge you not to say anything to Mr. Parker about your true identity. I can speak with Miss Le Blanc if you'd like. Make sure she understands how important discretion is. If you don't feel comfortable, I have another place I can send you. I have a new identity for you in here." He took out a manila folder and slid it across the table to her. "New name. New state."

"A new identity?" Tears pooled in Lily's eyes as she fingered the edge of the folder. She liked who she'd become. Lily Novak from Crystal Cove. Owner of the Sea Salt Spa. Part of a book club. Friend to many. And in love with Ty Parker.

She had it all. She wouldn't leave. Unless her friends were in danger.

"I can't leave," her voice, barely audible, croaked.

"It's your choice. For now."

"You'll tell me if you think anyone's in danger?"

"Of course."

"Have there been any leads?"

"Nothing." Thorne shook his head. "Chances are there aren't any leaks. Everyone involved in Gervais' crime circle may already be dead or in custody. We'll never really know."

"So no news is good news?" Lily ran her hand across the folder before sliding it back to Thorne. "I'm staying. But you have to promise me you'll tell me the second you have any suspicions."

"I'll need my telephoto lens and spy cameras to keep me informed."

Was that a joke? Now? There was no inflection in his voice and no lift in his lip to reveal if it was.

"Spy on the bad guy. Leave the rest of us out of it."

"You have my word."

"Thank you."

"I need your word as well."

"Of course. For what?"

"Don't tell anyone else. Especially Parker. If things go sour between you and you break it off, there's no telling what he'll do."

"We're not going to break it off. We love each other."

"People don't go into marriage thinking they'll end up in divorce. It happens. Don't let love blind you."

"That's cold."

"It's fact."

She refused to believe Ty would ever do anything to betray her. Even if somewhere down the road they went their separate ways, he'd never out her. He wasn't like that.

But then, she never thought her husband would have her murdered.

Or her father would be part of the master plan.

CHAPTER FIFTEEN

ALL DAY LONG TY COULDN'T get the image of Lily climbing into some fancy black sedan out of his mind. She had her head lowered as if trying to hide as she'd slipped into the stranger's car.

Hell. Stranger to him, apparently not to her. He'd flattened himself against the front door to Chambers Accounting Firm as he watched the car turn in the opposite direction, driving out of town.

Old, bitter bile worked its way up his throat as he remembered kissing Kristi goodbye as she went on her leave to Dallas. He'd pined away for her during her four-week leave and when she'd returned, he was so caught up in seeing her again that he didn't see the signs. Her distance. Her evasiveness. The quick hang-ups when he'd surprised her in her tent, brushing off the calls as idle chitchat with her friends back home.

How would Lily handle her betrayal? Ty had caught a glimpse of the man when he'd pulled into the Sea Salt Spa parking lot. Dark hair. Dark suit, from what he could see through the tinted windows. Polished, if he was anything like the Lexus he drove.

Which was the exact opposite of Ty.

Which was the same as the Dallas oil guy.

Needing to work off his steam and figure out what to do about what he'd just witnessed, he'd dragged his feet back to his truck, which was parked at his mom's bookstore. He and his father had finished up the Winston house ahead of schedule and had stopped by to visit his mom.

While his dad flirted with the elderly patrons, Ty had thought walking downtown to see Lily was a better use of his time.

His head hurt, and if he was honest with himself, his heart burned as well. Served him right for doing exactly what he'd told himself he'd never do again.

Fall in love.

Wanting to avoid his parents, especially after their knowing looks when he said he was going to take a walk earlier, he snuck into his truck and sped home. Tempting as it was to drive around searching for the black Lexus, he really didn't want to come to terms that Lily was seeing someone else.

There'd been signs all along. Maybe not of her being with another man, but secrets. Lots of them. She'd evaded any question about her past, her family, where she lived before Crystal Cove.

While he totally understood wanting to move on and not talk about the pains of the past, he'd opened up to her. At the time, he hadn't thought about her doing the same, airing her dirty laundry before him. Hell, he wanted her laundry on the floor and Lily naked.

Served him right for having a one-track mind. Ty pulled to a quick, hard stop in his driveway and shoved the door open. Needing to let off steam, he didn't even bother going inside and went around back to the shed in search of his chainsaw.

Today was as good a day as any to cut down the tall oaks out back that dropped more acorns than a drunk acrobat. He was sick and tired of raking up the thousands of acorns every fall and spring. Maybe with the tree gone his lawn would finally grow.

He checked the chain and oil then pulled the ripcord, starting up the chainsaw with a satisfying purr. The smell of the oil and the raw feeling of destruction under his hands did nothing to soothe the churning in his chest, but he'd keep pretending anyway.

Shutting the chainsaw off, he rummaged through his workbench until he found his safety goggles. He still wore his steel-toed boots and crummy jeans. The hot afternoon sun would be a bitch, though. Ty shucked his shirt and put on his glasses as he marched over to the giant oak.

It didn't take long to fell the tree and slice through the branches. The worst part of the job was dragging the limbs to a pile away from the woods where he'd burn it in a few months, once the wood was good and dry.

And the temperature wasn't so hot. Ty swiped the sweat from his forehead with the back of his hand and continued with his trips until all that was left was the bare trunk of the tree. It had to be at least two feet thick.

Revving the chainsaw again, he stuck his left foot on the tree for support and sliced through the wood. He cut three-foot lengths that he'd run through the wood splitter later. The tree would provide enough wood to keep the house heated for most of the winter.

Which he'd spend alone with only Meatball for company.

The humidity and blackflies stuck to his skin making the chore he usually saved for fall even more miserable. Which fit his mood perfectly. As he neared the end of the tall oak, he caught a glimpse of movement to his left.

Lily.

Not ready to see her, to talk to her, he pretended he didn't see her and continued working, the vibration of the chainsaw growing heavy in his hands. At least she was smart enough not to get too close or call out to him. It was another ten minutes before he came to the top of the tree. With no more to cut, he flicked off the chainsaw and let it hang from his hand by his side.

"Hey, sexy lumberjack," Lily called from behind.

He still hadn't figured out how to handle her. Ty avoided confrontations. He wasn't a fighter. Wasn't one to argue. He'd rather ignore the problem at hand and walk away. Hard to do with her standing in between him and the house.

Slowly, Ty turned.

Shit. Why did she have to look so gorgeous? With her wide grin and those tight pants that stopped below the knee, and a sleeveless top that accentuated her curves, he'd have a hard time pushing her away.

"You look like you could use a shower." Lily stepped closer, her floral scent billowing in the wind, covering up the smell of sweat and woodchips that covered his body. "I'd be more than happy to help you with that chore."

When she reached out to touch him, he held up his hand to stop her. "I'm a mess."

"I don't mind." That wicked, salacious grin that drove him crazy curved her lips.

And then he remembered why he was pissed. Just a few hours ago she'd been out with another man.

"I need to put this away." Ty held up the chainsaw, putting it between them so she wouldn't step closer, and headed toward his shed.

Time. He needed more time with his thoughts before he confronted her.

To be fooled again, and in almost the same way, made his already hot temper boil. And he didn't even have a temper.

Kristi had returned from Dallas and hadn't acted any differently at first. Cute. Flirty. Friendly. She'd made excuses when he wanted to be intimate, for that he was grateful. It would have been a thousand times worse if they'd slept together after she'd been with another man. Hopefully, she stayed faithful to the baby's father. The kid didn't deserve to be brought up in a home with parents who didn't love each other.

Lily, however, had offered to help him shower. In other words, sex. No, he wouldn't be touching her after she'd been with another man.

Aware of Lily outside the shed, he took his time cleaning up the chainsaw and storing it. He straightened his already organized tools and then braced himself for the lies.

"Have you eaten yet?" she asked as he closed the shed doors and held out a glass of water.

"I'm not hungry," he lied. His stomach betrayed him and growled. Knowing the Winston project would be done early, he worked through lunch and had hoped to grab a bite to eat when he stopped by Lily's. That seemed so many hours ago. The sun had dipped below the tree line, still filling the sky, but working its way toward sunset. It had to be close to seven. If Ty didn't eat soon he'd pass out.

"I bet you haven't stopped to rest all day. You need to stay hydrated. Drink." She forced the water on him and he took the glass, ignoring the sharp sting of deceit as their fingers brushed.

In three big gulps the glass was empty. He needed about four more glasses to replenish what he'd sweated out all afternoon. And another gallon of ice water to cool his boiling blood.

Without saying a word, he brushed past her and into the house. Forgoing manners, he didn't hold the door open for her and made his way to the bathroom, even locking the door behind him.

It wasn't an asshole move. It was necessary. If Lily joined him in the shower, he didn't think he'd have enough strength to ward her off. He took his time washing up. No point in shaving, although that would have eaten up more time. Making sure his towel was wrapped tightly around his middle, he padded across the hall to his bedroom, thankful Lily wasn't waiting for him in there.

Sounds from the kitchen and the smell of ground beef cooking on the stove worked its way down the hall. Food hadn't been on his mind until Lily brought it up. He'd eat and then send her on her way.

Dressed in jeans and an Army shirt, he braced himself for the inevitable as he joined Lily in the kitchen.

She stood at the stove, stirring meat in a pan with one hand and holding a box of pasta with the other. She must have heard him and looked over her shoulder with a smile. "You know I can't cook much. I can manage spaghetti and jarred sauce. Looks like you've put in a long day and need something more substantial, so I'm mixing in some burger. Sit. It's almost ready."

He didn't like her pretending to be nice. Guilt. It had to be. Kristi had done the same thing.

Words hadn't come to him yet so he grabbed a beer from the fridge, biting back the words to offer Lily a drink, and sat. Another asshole move. If he got her a drink she'd read it as a sign of interest. Of him wanting her to stay longer. She needed to leave sooner rather than later.

"By the way, I fed Meatball. He actually scratched at the door after his meal and came close to trotting down the stairs."

Shit. Too caught up in his own depression, he'd completely forgotten about his dog. The poor mutt had been shut up in the house all day. This was why he wasn't cut out for the relationship thing. Women got to him. Made him brood. Distracted him from what he wanted. Hell. He didn't have a clue what he wanted.

He watched as Lilly strained the pasta in the sink, the steam billowing up around her.

Dinner. That's what he wanted. He'd shovel down the food and tell her to be on her way. *Don't let the door hit you on the ass on the way out.*

Ty sipped his beer and watched Lily move around his kitchen. Yeah, her ass did look good in it. Not in a chauvinistic way. Hell, Ty had done more cooking in their relationship than she had.

There was no arguing the woman was gorgeous. Stunning, actually. And charming. The woman was always so pleasant around everyone.

It was a farce. A big flipping farce. That's how they did it. Two-timers, backstabbers, conniving witches knew how to put on a front. The sweet, angelic, pure as white show to cover up the ugly, muddy mess underneath.

Ty clenched his jaw and flinched when Lily leaned over him, placing a plate piled high with spaghetti and meat sauce in front of him. Once again his stomach betrayed him—betrayal seemed to be everywhere—so he dove in without waiting for Lily to sit.

Rude and he didn't care. If he waited for her she'd smile at him, touch his hand, kiss him. Ty couldn't have any of that. He didn't care if he looked like an animal, scarfing down his food, not coming up for air.

"I guess my cooking can't be that bad." Lily laughed. Her sweet voice pierced his ears causing him to wince. "Or maybe it is and you're too hungry to care."

Yeah. Something like that. Only he couldn't taste the spaghetti until it turned sour in his stomach. Scraping his chair back, he stood and brought his plate to the trash, dumping the rest of the remnants. He rinsed his plate and would have put it in the dishwasher but Lily stood in his way.

"Ty?" She placed a cool hand on his forearm. "Something's wrong. Do you want to talk?"

For the first time since she arrived, he met her stare with his. Her eyes read like a mixture of worry and fear.

Fear of what? Being discovered. Damn, he hated this. Even with Kristi he didn't have to confront her. She came clean when she told him about the pregnancy and the due date. There weren't many words exchanged after that. Embarrassment. Wounded pride and ego. Hurt. A broken heart. Nothing words could fix. Only time.

Ty dropped his plate in the sink and stepped away from her to the other side of the kitchen and crossed his arms.

"Let's talk."

"Okay." She looked at him with compassion and he turned his head, staring out the backdoor window. "What's going on?"

"How about we start with *you* doing the talking?" He didn't want to start this, just end it. His heart couldn't take much more.

"Okay."

What did he really know about Lily Novak? Nothing. At first he'd been fine keeping the talk of their pasts to a minimum. But he'd come clean, telling her of his skeletons, of personal hurt that not even Hope knew about. And she'd given him nothing.

All he knew was she'd lived in Arizona and she wasn't close with her parents, and her mother died when she was young. She'd gone to college and probably worked. Not a heck of a lot to go by. Her twenties happened and now she was thirty. End of Lily Novak's story.

"What were you doing when you were twenty-six?" It was a random question, but it irked him that he didn't know anything about her life.

Lily gasped, and her eyes grew round before looking away. Interesting. There were secrets.

"Married? Kids?"

"What?" She clutched at her chest and averted her gaze.

Guilt.

Ty didn't want to believe that she could betray him this way. She'd seemed so... innocent. The knife in his heart twisted and tugged and twisted again. Her stiff shoulders and silence spoke loud and clear.

"Who's the suit?" He kept his arms crossed, his body rigid as well. Only he wasn't hiding anything, except his vulnerability. "With the fancy car."

"Ty." Her eyes pleaded with him before she closed them. "I... I can't talk about it right now. I want to, but I can't."

A loud sarcastic snort escaped his lips. "Not good enough."

"It's not what you think." She opened her eyes and inched toward him. "I promise."

Shaking his head, he rubbed his hand across his face and sighed. "Then tell me who he is."

"I will. I promise. When the time is right."

"And when will that be? After you suckered me out of"—his love—"my house, my money, my job?" She didn't seem like a gold digger, but his track record with women sucked.

"I love you, Ty. With all my heart."

"All your heart except the part that holds secrets."

"There are no secrets in my heart."

"That's a good one." He pushed off from the wall with his shoulder and went to the front door, holding it open. "You should go."

"Please. I love you. This... what you saw, what you *think* you saw, has nothing to do with us."

"If it's coming between us, it has everything to do with us." Ty wouldn't look at her even when she stopped in front of him, her body only inches from his. He could feel her breath, smell her tears, taste her lies. She needed to leave before he broke down and did something stupid.

Like tell her he loved her too. That the past didn't matter. That he hated her for keeping secrets from him.

"When the time is right," Lily whispered, "I'll tell you everything. It won't change the love we have for each other. I promise." She kissed her fingers and touched them to his lips before walking away.

She promised. Too many damn promises and not enough truth.

CHAPTER SIXTEEN

SOMEHOW SHE MADE IT back to her apartment without completely falling apart. As soon as she dragged her body up the stairs and closed the door behind her, she stripped out of her clothes and put on a pair of cheap sweatpants and a loose long-sleeved shirt. It didn't matter that the night air was still thick with humidity.

The chills running up and down her spine weren't from the temperature. The cold, emotionless shut out Ty had given her chilled her to the bone. Crawling into bed, Lily pulled the covers tight around her neck and curled into a ball.

This is what Thorne had predicted would happen. Love didn't last forever and could turn on a dime. Was it only this morning she'd been nestled tight in Ty's embrace after making love as the sun rose and lit up his bedroom?

It seemed so far, far away. Like the look in his eyes when his gaze finally met hers. She closed her eyes, attempting to keep the tears at bay.

Of course he'd think she was cheating on him, especially after the betrayal from his fiancée. Only he didn't let her explain. Ty had already made up his mind she was a cheater and, as if their love didn't mean a thing to him, kicked her out of his house without a second glance.

It was the cold, hateful stare that had made her not tell him the truth right then and there. If he could so easily dismiss her, could she really trust he'd keep her identity safe? She'd trusted her father, trusted her husband. No, she never loved Damian the way she loved Ty; they both knew the marriage was more so out of convenience. A business merger in a way. While they'd enjoyed each other's company and were more interested in growing their business than a family, she never in a million years would have believed him to be a criminal. And a murderer.

One moment changed everything. Her future, her goals, her values. Not that she'd been longing for a husband, kids, and house with the white picket fence. Success, however, had been redefined.

Happiness. That's what made one successful. The months and months of living in fear and being housed in hotels and under watch twenty-four-seven, gave her time to think about her future, whatever that would look like.

One thing for sure, she didn't want to have any part of the cutthroat business world. Since she had to lay low for the rest of her life, that wasn't an option anyway.

Lily rolled to her back and stared up at her ceiling. She'd been more than content with her new life. Servicing others in her salon, hanging out with her new friends at book nights, or going out for drinks, building a relationship with Ty. It had all been such a blessing. One she never expected to have in her life.

Friends had a different meaning growing up. They were the people her father associated with. Business partners. Not that she or her father had ever called them *friend*. Not knowing anyone other than the girls she attended private school with, and the women she golfed with, she'd never realized what she was missing.

Lily hadn't ever *needed* a friend to lean on, to confide in, until she'd learned of her husband and father's illegal activities. And then she had the FBI and Agent Thorne.

But she didn't want to lean on them anymore. She wanted her true friends. Hope, Mia, Alexis and Jenna. The only times she'd spent with Grace were in group gatherings and then when she'd confronted Lily last week. Grace was the only one she could safely talk to, even if they didn't have much of a friendship yet.

The one person she wanted to talk with refused to see her anymore, thought of her as a cheater and a liar. Once Lily told Ty the truth about her past, he'd forgive her deceit and they could build a future together built on open honesty.

She hoped. She prayed.

She regretted not telling Ty the truth tonight and clearing up the misunderstanding. But the way his eyes turned so dark, so cold, scared her. It wasn't Ty she feared, but the lost look in his eyes.

She'd clammed up and went on the defensive instead of telling the truth. The niggling bit of doubt Thorne planted in the back of her brain took over, and she caved instead of following her heart.

Lily followed the lines in the ceiling. The cracks were like a mirror to her soul. Fissures that didn't seem too harmful until closer inspection showed how they grew in length and depth with time until eventually the building—or her insides—crumbled.

Damian and her father caused the first crack in her, and Ty's rejection was like a chisel opening the wound even more. She wasn't worth anything to her father; money and greed trumping her importance in his life. The same could be said for her husband.

She thought she was worth something to Ty, though. Something worth fighting for.

The chisel dug deeper into her chest, and Lily rolled over into a tight ball again. This time she let the tears pour out. She cried until her gut clenched and contracted into involuntary spasms over and over and over again.

The muscles in her sides ached, and she continued to sob until the sliver of the moon peeked through the slits between her blinds. The last thing she remembered before finally drifting to sleep was the wetness of the pillow beneath her cheek.

• • • •

THE RINGING OF THE alarm on her phone chimed from the living room where she'd dropped her purse before crawling into bed. Her body was numb yet ached at the same time. She didn't want to move, to get up. Ever. Knowing the phone wouldn't stop until she turned it off, she dragged her lifeless body out of bed and fumbled in her purse for her phone, turning it off without looking at the caller.

Barely opening her eyes, she went to the kitchen to make coffee. It would be a four-cup minimum morning. She leaned against the counter and swayed while the water heated. Too impatient to wait for the entire pot to brew, she took two cups out of the cabinet and filled one while the other caught the dripping coffee.

Without the caffeine fueling her body, she moved sluggishly, making a mess on her counter. And she didn't care. Returning the pot, she yanked open the fridge for her creamer and stirred her coffee.

It burned her throat and lips as she guzzled, and she didn't care. Ty didn't want to kiss her anymore anyway.

Slowly she made her way to her tiny bathroom and set her mug on the counter. She left the folding doors to the laundry area open and closed them, remembering the first time Ty had been inside her apartment. Crouched on his knees and holding her black thong between his fingertips in an expression of shock, horror, embarrassment, and maybe a tinge of lust. Or so she'd hoped at the time.

Pushing back the memory, she glanced up and gawked at her reflection. Eyes red and puffy and hair matted against the side of her head, she'd seen better days. Hoping a shower would make her appear more put together than the mess going on inside, she turned on the tap and stripped while waiting for the water to heat.

Twenty minutes later, dressed in black leggings, a long, loose black top and black flats, she pulled her dry hair back in a ponytail and checked out her reflection again. Despite her summer tan, her skin was ashen. If she showed up to work looking like this, everyone would ask what was wrong. And since the whole freaking town knew about her and Ty, they'd all know they had a lover's quarrel.

That's what they'd assume, at least. A lover's quarrel meant two people were in love. It seemed the love was only one-sided. If Ty loved her, he'd have had more patience with her. His eyes wouldn't have glossed over blocking her from seeing inside. She'd promised him she'd tell him later. With something as major as her past, she wasn't about to blurt it out while he was in such a mood. He needed to understand that.

Despite being married for five years, relationships were a new thing for her. Her family didn't exactly model effective communication. She'd screwed up, but once she told Ty everything he'd forgive her.

Yes. She'd tell him. Lily took out her makeup bag and made up her face with a new determination. She'd had all night to wallow in her pity party, to cry, to process, to make decisions.

Screw Agent Thorne. Lily knew what was best for her and Ty was the answer. After work she'd force her way back into his life and tell him everything. If he couldn't handle knowing about her past or if he threatened her safety, she'd pack up and leave.

With new confidence, she marched downstairs and opened the spa, ready to take on a new day.

"Are you sure you're okay?" Mia asked after her last client left. "Even Willie asked me what was up with you."

"I'm tired is all." Lily swept her station, turning her back on Mia. She thought she'd done a decent job of hiding the hurt, the fear that Ty wouldn't want to see her. Apparently not.

"Normally I'd roll my eyes and scoff at your sex life with my brother, but you don't have that morning afterglow, so I'm gonna say you being tired isn't from doing the nasty."

If nasty meant crying until snot streamed out your nose and you looked like the bride of Frankenstein in the morning, then, yeah, it was from doing the nasty. Ignoring Mia, Lily swept up the hair and dropped it in the trash.

She had twenty minutes before her next client was due to arrive and used it to clean her already organized station. When she felt

Mia's stare looming over her, she moved to the cash register and pretended to go through the appointment calendar.

A highlight coming in would keep her busy for a few hours. Then a trim, an eyebrow wax, and... crap. Ruth Bergeron's hair. Even though Thorne said his grandmother didn't know about his connection to her, Lily still worried. Not so much for herself, but for the Bergerons safety.

They were what connected Thorne to her. Hopefully they'd be moving sooner rather than later. Grace made it sound like opening her shop in the fall was a possibility, if all went according to plan.

"Tired of him already?"

"What?" Lily blinked away her thoughts and looked up at Mia.

"Ty's a pretty boring dude." Mia leaned on her elbows across the counter, her chin cupped in her palms as her eyes scrunched in scrutiny.

Lily shook her head and glanced away. "Ty's not boring."

He's amazing. Talented, funny, sweet, loyal, kind.

"Then you're just as boring. All the guy does is work. He needs some excitement in his life. I thought you'd be the one to give him that."

Lily snorted. Oh, her life before Crystal Cove was exciting, terrifyingly exciting. It had been nothing but mundane since she moved here. Which was perfect.

"You're the one with the active life, Mia. I have the spa and our once a month book club meetings."

"Which is why you're perfect for my brother. I know he'd never give you up. So you did the dumping, huh?"

"What makes you think that?"

"Like I said. Ty hasn't had a girlfriend in... forever. So what did he do to piss you off?"

"I'm not having this conversation with you, Mia." Lily closed the appointment book and walked away.

Thankfully Mia only worked Tuesday and Wednesday mornings and would be leaving soon. Annie was busy with her pedicures in the next room over, and Kendra was tucked away upstairs in the massage rooms. Once Mia left, Lily could distract herself with work and keeping the conversation about her clients' lives instead of her own.

An hour later, Lily's hands busy on Nancy Thimbleton's highlights, Mia came over and rested a hand on her shoulder.

"I'm done, but you can come over later if you... need to talk or anything." She gave a reassuring squeeze and left.

"I hope someday Mia can settle down the way her brother has with you. You two make a lovely couple."

"Um. Thank you." Lily had never talked about Ty with Mrs. Thimbleton and didn't think the sixty-year-old woman would care much about her personal life.

"Celeste Parker is a gem. Isn't she? She's just itching for grandchildren."

Lily bit her lip as she listened to her ramble on about the Parker family and how wonderful they were. As if Lily didn't already know this.

Her next two appointments were more of the same, Lily dodging the subtle and not-so-subtle questions about her love life. She couldn't imagine the town being so nosey with Ty. Granted, he didn't leave his house much unless it was for work or to hang out at The Happy Clam.

Now that Hope had Cameron to watch over her, he spent less time at the restaurant and more time at Lily's. Or at his home with Lily. Now that he wanted nothing to do with her, she wondered if he'd go back to his usual stool at the bar.

Hope said he never drank much. Maybe a beer. It was mostly to hang out with her while she worked. Hope would know how to handle the situation with Ty, but then Lily would need to tell her about her past, something Thorne had said the less people knew the better.

It weighed on her. The pressure of doing what was right based on what the FBI agent said was right and what she felt in her heart.

Finally, her last client was done, Kendra and Annie were gone, and she locked up the spa. Running up the stairs to her apartment, she changed into a cute skirt and blouse, slid into flip-flops, and hurried back down the stairs again.

She thought about calling Thorne first, letting him know she was going to tell Ty everything, but she didn't want to risk the chance of being talked out of it. Fifteen minutes later she pulled into Ty's driveway, and her heart sank. His truck wasn't there.

Maybe he was still at work. Or eating dinner at his parents' house. Lily got out of her car and sat on his front steps. When the sun got too much and her underarms started to sweat, she let herself into his house. He hadn't asked for his key back, so technically she wasn't intruding.

Something was off. All was quiet, which was normal, but a cool shiver ran down her arms even though the air in the house was thick with heat. The windows were closed up. Odd. He wouldn't do that to Meatball.

Lily spotted the empty dog bed in the corner of the living room. Not uncommon. Meatball didn't always sleep in it.

"Meatball," she called, not expecting to hear the *tick tick* of claws on the hardwood floor. He wasn't the type of dog to come running when called. Searching the kitchen and coming up empty, she checked Ty's bedroom.

His side of the bed was in tangles while her side was still neatly made from the night before. A pile of dirty clothes sat on the floor next to the bed. Very out of character for Ty who always put his clothes in the laundry basket in his closet.

Tempted as she was to clean up after him, she left the mess and continued her search for Meatball. There weren't too many places to hide.

Coming up empty, Lily figured Ty must have brought the dog with him. Good. They needed each other. And she needed them.

Another hour went by and still no sign of them. At nine o'clock, her hunger pains jabbing at the hollowness inside, she picked up her keys and left.

That night and the following day were more of the same. Empty, painful tears followed by a mask of *everything's alright* while working. She didn't want to go to book night, but not showing up would make the girls talk even more.

Making sure she looked and dressed the part of normalcy, Lily stuffed her book in her purse and walked downtown to Books by the Ocean. Jenna was already there, setting out the chips and guacamole and plate of cookies she'd made.

"Oh. Crap." Lily had been assigned drinks this week, and she'd come empty-handed. Whoever was on drink duty *never* forgot her job.

"What's the matter?" Jenna flicked her long hair over her shoulder and looked up at Lily.

"I, uh..." She could rush over to Boon's General Store real quick, if she had her car. It was only two miles down the road, but by the time she ran back home to grab her car and rushed to the store, she'd be late. Not that it mattered, but she'd make an entrance and everyone would tease her about getting it on with Ty.

It was either that or have no alcohol and *really* be the center of attention.

"I left the drinks in, uh, my car. I'll be right back." Lily turned and crashed into Hope.

"Hey. Woah. Where're you going?" Hope grabbed on to Lily's upper arms for support.

"The drinks. They're in my car."

"I'll help you with them."

"No." Lilly slipped from her grasp and shook her head. "I'll be right back."

Mia came through the front door, blocking her path. "Leaving so soon?"

"She forgot the drinks," Jenna called from behind them.

Mia's eyebrow shot up, and her eyes squinted in that scrutinizing manner she gave the day before. "No one *forgets* the drinks."

"We're not all alcoholics," Lily tried to joke. "My life doesn't revolve around having a drink in hand."

None of them were alcoholics. Sure, Mia spent many Friday and Saturday nights at clubs and bars, but that was the way she socialized. The rest of them enjoyed a cocktail or a glass of wine when they got together, that was all. Still, her attempt at humor fell flat.

"Sorry I'm late." Grace sauntered through the door, nearly crashing into Mia. "We hanging by the door tonight? My feet are killing me. I was hoping to lounge on the couch with a dry martini in hand."

Grace looked from Hope to Lily to Mia and back to Lily again. Her perfectly arched eyebrow lifted, and her carefree attitude shifted to something more intense. Serious. UnGracelike.

"What's going on?" She gave props to Grace for keeping her voice nonchalant, even when her eyes met Lily's, the fear evident in the intensity of her stare.

"Lily left the booze in her car," Jenna said so innocently from across the room.

"Yeah. And my car's at the spa. So"—Lily shrugged—"I'm going to hoof down the road. I'll be back in a few."

"I'll give you a hand," they all said in unison.

"I appreciate it," Lily said, fiddling with the hem of her shirt. "You girls start in on Jenna's goodies. I'll be right back."

"I don't think so." Mia blocked the door and crossed her arms, trying to appear intimidating in her five-foot-two frame.

"Lily? Mia? What's going on?" Hope, the voice of reason, stepped in front of Mia and faced Lily. "Are you okay?"

"Sure." She laughed it off. "Silly me. Busy day and I forgot the drinks. It's no big deal."

"It's gorgeous out. Why don't we all walk together? Burn off the calories before we eat and drink them," Jenna said as she joined them by the door.

"Good idea," this from Mia, the guard dog.

"Why don't we give the poor woman some air?" Grace draped her arm across Lily's shoulders. "I'm sure she has bigger things to think about than book club." Lily tensed under her hold. "Like her gorgeous boyfriend. If I had him at my beck and call, book club would sure as hell be the last thing I was thinking about."

Lily knew she meant well, and most likely assumed her forgetfulness was due to the stress of her past coming out. That was partially true. Right now she worried more about losing Ty than losing her new identity.

How she wanted to unload the burden of it all on to her friends. Not before she told Ty. He'd be even more hurt if he found out he was the last to learn about Veronica Stewart.

The last to know. Without realizing it, Lily had made a decision. She didn't want to hide anymore. Well, hide from the bad guys, yes, but not from her friends and loved ones in Crystal Cove.

She wouldn't take out a newspaper ad or make an announcement on social media, but her close circle of friends needed to know the truth. More than that, she needed to tell them.

But not before Ty.

"The truth is," Lily started, "I completely forgot I was the booze girl tonight."

"Love will do that to you," Jenna sighed.

"I can call Alexis. See if she's left yet," Hope offered. Living on a winery, Alexis had an endless supply of liquid therapy at her fingertips. "Or I can grab a bottle of tequila from the bar."

"I'm okay skipping the drinks tonight." A collective gasp came from all of them as they turned to stare at Mia. "What?" She lifted her hands. "You girls are the ones who need to get out more. Loosen up a little. Well, maybe not Grace. I hear she's already—"

"Mia!" Lily reprimanded. Alexis wasn't here to come to her sister's defense, so Lily took it upon herself to stand up for the only person, other than the FBI, who knew who she really was.

"That's okay." Grace laughed and dropped her arm from Lily's shoulder.

"Besides. Tonight was an extra book night thrown in the mix. We just got together last week knowing it would be hard to get away on back-to-back weekends. I brought tons of food. Maybe tonight we'll actually talk about the book. Which is why we are here anyway."

Even the escape of Lisa Gardner's latest suspense wasn't enough to distract her from the dangers that could be in store for Lily. And anyone close to her.

Grace tugged at Lily's arm, and she followed her to the grouping of chairs and sofa. "This is the first book I've read cover to cover in less than three days. Anyone else stay up all night reading?"

Jenna chimed in, rambling on about the main characters, and Lily let out the breath she didn't know she'd been holding. During the encounter by the front door, she'd avoided direct eye contact with everyone. Hope's gaze across the table burned into her, and she tried to ignore it by diving into the snacks.

They discussed nearly the entire book and even made suggestions for a sequel, and then Mia brought up the elephant in the room.

"I'm actually surprised to see you tonight, Lily. Figured you'd be with Ty." Mia scooped her chip through a mound of guac and shoved it in her mouth. Lily fidgeted in her seat while they waited for Mia to finish chewing and finish her thought.

Better to control the conversation and be on offense rather than the defensive end all night.

"Ty and I don't spend every waking minute together. We both have our own separate lives."

"Guess so. Still. When he told Dad he needed a few days off and was leaving for a long weekend, I assumed he was taking you with him."

The stinging behind her eyes burned, as did the final thread of hope she held on to.

"Mia. Be nice. If she and Ty need time apart, it's none of our business." Hope may have come to her defense, but her wrinkled brow and tilt of her head told Lily she was wondering the same thing.

"I..." Deciding on honesty instead of more lies, she told them what she could. What she hoped was true. "Ty and I need some time apart. As Mia said, if we're not working we're always together. I have my time with you all and he... Ty has Cameron and Ben, but they're so busy with work and... wives. I'm glad he could get away."

"Ty didn't go with Ben or Cameron. He went by himself."

"Alone time is important too."

"Oh, honey. Are you and Ty having problems? I'm sorry to hear that." Jenna seemed to be the only clueless one in the group. Alexis was probably out of the loop as well, but the winery had been busy so she stayed home tonight.

"It's okay. I'll talk with him when he gets back." Waiting until Sunday night would kill her, but maybe time was what they needed. He could gather his thoughts, come to his senses and realize he needed her, and Lily could prepare herself to tell her sordid story again.

And pray he could handle being with someone who had a target on her back.

CHAPTER SEVENTEEN

EVEN A WEEKEND AWAY with nothing but a tent, his fishing pole, and Meatball wasn't enough to clear his mind. Ty was a son of a bitch. Never had he been so rude to a woman. To anyone.

Lily's deception angered him. He couldn't help his irritability. Wednesday at work he was a bear to his crew. He didn't yell, that would be completely out of character for him; instead, he'd snipped passive aggressive comments their way.

"Hey, Ty. Framing's done on the windows. What do you think?" Greg had asked.

"Looks good for a first-timer." Which he wasn't.

Greg had been with him for three years and did quality work. The window framing was fine, as far as Ty could tell, but he didn't have the patience to inspect it as thoroughly as he usually did. Tossing that comment out made Greg second-guess his work. Ty trusted him to do a good job but didn't have it in him to dole out compliments.

Knowing he needed to get out of Dodge, he told his crew he was taking some time off. Something he never did. Something he never *needed* to do. His father didn't question him. Just gave him a slap on the back and told him to have a good time.

Most likely they thought he was taking off with Lily. Mia assumed so. When she saw Lily still in town, hanging out with her suit, she'd understand why Ty needed to leave.

The fish didn't bite all weekend and Meatball was nothing but a menace, wanting to be by his side and even sleep on his sleeping bag in the tent. Normally the mutt wanted nothing to do with him.

Same as Lily.

The sun had begun to set over the treetops as he turned down Cranberry Lane and headed toward home. Before he knew it, the sun would be up and he'd be embarking on another morning. Another day without Lily.

She said she still loved him. So what was with the suit? Jealousy reared its ugly head and flowed through his body. He'd wanted nothing to do with her excuses or explanation. At least Kristi didn't drag it out. She'd come clean, admitted to wanting to be with someone who had a substantial financial future, and left. She didn't string him along, tell him she loved him, keeping hope alive inside.

No, he had no hope for Lily. Whatever explanation she had, she could keep. If the suit was a business meeting, a friend with no strings, she'd have come clean right away, extinguishing any need of jealousy or insecurity.

But she hadn't. She'd said it wasn't what it looked like. So why the hell hadn't she said exactly what it was? If her slipping in the fancy car with a man who had everything Ty didn't meant nothing, why the secrecy?

It was about her past, it had to be. The way she shut down when he asked her if she was married. The suit was involved, knew more about her life than he did and that caused another ripple of rage to flow through his veins. If he was her ex...Ty couldn't compete with that.

Pulling into his driveway, he shoved his truck into park and scooped up Meatball.

"Do your business in the woods and make it fast. I don't have time for your finicky habits tonight."

As if he understood, Meatball trotted off to the woods. How Ty would spend his time tonight, he didn't know. There was nothing but time on his hands.

It was no different than life before Lily. Work. Check up on Hope and Delaney who no longer needed him to check up on them, check in with his mom and dad, who were still happy in love even after thirty-five years of marriage. Check in with Mia who would tell him to mind his own business.

Ironic since she made it her goal to butt into everyone else's business. He hadn't responded to a single one of her fourteen texts while he was away.

Gathering his tent and sleeping gear, he plodded to his front door and dropped his gear inside. He made one more trip, gathering his cooler, backpack and fishing gear. Back in the day he'd looked forward to his weekend fishing trips with his father. In the fall they'd hunt deer, and moose if they got a license. And in the spring they'd turkey hunt.

Other than that, Ty didn't do much. Didn't need much.

Until Lily.

She made him need more than he wanted to. Despite her dishonesty, he missed her. The way she teased him when they watched movies together. The way she treated Meatball as if he was the most loving dog in the world. The way she smelled, and sighed, and said his name while they were making love.

Ty pushed through the front door with the rest of his load and dropped it all in the hallway. Food, beer, then a shower were on tap for the evening, and then back to the grind.

He paused midway to the fridge and pulled a deep breath to his lungs.

Lily. He could still smell her in his house. Just like he could smell her on his pillow, on his sheets. Tuesday and Wednesday night he'd rolled over and avoided her side of the bed, not getting an ounce of sleep. That's when he knew he needed to take off.

Her scent, memories of their good times together, swarmed him. Had it only been a few months since they'd been in a relationship? Not even.

And in that short time, she'd ruined his perfectly planned out life by falling in love.

Almost forgetting about Meatball, he opened the backdoor and called out, "Come on, dog. Suppertime." As if he knew the struggle Ty was going through, Meatball lifted his head from the rhododendron bush and waddled his way to the back steps. "Good boy. You're finally learning. Took you long enough," he mumbled.

Ty filled the dog bowl with chow and rubbed Meatball's head. What to make for himself? He'd dined on chips, beer, and beef jerky for the past three days. Real food was in order. Finding a package of boneless chicken breasts in the freezer, he tossed it in the microwave and pressed defrost. Not ideal, but it would work. In the meantime, he scrubbed two potatoes and pricked them with a fork.

While the chicken defrosted, he went outside to fire up the grill; the *swoosh* as the flame ignited the only sound coming from his property. He liked it like that. Alone. Quiet. Still.

At least he thought he did. There was something missing. Some*one* missing. No matter how wrong it was, he missed Lily. Longed for her. God, he was a sucker. He stilled at the sound of tires on his gravel driveway. It was too soon. He needed to have a stronger hold of his feelings before seeing her again.

If she came too close, touched him with the softness of her voice, he'd cave and throw everything he'd worked so hard for, his pride, out the window. Maybe when he didn't answer the front door she'd take the hint and leave.

No such luck. He caught the sight of her coming around the corner of his house and had the urge to run inside and hide.

"Ty?" Relieved at the voice, he turned.

"Hope. Haven't seen you around in a while." It wasn't a random social call, he knew. She probably sided with Lily and would read him the riot act for being an ass to her, for not listening to her side of the story.

"Smells good."

"Nothing's on it yet. Just heating up the grill."

"Well, whatever you cooked last smells good."

Steak and grilled asparagus. Lily practically swooned when she cut into the tender meat and praised him for his grilling skills.

"Am I interrupting dinner?" Hope jerked her head toward the backdoor.

"Nope. Just me and Meatball tonight. Care to join us?" He wanted her to say no. Not that he didn't want to hang out with Hope, it was the interrogation he wasn't looking forward to.

"It's almost eight. I ate an hour ago."

With her family. Something Ty didn't have. Sure, he had awesome parents and a bratty sister, but a wife and kid he did not.

He hadn't been searching for the Rockwell image around a dinner table, not until Lily came into his life, filling his house and heart with her gorgeous smile, and now he couldn't get the image out of his head.

"How's Delaney?" Better to make her the center of attention than him.

"Amazing as always. She and Cameron are playing UNO."

In other words, she left her family to seek him out with a purpose. "Come on in. I need to grab the chicken from the microwave." He held the door for Hope and offered her some wine from an open bottle he and Lily had shared on Monday. "I don't know if it's still good."

"I'm not picky." Hope knew where the glasses were and helped herself to one, pouring the rest of the Merlot.

Ty got out a cutting board and fileted the chicken until he had eight thin pieces. He found the bottle of honey barbeque sauce in the fridge and grabbed the tongs from the drawer. "This won't take long."

"I don't want to interrupt your dinner plans." Hope held the door for him, and he set the chicken down next to the grill.

"I don't think Meatball minds your company."

"No Lily tonight?"

"Why are you here, Hope?" He knew her too well to play games.

"For a friendly visit?"

Ty snorted. "I know when you have an ulterior motive. What is it you know, and what is it you think you know?"

"And what do I want to know?"

"I'm not offering any information."

"And here I thought we were best friends."

Shit. He didn't mean to hurt her feelings. Ty shut the lid to the grill and hung the tongs on the hook underneath. "I'm sorry. I didn't mean to take... to take this out on you."

"That's what friends are for. Want to talk about it?"

"Not really."

Hope laughed, "Yeah. Dumb question."

Even though they'd been best friends for more than a decade, Ty never confided much in Hope. It wasn't because he didn't trust her, he simply kept his private life private. Besides, Hope always had a lot on her plate, first with her pregnancy and then being a single mom. His role was the listener. The supporter. Whatever Hope and Delaney had needed, Ty provided. Revealing his ugly secrets wasn't part of the deal, and Hope had always seemed fine with that.

"In all the years we've been friends, you've never been serious about a woman."

"I'm not the relationship kind of guy."

"Bullshit. You have *family guy* written all over you. The house, the dog, the quiet, loyal friend who is there in a heartbeat. You're every woman's dream."

"Not yours." The chemistry simply hadn't been there. Not like with Lily.

"You know I love you, Ty."

Yeah, he did. And he loved her too. Always would, in that familiar way. The words were hard to say, but she knew. As did Delaney.

"So what did Lily tell you? Everyone in town think I'm an ass-hole?" The only thing he'd done wrong was send her away without a chance to tell her side of the story. Other than that, he was complete-ly innocent in this... in whatever they were in. Break up, he'd called it.

"She didn't know you went fishing. Mia dropped that bomb on her during our book meeting."

"I thought you guys met last week?"

"We did, but something happened..." Hope leaned against the railing and sipped from her wine. "Lily was off. Something spooked her, and she left saying she didn't feel well."

"Last week?" Ty picked up the tongs and turned over the chick-en. She didn't come over after book club, but he hadn't expected her to knowing it would be a late night. Had he wanted her to? Hell yeah. She'd sent him a text with an apology saying she didn't want to wake him and couldn't wait to see him Friday night. Their weekend together had been perfect. Or had it all been a cover? Had she been out with the suit Thursday night, which was why she left the book-store early?

"Did you guys have an argument?"

"Kind of."

"I'm assuming you don't want to talk about it, but I think you should. If not with me, with someone. It's not healthy to keep things bottled up."

Uncomfortable with the attention on him, he checked the chick-en again. "I need a clean plate." She didn't follow him inside, and he stalled for time. He put the dirty dish in the dishwasher and took out a clean plate and fork for his chicken. The potatoes would be done soon so he dug around for a can of corn, opened it, dumped it in a bowl and nuked it.

It was either let the chicken burn and avoid Hope for a few more minutes, or suck it up and face her, and salvage his dinner. Manning up, he went back outside and turned the grill off. "Sure you don't want any? There's plenty."

"Nope. I'm gonna hover and watch you eat. Hopefully you'll be so uncomfortable you'll spill your darkest secrets," she teased, obviously unaware what any of his were.

Not that being ditched by your fiancée was a deep, dark secret. Which it wasn't. Ty plated the chicken and thanked Hope when she held the door for him.

She didn't say anything, yet her curious stare made him fidgety while he prepared his potato and scooped up some corn, piling it next to his chicken. They sat next to each other at the table, and Hope remained quiet while he cut his food, chewed, and swallowed. Damn, the woman was patient.

When his plate was empty, he sat back with a loud sigh. "I was engaged when I was in Afghanistan."

"You what?" Hope nearly shot out of her seat. "Don't tell me it was Lily?"

"No." Although history had a way of repeating itself. Last week he could see himself engaged to her. Now... not so much. "Another soldier. I had plans to tell the family during my next leave."

"We talked every week and you never told me you were dating anyone, much less were engaged."

"We tried to keep it on the down-low." Her idea and he hadn't seen through it back then.

"I'm sorry it didn't work out. Oh." Hope covered her mouth with one hand and reached for his with the other. "Did she die?"

"No. Nothing like that. She went home on leave and came back pregnant. Baby wasn't mine."

"Oh, Ty. That sucks. I'm sorry. And you never told me? Why?"

"You had your own stuff going on. Delaney, trying to make ends meet. Hearing about my pathetic life wouldn't have done you any good. You'd have felt helpless and miserable for not being able to do something."

Hope cocked her head. "I guess that's true. Why not tell me about the little witch when you came home?"

Ty laughed. He could always count on Hope to be on his side. "I was trying to move on."

"Okay. I can respect that. Thank you for telling me. I know how private you like to keep your life."

"Yet here you are trying to pry secrets out of me." Ty picked up his beer bottle between two fingers and wiggled it. Empty. "Need a refill?" he asked as he got up and got himself another beer.

"No, thanks."

He opened the bottle and tossed the cap on the counter and sipped the cold ale. Hope fidgeted in her seat, most likely processing and trying to figure out what to ask him next.

"So what does this former cheating ex of yours have to do with Lily?"

"Nothing." Ty shrugged and sipped again.

"Then why are you telling me about her now? There has to be a connection."

He didn't respond and sipped again.

"Don't tell me she cheated on you too. I wouldn't believe it for a second. That woman is so head over heels in love with you."

When he didn't respond, Hope shot out of her chair and gasped. "No!"

Ty shrugged and finished his beer.

"No," she said again. "You should have seen her this week. The woman's miserable. What happened?"

"I really don't want to talk about this."

Hope ran her hands through her hair and paced his kitchen. "Okay. I get if you want to tell me to mind my own business."

"Mind your own business."

She lowered her lashes at him and pointed her finger into his chest. "This is my business because you're both my friends and you're both miserable. However, I get if you don't want to talk to me about it. You do, however, need to talk to Lily. I'm assuming she knows you know about this other guy?"

"Yup."

"I still don't believe it." Hope shook her head. "What did she say?"

Ty shrugged again.

"What does that mean? That you don't know or you didn't listen?"

Done with the interrogation, he tossed his bottle in the recycle bin and would have reached for another if Hope hadn't leaped in his way.

"Ty Parker. Don't you dare walk away without a fight. You keep your emotions locked up tighter than a clam. I'm guessing you're putting her in the same category as your cheating fiancée." Hope gripped on to his shoulders forcing him to look at her. "If Lily means anything to you, listen to what she has to say. If it's true, if she really is cheating on you, hell, I'll help you drive the woman out of this town. She'll have fooled us all into believing she was a good person. But if there's a misunderstanding, which I really want to believe is the case, you need to talk to her. Don't let your pride get in the way of what could be something amazing. I almost lost Cameron because I refused to listen to the truth. Don't do the same."

She cupped his face in her hands and kissed his cheek.

"You've already let her in, given her your heart. Don't let her run away with it without a fight."

A few minutes later when Hope's taillights vanished in the distance, he turned off the lights inside and headed to the bathroom to take a shower. He'd call Lily tomorrow and give her an opportunity to say her piece.

But he'd come prepared to battle, with a shield around his heart

CHAPTER EIGHTEEN

THE DAYS DRAGGED, AND no amount of caffeine or *Ellen* reruns could get her out of her slump. Lily flipped the sign on the front door to the spa to *Open* and shivered, even beneath her long-sleeved black shirt and jeans.

Fitting that the forecast for the next five days was back and forth between cold, miserable rain, and glimpses of sunshine. Mother Nature didn't care that the calendar said July. Weather in Maine, especially central coastal region, changed on the dime. Summers were short. You enjoyed the warm, cloudless days when you could.

And it seemed like those were over. Lily refused to believe things were over with Ty. She understood where he was coming from. Had she witnessed him getting in a car with a woman and being evasive about it, she'd question his intentions as well. And if he refused to explain... yeah.

Lily's stomach tightened in pain and guilt. Ty had suffered so much already. It took a great deal of emotional effort to tell her about Kristi, and here she was doing the same thing to him. Well, the same thing in his mind.

Never. Never would she cheat on Ty. Deep down inside he had to know, to feel her unconditional love for him.

Scrolling through her appointment book with no enthusiasm whatsoever, she was grateful for the under-booked Tuesday. Annie would be in any minute, and Mia was scheduled to work in an hour. Hopefully Margo Reed would actually arrive early for her color and cut and fill the room with her non-stop chatter.

When Margo was in the house, no one else could get a word in. Lily needed the obnoxious grandmother to distract her from her thoughts.

Looking further down the appointment book she sighed in relief to see Priscilla had left a message to reschedule her appointment.

While the waitress from the Sunrise Diner was a sweet lady, Lily didn't need her reading the aura around her today. Even without special psychic—or whatever they were called—powers, it was obvious to the world Lily was down. Depressed. Her heart and head rolling around in guilt and anguish.

Right and wrong. It wasn't supposed to be this difficult to distinguish between the two. This was her life. If she wanted to tell Ty about her past, about her new identity, it was her prerogative, not Agent Thorne's.

It was her right to live her life how she wanted. Screw the agent and his advice. What did the cold-hearted man know about love? About honesty?

Lily lowered her head to the desk and whimpered. In only a handful of years, she went from a spoiled socialite to an abused wife and turned herself into someone genuine and kind who didn't judge others. She knew all too well what you saw on the outside wasn't necessarily representative of what was going on inside.

Agent Throne acted cold and callous, but she didn't really get those vibes from him. Still. He was the only one she could truly talk to, and he wasn't the touchy-feely kind of guy.

There was Grace, but Lily didn't want to involve her any more than she already had. Keeping a secret of this magnitude had to be difficult. Especially in a small town like Crystal Cove.

The bell chimed above the front door, and Lily lifted her head and turned on her hospitable smile.

"Hi, Annie."

"Good morning, Lily." Annie set her giant pocketbook behind the counter and hung her raincoat and umbrella on the coatrack. "Can't believe I brought a coat with me this morning. Channel Six News said it's going to be a nasty one."

Lily looked out the front windows at the dark clouds rolling in. The wind had picked up, blowing the leaves on magnolia trees across the road.

"I'm not expecting many walk-ins today." At least she hoped not. Her last appointment would be done at three. Lily planned on letting Mia close up and going to Ty's for their heart-to-heart.

"I'm booked pretty solid today. The early summer pedicures are wearing off and everyone wants new toes."

"I'm glad business has been so steady for you, Annie."

Annie had been a godsend. She'd been working in a popular salon in Rockland, but had wanted to work closer to home and slow down a little as she got older. Not that fifty-two was old. Annie was the perfect blend of social when you wanted to chat and quiet when you wanted to be alone.

The woman understood boundaries, and her clients loved her. She was mothering without smothering, and Lily appreciated the privacy she gave her.

"I love it here, Lily. You've done a fantastic job with the spa. Oh, while you have the appointment book open, I need to cash in on my gift certificate my children gave me. I'd like to book a massage."

Lily's massage bookings had been slow. Another reminder to update the Sea Salt Spa's website and put an ad in the local paper. She'd had her masseuse license for five months and hadn't done nearly as much with it as she had hoped.

When she took courses to get her license, she hadn't been as busy and wanted to expand the spa. Now she wondered if she bit off more than she could chew. She wanted to do it all, except for the nails. While she loved a good manicure and pedicure, she didn't particularly care for scraping, scrubbing, clipping, and painting.

The art of doing hair and learning the pressure points in the back and legs, she could do. Balance, though. Lily needed to balance it all. Which meant she needed to hire more help.

Maybe she should give up on the hair and work fulltime upstairs in the massage rooms. It would give her more privacy. She wouldn't have to talk as much. Risk being found. Discovered.

"Are you okay, honey? You seem distant."

"Hm?" Lily returned her gaze to Annie's. "Sorry. A lot on my mind. Bracing myself for Mrs. Reed in a bit."

Annie chuckled. "Even from the other room I can hear every detail of her grandchildren's lives. If I get that self-absorbed when I finally have grandchildren, smack me a time or two, okay?"

"I highly doubt you'll be as obnoxious as her."

"It's one thing to brag about your grandchildren and show pictures to everyone you see on the street; it's another to put down other children because they're not as 'good at life' as yours."

Margo had a way of passive-aggressively insulting other parents and children. Never wanting a roe, Lily usually ignored. With today's mood, however, she hoped she could do the same.

An hour later Mia buzzed twelve-year-old Caleb Lundry's head two stations down while Lily zoned out pretending to listen about Margo's perfect grandchildren.

"Hunter is already walking. Only nine months and four days old. He's bright, that's why. Helen Doty's granddaughter is fourteen months and still can't walk. Poor thing. She'll probably need special services in school when she is older as well."

"Easy there, Mrs. Reed." Mia pointed the razor at her. "I walked at ten months and couldn't read until I was in fourth grade. I went to Title One for help and hated it. Now I can't put a book down."

"I'm glad you got the help you needed. I'm surprised your mother didn't do more to support you when you were younger. Ironic that she owns a bookstore, isn't it?"

Mia gasped, and Lily tugged a little more roughly than necessary on Mrs. Reed's hair.

"Don't you—"

"Mia!" Lily shook her head and cast her a warning stare.

"Ty walked late in life and graduated with honors," Mia countered.

"I'm surprised he didn't go to college and do something better with his life." Margo picked up her vibrating phone. "Hi, Colleen. How's my precious granddaughter today?"

Lily held up a hand to stop Mia and went back to coloring the cruel woman's hair.

It was a good thing her phone had rang; otherwise, Lily would have come to Ty's defense, making a spectacle of herself. Better to let the woman be, knowing no one paid much heed to her words.

The winds had picked up outside, but the rain held off. When the clouds opened, visibility would be scarce. Two hours later after Cruella De Ville had left and Mia buzzed and trimmed a line of boys and men's hair, Lily busied herself sweeping and cleaning her station.

"I don't like the brooding. At first, I thought the lovey-dovey crap was sick, but you and Ty moping around is depressing. Normally I wouldn't admit this, but I miss your perky little self. What's going on with you two?"

"We're fine, Mia. Really." At least she hoped they would be once she talked with him.

"Uh, huh." Mia lifted a skeptical eyebrow. "You're off the hook for now. I don't have any more appointments today, mind if I take off? I'm gonna stop by The Happy Clam, see if Hope needs me earlier. I can bring you lunch."

"It's going to pour any minute. I'm sure I can find something for you upstairs in my fridge if you're hungry."

"Not likely. I've seen your fridge. No wonder you're so skinny. You need to eat better."

She had been eating better. Sipping wine while Ty grilled their dinner. Or talking and laughing over long, leisurely dinners somewhere outside of town. The past five nights she'd dined on oatmeal and cookies. Not tonight, though. Tonight whether he wanted to or not, Ty was going to listen to everything Lily had to tell him.

And then they'd make up and live happily ever after. She let out a heavy sigh and waved to Mia. "Be careful."

"Seriously. It's rain. It's not like it's a blizzard. See ya in the morning. Or if you're not... busy with Ty, come over to the restaurant for dinner. Or a drink. On the house."

"So kind of you to offer Hope's alcohol," Lily teased.

"I know. I'm nice like that." Mia paused, one hand on the door. "Seriously, though."

"I'm good. Thanks."

Lily did two more highlights then had Diane Windward's massage before she could call it a day. Annie left before Diane showed up and Lily went through her inventory, making a list of products to order and those to discount for the summer.

"What a storm we're having," Diane said as she shook the rain from her raincoat and closed the door behind her. The gust of wind blew the receipts on the desk, and Lily slammed her hand down to keep them from flying away.

"You're soaked." Lily took the umbrella from her and propped it against the wall. A crack of lightning lit up the sky, followed by a rumble of thunder that shook the building. "Are you sure you don't want to reschedule? A massage should be relaxing."

"This doesn't bother me a bit. I've always loved thunderstorms. Hope and her father were the scared ones, huddling together while I'd run around closing up the house. Thankfully, Delaney takes after me."

"I wonder where Cameron stands on them." Lily could picture the cozy family of three cuddled together on the living room couch watching the lightning and counting the seconds for the thunder that followed. It wasn't something she'd ever thought about, tucked away in her family's penthouse or summer home.

"According to Hope, he and Delaney are practically twins. So if I had my guess, I'd say he's a trooper."

"Well, good for Hope for scoring him." Another streak cut through the dark afternoon sky. "It's not a problem to reschedule."

"Nah. This is nothing. Besides, if you lose power it will only make it more calming. I've been looking forward to this massage since Hope and Cameron gave me the gift certificate for Mother's Day."

She'd sold nearly forty gift certificates with that promo, giving customers a free haircut with the purchase of one. Slowly, her clientele was growing.

"Well, right this way then." Lily led Hope's mom up the stairs and into the first massage room. "Would you prefer lavender, citrus, or sandalwood essence?"

"Lavender sounds heavenly."

Lily lit the wick and reached for the portable iPod. "Normally I ask if you want the sound of waves, rain, or birds. It'll be hard to drown out this downpour, though."

"I guess rain it is."

"Perfect." Lily gave her instructions on where to put her clothes and how to lie down on the table. "I'll knock before coming back in."

She slipped out giving Diane privacy to change. Lily went into the second massage room and peeked out the window. Visibility was next to nothing and the rain came down in sheets. The lightning seemed to be moving away, still visible in the distance.

After one more rumble of thunder, Lily went to work on Diane. The rain in the background, lavender filling the air, and the dimly lit room was enough to put Lily asleep, if she didn't have so much on her mind.

This was what she loved about giving massages. The inner peace it brought not only to her clients, but to Lily as well. It wasn't quite the same as being on the table herself, but Lily left each massage feeling more relaxed than when she started.

"That was heavenly," Diane said as she sat up, holding the sheet around her. "I nodded off a few times."

"I'm glad you could relax. I'll wait for you downstairs."

Lily gave her privacy again and went to the main floor to wait for her. With everything cleaned up and ready for the next day, there wasn't much to do. Her phone lit up on the receptionist table signaling a text. Maybe Ty had been trying to contact her for the past hour, anxious to see her.

Nervous butterflies danced in her belly.

"Not even this rain can take away how wonderful I feel," Diane said from behind her.

Lily turned and smiled. "You deserved it."

"And so do you. I'm sure if you ask, Ty would give you a nice foot massage. You're on your feet an awful lot."

Lily swallowed, the lump in her throat making it difficult to go down, and looked away. Again, her phone lit up.

"I'll let you take your call. I turned my cell phone off so I wouldn't be bothered. I don't think I'm going to turn it on until I get home. I'm feeling too good." Diane slipped into her raincoat. "And this is for you." She slipped some cash in Lily's hand.

"You don't have to tip me, Diane."

"Of course I do. That was fabulous."

"Thank you." Lily tucked the money in her pocket. "Drive safely." She handed Diane the umbrella and opened the door for her.

Not wanting to seem desperate, she told herself she'd wait until she was up in her apartment to check her messages. Lily pocketed her phone and took deep breaths as she mounted the stairs.

Stepping out of her flats, Lily pulled out of her bun with one hand and turned her phone on with the other.

Eleven unread texts. Lily licked her lips in anticipation and frowned when she saw none of them were from Ty. Nine from Hope and two from Jenna. They really wanted to hear the gossip.

Settling into the couch, Lily opened the first one from Hope and gasped.

Mia's in the ER. Hit by a car.

She continued reading through them. No details except the name of the hospital. Jenna's text said the same thing. Lily jumped up and dashed to her shoes, grabbed her keys from the table, and fled down the stairs and outside into the pouring rain to her car.

The sky had grown darker and the rain heavier, making it difficult to see ten feet in front of her. Lily unlocked her car and climbed behind the wheel, shivering from the cool air or from worry, she couldn't tell. Both, most likely.

The small hospital Hope named was twenty minutes away. By the time Lily pulled into the lot she was semi-dry. Not that it mattered. She hadn't even thought of bringing a raincoat, too concerned about Mia.

Of course, on a night like this there wouldn't be any close spaces either. She drove around until she found one in the fifth row. Once parked, she gathered her purse and dashed toward the emergency room entrance.

The waiting room was crowded, but Lily made out Ty right away. His arm was anchored across his mother's shoulders, her face pressed into his chest. He talked to his father over his mother's head and didn't notice Lily.

She longed to run over to him, to his parents, and hug them tight, but didn't know how she'd be received. Ty's brush off this past weekend hurt deep to her core.

"Finally. I was tempted to drive over and get you myself." Hope pulled her in for a hug.

"I didn't have my phone on me. I was giving your mom a massage."

"Crap. I forgot about that." Hope squeezed her eyes shut. "I sent her a ton of texts as well. Celeste could use her shoulder to lean on."

"At least she had Ty."

Hope opened her eyes and took Lily's hand, yanking her around the corner of the waiting room into an empty hall. "My first reaction when I heard about Mia was to contact everyone close to her. Including you. I wasn't thinking about... you and Ty."

Her eyes narrowed as if untrusting and searching for the truth inside of Lily.

Lily squirmed under the intense scrutiny and pulled her hand away. "Thank you for texting me. How is she? What happened?"

"Hit and run."

"What?"

"Yeah. She parked on the other side of the lot and some asshole came out of nowhere and mowed her over. Took off. Didn't even stop to see if she was okay."

"Oh my God." Lily covered her mouth with her hand. "How bad is she hurt?"

"Broken leg. Maybe some internal damage."

"A hit and run?"

Hope nodded. "Wasn't a customer either. He didn't have Maine plates. Witnesses couldn't make which state and said it looked like he was aiming for her."

Chills ran up her spine. A hit and run in Crystal Cove? The timing. It was too... Lily tightened her arms around her middle and bent over. They were coming after her friends. No one was safe. She needed to warn them.

Or leave.

"Lily? Are you going to be sick?"

"Maybe. I need some air."

"You're not going outside. Let's go back to the waiting room so you can sit."

No. Ty was there. She needed to separate herself from everyone she cared about before they became the next victims of... hell, she didn't even know who she was running from.

"I'm going to sit here for a minute. I'll be okay." Lily leaned against the wall and slid to the floor, drawing her knees to her chest.

"Does this have anything to do with...?"

Either Grace had told Hope and she wanted to pretend she didn't know, or Ty had told her about his suspicions. Since Hope wasn't freaking out about the prominent danger, she must believe Lily was cheating on Ty.

"I—" What? She couldn't tell Hope how much she loved Ty. Damian's guys already hurt Mia, a message Lily wouldn't ignore. Knowing the type of men he associated himself with, they were just getting started.

Severing the ties with the people she loved was the only way to keep them safe.

"I need some time alone."

Hope crossed her arms and sighed. "Don't hurt him. Whatever you do or say, don't hurt Ty." She walked away without looking back.

"That's what I'm trying to do," Lily whispered. Hating to make the call but knowing it had to be done, she took out her cell and dialed Agent Thorne's number.

After a quick call where she relayed the little she knew about Mia's accident, Lily chucked her phone in her purse and rested her forehead on her knees. She had no idea how much time had passed. It wasn't until a pair of shiny black shoes appeared beneath her nose that she looked up.

"Did you seriously just fly here from New York or DC or wherever super spies hangout?"

His expression didn't change, but she knew Agent Thorne mentally rolled his eyes. He held out a hand for her and she took it, thanking him for his strength. Her knees were wobbly, and she knew she wouldn't make it far on her own.

"I'm not a spy."

"Sure. Do you have a teleporter or something?" Her feeble attempt at humor wasn't likely to lighten the mood of the agent's or hers.

"You did the right thing by calling me."

"Evading. You must have super secret spy gadgets to get you here this quick." She followed Thorne into a small waiting room down the hall.

"I was at my grandparents' place."

"Why?"

Not a raised eyebrow or a flick of his head. Nothing. Stoic. Yeah, Thorne made a good spy. Lily supposed she should follow his advice on her next move.

"Since you seem to know everything, can you tell me how Mia's doing?"

"You didn't see her?"

"She was having tests done. The family was in the waiting room."

"They're all in her room now. I was surprised you weren't in there when I walked by."

"How did you find me in the hall?" If he asked Hope or—God forbid, Ty—about her, their speculation on her being a cheater would be solidified.

"The hospital is small."

"Did anyone see you?"

There was a slight tilt of his head that made her feel stupid for asking such a ridiculous question.

"So tell me how Mia's doing. Will she be okay?" Lily curled her bottom lip under her teeth and bit down.

"She has a broken leg. She may need surgery; only time will tell once the swelling goes down. A cracked rib and a concussion. No major permanent damage."

"They'll go after Ty next. And Hope. I'm closest to them. Please promise me you'll keep them safe."

"How do you know this is the work of Gervais? Is there something you're not telling me?"

"Me? More like there's something *you're* not telling *me!*"

Again Thorne stood motionless. His gaze darted to the open doorway before he moved to close the door.

"Why don't you think this is a random hit and run?"

"Because there are people who want to kill me," she whispered angrily.

"Exactly. They want to kill *you* not your friends."

"I'm not stupid. I know how these people work. They hurt the ones closest to you before they come for you. It's psychological terror or something like that."

"You watch too much television."

"I don't watch TV."

Thorne took her by her shoulder and pushed Lily into one of the plastic chairs. "I've been watching you. Watching the town. I'm not going to lie. Tonight's accident took me by surprise. It may just be a random hit and run, but I'll look into it."

"It's not random. I can feel it. Everything is going wrong. Please just make sure they're safe. If I leave, Damian's men will leave town as well to track me down. Can't you send me somewhere for a while?"

"And when they can't find you, who are they going to turn to for your whereabouts?"

Lily placed a hand over her stomach in a poor attempt to calm the storm raging inside. "There's no escaping them, is there?"

What had she brought on these good people? No matter what she did, where she went, Damian's men would cause trouble for them because they were friends with her. Bile worked its way up her throat and she gagged, choking it back down.

"Why don't you stay at the Emerald Pond for a few days while I investigate. That way you're close, but out of sight."

"How will that keep Ty and Hope safe?"

"There's no reason to believe they're in danger."

"Are you kidding me?" Lily jumped to her feet. "One of my very good friends is here because of me. Of course there's reason to believe they're in danger. How obtuse are you?"

"We'll leave your car here so it can't be traced back to my grandparents' place."

"Emotionless, insensitive robot. That's what you are."

"Are you going to make a scene as we leave here? I highly suggest you don't. The less attention we bring to you the better."

Her body shook with fear, with shock, with adrenaline. She nodded, her shoulders slumping in defeat. Thorne opened the door and escorted her out with his hand on her lower back as if guiding her through the halls.

Her feet dragged down the hall. She would have collapsed if Thorne wasn't there to lean on. Somehow they'd made it outside. It wasn't until he closed the passenger side of his car door that she realized he'd draped his suit coat over her shoulders. No wonder she didn't feel the rain.

Lily didn't feel anything. Except emptiness.

CHAPTER NINETEEN

THE ONLY THING STOPPING him from chasing down the asshole who had his arm around Lily and his coat on her shoulders was knowing his sister was on the third floor in recovery from a hit and run. Hell. Ty was a magnet for misery.

This was why he didn't date. Didn't do relationships. Why he and Meatball were a perfect pair. Socializing, being part of the cheating world, was not for either of them.

Ty could feel his depression setting in again. Not that it ever went away. Sure, the pills helped him come out of his stupor faster than when he was off them, but right now he wanted to crawl into a hole and never come out again. Being angry was good. It was better than being sad and retreating into his shell again.

Hell, he'd barely come out of it. Lily had helped him see the light. She brought happiness to his life, to his house. She made him see a hopeful future. And then she pulled the rug out from under him, stabbing him where he was the most vulnerable.

Damn, he felt like a sissy. A woman shouldn't have a strong hold on his life like this. Ty had everything going for him. A solid work ethic, good employees, and now that his father was working on retirement, Parker Construction would be his.

The company had a solid reputation, as did Ty. He even had friends now beyond Hope and Delaney. Guy friends. Cameron and Ben were good guys who seemed to get him. It was okay that Ty wasn't much of a talker. They could chill. Be guys. All was good.

Except the woman he loved walked away in the arms of another man.

Determined not to let depression—or a woman—get the better of him, Ty spun on his heels and marched back to his sister's room.

Hope, Cameron, Jenna, and Grace stood close together, talking quietly outside Mia's room.

"She awake?"

"Yeah. Groggy. Grumpy. So basically she's back to her usual self," Hope teased, but the smile didn't quite reach her eyes.

"Your parents are in there now. We're going to head home, but we'll be back tomorrow. You'll call us if you need anything?" Cameron asked.

"Why would I need anything? Mia's the one who got left for dead in the middle of the parking lot."

Grace gasped and clutched at her throat. Ty didn't know much about the woman, other than she was Alexis' younger sister who turned her head at anything resembling responsibility. Or at least that's how Ben and Alexis had described her.

"Are you saying someone intentionally ran her over?" Grace scratched at her neck, fear etched around her eyes.

"That's how it was explained to me. A hit and run. I thought you all knew that."

"No. I didn't." Grace looked to Hope, then to Jenna, before returning her concern to Ty. "You should all be careful out there. We live in a dangerous world."

"No need to be dramatic, Grace. This was a fluke accident. It sucks it happened to Mia, but she'll pull through."

Grace's reaction wasn't what he expected. Concern for Mia, yes; concern over the reckless drivers out there, not necessarily.

"Tell your parents we'll keep our phones turned on all night if they need anything, or if any other news about Mia's accident comes up."

"Thanks, Hope. It's getting late, so I doubt we'll hear any more tonight. You guys head home."

"Don't forget to take care of yourself as well." Hope hugged him before walking away with Cameron and her friends.

The best way for him to take care of himself was by busying himself with Mia and her care.

Tapping softly on the door, he opened it and stepped inside.

"It's about time. I didn't think you even cared. Probably hoping the douchebag offed me so you could claim my inheritance."

"Mia. Language," their mother scoffed.

Ty chuckled. "It's too bad the douche didn't knock the attitude out of you." Ty leaned down and kissed his sister on the top of her head. "And Mom and Dad are gonna live until they're a hundred, so we have a ways to go before claiming their inheritance."

"You know what I mean."

"I usually don't." Ty took in the contraption holding up her right leg and the IV bag, following the tube to her arm where it fed her painkillers. "You feeling okay?"

"For now." She held up her stuck arm and wiggled her eyebrows. "Got some good stuff pumping through my veins right now."

"You gave us quite the scare, Mia."

"Sorry, Dad. Had I known that douche—jerk wasn't going to stop for a pedestrian running across the parking lot in the pouring rain, I would have leaped out of his way sooner."

"What exactly happened today?" Ty sat at the edge of her bed and read through the 'it's not so bad' mask Mia wore.

"Go chase down the police officers if you want to know more. I don't feel like going through it all again." Mia closed her eyes and sunk deeper into her pillow. In seconds, she was out, a soft snore coming from her lips.

"We should let her sleep." Celeste stroked Mia's arm and kissed her cheek before doing the same to Ty. "You should go home as well. We'll visit in the morning when we're all rested."

"Drive safely, son. It may not be winter, but the wind knocked down a lot of debris. The roads will be slick with leaves and twigs."

"You too, Dad." He hugged his parents and after they left, he went back to watching Mia sleep.

Sometime later a nurse came in to read Mia's vitals and strongly suggested Ty go home.

The rain hadn't let up, and even with the wipers on full speed he could barely see ten feet in front of him. The slow drive gave him too much time to think about Lily and what she was probably doing with the suit right about now.

Something deep inside him didn't sit right, and it wasn't just the image of Lily with another man. That would never sit right. It was the expression she wore on her face. Ty only caught a quick glimpse, but the dark shadow under her sad eyes on her pale face shouldn't be there if she was having an affair with another man. He was too familiar with that expression; he'd seen it in the mirror too many times.

The man had his arm anchored around her back as if she needed his support to leave the hospital. It wasn't the sight of a woman being whisked away into the night by her lover.

Ty pulled into his driveway and shut off the engine. He didn't like the directions of his thoughts. A cheating woman didn't deserve his sympathy. He wanted nothing to do with her.

The downpour greeted him when he opened the driver's side door, and he didn't even attempt to shield his head or dash for his front door. Instead, Ty dragged his feet up the steps and unlocked the door, bringing in a gust of wind and rain, which puddled on his hardwood floors.

And he didn't care. Depression. It was back, and for some reason it worked its way into Lily's life as well. If she was depressed, he wanted nothing to do with it. He had a hard enough time fighting his own dark demon.

Meatball trotted over and lapped at the water around Ty's feet.

"You have a nice water dish, yet you prefer toilet bowls and puddles. Damn dog." He closed the front door and knelt to rub behind his dog's ears. "Looks like it's just you and me, kid."

A flash of lightning lit up the living room and Meatball began to shake, cowering at his feet. "I'm gonna change and then we'll hang on the couch and watch Captain America or something for a bit, 'k?"

It was late, too late to start a movie, but Meatball needed comforting, and he hated to admit it, but so did Ty.

Ty woke some hours later, a cramp in his thigh, a heavy weight on his chest, and smelly hot air panting in his face. Opening one eye, he cringed when Meatball's tongue lolled from the corner of his mouth, a thick line of drool hanging from it, ready to land on Ty any second.

"Seriously, man." Rolling his shoulders, he moved his head to the side as the drool dropped, running down Ty's neck. "And here I was feeling bad for you."

He bent and stretched his legs, patting the hardwood floor. "Get down and I'll make you some breakfast." Meatball scooted back, sitting firmly on Ty's bladder, and stared at him. He knew that look. No one could make Meatball move if he didn't want to. "We're on the couch. You can hop down by yourself." Still, the dog didn't budge, and Ty needed to go to the bathroom. "Fine."

Grunting, he shifted to a sitting position and picked up Meatball, placing him on the floor. "Just for that, I'm taking care of my needs before yours."

Of course his dog would want to prove a point and trot to the backdoor. He'd been too scared to go out yesterday in the rain. His bladder had to be on the brink of explosion as well.

"Fine. You win. But when I call you, you better run your fat ass off to come back inside, or I'll leave you out in the next storm."

Meatball would call his bluff, and Ty would lose again.

They went through their morning rituals, and then Ty stopped in to see his sister at the hospital before heading into work.

"Are you sure you're okay to go home today?" He looked his sister over, happy to see the color back in her cheeks.

"You guys gotta chill. It's a broken bone, not the end of the world."

"Your apartment's on the second floor. How are you going to manage that with crutches?"

"Does this mean you want me to stay with you?"

Ty's upstairs wasn't finished, but he could blow up an air mattress and sleep up there, giving Mia his bedroom if she needed it. They'd kill each other by the end of the week.

"If you—"

"We barely survived our teen years. There's no way in hell we could live together again."

Relieved she'd been thinking the same thing, Ty thought about her options. The bedrooms at their parents' house were upstairs. Hope had a nice place, but her spare was upstairs as well. Grace lived with her parents and Jenna lived with an elderly man, and while Ben and Alexis had an office space off the living room, they also had a baby.

There weren't many options for Mia.

"How are you going to get around?"

"Single people manage all the time. I'll be fine. Mom and Dad are swinging by in a bit to drive me home. That's one thing I won't be able to do until I get this cast off." She knocked on the plaster. "Looks like you and the girls will be my designated driver for a while."

"That's fine."

It's not like he had anything better to do.

* * * *

LILY WOKE TO AN UNFAMILIAR sound. A creak and a light tap of a screen door clapping against the frame. Remembering where she was, she rolled over and stared at the blank wall.

Ruth and Herb Bergeron's house. Thorne had all but insisted she stay while he did some investigating into Mia's accident. He'd been aloof last night. Nothing out of the ordinary for him.

She reached for her cell on the nightstand and found nothing. Peeking over the side of the bed thinking it had fallen during the night, she didn't find it on the floor either. Pulling back the covers, Lily sat up, a wave of fear and embarrassment rippling through her body.

The sweatpants and shirt were Thorne's. He'd offered them to her last night when they'd arrived soaking wet from the rain. It was better than sleeping in wet jeans, and much better than sleeping naked.

Thorne didn't give her the heebie-jeebies, but it was still awkward being in the house alone with him. Especially when Ty had the wrong impression about them. She needed to explain it to him before he lost all hope in her.

Not caring how her hair or face looked, she padded across the room, opening the door and peering down the stairs. She could hear Thorne's quiet voice in the distance and hurried to the bathroom.

A few minutes later, she made her way to the kitchen and poured herself a cup of coffee. The screen door creaked open and Thorne stepped inside, dressed in business slacks, a shirt, and tie. He was incongruous to the summer camp setting, looking more out of place than Lily felt.

"Did you sleep well?"

After tossing for hours and hours, maybe. "Sure. I need to go to work now. My first client will be there soon."

"Annie called and rescheduled your appointments."

"What... how... what did you say to her?" Part of her was pissed for him taking over her life, and the other part was grateful. She was too drained, emotionally and physically, to put on a fake smile and make small talk with her clients.

"Don't worry about it," he said calmly. The man could make things happen without raising suspicion. She'd watched him do his job, and do it well, two years ago.

"Have you seen my cell phone?"

"Yes."

Lily sipped her coffee and waited for him to elaborate. Which he didn't. He wouldn't. "Where is it?"

"I have it." Thorne poured a cup of coffee for himself and sat at the table in front of his laptop.

"Can I have it back?"

Thorne reached in his briefcase and handed her the phone. It felt lighter. Lily powered it on and got nothing.

"Did you drain my battery?"

"I took it out," he said without looking up from the screen.

"Um, why?" Lily set her coffee down on the table with too much force, not caring as it sloshed over the side.

"So you can't be traced."

She opened her mouth to argue and then shock set in. Traced. Someone *was* after her. The same someone who mowed down Mia. Her heart hammered in her chest and the buzzing returned, cramping in her side until her eyes blurred.

"My friends. Ty," she whispered, dropping to the chair next to Thorne. "Please tell me they're safe. You need to... to protect them."

"They're safe." Thorne closed his laptop and picked up his coffee, appearing all too calm while a tsunami of feelings drowned her insides. Fear. Guilt. Anger. Sadness. Rage.

"Where are they?"

"Home. Working. They're safe."

"Do you have people watching them?"

"I need to ask you a few questions."

He wouldn't give her answers, yet he wanted them from her. It was unfair, yet Lily knew he was only trying to keep her safe.

"I don't know anything."

"How much have you told Ty?"

"Nothing." Lily pushed back her chair and paced the small space. "I've told him nothing, and he thinks I'm a cheating whore. I want my phone battery, and I want to see Ty. I need to tell him. He needs to be careful, to be on the lookout for danger."

"He doesn't know about Gervais?"

"Of course not!"

"Does he know Veronica Stewart?"

"No. You're ruining my life making me keep things from him." Lily swiped at the tears with the back of her hand and sniffed. "I don't want to lie to the man I love. I deserve a nice life. A quiet life filled with love and family and friends. And you're taking it away from me. I hate you for that."

It hurt like hell keeping secrets. She hated the double life. Hated the secrets. Hated not being with Ty. "I'm telling him. Today. You can't stop me." Lily marched out of the kitchen, finding no satisfaction when the screen door slammed behind her. The grass was wet under her bare feet, and the sun reflected so brightly off the lake blinding her as she made her way down to the dock.

She sat on the dock not caring that it was still slightly damp from yesterday's rain. The start of an engine had her lifting her head and turning around. Thorne was leaving. She was trapped at the cabin with no phone, no car, and none of her belongings.

A blue kayak sat tied to a tree not far from her. She could paddle her way to freedom, if she knew which way to go. Lily had no idea how much time passed as she sat, deep in her thoughts.

When she heard Thorne's car again, she shot up and stormed into the house. She was already yelling at him before the front door opened all the way.

"Don't you ever leave me again—"

Broad shoulders filled the doorway covered in a navy t-shirt, and a just as confused expression played on Ty's face.

"What's going on here?" He looked back over his shoulder where Lily spotted Thorne.

"You two can talk." Thorne turned away and got back into his sleek car.

"What the hell?" Ty placed angry hands on his hips as he looked from the black car already halfway down the driveway to Lily. "I don't want any part of this. Where the hell is your suit going?"

Conflicted between wanting to jump into Ty's arms and wanting to slap him for ever believing she'd cheat on him, she clenched her teeth and bit back her words until she figured out what to say. Or at least, how to start.

Ty cursed and took out his cell.

"No. Don't." Lily reached out and placed her hand over his, stopping him from texting or dialing.

"I don't want to be part of this."

"You are whether you want to be or not."

"If you're having a lover's spat, you can figure it out with your suit on your own."

"My *lover's spat* is with you, you big idiot. Thorne is not and has never been my *lover*."

"Thorne? What a fitting name." Ty walked out the front door and stood in the driveway turning in a three-sixty, most likely looking for a way out. Lily had done the same thing earlier.

"Ty, we need to talk. Will you come inside?"

"I'm not stepping foot in a place where you've been with another man."

"I told you—"

"You're wearing his clothes. I'd say you're more than a casual acquaintance."

Lily looked down at her attire and grimaced. It looked bad. She needed to put herself in Ty's shoes. Yeah, she'd be pretty pissed if she stepped into a similar situation. The best approach here would be the band-aid way. Fast.

Stepping outside, she took a deep breath and looked straight into his eyes. "My name is Veronica Stewart. I'm in the witness protection program, and Agent Thorne is responsible for my safety."

"You." Ty cocked his head and studied her. "What?"

"My ex-husband is in jail for espionage, grand theft, and murder. And my father, being his right-hand man is dead. Either as a result of my husband—my ex-husband—or his own hand. I don't know and I don't care. Damian thinks I know more about their business than I really do."

Ty opened his mouth to speak, but no words came out. He closed it again and closed his eyes. Lily waited, giving him time to process. When he opened his eyes, they were distant and unresponsive as he looked past her toward the lake. Without glancing at her he walked away toward the water.

Lily watched as his normally strong shoulders sagged, his head hunched forward, and his gait tired. The pang in her chest grew stronger as she hurt for him. For them. She gave him a minute of alone time down by the water and then followed his path, stopping at his side, keeping a solid five feet of space between them.

"Agent Thorne was assigned to me when I returned to the States."

"Returned?" Ty asked, still keeping his focus out on the water.

"I lived in Europe with..." She hated saying his name but Ty needed to hear it all, and she needed to tell him. "Damian Gervais. We moved there after we married."

Lily poured out the whole story from the marriage of convenience to discovering her husband's illegal business activity, and his and her father's illegal activities and even murders.

"Is there any truth in you at all, or have I been sleeping with a fake person for the past month?"

"I'm not fake, Ty. You have to understand the danger I am in. I couldn't tell you who I was."

"Why?" He turned and peered down at her, the wall of tension thick between them.

"I started over. A new life. I don't want anything to do with my past life. Can't you understand that?" Tears of frustration streamed down her cheeks.

"Why didn't you tell me?"

"I couldn't. I couldn't tell anyone. I don't know if Damian has men out there trying to find me. "

"And you thought I could be one of them?" His eyes darkened and went from peering to icy cold. All emotion washed away from Ty as he watched her with a face as still as stone.

"No."

"Yes."

"I didn't tell anyone. I don't want to live in the past. Can't you see?" Lily balled her hands into fists and clenched her jaw. "I don't want to be Veronica Stewart-Gervais, the socialite and heiress. I want to be Lily Novak who owns a small town spa and falls in love with a kindhearted man."

"You can't change who you are, no matter how hard you try. You'll always be... you." Ty ticked his jaw. "And I'm not a kindhearted man."

"So this is it? You're ending something special between us because I didn't tell you about my dangerous past? I know your ex-fiancée hurt you, but don't clump me in the same category as her. I never cheated on you. You need to get your head out of your ass and think about someone besides yourself."

Ty's shoulders stiffened, but he didn't respond.

"Mia's accident was no *accident*. My identity may have been dis-covered by the wrong people, and now they're trying to scare me by hurting my friends. You could be next, Ty. And Hope. And Grace and Jenna. Damian's people are dangerous. Forget your male pride for a second and think about those around you. I didn't tell anyone who I really was because I wanted to keep you safe."

His eyes grew wide with a new emotion Lily couldn't read. The sound of a car pulling in had them both looking up toward the drive-way. Thorne appeared looking casual and out of his element next to the house.

"Your suit better know his shit. I won't allow Hope or anyone else to be hurt." He marched off up the slope toward Thorne and grabbed his shoulder, forcing him around the corner of the house.

Thorne may not have the muscle packed on like Ty, but Lily doubted he'd let himself be pushed around if he didn't want to be. The agent was smart and must have known now was not a good time to mess with Ty.

Instead of getting involved in the alpha verbal war she was sure was happening inside the house, Lily sat in one of the Adirondack chairs and wished the breeze could blow away her troubles.

The ripples in the water ended once they hit the sandy shore and more followed behind in a never-ending gentle current. Lily longed for those nights when the water was still and flat as glass. Nothing moving or breaking the tranquility and inner peace.

Instead, the world was crashing down on her like waves before a storm.

The storm. Mia. Hell. She'd been so caught up in Ty and wanting him to believe in her again that she'd forgotten about her friend. Lily shot out of her chair and jogged to the house. As the screen door closed behind her, she heard the start of an engine. Running to the front, she whipped the front door open and watched Thorne drive away. The silhouette in the passenger seat belonged to Ty.

It was one thing to learn the man you married was a murderer and wanted you dead. It was another to learn the man you gave your heart and soul to no longer wanted you.

Her throat tightened, burning with tears she couldn't shed. His lack of understanding and sympathy shattered her already fragile heart into a million pieces. No new identity could replace that.

Ever.

CHAPTER TWENTY

TY ROUNDED THE CORNER of Hemlock Drive and changed gears as he pedaled up the hill. He'd passed the twenty-five-mile mark and had yet to burn off the hostile steam that had built up inside his chest and head.

When the suit had shown up at his jobsite a few hours ago, Ty was ready to punch him in the gut, or at least do something to mess up his stiffly ironed shirt and pants. Ty wasn't a violent guy, and the urge to hurt the man was unsettling in his stomach.

"You need to come with me," the suit had said, holding open the passenger side of his slick car.

"Not a chance in hell."

"Lily needs to talk to you."

Ty gritted his teeth and practically growled. "I don't want to hear it." He'd turned and the suit reached out, grabbing Ty's forearm. Ty stiffened then yanked his arm away, nearly knocked the man on his ass. "Keep your hands off me."

"It's about your sister."

"What the hell do you know about my sister?" The suit didn't flinch, still holding the open passenger side door.

Was that why he was at the hospital last night? Did he have something to do with Mia's hit and run? Or was he there to comfort Lily? But why would she need comforting? She hadn't even stopped in to see Mia.

Too many questions that needed answering. Ty unbuckled his tool belt and tossed it in the back of his truck. "I'll follow you."

"That won't work."

Ty grabbed on to his hair in frustration and tugged. "Who the hell are you?" He didn't move, didn't quirk his lips, and his eyes were unreadable behind his dark sunglasses. Hell, if it hadn't been about his sister he wouldn't have even thought about getting in the car with the asshole.

He hadn't been ready for the reaction his body had when Lily had opened the door to the camp. Her face was void of any makeup and her hair had seen better days, pulled back into a mess of a bun. Ty loved her like that. Fresh and rumpled.

And then he'd noticed her outfit. Men's clothes. And not his.

For the second time in less than an hour hostile rage had fed on his body.

Ty stood up on his pedals and leaned forward as he neared the peak of the hill. After the next bend he'd be able to coast the last three miles to his house. In the meantime, he needed the pain, the sweat, the escape.

But the exercise hadn't taken his mind off Lily or the revelation she'd dropped on him. Witness protection? An ex? A murderer? And shit, her father tried to kill her?

He was a hot mess of guilt and shame for the way he'd reacted to the bombshell. Lily was frightened, not only of her ex but of what he could do to her friends. To him. And instead of comforting her as she'd cried and admitted to her lying, he'd clammed up and ran off like a coward.

If she refused to have anything to do with him again, he wouldn't blame her. His dammed freaking ego got in the way, blinded him from seeing, blocked his ears from hearing and feeling what Lily had experienced.

He changed gears and sat back on his seat as he coasted, the wind cooling the sweat that clung to his body.

He needed a do-over in the worst way. Instead of caring about Lily, he'd only thought about himself. A selfish asshole.

Thorne had assured him on the drive back to the worksite that Mia's accident was completely unrelated. The geriatric man had a stroke and his wife had yanked the wheel, missing hitting Mia full on and only nicking her. They were as shaken up as Mia and the rest of them.

What Thorne couldn't assure him of, however, was Lily's safety. He'd explained in short sentences why she was at his grandparents' lake house and that he could find no evidence that her life was currently in danger. He'd be leaving for New York in the morning and asked Ty to keep an eye on her.

The man was either really good at his job or sucked ass. Ty hoped it wasn't the latter. Either way, he had Thorne's business card in the glove box of his truck and prayed he'd never have to use it.

In the meantime, he needed to check in on Mia, make sure she was settled in okay, and then grovel at Lily's feet.

Even if she didn't accept his apology, he'd spend the rest of his life looking out for her, keeping her safe from her asshole ex-husband.

He looked over his shoulder for traffic before crossing the road and pedaling down his driveway. His legs shook when he got off his bike. It had been too long since he took his mountain bike on a good ride. Unbuckling his helmet, he hung it on his handlebars and grabbed his water bottle, chugging it down before going inside.

Meatball lifted his head a fraction of an inch from his dog bed in a weak greeting and went back to doing what he usually did. Which was nothing.

Ty headed to the bathroom and stripped off his sweaty shorts and shirt, turning on the taps to his shower. If only he could wash off his stupidity.

This time he couldn't blame it on his depression. Pure selfish arrogant pride made him treat Lily poorly. She'd suffered enough, and he hated himself for being the cause of more pain in her life.

He showered and threw on work clothes, checking his text messages on his way to his truck. Between being gone all day and his dad at the hospital with Mia, he still had a shit ton of work to do and the Cummings jobsite.

Josh had left four messages. He was Ty's hardest worker but, he was young and still had a lot to learn. On his way to the jobsite Ty called him back, thanking him for putting in extra hours and got the lowdown on the progress.

He'd have to put in some long hours this week and find time to check in on Mia and talk with Lily. There was no time to mope, to wallow in self-pity, or to let his depression get ahold of him.

Ty pulled into the site, checked the work that had been done, and added to his list of things to do. An hour later, his crew left and he stayed behind to finish the window casings. It was nearly dark before he headed home, and with the sun not setting until well after eight, he knew he needed to get home to feed Meatball.

And figure out how the hell to make things right again with Lily. That is, if she'd ever forgive him. Was he even worth it? Why would a woman with her background want to settle with a middle-class carpenter from the middle of nowhere?

Self-doubt continued to creep its way into his head. This was too big for him to handle on his own. Lily was worth the fight. Worth the effort. Worth groveling. In the morning he'd call his therapist and refill his prescription that had expired a month ago.

He'd do anything, absolutely anything to make things right again with the woman he loved.

• • • •

LILY CHANGED BACK INTO her clothes and ate a bowl of oatmeal, forcing it down, knowing she needed some food in her body, by the time Agent Thorne came back to get her.

"How dare you leave me here stranded!" Lily slammed the door behind him when he stepped into the living room. "What if Damian's men found me while you were gone? How would I have contacted you? I could be dead, laying in a puddle of my own blood on your grandparents' floor, and you'd have no idea."

"You seem alive and well. Get your things. I'll bring you home."

"What?" She planted her hands on her hips and shook her head violently. "No. Tell me what's going on first. Where's Ty? Is he safe? Is Mia safe?"

"Yes."

"Yes?"

"Let's go."

"Not until you tell me what's going on."

"Nothing." Thorne brushed past her into the kitchen and locked the backdoor. "You have your things?"

"Things? What things? I have nothing, including the battery to my phone." She dug out her phone from her pocket and held it up to him.

Thorne paused for a moment before reaching into his shirt pocket. "Here." He held out his hand, the battery in it.

Lily stepped back afraid to touch it. If her phone had been traced to her, as soon as she turned it on Damian's people would know where to find her. Her eyes grew wider with fear, and she looked up at Thorne and swallowed. "What if..."

"It's clean. Your phone. Take it." He held her wrist and turned her hand over, placing the battery in her palm. "Let's go."

He walked out leaving Lily standing alone and confused in the empty living room. When she heard the start of the engine, she jogged out the door and slid into the passenger seat.

"Is Mia in a safe house?"

"No."

"Why not?"

"There's no threat to her."

"The hit and run?"

"An elderly man had a stroke. There's no connection to Gervais."

"How can you be so sure?" Lily picked at her nails as she watched the scenery speed by. The nervous churning in her belly was back.

"I looked into it." He continued to drive, taking the corners with ease, keeping any emotion from being revealed on his face.

She wanted to believe him, to believe her friends were safe. If Thorne thought they were in danger he wouldn't be so blasé, would he? Yet he'd held her prisoner for nearly twenty-four hours. But he also brought Ty to her. Too bad being upfront and honest with him had totally backfired.

"So, uh. Thanks for bringing Ty." She waited for Thorne to say something in response. Which, of course, he didn't. "He wasn't too happy to learn I'd been lying to him." And he'd hurt her more than she thought a man could.

Damian and her father's plot to kill her hurt and angered her. But mostly she felt like a fool for being so gullible.

The hurt Ty brought on was an entirely different kind of pain that ripped at her soul. She didn't hate him; she hated what he'd said to her, how he looked at her. Like she was the spawn of Satan. He'd ripped away a piece of her soul and even so, Lily still loved him.

She understood his pain and he had every right to be mad at her, but it hurt to her core. Sticks and stones. Those were thrown at her by her father and Damian. She'd never really loved either of them. Their relationships were centered around business, not around love or emotions.

But words can never hurt me. Yeah. Wasn't that a big, fat lie? Words didn't heal with time. They stayed forever. And while what Ty said wasn't necessarily cruel, his intentions were deliberate. He wanted to hurt her, and he did, by calling her a liar.

"I'm flying back to New York. Call if you need anything."

"Like a comforting shoulder? Someone to talk to?"

His lower lip quirked a fraction of a millimeter before he turned to her. "Sure."

"Who is going to keep me safe?" She didn't mean to sound so pathetic, so weak. She hadn't needed Thorne by her side for the past two years and was proud of the independent woman she'd become.

"Ty."

Lily snorted. "Not likely. He's not impressed with me right now. Besides after the way he... I won't be calling on him." She'd read the pain in his eyes when she told him about her heritage. The wealth. She wanted to gloss over it, but it was part of the mess that got her to where she was. After being left for a man who made more than him, Ty was extremely insecure when it came to financial status. The last thing she wanted to do was rub her wealth in his face.

Yet that seemed to be the thing he focused on. Her secrets and her supposedly lowering her standards by being with a common carpenter.

Fury bubbled up inside her once again as Thorne neared the hospital. Annie had rescheduled her appointments and closed up for her, for which Lily was very grateful. If rumor hadn't already spread like wildfire throughout the town, they'd surely start to spark soon enough.

When Thorne stopped in front of her car in the hospital parking lot, Lily unbuckled and reached at her feet for her purse.

"Just so you know, I'm telling Mia and Hope. I trust them. They deserve to know."

"Okay."

Lily scrunched her face in shock. "*Okay?* You're not going to try to persuade me to button up?"

"It's your choice."

"Really? Because you didn't want to give me a choice last week when I told you I wanted to tell Ty. Why the sudden change of mind?"

Thorne kept his hands on the steering wheel and his focus forward not responding to her question.

Letting out an exasperated sigh, Lily looped her fingers through the door handle and opened the door. She had one leg out the door when Thorne spoke.

"You're safe here, Lily. I'm glad you have Ty and your friends around you."

"If anything happens to—"

"It won't. If anything changes, though, I'll be here in a heartbeat."

"You have one?"

Thorne glanced at her keeping his face stoic, yet she could see a trace of laughter in his eyes. The man needed to lighten up, but she was extremely thankful for him in her life.

"I guess I hope I don't have to see you for a while. Or ever. No offense."

"None taken."

She climbed out of the car and unlocked her own. Had it been only twenty-four hours since her life once again turned in an instant?

Even though Thorne told her there wasn't a connection, she still felt obligated to tell Mia what could have been. Not wanting to lose her ambition, Lily picked up her cell and dialed.

"Hello?"

"Hey, Mia. I heard you may be home by now."

"'Bout fricking time. Those damn nurses were pricking and prodding at me every other minute. At least now I can get some rest."

"How are you feeling?"

"Annoyed. Tired."

Maybe now wasn't a good time to come over. "Are you in any pain?"

"I'm still pretty doped up. My parents brought me home, and Ty came over and hovered. I kicked him out. He's annoying. You two still having a rough patch?"

Patch? No. It was worse than that. "I'm more concerned about you. I'd like to come visit, but if now isn't a good time..."

"Now's great. Bring some wine. And ice cream."

"Should you be drinking while on medication?"

"Great. Ty's been rubbing off on you. He said the same thing."

Lily really didn't want to talk about Ty. Once she started the story of her past, she was pretty confident Mia would be sidetracked. "I'll let you rest. Tomorrow, though. Can I come by after work?"

"You okay? You don't sound your usual perky self."

"I, uh..." Lily played with her keys and then stuck them in the ignition. "I need to tell you some... stuff about the accident."

"About the old couple?"

"Well, no. Not really. It's just that... it's just... I thought your accident was because of me."

"What do you have to do with them?"

"No." Lily rested her head on the steering wheel. "I didn't. I don't know them. The accident was just a terrible accident, and thankfully I didn't have anything to do with it but I could have."

"It could be the lovely drugs I'm on right now, but I'm not making heads or tails over what you're saying."

"I know," Lily groaned. "I don't mean to sound so evasive, so edgy. It's just not something I want to talk about over the phone."

"So come over."

"You need to rest."

"I can't rest now. You're freaking me out. You sure you're okay? Is this about Ty?"

"No. Ty has nothing to do with this." Absolutely nothing.

"If you won't pick up wine at least grab a tub of ice cream. Rocky Road or cherry chocolate chip."

"I'll be there in a bit." Lily hung up and called Hope, asking her to meet at Mia's as well. Better to get the story over in one tell instead of two.

CHAPTER TWENTY-ONE

"OH. MY. GOD." MIA'S jaw dropped, her eyes filled with shock.

"Lily," Hope gasped. "This is the most terrifying thing I've ever heard. Are you safe? Are you okay?"

Lily nodded, tears filling her eyes. "You are too." She filled them in on her initial fear of Mia's accident being connected to Damian in some way, and of Thorne's thorough investigation into it.

"Oh, honey." Hope drew her in for a warm hug and sniffed. "I can't even imagine what you've been through."

"I'm sorry for lying to you. To everyone. I—"

"Sorry? Hell, you have nothing to apologize for." Mia straightened, unable to move too much on the couch. "Shit. I'm touched you're telling us. I swear I won't tell a freaking soul."

"We'll keep this between us. I'm assuming Ty knows?" Hope pulled back and stroked Lily's hair.

Lily stepped out of her embrace and wrapped her arms around herself. "Grace knows. She suspected for a while. Our last book meeting..."

"You were off. Said you were sick and Grace left shortly after."

"Yeah. Damian and I had visited the boutique where she worked. She'd followed us in the magazines and online and made me out. I'm sorry I didn't tell you then as well."

"Honey. Seriously. Why are you apologizing? The FBI worked hard to help you with a new identity. It would counteract what they'd done if you started telling everyone who you used to be."

Their acceptance warmed her insides, and also made her realize what a jerk Ty had been. "You're not mad? You don't feel betrayed by my secrets?"

"Of course not," they both said at once.

"Well, your idiot brother seems to think I'd committed the worst crime of all by keeping this from him. He didn't even ask about my safety and, instead, went on a tirade about my dishonesty."

"He's a shit." Mia smacked the couch next to her. "This is why you two have been off?"

"Sort of. It is now. He'd seen me with Agent Thorne and thought I was cheating on him. And then when Thorne brought him to the camp this morning so I could tell him about everything, he treated me like a lying, cheating traitor. Like I'd hurt him."

Lily snagged the bottle of wine Hope had brought over and filled her glass, sloshing red liquid on Mia's countertop. The blood red color matched her temper. Matched the rage inside her chest.

"The next time I see him I'll give him a piece of my mind."

"You do that every time you see him, Mia," Hope said. "Besides, I think it best for Ty and Lily to work things out on their own. We shouldn't meddle."

"Meddle my ass. My brother is a dickhead. Lily's the best thing that ever happened to him, and he put his stupid pride ahead of her feelings. I knew he was socially awkward but didn't think he'd ever hurt his girlfriend like this."

"He's not socially awkward. He has de—" Lily stopped herself by bringing her wine glass to her lips. She didn't know if his sister or Hope new about Ty's depression, so she cut herself off. It wasn't her secret to share. Ty had been fairly closed mouth about it and even embarrassed, as if his depression made him less of a man. He may have hurt her, but she wouldn't share what he'd told her in confidence.

"You still love him." Hope joined her at the counter. "And he loves you. I've been his best friend since high school, and I've never seen him look at a woman the way he looks at you."

"Granted, Ty hasn't dated a girl since high school," Mia added.

Lily continued to sip her wine, not wanting to confess how much she still loved Ty.

"He shared stories with you about... his time overseas. He told you before he told me." Hope gave her a knowing smile and lowered her voice so Mia couldn't hear from the other side of the room. "We talked one night about it. At first, I was a little put off that you were the first to know about *her*, but then I realized the implication. It meant his feelings for you were strong. You've changed Ty for the better."

Lily's eyes filled again, and she wiped them on her shoulder. "I'm pretty sure it was a temporary change. He's back to the surly, closed-off man he once was."

"He'll come around. Give him time."

"I don't know if it will matter, Hope. He hurt me. If Ty doesn't trust me, we can't have a relationship. I won't live like that. Ever. I'd rather move on." And hopefully find a man who could love her for *her* and not be caught up in what she once was or could be.

"I can talk to him—"

"No." Lily placed her hand on Hope's arm. "I appreciate it, really, but what's done is done. Ty said some... some hurtful things to me. If that's how he feels then we're done. I don't want you or anyone else trying to persuade him to apologize. Forced apologies are meaningless, in my opinion."

"I agree," chimed Mia from the couch.

Lily let go of Hope and sat on the coffee table in front of Mia. "I didn't mean to bring any pain to you or your family."

"Don't ever apologize for your murdering asshole of an ex or what you had to do to protect yourself. I'll take this to my grave, swear to God."

Her heart swelled with love. She had friends. Real friends who didn't care who her father or ex-husband were. They didn't care about her name or heritage. They didn't judge her by her clothing or jewelry. Instead, they cared about what was inside. They cared about Lily.

Veronica Stewart would never surface again. There wasn't a single aspect of her life Lily missed or wished to relive. Had she been older when her mother died she might have felt differently, but with no familiar love or relationship other than the business sense, there was nothing Lily wanted other than to start over.

Everything and everyone she cared about lived in the tiny, sleepy town of Crystal Cove. This was the life she never knew she wanted. It wasn't just about how the other half lived. Heck, she never thought about the other half other than the times when she wrote checks for charities to help the poor.

Not once had she or her father, and definitely not Damian, thought about the people receiving the donations. Not once had she thought about the middle class. Not once had she thought about having friends. Or falling in love.

Life was a series of business deals and acquaintances right up until it all came to a crashing halt. The past was dead, and she never wanted to relive it or unbury it. Out with the old and in with the new.

Lily Novak of Crystal Cove, Maine, owner of the Sea Salt Spa and friend to many. This was who and what she wanted to be known and remembered for.

And if Ty Parker couldn't accept the new her without Veronica Stewart getting in the way, then well, he wasn't for her.

"You okay? Looks like you're as spaced out as I am. You been kicking back my pills?" Mia rotated her foot and cringed. "Speaking of, I think they're wearing off."

"I'll get you some more." Lily stood and turned.

"Nah. I'll survive. I'm exhausted anyway. If I need to I can take some later."

"I'll put them and a bottle of water next to your bed," Hope said, picking up the prescription and opening the fridge.

"You gals rock. Don't tell my mom and dad, but I was pretty nervous when they left. I'm glad you guys came over. Don't take this the wrong way, Lils, but your story did a hell of a job distracting me from the searing pain in my leg. I'm past it now and am ready to crash."

"I'll help you up." Lily held out her arm to steady Mia, and Hope came around to the other side.

Ten minutes later, after Mia was tucked in with her cell phone charging at her side, Hope and Lily left.

"I'm serious," Hope said at the bottom of the stairs. "You need anything and I'm there. That includes giving Ty a swift kick in the ass. I can get Cameron to do it for a bigger effect."

Lily smiled. "I'll let you know if I need to cash in on that."

"I won't say anything to Cameron. I tell him everything, but this isn't something he needs to know."

"It's okay. I trust you and him. It's a pretty big secret to keep to yourself. Besides, you have Delaney to worry about. That's what killed me, thinking Mia's accident was the work of Damian's men. I thought it was a warning and feared they'd come after you or Delaney next."

"Why Mia? If anything I'd think they'd go after Ty."

Lily nodded. "That's what I thought too, which is why Mia's accident came as such a shock. My imagination went into overdrive. If you ever worry about your or Delaney's safety, I'll leave town. I could never live with myself if anything happened to you guys because of me."

"I appreciate the warning."

"Which is why I want you to tell Cameron. He can be on the lookout too."

"Are you worried for your safety, Lily?"

"I wasn't when I came here. I was cautious, but not worried. The past year I've been more and more comfortable. I hadn't even thought about my past until I got close to Ty. I didn't like keeping secrets from him."

"And now?"

"Agent Thorne is extremely cautious. You could say he's overboard with safety. If he says I'm safe, I believe it. I can't live in fear for the rest of my life, but I don't want anything to happen to—"

"You can't live in fear for our lives either."

"I know. Actually, this past winter when Delaney was kidnapped, I hadn't even thought about there being a connection to me."

The whole town had been on high alert, and the police had pointed their finger at Cameron. What a nasty mess that was. His mother had taken Delaney, claiming she wanted to be part of her granddaughter's life, even after disowning Cameron.

Thankfully, the police had seen the craziness in her and Cameron's family and exonerated him when he found Delaney.

Even then she hadn't thought her identity had been discovered, or Damian was involved.

"But you thought Mia's accident was connected? Why?"

"Good question."

"I think you know the answer." Hope hugged her. When she pulled back she had a knowing smile in her eyes. "You're attached now. To the town. To your friends." She opened the front door to the building and gestured for Lily to go first. "To Ty," she said from behind Lily as they crossed the parking lot.

Lily didn't say anything until they reached their cars. "Maybe."

"The stakes are bigger now. There's more to lose when you've opened your heart and let others in. From what I gather, you didn't have many close relationships before you became Lily Novak."

Lily folded her bottom lip between her teeth and furrowed her brow. She'd told Hope everything about the night she'd witnessed the murder and her fear for her own safety, but never said anything about her relationship with her father. Or her lack of friends. Or a loving marriage. Obviously, if they'd been in a loving marriage, Damian wouldn't be trying to kill her.

The fluttering in her belly wasn't from fear or nerves. Instead, a rush of something new and calming warmed her insides. This was friendship. This was family. When someone knew you so well you didn't have to use words to express what you were feeling.

If she could handpick a sister, Hope would be her. Her intuitiveness, her comforting words, her strength were all admirable qualities that Lily wished she had.

The strength she once possessed was only in the business sense, not in the quality of her character. Not in understanding feelings and needs in those around her, which was more important than knowing when to drop the right buzzwords to charm a client, or manipulate numbers in a contract to make a bigger profit.

"Am I wrong?" Hope leaned against her car and crossed her arms against her chest. She had the big sister look down to a T.

Tears surfaced, blurring Lily's vision. Closing her eyes, she nodded. "I'm new at this," she croaked, her throat tightening with emotion.

"Oh, Lily."

Seconds later, Hope's arms wrapped her in a tight embrace, and they cried on each other's shoulders. "I've never," Lily choked on her words, "had a girlfriend before."

"That makes me sad. And mad. But I get it. I didn't have many either, but at least I had my parents. Ty. Delaney. You." Hope squeezed her tighter. "You've been all alone your entire life, I assume. But never again. No matter what happens, we're your family. Crystal Cove is your town. We're your tribe."

Lily's heart exploded with... love. She'd read about it, witnessed it between Hope and Cameron, Alexis and Ben, and seen it in their group of girlfriends, always supporting and encouraging each other.

She'd like to believe what she felt with Ty was love as well and that the feeling was mutual, but there was nothing but distrust and scorn when she'd last seen him.

Pushing those feelings aside and focusing on the love in front of her, Lily gathered her trembling breath and sniffed back the rest of her tears. From here on out she'd only focus on the good. The positive.

"You okay?" Hope asked, wiping her tears away.

"I don't know what I'd do without you. You're the best friend I've ever had. The only one, really."

"Great." Hope laughed. "Not much of a compliment then."

"That's not what I meant."

"I know. I'm only teasing. I'm honored to be your friend, Lily. Honored that you confided in me. I really admire you. I'm glad Ty has you in his life too."

"Let's not go there." Lily pulled her keys from her pocket. "I should let you get back to your family."

"Delaney's hit puberty so rushing home isn't high on my list right now. She's giving Cameron and me a run for our money lately. We never know what mood she'll be in."

"Your daughter is adorable."

"That, she is. And lately it's gone to her head. Middle school years. Ugh. I'm having a harder time with this than Cameron. Thank god I have him. That Delaney has him. I don't..." Hope clamped her mouth shut and clutched the hair on her scalp with both hands. "I'm so insensitive right now. I should be comforting you and, instead, I'm going off about my problems."

"Don't apologize. It's a great distraction. I don't remember much about my pre-teen years. Boarding school and strict rules. I don't wish that on anyone. I'm nowhere near ready to even start thinking about a family of my own. But, in the meantime, I'm soaking all of this in. Learning from the best. You're an awesome mom and will figure it all out. And if not, I'll have a bottle of wine and a tub of ice cream waiting for you in my apartment."

"I like the sound of that. Call me if you need anything. *Anything*."

"I will."

Her short drive home was much more pleasant than the drive to Mia's. When Lily was settled into bed, she sent Mia a quick text offering to bring by breakfast in the morning before her first client, then sent Hope a meme about girlfriends and wine.

Sleep didn't come easy, but she had a full day ahead of her and a new life to come to terms with.

There'd be changes. The balls and gumption Veronica Stewart had would come back, but other than that, she'd bury her past for good.

CHAPTER TWENTY-TWO

SON OF A BITCH. He was a dickhead. Ty knew it, his sister had told him over and over again, and by the stoic expression on Hope's face lately, she knew it too. Even Meatball treated him like yesterday's trash.

Ty pushed the lawnmower across the back lawn, stopping only to swipe the sweat from dripping into his eyes.

Work had been a bitch, but he had no one to complain to. Even if he did, he wouldn't. His father and mother switched off caring for Mia and bringing her to her doctor's appointments, which made Ty shorthanded at times. He needed to get used to it if his dad was going to retire in the fall.

Work slowed down in the fall and winter, or at least the projects got smaller. He wouldn't need to hire more crew until the spring, unless Ty kept flubbing up like he'd done the past week. Measure twice, cut once wasn't working. Measure four hundred ninety-eight times, maybe.

He'd measure the trim for the new windows, measure again, then cut. And damn if he could get it right the first time. Or the second. Sometimes the third. His memory was shit. He'd write the dimensions with his carpenter pencil right on the wood, and somehow his brain couldn't process fast enough to his fingers.

Lily monopolized every other second of his thoughts, with a dash of Mia and his father thrown in as well. But it all came back to Lily. He wanted to know more. How the hell did she allow herself to marry an asshole criminal like the Gervais guy?

And an heiress? Shit, if he hadn't already lived through one rejection over money and status that might not have hurt so bad. He couldn't wrap his brain around the story she had told him. It was all too... too surreal. Too unbelievable.

People in Crystal Cove didn't have backstories like hers. Sweet, innocent, beautiful Lily had a dark, dangerous past he couldn't wrap his brain around.

And so he treated her like shit, running away like a fool. By the time he'd woken up the following morning, he was back into his deep depression. He never made the call to his therapist; he forgot to take his medication, wouldn't talk to anyone, and was a bear at work.

People stayed away, except his friends and family who openly told him he was an ass. It had been five weeks since he'd seen Lily or talked to her. The morning Thorne dumped him back at his truck and he'd gone for the bike ride, Ty thought he was brave enough to beg for forgiveness at Lily's feet.

But then his mind went into overdrive imagining all the ways she'd reject him, turn him down, kick him to the curb. A place where he belonged.

He wasn't good enough for Veronica Stewart. He'd googled her and read about the millions. The silver spoon she was born with. The fancy schools. The famous men she'd been associated with. The billionaire husband.

Then the scandal and her supposed death. The more he read the more inferior he felt. No matter how much she wanted to believe she was Lily Novak, she'd always be someone else as well. The first twenty-eight years of her life were lived in luxury beyond anyone's imagination. She couldn't just forget that and be happy with Ty's small, unfinished house.

With his middle-class standing. He'd invested well over the past decade, but even if he worked until he was seventy-five, his retirement wouldn't be anywhere close to what the Stewart or Gervais families made in a day.

He couldn't give her any of that and the more he thought about it, the deeper he fell into his depression. It had only been the last week, after a verbal ass kicking from Hope and Mia, that he started taking his medication again and had even met with his therapist.

When he'd gotten an invite to the Coastal Vines Labor Day event and realized the entire town would be there, including Lily, and he'd rather stay home and mope with Meatball, he knew he needed to get back on his meds.

Ty whistled for Meatball, who lay in the shade by the woods, and pushed the mower toward the shed.

"We're going to the ocean to cool off. Don't make me carry you." Maybe watching Meatball play in the water would lift his spirits. Both of theirs.

He couldn't ignore everyone, including his family, because he felt sorry for himself. Ty was surprised Mia hadn't come over and kicked his ass. She was hobbling around better now that her cast was off. Instead, she gave him the cold shoulder. That hurt almost more.

Even Hope and Cameron were different. They reached out to him and invited him to dinner, which he declined every time. Hope would stop by his house and read him the riot act for blowing everyone off, and he did just that. Blew her off.

There were no words to say. He didn't argue with her or anyone else. Instead, he remained mute. Aloof. Distant. And he hated every damn minute of it. Solitude hadn't bothered him before. But now that he had friends, had a brief glimpse at what being in a relationship could be like, he didn't like being alone.

He'd put himself in quite the conundrum. Not wanting to be alone yet keeping everyone at their distance. Thorne had asked him to keep an eye on Lily, and he couldn't bring himself to do that either. He was a selfish bastard and not proud of it.

After his appointment with his therapist last week, he'd called Thorne and admitted to his negligence. Thorne had once again assured him things were under control and even had the decency to thank him for the call. The agent's manners and civility only made Ty feel like a bigger ass.

"Let's go. I don't have all day." He did, actually. Ty would have finished up the Cummings remodel today if it wasn't Sunday and they weren't having a family birthday party at the house.

Surprisingly, Meatball followed at a distance, and he waited at the truck with the door open. He normally wasn't one to go into the ocean, but he needed to cool off. Hopefully it wouldn't be too crowded at seven at night, even if it was the last weekend in August.

He lifted Meatball into the cab and rolled down the windows, letting the breeze dry the sweat from his body. "You and I are a miserable lot. But we'll get through this." He backed out of his driveway and continued talking to his dog, even though he'd gone immediately to sleep.

"We're going to act like normal, civilized people." Ty glanced at his snoring pug. "Or dog. We'll smile and make small talk if people come up to us. You can wag your tail instead. We're going to stop feeling sorry for ourselves, understood? Once we clean up our act, we'll figure out a way to get Lily back in our lives."

At the sound of her name, Meatball picked his head up. Ty's stomach did that clenching thing. Yeah, they both had it bad for the woman. She made them better people. Well, better person and dog.

It would be hard, but it would be worth every ounce of mental energy he had to work through his issues and give him and Lily another chance. If she'd have him. He'd made more appointments with his therapist. Weekly appointments. He was determined as hell now to get his life back.

Truth was, he missed people. He missed being happy.

Ty parked the truck and opened the door, realizing he forgot to bring a towel or swim shorts. That was him lately, distracted.

"The truck needs a good cleaning anyway. We'll clean it out tomorrow after work," he said to Meatball as he lifted him out of the truck. It wasn't fit for Lily... Nope. Ty shook that thought away. He had to separate Veronica Stewart's wealth from Lily Novak or he'd never make headway.

He'd clean his truck because it looked more like a bachelor pad with wrappers in his cup holders, dirt from construction sites on the bench and floor, and a layer of dust and spring's pollen covering his dash. He needed to clean his truck to make it presentable to a lady, be it Lily or Hope, or even his mother.

There. He'd done it. Redirected his thoughts before he let the depression skew his thinking. Feeling proud, he closed the door behind him and looked down at his feet to tell Meatball about his newest accomplishment, only his dog had trotted off ahead of him toward the beach.

"Well that's a first," he muttered to himself.

Quickly scanning the small beach area, he spotted a woman to the left sitting in a beach chair reading a book, an elderly couple packing up a cooler, and a family with two small children building sand castles closer to the shore.

Meatball headed straight toward the woman. "Another first." Ty chuckled to himself. Those short, stubby legs of his dog's had never moved so fast. Maybe Ty wasn't the only lonely one in the house.

When Meatball neared the chair, the woman turned her head toward him and Ty felt a punch in the gut.

Lily. Her lips turned into a smile as she reached out and rubbed Meatball's ears and neck as he licked her face. Her laughter carried across the beach and filled his ears and heart with chills. Good chills. Warming, emotional tingles.

She must have sensed him nearing. Her smile wavered, and she spoke soft and low so only Meatball could hear. He plopped himself in the sand next to her and rested his head on her bare thighs.

"Hi," he finally said, tucking his hands deep in his pockets so he wouldn't be tempted to reach out to touch her. God, she was beautiful. Her face free from any makeup and her hair pulled up into one of those messy bun things, like the last time he saw her. She'd opened the door to the FBI agent's lake house looking the same, only then she'd been wearing his clothes.

Not because they were lovers, Ty reminded himself. Not because she had done anything wrong. Because she feared for her life.

Ty swallowed and took in a deep breath through his nose and let it out his mouth. Calming breaths, giving himself time to refocus. He watched as her blue eyes dipped, hiding now behind lowered lashes as she ran her hands across Meatball's back.

Tonight she wore her a teal tank top and dark running shorts. The same outfit she'd worn one Sunday afternoon when they'd gone for a hike and stopped for ice cream afterward. They'd talked and laughed while hiking and swapped ice cream cones so they could taste each other's.

He missed those days. Those simple moments. He wanted to ask her if she missed them too, but he didn't.

"I'm sorry he disturbed you. Is that book for your book club?" He nodded toward the closed book in her lap next to Meatball.

"Yeah. My apartment is stifling with all this heat. I've been reading down here at night."

"I can put in an air conditioner for you," he offered quickly. Too quickly. Did he sound desperate? Clingy?

"That's okay. There aren't many nights left like this. The weather report says the humidity is supposed to break tomorrow."

"Oh. That's good." *Damn,* he was an idiot. It had been too long since he'd seen her, talked to her. His last words were hurtful, and here he was sounding like a moron. "Lily. I, uh... the things I said..."

"No. Don't." She gently nudged Meatball's head aside and stood, brushing off sand from her legs. "You made it quite clear then and you've made it quite clear over the past month how you feel about me. I'm sorry you think I was wrong not to spill my deepest, darkest secrets in your lap the first time we had sex, but if I had to do it all again, I still wouldn't change a thing."

"Not change a thing as in you'd still sleep with me or still wouldn't tell me?" Lily's mouth hung open in stupor, and Ty cringed at what a stupid thing to say. He wasn't good at this. Talking. Feelings. Apologies. Women. "That's not what I meant."

"Yeah, well, it's nice to know all you cared about was the sex." She folded her chair and tucked it under one arm as she slid her feet into her flip-flops.

"No. Lily, please. Listen. I'm sorry." He reached out and wrapped his hands around her forearm, holding her in place.

"Listen?" she scoffed. "You haven't said a word to me. I would've listened to your apology weeks ago, had I thought you meant it. I don't want to listen to anything you have to say now. If you hadn't run into me tonight you wouldn't be apologizing. You're only saying you're sorry because Meatball brought you over here. If you were truly sorry this wouldn't be an accidental run in. So take your words, whatever few and miniscule they might be, and shove it."

Lily tore her arm away from him and fled. Ty sank to the sand and covered his face with his hands. If he was a crying man, he might have shed a tear. Instead, he did as his therapist had instructed and breathed deep through his nose and out his mouth, pushing away his self-doubt and focusing on the facts.

Fact number one: He was an idiot.

Fact number two: He hurt Lily. Badly.

Fact number three: He needed to figure out how to make it up to her.

Fact number four: He loved her with all his heart.

Meatball shoved his head between Ty's legs, kicking up sand onto his shorts. "What?" Ty growled, softening when he opened his eyes and saw Meatball's pathetic sad face. "Yeah. I miss her too."

As Meatball moved around, kicking up sand, Ty spotted something shiny in the sand. Keys. He picked them up recognizing the teal sea glass hanging from Lily's keychain.

He could play this a few ways. Leave the key and walk away, giving Lily her space when she returned. Or he could bring them to her, knowing she stood stewing mad outside her car somewhere down the road.

Not prepared with the right words to say, he left her keys in the sand and stood. "Let's cool off in the water." He kept his back to the sand as he waded in to just below the knees. Meatball barked behind him, so Ty walked backward until only his toes were covered with the cool water.

"It's not scary. You can go out a little further than this." Meatball got his paws wet then retreated backward, following the tide go in and out. Ty wished he could say he sensed Lily as quickly as his dog did, but when Meatball turned and trotted up the sand, Ty knew it was to greet her.

His first instinct was to keep his back to Lily, allowing her to grab her keys and escape without having to see him. That was the coward in him talking. If he wanted to keep Lily in his life he'd have to fight for her. It would be an uphill fight, but she was worth it.

Turning, he couldn't help but crack a smile at Meatball's stub of a tail wagging furiously as Lily rubbed behind his ears. The key was still a good twenty feet away from them. Flying by the seat of his pants wasn't his specialty, but he'd have to wing it.

Ty headed toward her keys and picked them up, slipping them into his pocket. Meatball wandered back to the water, and Lily followed behind him. He watched them play in the water, the first sign of life in Meatball since she left them.

Since he pushed her away.

Even with Lily's presence, Meatball's energy never lasted long. Minutes later he strolled just far enough away from the water so he couldn't be reached and sprawled out into the sand to take a nap.

The sun had begun to set, and the breeze off the ocean brought some relief to the humid night. If there wasn't so much tension in the air, it would have been the perfect night. Lily looked so right standing on the shores of the town beach. A place only locals knew of and visited.

She belonged here in this town as if she was born and raised here. And in a way, she was.

Swallowing his pride and praying for strength, Ty slowly prodded toward Lily. "You looking for your keys?" He held them out in front of him.

She snapped her head to her left and scowled at him. "Yes." She held out her hand but instead of returning them, Ty shoved them back in his pocket. "That's immature."

"I'm not done talking."

"I hadn't realized you started." She crossed her arms over her chest and lifted an eyebrow. He'd never seen her like this. Feisty and full of spunk. While he hated being on the receiving end, he was proud of her for holding her own and not cowering like he'd done too many times.

Feeding off her energy, he fired back, "I'm trying now."

"A little late for that."

"Better late than never." He watched Lily fold her upper lip between her teeth. Biting back words, most likely. "You're right, though. I've been a... coward. I was mad, afraid, hurt, depressed. That still doesn't give me any right to treat you poorly or accuse you of lying. You didn't do anything wrong. I did. For that, I'm sorry. I know I can't take back the words I said and that they'll be with you forever. It kills me knowing how badly I hurt you, how I ruined the best thing—"

Ty scrubbed his hands across his face and rubbed his eyes, hoping for the right words. "You're not a *thing*. You're a person. A beautiful person inside and out. You're the most honest, kind, caring, wonderful human being I've ever met, and I treated you like shit instead of talking to you about my feelings."

Lily's arms remained crossed but instead of tight, tense shoulders, she appeared to relax a little. Her teeth no longer held her lip hostage, and it plumped as she released it. Kissing those lips was another thing he missed.

Lifting his gaze from her mouth, he swallowed and continued. "The past month I've been in hell. I stopped taking care of myself or caring about anyone else. I let my depression and my feelings get the better of me."

"Ty." Lily unfolded her arms and started to reach for him, but pulled back. "I don't want to be the cause of your depression."

"What? No. Don't ever think that. *You're* not the cause for my depression. It's there. It's a chemical thing. I have medication for it, you know that. I know that. I stopped taking my pills—"

"Why? I'm sorr—"

"No." Ty held up his hand, stopping the apology. "No one is to blame for my depression except my body make-up and me. I'm handling it better." The next was hard to say out loud. He questioned his masculinity, which was ridiculous. Needing therapy didn't make one weak, admitting you needed help took strength. He'd learned that as well and only now believed it. "I'm taking my medication now and even seeing a therapist again."

"That's... that's good."

"It's not going to be easy. I'm going to doubt myself a lot and I know it will take time, but I'm hoping with time you'll learn to trust me again and give me a second chance." He took her keys from his pocket and picked up her hand, placing them in her palm. "I've never stopped loving you, and I'm going to do my damnedest to win you back. To be worthy of your love."

Knowing he was out of words and had probably already pushed his luck, he pushed it one more step further by leaning in and placing a gentle kiss on her cheek. He called for Meatball and walked away praying his lazy dog would follow.

CHAPTER TWENTY-THREE

TY'S APOLOGY LAST NIGHT left her in knots. And speechless. For the past few months she'd experienced anger, grief, depression, love, and loss. Just as Ty had.

Her morning had been a mess. Her first appointment was early, and Lily was running late for the first time ever. Her eleven o'clock was twenty minutes late, which made Lily fall behind for the rest of the afternoon, and then Annie informed her of a new massage client at five.

It was their impromptu book club night, and she had forty pages left to read. After running into Ty on the beach last night she couldn't read anymore, no matter how engrossed she was into the story, and she still hadn't figured out who the arsonist was.

There was so much to do, so much idle chatter to be had, and her head was not in the game.

Her argument with Ty didn't have to mean it was the end of their relationship, yet they'd both been too stubborn to work through it. Lily's heart broke for him and his battle with depression. She should've been more sensitive to him, yet she had no way of knowing if he truly meant those words or if they came from the heat of the moment.

Hope and Mia had told her how surly he'd been. She should've figured he'd relapsed in his depression. If relapse was even the correct term. Lily wanted to talk to him about it so she could help him, support him, but by the time they got close enough in their relationship to have that conversation, he'd seen her with Thorne.

She should've told him everything the moment he saw her with Thorne. Maybe then he never would've gone down the rabbit hole of distrust.

Should've, would've, could've. All she could do now was move forward. And she really wanted to move forward with Ty, as long as he truly meant what he said about believing in her and taking ownership for his role in what happened. Whatever that was. An argument? A breakup? It just sort of ended.

He still thought he had to work hard at being *worthy* of her love. She hated those words and what they implied. They'd need to work on their communication skills, and he'd need to get past his feeling of inadequacy if they were going to have a future together.

Lily had her station cleaned and new inventory stocked at five minutes to five. Her new client had better be on time. The day needed to end. She needed book club for the distraction, the connection with the girls, and hopefully, some time with Hope at the end to talk about Ty; something she hadn't done since the night Mia came home from the hospital.

"I got your client all situated in room one upstairs. If you don't need anything, I'm heading home," Annie said, getting her purse from the bottom drawer of the front desk.

"She's here? I didn't see her come in?" Lily hadn't left the front other than to go to the bathroom twenty minutes ago.

"Hmm. Funny you missed him. I already did the usual check-in. No injuries. No areas you need to focus on."

"Him? Do you have his name?"

Annie grinned. "Oh, don't look so worried. He's a friend of the family's. Total gentleman. He already paid and tipped, so you don't need to worry about that."

"Tipped?" Lily didn't like the feeling of this, being alone with a strange man in the spa.

"Would you feel better if I stuck around?" Annie set her purse on the desk.

"Um, I don't want to inconvenience you."

"Not at all." Annie sat in one of the guest chairs and flipped through a magazine. "Let me know if you need anything."

Wanting to get the next hour over with, she trudged up the stairs and tapped lightly on the door to the first massage room. Annie had dimmed the lights, turned on the sounds of the ocean, and lit the citrus incense burner. Seeing everything was in place, she eyed the man on the table. He was on his stomach, his face looking down at the floor, and a towel draped across his rear.

Her skin flushed at the sight of his back. She shouldn't be affected by the stranger, yet there was a familiarity to him. She'd given massages to men before and never felt the zing to her chest.

She moved her gaze to his legs, strong and firm. The man was younger than she expected. When Annie said he was a family friend, she pictured the man in his fifties. Lily didn't look at the back of the man's head, but she didn't imagine him to be that old.

"I'm Lily, I'm sure Annie told you. You can let me know how much pressure you like, or if I'm hurting you."

The man didn't move. Didn't say anything. Maybe he'd already fallen asleep. Lily liked when she could put a client to sleep. It meant she—or he—was truly relaxed. Starting with his calves, she applied citrus oil to her palms and rubbed his muscles. The man stiffened before quickly relaxing.

By the time she'd finished his lower half, she swore she could hear him moan, especially when she worked on his hamstrings. Her skin flushed, from the heat, she'd told herself.

Applying more oil to her hands, she skimmed her touch across his lower back, and he sighed, "Lily."

Her breath hitched and her gaze quickly jumped to his neck, to the back of his head, and to the little she could see of his ears and cheeks. Her heart skittered when he picked his head up and gave her a cheeky grin.

"This feels amazing."

"Ty? Why did you—How did you—What are you doing here?"

"I'm here for a massage. I hear you're the best in town."

"I'm the only one in town."

"You're doing great. Don't stop." He lowered his head to the rest again and let out another loud sigh.

Lily stood there, frozen, passion igniting inside of her. Heat pooled in her, and she was tempted to do more—so much more—than just rub his aching back. Pretending to be professional, she continued rubbing, disguising her shaking hands by pressing harder into his muscles.

"Why so secretive?"

"Mm. Feels good."

Okay, she could understand if he didn't want to talk in the middle of a massage, and because he already paid for it, she'd finish the job. Lily worked his shoulders and his triceps, ending at his palms and fingertips.

The last ten minutes of his massage would be tricky.

"If you, uh, can roll over I can massage your chest." She hadn't given many men massages, but had learned what they can do to a man's anatomy. They couldn't necessarily control their erections, and as long as they didn't do anything about it, she dealt with the uncomfortable air in the room.

By the way he was moaning, and the wicked glint in his eye before he rolled over, Lily knew what was underneath the towel would be impressive.

She couldn't help her eyes from glancing south when he'd finally turned. Ty brought his hands to his front, covering himself. A shy redness filled his cheeks. "I'm sorry, Lily. I didn't mean for... *this* to happen. That's not why I'm here."

"It's okay." She cleared her throat as her body sizzled. "It's a natural reaction. Happens to a lot of men."

"What?" Ty shot up into a sitting position, apparently forgetting about the sheet and what he was trying to hide underneath it. "What men?"

"Clients. Most are grandfathers who need their muscles worked on, that's all."

"Has anyone ever... I'm sorry. It's not my place." He settled back down onto the bench and let his arms relax by his sides.

"No. No one has ever done anything or said anything to make me feel uncomfortable. I appreciate your concern, though." Lily applied more oil to her palms and worked it into his shoulders. "When I found out my client was a man, I asked Annie to stick around. She's downstairs."

"That's good. I mean, she doesn't need to stick around. I won't... I'm not... that's good that you're careful."

"I'm very careful. About a lot of things," she said softly.

Ty lifted his hand and rubbed it up and down Lily's arm as she massaged his shoulder. "I like that you're careful."

"I don't think Annie actually stuck around. It makes sense now. Why she was acting so nonchalant and kind of giggly."

"I made her promise not to tell you it was me."

"I figured." She moved to his other shoulder avoiding his gaze that she felt on her. "So why the secret massage?"

"I wanted to be near you with no way to escape."

"Oh."

"Well, for me to escape. You can leave when you want. I, on the other hand, am at your mercy." He lifted his head slightly and nodded at the sheet draped across his waist.

Lily didn't need to take her eyes off his shoulder. She could very well see his rising erection in her peripheral vision.

"I've never had a massage before. I didn't know it would be so..."

"Arousing?"

"Lily." He dropped his hand from her arm and closed his eyes. "I didn't mean to put you in this uncomfortable situation."

"Looks like it's probably more uncomfortable for you than me," she tried to tease. She needed a moment to process Ty's words. His actions. He was absolutely adorable with his vulnerability. For a man who had a hard time communicating, he was doing a pretty darn good job in making his apology.

"Which was my intention. Well, minus my evident desire to be with you in every possible way."

"I realize men can't always control their... reaction *down there.*" She didn't like speaking in euphemisms but needed to simmer down the heat in the room. "It's a normal reaction to stimulus. It doesn't mean you're in love, that you want to have sex, or that you're even interested in a woman. It's science. Body chemistry and all."

Ty scrubbed his hands across his face. "My intent was to let you have the upper hand. To be at your mercy."

"Well. When you put it like that." Lily grinned and pressed hard into his clavicle.

"Ouch." Lily chuckled and let up the pressure. "Brat," he teased. "I like the sound of that. Your laughter. I'm hoping I can hear more of it."

"Me too." She skimmed her fingers down his chest and worked her palms in circles.

"Shit. You need to stop." Ty grabbed on to both wrists and stopped her from moving.

Lily's face softened as she let up the pressure. "Am I hurting you?"

"Not in the way you think." Ty sat up, still holding her wrists, and swung his legs to the side of the bench. "I didn't mean to—"

"You've already said that. A few times. About a few different things. Why don't you instead tell me what you did mean to do?" Lily wiggled her wrists free and stepped back, hoping he'd readjust the sheet. His right thigh and hip were naked and free, the corner of the sheet slipping away.

"I..." Ty stood, obviously forgetting he was naked underneath and grappled for covering. He stepped on the sheet and tried to yank it up at the same time, bumping into the table that held the music and incense, knocking it over. He reached to pick up the bottle of essential oils, and the sheet dropped to the floor again. He bent to pick it up and looked up at Lily, locking his dark eyes with hers.

Lily chewed on her bottom lip to stop the laughter threatening to erupt. Her body shook, and she bit harder.

"You think this is funny?" He wrapped the sheet around his body like a bath towel and sat back down on the massage table.

"Kind of," she giggled.

"I'm glad I can amuse you. Like I said, I like your laughter, even if it is at my own expense."

"It's not like there's anything I haven't seen before." She bit her lip again, not intending to sound so... sexual. Or intimate. While it was the truth, Ty's visit today wasn't about sex.

"That's not what I—"

"We've established that. Which brings us back to my question. What did you hope to get out... of this? Besides a massage?"

"You're very good, by the way." Ty rolled his shoulders and placed his hands on his lap, his smile softening to a serious flat line. "Like I said before, I caught you at a weak moment and took advantage of that. I dumped my insecurities on you, trying to make you feel at fault when really I didn't know how the hell to process it all. I never asked about your safety. What I could do to help. I was a selfish bastard and will never forgive myself for treating you that way."

Lily toyed with the hem of her shirt, unsure how to respond or what to do. Ty stared at her with an intensity so strong it almost scared her. He'd beaten himself up over this as much as she had.

"I'm not going to use my past or my depression as an excuse for treating you that way; I took the easy way out. And instead of talking to you about my suspicions with Thorne, I cast you aside. I didn't want to love you because it hurt too much. If I pretended you didn't matter, I could go on making myself believe I was better off without you. That you were just like the others. Or other. Shit. No wonder I could never get a girlfriend."

"Ty, you're not fully to blame. I walked away as well. I should've stormed down your door and made you listen. Made you see the truth."

"No." He stood, framing her face in his hands. "You told me the truth. It was up to me to believe it. You gave me the space I needed to process, to be angry. To heal. I'm still healing. Not from anything you did, but from myself. So much of this is self-inflicted. I'm learning to cope, to handle my self-doubt, to ask for help when I need it. When I'm stronger, when I'm not as needy, we'll figure this thing out. All I'm asking is for your patience."

He kissed her lightly on the lips, scooped up his clothes from the chair in the corner, and walked out the door, leaving her speechless once again.

She heard his heavy footsteps go down the stairs, and the squeak of the bathroom door closing. Noticing an article of clothing he missed, she picked it up and shook it out. A Parker Construction pullover.

She held it close to her heart like a teddy bear and then slipped her arms through the sleeves, inhaling his woodsy scent and replaying what just happened between them.

Ty wanted her back. She wanted him back. He took ownership for treating her badly and asked her to wait patiently for...

Lily jerked her head back as if the answer would be written on the wall in front of her.

Wait? Wait for what? She jogged down the stairs and stood outside the bathroom. Ty emerged a minute later dressed in khaki shorts and a Parker Construction shirt and a warm smile on his face.

"Wait?" Lily poked him in the chest. "I've been waiting for over five weeks for you to talk to me. What is it I'm waiting for now?"

"I'm not mentally healthy. I've only been back on my medication for a week. I've had two therapy sessions. In time I'll get better. I'll be sure of myself. Of you. Of us. In the meantime, I don't want to risk hurting you again."

"How exactly do you think you're going to hurt me?"

"By questioning why you're with me. By asking you if you could settle down with a middle-class construction worker from central Maine when you're accustomed to fine dining, expensive jewels, and a ton other crap I'm completely ignorant to."

"First. *I,* Lily Novak, am not familiar with any of that other *crap.* You're referring to a woman I want nothing to do with. I don't want to be her. Ever again. You're the one putting *her* between us. Not me." Lily held up two fingers, and Ty flinched in surprise. "Second, if I didn't want to be with you, I wouldn't. If you're so set on picking apart my past, know that *she* nor *I* have ever done anything we didn't want to do. If I want out, I get out. Got it?" She poked him in the chest again.

"And that's why I need time. I'm going to keep pissing you off with my doubt."

"No. You're going to keep pissing me off if you don't *talk* to me about your feelings." She softened her voice and placed a hand on his chest. "You're going to keep pissing me off if you keep pushing me away. I'm here for good. The Sea Salt Spa is my business, my home. I have friends here. I have nowhere else to go. So if that's what you're worried about, stop. And if you can't, then talk to me. Don't make assumptions or decisions for me because *that* will piss me off."

"You're mad." Ty shoved his hands in his pockets again, his sign of retreat.

"Yeah, I am. Who said this was going to be easy?" She slid her hands down his arms, joining their hands together in his pockets. "We're going to argue. Do you think Ben and Alexis never argue?

Hope and Cameron? That's what couples do. But they talk. They compromise. They figure things out. They make up."

"You still want to be a couple?"

"Is that doubt I hear in your voice?" She squeezed his hands in hers and tugged him toward her.

"I thought you'd need more time."

Lily slowly shook her head from side to side. "You assumed. Ass. You. Me. Don't." She lifted herself up on her toes and kissed him on his lips.

He pulled their joined hands out of his pockets and brought them behind her back. Her chest lifted and pressed into Ty's. This. This was what she missed. Being in his arms. Being on the receiving end of his gentle touch. He was such a good, good man. More than anything in the world she wanted a relationship with Ty.

She had the physical baggage and he carried more mental baggage, but together, they could get through anything. Releasing her hands from his, she lifted her arms and draped them over Ty's shoulders.

"I missed you so much," she whispered into his mouth, taking their kiss deeper. He electrified her with his kiss sending bolts of desire through her body, and his hands hadn't even moved from her lower back.

Again, Lily pressed her body harder into his, feeling his strong desire for her, yet he didn't move his hands.

"Ty," she moaned, wiggling in his arms.

He released her lips from his and left a trail of kisses up her cheek and into her hairline, resting his cheek on her head. "Lily." His voice raw, yet tired. "We should stop."

"We should not. We should take this upstairs."

"Don't tempt me," he growled. Squeezing her hips, he placed a hard, swift kiss to her lips and stepped back.

"What's wrong?" She immediately missed the heat between their bodies.

He picked up her hands in his and kissed her knuckles. "As much as I want to continue this, I'm suggesting we take things slow."

"No." Lily shook her head aggressively making Ty laugh.

"Yes."

His smile took her breath away. She wanted him more than ever before. It used to be the sizzle of chemistry and heat between them, but now with the added element of love, she thought she'd spontaneously combust. Her heart raced, and she was dizzy with love.

"Twenty-four hours ago you hated me," he said with a sad smile.

"I never hated you." He cocked his head to the side. "I was mad at you, yes. I hear make-up sex is amazing."

"You're a brat. Stop tempting me." He laughed again.

"I don't ever want to stop tempting you," she said with a long sigh, hooking her fingers through the belt loops in his jeans.

"I like that." He kissed her lips and pulled back before she could take the kiss deeper. "I also like this on you." He traced his finger across the embroidery over her chest.

"Your sweatshirt?"

"My name," he said softly, still tracing the lettering with his fingers.

Lily's heart thundered in her chest as she gasped. "Oh." Did he just...?

"You have your book club with my sister and your friends tonight. Go have fun." He kissed her chastely and stepped back. "I'd like to take you out to dinner tomorrow night, though. If that's okay."

"What?" He couldn't do that. Almost propose one second and then send her off to book club the next.

"A date. A real date. I want to pick you up, take you out to eat, maybe even bring you more flowers, if that's okay. I think I actually like this dating thing. As long as it's you I'm going out with."

Damn Ty and his sweet, sensitive side. She was so doomed. So head over heels in love with him she couldn't care less if she ever went to another book club. Being wrapped up in his strong arms and warm kisses was all she'd ever need for the rest of her life.

"We can order in." Having Ty to herself sounded much more attractive than sharing him with a waitress and customers.

"There's plenty of time for that."

"We can take things slow if you want, but I'm not walking away from you, Ty. I love you. This... what happened between us didn't destroy our relationship. It made us stronger. I love you even more than I did before."

"Lily," Ty sighed. "I don't know how I got so lucky. That's not doubt. That's a fact. I love you too. I never stopped. I'll admit I tried. I tried not to think about you. I tried telling myself it was never love between us. That it was fake. We both know it wasn't."

Ty framed her face in his hands and sipped at her lips. She kissed him back with passion and desire as every inch of her craved him.

"My love for you keeps growing every damn day. That whole cliché about absence making the heart grow fonder? One hundred percent fact. I love you even more for giving me a second chance. You feel so right it scares me."

"You still going to turn me down on my offer to go upstairs? I can *really* show you how right we feel together." She had never been so flirtatious or suggestive before, and she liked it. Especially seeing the reaction she got out of Ty.

His eyes lit up as he raked his fingers through her hair. "I've already kept you, and if I know my sister and Hope, they're going to give you a hell of a time for being late."

"It's not like they know what I've been up to," Lily said with a sly smile.

"Sweetheart, they'll know."

CHAPTER TWENTY-FOUR

"OH MY GOD. YOU HAD sex!" Mia yelled from across the bookstore.

"What?" Hope snapped her head around and stared at Lily, who couldn't help but blush. "You and Ty made up?"

"Or she took my advice and went out to sow her wild oats."

"Mia! You did not tell her to do that," Grace reprimanded.

"Oh, lighten up. You're just worried about the competition."

Lily didn't say a word; there was no need to. She grinned from ear to ear listening to her friends' banter, to take her defense in their unique ways.

"I'm hoping that glow means you and Ty are back together." Jenna hugged her and offered a spiked seltzer.

"Ben's been trying to get Ty to go out with him and Cameron, but Ty wanted nothing to do with the guys. He misses his new friend. I'm hoping this also means he's going to come out of hiding. Ben needs a friend. He's crowding me and moping all day." Alexis put her arm around Lily and led her to the overstuffed chair.

"I walked through the door thirty seconds ago. What makes you guys think Ty and I are back together?"

"You're blushing."

"You're lips looked like they've gone through a major make-out session."

"You're smiling."

They said one after the other. Lily giggled and sipped her drink. Yeah, there was no amount of money in the world that could tempt her away from this town or her friends.

"I heard about Ty's surprise visit in your massage room," Mia admitted.

Grace crossed her legs and wiggled her butt in her chair. "This, I have to hear."

Lily couldn't contain her joy anymore and told them about their run-in at the beach last night and her surprise at finding him naked on her massage table.

"Those tables are pretty sturdy. Did you test it out?" Jenna asked, shocking them all.

"Oh, my ears. I don't want to hear this." Mia covered her ears with her hands.

"I agree. No details in that department. Ty's too much like a brother to me. I can't do it. I'm going to assume by the smile on your face that your clothes hit the floor."

"Actually," Lily said, setting her drink down and curling her feet under her bum. "My clothes didn't come off. His did, though."

Grace howled with laughter, and Mia ducked her head between her knees. Alexis and Jenna giggled, and Hope unsuccessfully bit back a smile.

"Ty was there for a massage, remember? Of course his clothes were off."

"And here I thought the Sea Salt Spa was a reputable place. Wait until the townsfolk hear there's hanky-panky going on in those upstairs rooms of yours," Alexis teased.

"There was actually no hanky panky at all." Lily picked up a whoopie pie and licked the creamy filling oozing out of the sides. "Ty was a perfect gentleman. Much to my dismay."

"Oh, I like you." Grace pointed at Lily with her drink. "I can't wait to be your neighbor."

"Neighbor?" Alexis gasped. "You're moving?" She looked at her sister in surprise.

"Not yet. I'll keep my room at Mom and Dad's until I've saved up more. I'm renting the space next to the spa and opening a boutique. I'll be featuring graduate students and new fashion designers. Giving them a place to start out. I'm thinking of making it like a thrift shop or maybe a library. Where women can borrow high-end clothing and either return it or buy it. Still brainstorming."

"Crystal Cove isn't exactly a fashion mecca, Grace."

"Someone tell my sister to have a little faith in me. I've done my research. Ben has given me some pointers as well. At least my brother-in-law supports me."

Lily wasn't sure of the animosity between Alexis and Grace, but she knew it ran deep. They'd done well to act civil around each other, and Alexis didn't seem to mind Grace joining their group of friends. It wasn't any of Lily's business, but she'd be an impartial friend to both of them and pray the sisters could rebuild a relationship.

Growing up, Lily never minded being an only child. Less people to deal with. Less responsibility. Her focus had been on her studies while in private boarding schools, and when home, her nannies continued her education, and her father only talked business. If she wanted to be part of any conversation, she had to learn about numbers and financing, marketing, strategies, schmoozing.

She fell into the trap of having a single goal: making more money. Too bad she and her father never actually enjoyed what they did or even enjoyed their earnings. There were no vacations. A trip to Europe meant a potential business deal. The house in the Caribbean was a business investment. Clients from all over the world would meet there. More business transactions were made on the golf course than strokes.

That was normal. Or rather, that was Veronica Stewart's normal.

Lily Novak's normal was sitting around a small bookstore on tattered furniture talking about friendships, relationships, food, and sometimes books. The new normal was having arguments and making up. Walking the beach and tracking sand through the house and having to clean up after yourself, not relying on a maid.

Normal was going on dates to the drive-in. Grilling in the backyard. Sitting around campfires.

Laughing. Crying. Smiling. Hugging. Loving.
Normal was simplicity. Normal was this.

MARIANNE RICE

THE END

ACKNOWLEDGEMENT

WOW! THIS SERIES WOULDN'T be what it is without the love and support of my readers, especially my Ricecakes. I love you all for your encouragement and your constant nagging of me to write the next book!

And of course, *What Makes Us Stronger* wouldn't be what it is without my super fabulous editor, Silla Webb. You're fantabulous! My knack for cover design more than sucks, but thankfully I have the ever-patient J.M. Walker of Just Write Creations who puts up with my long rambles and constant changes. I love this cover!!

Lastly, thank you to my husband and kids who have finally accepted that Mommy's stories are important, and that her characters are real people.

Don't miss out!

Visit the website below and you can sign up to receive emails whenever Marianne Rice publishes a new book. There's no charge and no obligation.

https://books2read.com/r/B-A-LKSE-KTXU

Connecting independent readers to independent writers.

Also by Marianne Rice

A Well Paired Novel
At First Blush
Where There's Hope
What Makes Us Stronger

The McKay-Tucker Men
False Start
False Hope
False Impressions

Standalone
Smoke & Pearls
Marshmallows & Mistletoe

Watch for more at www.mariannerice.com.

About the Author

Marianne Rice writes contemporary romantic fiction set in small New England towns. She loves high heels, reading romance, scarfing down dark chocolate, gulping wine, and Chris Hemsworth. Oh, and her husband and three children. You can follow her all over social media, and keep up to tabs with her latest releases on her website: www.mariannerice.com

Read more at www.mariannerice.com.

Made in the USA
Middletown, DE
21 November 2022

15047257R00184